HARMONY

LILITH SAINTCROW

For Miriam Kriss, who knows why.

All God's children get weary when they roam.

— JOE SOUTH

PART I
PRELUDE

1

LITTLE BONES

Tires crunching on gravel is one of the worst sounds in the world. It's like thousands of little teeth grinding away at each other, a headache boiling right through your ears. With the windows—even the cracked ones—open for a little while to air the farmhouse out, it reverberated through dusty rooms and rattled in the kitchen, where I stood in front of the balky old stove trying to convince it to boil a pot of water. You had to watch and not let the element go for too long, or it would blow a fuse and you'd have to troop downcellar, past dusty shelves with non-dusty jars of preserves and pickled beets—*ugh*—to flip it.

There were other things besides beets down there, to be honest. For once we hadn't worked through all the string beans or the pickled garlic; winter had been pretty good. The woodstove in the living room was hot; I'd have to close everything up and sheet the windows before too much longer, or it wouldn't warm up and we'd shiver all through the night.

I flicked the burner off and headed for the front, because it wasn't just one car coming down the drive and it didn't sound like our old, rattling blue truck either. There was no quick tap on the horn to let me know Mom was bringing someone, either.

Neither of us liked to be surprised. Plus, if she was bringing a straight home for whatever reason, the joke was I'd have to put some clothes on. I'd grown out of my toddler nudity phase, but Mom acted like it might come back any second. Sometimes in the summer I was damn tempted, but... Well, Mom said it was Dad's influence, that I'd been cramped by living with the patriarchy in my munchkin years.

Maybe we both were, because she only went topless occasionally, when there were straights around to shock.

I pushed aside the cheap pineapple-stamped drapes in the front room; the curtain rod was askew, so they tended to creep during the day. I almost stuck my head out the window to get a better look, but then I saw the lights on top of the last two cars and a ball of ice, like when you fill up a balloon and freeze it, plopped into my tummy right between second and third chakra. Mom would prescribe a cleanse, maybe, or one of her rocks. Maybe hematite to ground me, to make my hands stop shaking and my heart stop the thump-thump it began as soon as I realized what I was seeing.

They came over the slight rise and dropped, one after another like ducks at the carnival. A yellow Dodge Charger leading the way, a car I didn't know. Then one cop car, followed by another.

Straights with guns. The po-po. Mom didn't call them *the pigs* like some of her friends, especially the older hippies who were off-grid most of the year, but she got this funny nose-wrinkled look on her face whenever they were mentioned. Dad told me later Grandpa Jack had been a cop. Mom never said.

My old, battered huaraches nailed themselves to the floor. My breath whooped out, and that's when everything started going haywire. Maybe I should have run away into the apple trees or hidden somewhere, anywhere. Instead, I stayed right where I was, as if I knew somehow. Like I suspected, despite having what Mom called "natural shields." I wasn't sensitive like she was.

No, I was the one who counted the cash and made change, who

held out my hand with just the right mixture of customer-service smile and don't-even-think-about-ditching frown. *Pragmatic*, Mom called me. I didn't want to be, I wanted to be like *her*, but the energy didn't talk to me.

Not then.

The bright yellow Charger pulled to a stop. The engine cut and the driver's door opened while the cop cars were still bouncing down the last small slope, the one that always said *home* under Mom's truck with a particular lift-and-drop. He got out, rising up and up like a beanstalk giant. Still in work overalls, the stitching that said *Earl* over his left breast pocket, and even though it had been a while and I couldn't see his face I knew those slumped shoulders, those big work boots, and those gentle, dangling, basketball-cradling hands. That short bristled ruff of black hair on his head, and those blue, blue eyes —all familiar.

It was Dad. With *cops*. My hands turned numb, and the rest of me too. All I could think about was going back in the kitchen and turning the burner on again, to make...what had I been trying to do? Tea? Maybe? Something else? Heating it up so I could wash my hair, since it was no longer cold enough to freeze damp strands to the pillow?

I couldn't remember for the life of me.

"Val?" Dad called, his shoulders coming up. "Val, honey, it's me." Maybe he saw the windows were open, or he figured I was outside running around. He knew Mom didn't like the police, why would he bring them here? They hadn't fought over her bagging out on the joint custody order, or at least, she hadn't told me, and that wasn't like her.

She told me *everything*.

It wasn't that Mom didn't want me to see him, exactly. It was just that meeting Dad and handing me over was a hassle, and she didn't want him driving out to the farmhouse and cramping her style either. I called him when I could get to a phone, like at at the Enlightened Source bookstore, and he always made sure I had both his cell and work numbers. Not like his work number had changed for years, ever since he moved here to be closer once Mom came into the farm and quasi-settled.

"Val? Dumplin girl, it's Daddy." He tried again, heading for the door with his big swinging strides, but he didn't stamp, instead putting each foot down like he wanted to avoid crushing anything small underneath. He always tried his hardest, even though the world was built too small for him and too large for Mom.

I was hoping I'd end up middle-sized, but I'd have to put on a growth spurt or two before that was even an option. The sweet, cold breeze of a spring day, winter-hardened fields blinking a bit before they really woke up and the apple trees about to bloom, washed over me. My hands were on a splinter-chewed wooden windowsill, and they gripped so hard I couldn't let go.

"Val?" He didn't know to avoid the second porch step, and its squealing sound broke the afternoon clean in half, from *before* into *after*. "Val, honey, it's Dad. You in there?"

I didn't say anything. He knocked, almost shyly. Mom didn't believe in locking the doors, not out here in our little refuge, our place away from the straights and their rules and their crimes. "Valentine?"

Here, I tried to say. *I'm in here.* The words couldn't squeeze past a wad of something dry and dark in my throat. Throat chakra. Communication, and...what else? It was responsible for something else, but for the life of me I couldn't think of *what.* A well-cleansed quartz crystal would help clear the blockage, right? That's what Mom would prescribe.

The door rattled. You had to lift it a little or it would catch on the peeling hall linoleum.

I tried to say something, to yell, to wrench my hands off the windowsill and run to the door, throw the ancient lock, clap my hands over my ears.

It didn't work. I just stood there, stupidly, and let them tromp right on in.

2

SOGGY TISSUES

IT WASN'T what she would have wanted.

Nobody was there—not Nadine from the yoga studio, not Bert or Coral from Enlightened Source where Mom did tarot readings and workshops on crystals and chakras and soul-stuff. Even bearded, blunt-fingered Feather, who was always saying how Mom had such a beautiful *soul*, didn't show. He was aiming for the boyfriend position, I guess, and had even made halfhearted attempts at giving me a male role model. I didn't trust anyone who had bought his quartz-topped walking stick online, though, especially when he kept staring at my chest when Mom wasn't looking.

Instead there were a bunch of people I didn't know or only vaguely remembered, like Dad's brown-bearded friend Henry Harding. Everyone called him Hooker, a horrible nickname but one he didn't seem to mind. His wife, a wide-set straight with her short reddish hair permed and frozen with some kind of goop, kept saying how it was such a *tragedy*, so *young*. Her avid little gaze would crawl all over me each time her lipsticked lips pushed the words out, and I could tell she didn't think Mom's long black velvet coat bought for $5 at the thrift store—a huge find especially since it only needed its

7

arm sewn back on—was proper funeral wear. Mom's black skirt printed with bright red roses probably wasn't up to her standards either, but in a shitty little Lutheran shed with a plain cross above the casket—*you don't want to look at that, dumplin'* was all Dad said when I asked why it was closed—it was all the straights were going to get.

The only pair of black shoes I had were combat boots, still too big for me because Mom expected I'd grow into them. Heavy socks would have helped, but I didn't have any. The steel toes were cold, my own toes were cold, and my feet slipped inside like peas in a dried pod.

Dad's face was a wall, dark circles under his bright blue, bloodshot eyes. Hooker stood elbow-to-elbow with him, and I pretended not to notice when the bearded man pulled out a silver flask and took a hit. One of Mom's friends might have asked for a drop—Gloria, maybe, who did shamanism retreats but didn't shy away from bringing a six-pack when she visited. Last time they'd set up tents under the apple trees in summer, and the drumming had lulled me to sleep at night. People paid four hundred apiece to come out and pick a spirit animal. I could never figure out if Gloria thought they were suckers or just amusing babies.

I thought at least Gloria would be there. Or Nadine. Someone. Anyone. A joint would have been better than the flask, too. Take the edge off, tune in, be groovy.

There were about half-a-dozen people from Dad's work, their names going into my head and right out again as I stared at the casket, willing it to...what? Open up like a butterfly, and show her in there?

The steering wheel hit her in the chest. One of the cops had started to tell me more, but Dad said something I didn't quite hear over the rushing in my ears and the buzzcut jerk in blue shut up. They'd stood in the farmhouse foyer like insults, with their guns on their hips and their bright shiny badges. Why the fuck they had to bring out two cop cars to tell me I don't know—did they expect me to fight? Or what? I kept wondering if they were going to look for the

weed stash or something, my brain fastening on that instead of...
anything else.

A coffin. A church. She would have hated it. Why did they call it
a "viewing" when the thing was closed? She probably didn't even
want to be buried. They were going to lower the box into a hole in the
ground, but she was all full of embalming chemicals. The straights
had gotten her at last.

God. Or Universe, as she would say. *The Universe wants you to
have it.* Smiling just a little, pressing a chunk of carnelian into a
client's hand. Giving away stuff. *They needed it more, Val.*

None of the straight "family" showed up either, assuming there
was any left. She didn't talk much about Grandpa Jack and Grandma
Stella, I wouldn't even have known their names if I hadn't found the
one photo album Dad put together, each snapshot carefully labeled
in his spidery chickenscratch handwriting. For some reason she kept
that, along with a fabric-covered one with my baby pictures.

"You've gotten so *big!*" Dad's friends said it like they remembered
me. And things like, "Your dad is always showing pictures of you, he's
so proud."

Did Mom send them? She didn't *take* pictures, she wasn't that
kind. If she was here, she would be standing near the back, and her
expression would clearly shout the energy was way too negative for
anyone even remotely sensitive.

There was a cop, too, in full dress uniform. The one that showed
up first at "the scene." Only it didn't mean a party, or a gathering or a
convention or a drum circle. *The scene.*

I tried not to imagine it. *Came right over the yellow line,* someone
murmured.

Who were the handful of other people, not from Dad's work? I
don't know. Dad's other friends, maybe. Did Nadine or Bert or Coral
even know Mom was gone, and not flaking on her tarot workshop or
her laughing almost-promise to teach a few more kundalini classes?
Nadine wanted it to be a regular thing, which would have been fine
by me, but Mom hated being nailed down.

Except now she was, nailed right inside the gunmetal-gray box. My hands kept shaking. I didn't know where to put them. In my pockets, in front of me, behind my back? I kept dropping my chin and sniffing, to catch the comforting rasp of patchouli from the velvet coat. My nose would fill and I wouldn't be able to smell it unless I snorted all the snot back up. Dad had a box of tissues, I wadded the used ones into a big ball and just stood there, wishing I could hide behind him.

The church was so empty it echoed. Finally we all trooped outside, and they really did mean to do it. They really did mean to slide her into a hole in the ground.

Maybe she wasn't really in there. Maybe it was a coverup, like Bill-the-veteran was always talking about. Maybe the energy had taken her, all the crystals and the healing getting rid of her physical form, vibrating it right into energy, but the straights couldn't let everyone know that was possible, so they closed the casket and pretended?

But Dad wouldn't let them, would he? He'd identified her, right?

You don't want to look at that, dumplin'.

It was a bright spring morning, the kind you go out into because it's too beautiful to stay inside. The kind where you turn over just-thawed garden dirt for a few hours, glad of the work and the breeze. The kind Mom would sometimes let me skip school on and we'd go in the truck for what she called a ramble, rolling over hills, singing along to the radio, avoiding the city. Sometimes we'd even get milkshakes, vanilla or chocolate. The strawberry ones weren't real fruit, and she agonized over the corn syrup and the growth hormones in the milk, but still, if I asked persistently, she'd roll her eyes and find a drive-thru.

I didn't look when they lowered the grey casket. I stared across the unreal green of the cemetery, at the line of winter-naked trees holding only the barest suggestion of green, a few evergreens at regimented intervals. What happened when they ran out of room to put people? Did they take them out? Stack them up, bury them deeper?

Dad put his arm around me. Next to him I was just as tiny as Mom.

The casket was too big for her. *Rattle around like a pea in a pod.* She would touch the big chunk of turquoise surrounded by silver scrollwork at her breastbone, grounding herself. I couldn't *breathe*, all the air was too thin.

There was no hematite in my pockets. Nothing but soggy tissues.

PART II
DISSONANCE

3

WASTE NOT

PARKING LOTS ARE STUPID. They're scorching except when they're freezing, full of garbage no matter who they pay minimum to clean up, and every time you cross one, someone looks at you like *you're* the trash. Even if you know you're not, it kind of stings.

"I'll just be a minute," Dad said, his forehead furrowed like whenever he forgot I wasn't six anymore. His stubble was dark as ever, but his hair had started to show a little grey. Salt-and-pepper, you'd call it, only heavier on the pepper. "Sure you don't want to come in, Val?"

"No thanks." I finished rolling my window down; he cut the engine. At least he waited until I was done before turning it off. Mom wouldn't have, if we'd ever had any vehicle with power windows. She had too much to get done, especially on a day like this, with bright sunshine pouring down and a good breeze shaking branches full of fuzzy nubbins or early blossom or the ones showing bits of green. *Spring cleaning*, she'd say. *Everything's waking up. Come on, let's go.* Trailing her brightly patterned broomstick skirts and her patchouli and the gentle music of bangles moving on her wrist. Nobody else's mom dressed like her, and I'd been proud and fascinated when I was little. Later, it was just the way things were, and I was still secretly proud. Even when she dressed "straight camouflage", as she put it, there were the small things saying it was just a costume, like the turquoise shield hanging against her breastbone or her Earth Shoes. Negative heel slope meant better back alignment, and all that.

I like my huaraches better. Except when it's cold. Since the funeral I put on the combat boots every time I had to leave the apartment; I needed the extra armor.

A lump settled in my throat. Dad might even have known what I was thinking, because he patted the gearshift as if it was my knee, twice, very gently. "Well," he said, and his bright blue eyes focused out the yellow Charger's windshield. It was a brand new car, and the color screamed *I need a trophy wife*, but it was a nice ride. Power everything, good suspension, and that heavy chemical smell of new upholstery. "Almond milk, right? And bread."

Why was he asking me? Unless it was because I was a girl, so I automatically knew what groceries we needed? Mom called him *patriarchal*, on the few occasions she talked about him at all. It was one of her biggest almost-insults.

"I guess." I let my own eyes—blue as his, blue as hers—unfocus, staring at the brick side of a Wendy's across the lot. For a second I wanted fries, forbidden and full of trans fats and tallow. Getting out of the car and actually walking over there seemed like a huge goddamn hassle though. Just like going to the grocery store at all, but *you need to get out*, Dad said. *You can't stay in the house until you go back to school.*

Even if I wanted to. I'd been doing pretty good so far. It was our first night cooking dinner together ever, because of the garage where Dad worked. You can't just change your schedule when you're dealing with the real straights. Even when your ex-wife gets in a head-on collision and…

No. I didn't want to think about that. So instead, I went back to mulling going-back-to-school, another stupid unhelpful train of thought. They wouldn't bus me all the way across three districts for the rest of the year, so it was a transfer.

Great. Just *fabulous.*

You had to hand it to Dad, though. He was trying so hard you might want to smack him. I didn't tell him I was vegan, because I'm not, that was Mom's trip, but he assumed cow milk wasn't going to do it for me. "It doesn't have to be almond milk," I said, finally. "Regular's fine."

"Oh." He looked at me, but I was busy watching the Wendy's. I could *feel* him wondering if he should make me come in. Half-moons of engine grease settled along his cuticles, his big callused hands loose and gentle. *At least he was never violent,* Mom had sniffed more than once. *There's that.*

I don't even remember them fighting. I was only five when Mom left him, taking me along. Sometimes I imagined her carrying me down a road at night, even though I knew she'd just picked me up from daycare and driven to a new apartment. "I'm not vegan," I clarified, just in case. "I just want to sit here a bit, you know."

"Okay, dumplin'." His hand on the gearshift moved a little, caught in my peripheral vision. "I'll be right out."

I nodded, still staring at the Wendy's. Counting the bricks in the wall sounded like a good idea, one at a time, no multiples. Counting is just taking little bites out of big time, just like breathing.

Mom was big on breathwork. It was how the energy moved. *Nothing a few good breaths can't fix,* she'd say, right before taking my hands and inhaling with me.

I counted forty bricks before Dad reached the sliding glass doors, started again and got to a hundred and twenty before two big white vans parked right between me and the goddamn Wendy's. The Charger was low-slung, so I couldn't look over the vans, and they each took up two parking spaces. They sort of had to, they were ginormous, and stuffed to the gills with a church group or something.

The doors opened, and out tumbled people who all looked like each other but not inbred or anything. Women and men, all in their twenties-plus, and all with long hair. The girls mostly wore long skirts, and it was hard to see the flutters and flares of fabric swaying.

Just a few bangles, though, and most of them had crosses on thin chains at their slim necks. The guys were all in jeans and chambray shirts under work jackets, hard-worn, and some of them wore crosses too.

Mom wouldn't be caught dead wearing a cross. *Symbol of state torture*, she called it. I moved uneasily in my seat, the car starting to collect heat even though the windows were down. Everything hitched in my chest again, a big smooth egg with something sharp tapping at it from the inside.

Mom would call it my heart chakra getting blocked, and have a whole list of things to *un*block it.

The group milled around for a moment or two locking up the vans before heading for the grocery store. A woman with long black curling hair in a half-braid—my chest squeezed down on itself, Mom would never have just done it up halfway—danced a few steps in her Birkenstocks, and a snatch of *a cappella* drifted through the half-open window on the driver's side. Their mouths moved, the singing unexpectedly sweet. It floated over the freshly painted parking stripes, mixed with a spring breeze full of car exhaust and the weird brown smell of dirt waking up after a winter nap, but it wasn't any song I knew. It sounded almost gospel.

They harmonized pretty good, like in a movie, a musical. When we stayed with someone who had a TV, I used to watch those. Mom always said television would rot your brain, and for a while after watching a movie or even some commercials I'd shake my head, sometimes, trying to see if I could feel anything not-right inside my skull, soft or spoiled, like an orange gone bad.

The singing people all looked, I don't know, just sort of *finished*. Day trippers, Mom would say. All glossy, like they ate organic, drank sustainable, and went to workshops on conscious crystal healing, driving up the cost of reasonable clothes at the thrift stores when they condescended to go in. Why they were in a Dandy Way parking lot instead of going to the Whole Earth Foods just up Martin Way was beyond me. Maybe they were slumming, or on a church trip. Did religious-college kids go on field trips?

I didn't know.

I *do* know it wasn't there my dad met Clover—she said later it was at the garage, when they took one of the vans in—but she probably saw him in there again, probably stopped to say hi. Maybe in the produce section, because he came out with a bag of apples, a big old handful of greens, some tomatoes, oatmeal, franks, spaghetti, two bags of beans, and a bemused expression, pushing an ancient rattle-squeaking cart. Or it could have been near the dairy case, because there was a gallon of whole milk. Or in the aisle with the rice and beans, because he had a bag of brown rice, too. Or maybe she didn't see him there. It doesn't matter, I guess.

Later I found out two more of their vans went around the back of the supermarkets on Food Days—and even the back of Whole Earth —to look for slightly bruised or just-expired stuff. *Waste not, want not*, was one of *his* biggest sayings.

That was the first time I saw the Harmony people. When Dad came out, he didn't say anything about them, and neither did I. Just filed it away and forgot it.

4

BIG ON BALANCE

DAD CLOSED the Smart Eating Cookbook and laid it down safely away from the stove, his entire face scrunched up over the sizzling. "They say brown rice is healthier."

"You used to make grilled cheese." I kept slicing the tomatoes, working the knife through tough skin, rocking it like Mom taught me. *Get the whole blade in on it,* she would say, pushing her hair off her forehead with the back of one fine-boned hand. Black hair, blue eyes, so pale she almost glowed in winter, there was nothing about her that was halfway. "All the time." *With Wonder Bread, even.* Mom believed in spelt instead. And sprouts. She never met a sprout she didn't like, from bean to Brussels.

"Well, you were five. It was all you'd eat." He reached again for the top of the heaviest pot he owned, and I clicked my tongue.

"Don't, Dad. The steam will escape." I wondered if I sounded like her, because I could hear her saying the same thing inside my head. You had to watch the stove at the farmhouse, like a hawk watching the field past the apple trees, bobbing gently on a branch, swaying in the breeze.

"Oh. Yeah." Bacon spat in a blue nonstick frying pan. Whatever health benefits we'd get from the rice would probably be destroyed by pork fat and nitrates.

Dad's kitchen was full of yellow linoleum and vaguely pink counters. His stove worked just fine on all four burners, and the oven door didn't need a yardstick to prop it closed. He had an actual bathroom instead of an outhouse, and *that* was a welcome change. There was hot water from un-rusted pipes and he didn't have to stuff towels around the windows if it was cold outside; the heat worked just fine. There was even a bedroom just for me, with a futon and a pasteboard dresser. *I got this place a few years ago, for if you ever came to visit.* He said it all hopeful and anxious, like he was thinking I'd be insulted or something.

On the one hand, it was nice. On the other, there were no apple trees, and I could hear people living on the other side of the walls. I mean, not precisely *hear* them, the Swallow Mills apartment complex was pretty quiet and respectable. But that sense of other people breathing in the same building as you? Like that. Not like the farmhouse where the wind seeped in through cracks and the long grass was full of burrs and bugs and interesting things. Mom always said living off the grid was best, and electricity was a necessary evil at best. Dad's place had no cranky woodstove for heating, no mouse poop in the corners, no attic full of ancient, shrouded furniture and moldering boxes. No jars of jam or pickled beets—no home-pickled or home-canned *anything* in his cupboards. The carpet was all one color, it met the walls everywhere, and he even had a tiny concrete balcony outside the glass French door, with two lawn chairs sitting chummily and a big heavy green hibachi between them. On the third floor you could only look out over the covered parking, but there were strips of grass and landscaping there too, caught between roofs and concrete.

It was just...weird.

"Mostly on my own I get the TV dinners." He poked at the bacon with a blue spatula, its taped-up handle friendly and well-used. "I'll check out more cookbooks from the library, maybe? Take notes."

"It's fine." There were cookbooks in storage. Deciding what to bring, what to box and put away was hard. I wished I could sneak back to the U-Store-It and just open up a box of Mom's clothes, smell them. Touch them, as if they weren't husks, cold and rattling. I had my own key to storage, too, since Dad said it was all my stuff now. "It's really nice." I searched for something else to say. "I mean, that's really good of you."

Then I felt stupid. He was my father, of course he was trying. It wasn't his fault there was a patch of melting ice on the road, or a drunk driver in the middle of the afternoon coming over the yellow line, or that there was no airbag in the old truck. He didn't want to tell me about that part of it, but I was used to listening around corners and filling in blanks. Going to festivals and coloring in the corner while my mom ran yoga classes or taught housewives how to to meditate and make cheese and candles was not only the best way to learn how to deal with the straights, but it was an education in how to be so quiet nobody even suspected you were filing away information for later. Besides, I was the one who calculated the sales tax and wrote out the receipts, made change and smiled when they asked for discounts or said they left their wallet at home.

You see a lot, that way.

My eyes were hot. Tomatoes weren't onions, I couldn't blame the stinging on them. I finished slicing, and stared at the plastic cutting board.

Red tomatoes. Conventionally grown, probably full of pesticide. The bacon smelled really good, though. I scrubbed at my hot, grainy eyes with the back of my left hand, swallowing hard. Opened the cabinet in front of me, looking for bowls, but they were in the next one over. His kitchen wasn't really arranged, it was just sort of thrown together. Mom would have had a fit.

Oh, God. It took a few seconds, focusing on the big black egg in my chest, before it was smooth and polished again, nothing leaking out.

My little rock, Mom sometimes called me. Not quartz, those were clear, solidified light. Just a plain pebble, with my hard head and my worrying over things like the electric bill or rent before some family I never heard of left Mom the farmhouse. *Come on, honey. Go with the flow.*

The timer beeped. Dad flicked the heat off under the rice and half-turned, still holding that spatula. The bacon was crisping up. "You all right, dumplin'?"

"Just hungry." I set the knife down, carefully, and got out two of the mismatched, plasticky bowls. One had cornflowers, the other one had harvest fruit. Complementary. "It smells good."

"All right." His voice cracked in the middle. "Should I open up the rice now?"

"Yeah. Fluff it up with a fork."

"All right." The same hitch. Just like the squeal-squeak under his boots, on the second step of the big wraparound porch of a farmhouse that was all closed up now.

He was being careful. So was I. Real grown-up. Real straight.

I pretended not to notice he was having trouble talking. "I'll do it. You can get the bacon." I sounded nice and steady. Not like the girl who saw the cop cars coming down a dirt driveway and froze. And that yellow Charger, ridiculous to go through spring mud in. I didn't know he'd gotten a new car. We didn't have a phone at the farm.

He never pushed the custody thing, and sometimes I wondered why, or if he even cared. He seemed to when I was right in front of him, but people do that and forget you as soon as you're gone.

Like how Mom almost never mentioned him once she left him. Just forgot, between one day and the next, after she picked me up from daycare that one day and didn't take me home but to the small walk-in above Martin's occult store on Therses Street in Pittsburgh, a long time ago and a long, long way away.

Dad switched off the burner under the bacon with a quick, hard flick of his big paw. "No. I got it, sweetheart. You just get your milk."

It was regular milk in a plastic gallon, more than I could ever drink alone. *Full of hormones.* Did it matter anymore? Probably not.

We sat at his tiny table, two narrow, slightly wobbling, high-backed chairs covered with sunflower-printed vinyl. Whether it was the floor or just that the chairs were older than me, I didn't know. Neat slices of bacon, still hot. A glump of brown rice, and the glowing ruby tomatoes. Probably shipped from Ecuador or something. Mom would call them soulless. They didn't taste like heirlooms from the summer garden, but maybe that wasn't fair to them. They were doing the best they could.

Just like Dad. A short, awkward silence wrapped around us as I stared into my bowl.

"Do you, uh...did your mom ever say grace?" His five-o-clock shadow was pretty intense. With his straight nose, heavy jawline, and his blue eyes, you could see a little of why Mom might have liked him. Her boyfriends tended to the tall, lean type instead of his bulk, but they never stayed.

He'd lasted the longest. Maybe that was just because of me, though?

"Not really." Should I explain that we just had a moment of silence for the food, to feel its energy? "Do you?" You had to conform when you were with the straights.

"I don't usually. Maybe we should, since it's our first?"

"If you want." I mean, it probably couldn't hurt, right? "You don't have to."

"Well, I suppose it doesn't matter." He picked up his fork; there wasn't a chopstick in the whole apartment. "So, uh. How was your day?"

"Fine." *You were here for most of it.* I had a brand-new library card for the city system as well as the county, and a bus stopped right by the apartments. He wanted to get me a cell phone, too. Bill-the-veteran swore they caused cancer, just like he swore there were government coverups everywhere. I kind of missed Bill's cranky old face. He came into Enlightened Source every few weeks, mostly to argue with Bert about philosophy. "I don't want to go back to school." It came out all in a rush. I poked at the rice with my fork. "Can I just home-study, or something?"

"Lady at the district said we'd have to wait for next year to do anything like that." His mouth turned down at the corners. "I'm sorry, dumplin'."

"God." I poked at the rice again. "Do I *have* to?"

"I know it's not the best." Well, wasn't that an understatement.

Dad went for the bacon first. He dwarfed his chair, and the fork almost vanished into his hand. I kind of wondered how he and Mom fit together to produce me, and that was one of the most uncomfortable thoughts in the world even if Mom probably would have told me.

She wanted to raise me without hangups. Maybe it might even have worked if I wasn't so practical-headed. "Okay." I jabbed at the rice one last time, and decided, just to balance him out, I'd start with the tomatoes. Mom was big on balance. My eyes burned some more.

"Honey..." Now he sounded anxious. I couldn't tell, because the bowl was blurring and running in front of me. "I can drive you to Valley High. You don't have to change—"

"No. It's fine." Nobody at Valley was my friend, anyway, not even the stoners I hung with at lunch. Nobody had shown up for Mom's funeral, and nobody would fucking ask me about it at school. I might as well just go somewhere else. Pack up and start over. Again. Even the farmhouse wasn't supposed to be permanent. *We're wanderers*, Mom said. *Nomads. Live lightly, Val.*

My chest hurt. But I chewed on tomatoes, and when I bit into bacon the salt and crisp fat tasted wonderful. That was when it really hit me, I guess.

I was eating. I was sitting and breathing and eating. So was Dad.

Mom wasn't. And she wouldn't, ever again.

5

MAXIMUM INCONVENIENCE

Cold Ridge High was built only ten years ago instead of thirty like Valley, and it still looked new. Blue roof, brick sides, bushes trimmed and a green space they called the quad, like a college. The Charger didn't look too out-of-place in a long line of SUVs and other glossy soccer mom carrying-cases. Dad waited until we got to the crosswalk, his car creeping almost apologetically along. An avocado-colored Acura had pulled right in front of him, cutting in line, but he didn't swear or even look perturbed, just shook his big head and clicked his tongue once. The parental *I'm so disappointed in you* sound scraped over my last nerve, and I suddenly wished I'd put my hair up or something. Or that I'd gone for jeans instead of Mom's black-and-roses skirt and the velvet coat again.

The only good thing was a warm, comforting weight against my breastbone. Dad had put the turquoise necklace in a box with a banged-up silvery ribbon bow held on with Scotch tape, and set it at my place at the table that morning. I didn't manage to get down more than a slice of dry toast, and I almost didn't put the necklace on. I didn't ask if the cops gave it to him, or if they washed it off.

I didn't want to know. But it was there, and I could rest my finger-tips on it if I needed to.

"You just go in the office," he repeated, "and talk to that lady Dixon. That's what she said to do."

"I know." But I just sat there for a moment, staring at the kids streaming by. School ended in June. I was showing up right at the beginning of the big push for finals. There went my GPA. The teachers weren't going to like this, and the other kids were set in their groups now with a whole year of history behind them. It was just like every other time I changed schools before the farmhouse. The best was a Montessori one, sixth grade, but Mom hadn't managed to keep a steady enough job for the tuition.

The straights kept messing with her, expecting her to fit in their boxes. It was easier for me, I wasn't sensitive.

Dad even packed me a lunch in a brown paper bag. Peanut-butter and jelly on white bread. An apple. A packet of cheese crack-ers, which are nasty. But he was trying, right? So the least I could do was try, too.

"Honey?" Uneasy, tentative. Someone behind us hit their horn, a light, irritated tap as if everyone in front of us hadn't taken their own sweet time too.

"It's fine," I said, numbly. "I'm a big girl, Dad." I grabbed the door-handle and floundered out. A group of boys in baggy pants and back-wards-turned baseball caps, all of them whiter than the Wonder Bread Dad used to make grilled cheese with, congregated near the corner of the right-hand building, one of them half squatting as he beatboxed, spit flying from his mouth. I looked in vain for any stoners or thunkers, but they were all straights, the girls with long flat hair and the bronzer that was in style, along with the really thin headbands. The boys were either bros or wannabe hiphop, and they all knew exactly where to go.

Later I learned that only the rich kids got dropped off. The ones riding the buses were more my speed, but that first day, I didn't have a clue. It hadn't been like that at Valley.

I kind of wished then I had at least one real friend at my old school. Or that I had headphones and a cellphone, like a few of the girls I saw, walking straight through the crush and not looking at anybody. Cold Ridge swallowed me whole, and I followed the signs for the office, where I'd sat and kicked my heels in an uncomfortable plastic chair while Dad registered me and dealt with paperwork.

I almost got turned around—everything looks weird when you're in the middle of a group of spazzed-out teenagers—and the first door to the office was locked. I tugged on it like a spazz myself, sighed, and finally saw a small sunbleached sign with an arrow, *Use Other Door*.

I was about to, when I heard something strange.

Light voices, blurring together in some sort of made-up language, or just one I hadn't heard before. They came into view down the long colonnaded path heading to what I later found out was the lot where the buses parked, moving together but not marching in time. Just... swimming along, each with their own distinctive step, their mouths opening and closing.

Singing. Like some sort of glee club on crack.

The other kids didn't really look at them. Well, some did, and a couple of the bros pointed and laughed the way they do with anything outside their little clique, big dumb troll-hahas like the neanderthals they are. I just stood there, my hands dangling, my bright embroidered backpack—it was Tibetan—slipping down right shoulder. Maybe my mouth was open, I don't know.

A few boys, four girls. The girls all had long hair, but none of them had the skinny headbands. Instead, it was hippie-style, pulled back from the forehead in a small braid, the rest left loose, you know the type. They looked vaguely familiar, though I'd never seen any of them before. They were all in long broomstick skirts, just like I was, but the two blondes were in peasant tops. The other two wore tank tops, one with a shearling jacket and the other with a big chunky blue cardigan that looked itchy but that I later found out was a silk and wool blend, surprisingly soft.

The boys were all in faded jeans and braided belts, vintage T-

28

shirts and old jackets. They had longer hair too, swoopy emo-fringes across the forehead, little bits fingering the collar in back. The tallest one was brown-haired, a gold cross winking at his throat. The leather thong carrying it looked too short for him but he made it work, dark eyes slightly narrowed like he dared you to notice. They all wore boots, too—Red Wings, real working shoes.

And they all looked...I don't know. Happy to be together, and like they didn't have a fucking care in the world. A series of loud chimes broke across their singing, and the crowd of kids took on a hurried, frantic pace I knew from experience.

Time to get to class.

I tugged on the office door, taking one last look over my shoulder, and almost ran into a skinny, blow-dried girl with a high ponytail and so much makeup she looked like a doll, any shadow of acne buried and plaster-smoothed.

Her blue plastic earrings swayed, and her smile was a grimace. "Oh, *excuse* me." The words dripped with venom.

"Sorry," I mumbled, and backed up so she could go first. Which she did, clipping along on a pair of cork wedges high enough to pass for a hooker's. The shoes looked flimsy like all artfully-frayed expensive stuff does, each strap arranged for maximum inconvenience. Her thin hairband matched her earrings, and she blinked her muddy eyes at me with profound contempt, marking me as most definitely *not* one of the pop-preppies. The judgment only takes a split second, and it's written all over a straight's face. Sometimes you see it at festivals, it's the mark of the daytripper, sizing you up for the cubbyhole they want you to fit, saving them the trouble of treating you like a human being.

"Sandy!" someone called, and she raised one manicured hand. Her blue nail polish was chipped, and that cheered me up a little.

I braced myself and plunged into the den of school bureaucracy.

6

SHORT-TERM MERCY

By the time they got my schedule all figured out, it was the middle of third period. I should have just gone to the library and hung out in there for the remainder of the school year. Librarians are used to the kids who don't fit anywhere taking refuge, and if I got in there and found a quiet corner they might just ignore me.

It would've been worth a shot. But, like all really good ideas, it only occurred to me when it was too late. I stood in front of a wide-open orange door, listening to a stout lady teacher in a gray and blue nylon dress drone about the Vietnam War. I had my schedule and a map of the school in one damp palm, my throat was full of something hot and acid, and the all-day hall pass with NEW STUDENT marked in red across the top made me think of *The Scarlet Letter*.

I hadn't made it all the way through that one, it was the scene with the mom going to the governor that did me in. I kept imagining her as *my* mom, begging a straight not to take me away. Nobody ever tried, but you heard things at the festivals and fairs, in the head shops and bookstores full of shelves like *Metaphysics* and *Shamanism* and that best of words, *Occult*. Straights using judges to get custody, women on the run with thin-cheeked, hungry-eyed kids, men with sullen lines around their mouths talking about the bitch who took everything and karma served when they were pretty sure nothing female was around to hear. Sometimes I used to imagine that I'd be in danger, and Mom would do something dramatic—walking barefoot on a highway, her face set and white and queenly, or standing in front of television cameras. *Give me back my daughter!* I imagined what she'd look like when she won me back, how she'd hug me and kiss my head and tousle my hair.

Each time I imagined it I felt guilty, but the whole idea was a mosquito bite I couldn't stop scratching.

The round-faced teacher didn't notice me, droning as she laid sheets of printed plastic on the overhead projector's flat, lighted face. Another projector hung from the ceiling, controlled by the computer on her desk, but that day she was using the overhead, blinking owlishly every once in a while when the swell of conversation from the back of the classroom got a little louder. I always like to look at things before I dive in, and there was only ten minutes until lunch. I was just about to step to the side and lean against the wall, out of sight, when she called on someone.

"Yes, Travis?" Her nose wrinkled a little, and she had the weary tone of an adult who knew a kid was about to be an asshole but couldn't do anything about it at the moment.

"Can I go to the bathroom?" A sullen, drawling boy-voice. I could just *see* the kid slouching in his seat, whether it was a desk or a table, probably with his baseball cap turned backwards and a cloud of body spray saturating the air around him. Bonus if he'd started shaving, even though he probably had nothing but a few wisps on his chin. He'd be sleepy-eyed and scuzzy, and his effective vocabulary was probably about three hundred words.

The pop-preppers probably loved him.

"Do you have any passes left?" As soon as she said it, though, the teacher probably realized it wouldn't do any good. Her cheeks were bright and rosy as waxed apples.

"I gotta *go*," the kid persisted.

31

No wonder teachers went grey early. "You'll miss the homework assignment." Her tone plainly said *you won't do the work anyway.* "If that's a risk you want to take, go ahead."

I could probably step to one side or the other, and nobody would know I was there. The only trouble was, I couldn't tell which way the closest bathroom was, or even what direction Travis-the-Bathroom-Bro would go. I couldn't just stand there like an idiot, either.

So I knocked on the side of the doorframe, tentatively. "Mrs. Shieldman?" I held up the pass, like a magic charm. An adventurer in the gnoll's den, like in the short story about selling rope and emeralds that always gave me the creeping willies. "Ms. Dixon at the office sent me here."

That got her attention. She blinked at me like I had just yelled something obscene, reaching for the glasses resting against her high-strapped chest on a bedazzled lanyard. Her tits didn't move; she was apparently one of the bigtime bra-believers. "Huh? Oh, come in. You must be the new student. Where have you been?"

On a Monday after Spring Break, she was asking me? "The office was really busy."

"They didn't send anyone to show you around?" She waved the question aside, irritably. "Come in, come in."

I braced myself and edged into the room. Twenty-odd pairs of eyes crawled all over me. I *hate* that. One of the kids was half out of his chair—they had separate desks instead of tables, which was all right. Sitting at tables always ups the chances of being stuck with someone awful when group project time comes around.

I hate group projects. They're just a way to make the kids babysit each other instead of having the teacher do it.

The Bathroom Bro was husky in a way that shouted *football,* and the only thing he was missing was the backwards baseball cap. Instead, he had an aggressive dark buzzcut and a sort of congested face, his eyes close together and his letterman's jacket straining to contain shoulders that *had* to be steroid-induced. His pants sagged, his belt pretty useless, and I was glad I was too far away to smell whatever body spray he'd drenched himself with. That was a short-term mercy, though, because he was heading for the door.

"Come on." Mrs Shieldman nodded sagely. "Come over to my desk. The rest of you, finish your notes."

"Who are *you?*" Buzz-cut demanded, over her last sentence. He bumped his way between the desks, casually flicking another kid's baseball cap off and sniggering. The other kid, a weedy dark-haired nerd, turned scarlet, and I longed to smack Travis the Buzz-Cut.

Mom would have said violence is never the answer, but man, it was tempting. I was always more Fight the Power than Summer of Love anyway.

I pretended not to hear him, following the teacher. Travis didn't like that. Well, maybe he just decided to show his appreciation by muttering "Bitch," as he passed me on a draft of chemical smell. I almost gagged.

He could have meant the teacher. Maybe she pretended not to hear him, too. I restrained the urge to wave his cloud of funk-smell away.

"Go ahead and sit next to Oscar, there." She pointed at the blushing kid—skinny, his shearling jacket hung on the back of the chair and his boots shouting *rural*, curly dark hair and a bit of fuzz on his upper lip. He had the nervous, oversized hands of a drummer, and there was an empty desk right next to him. "He'll share his notes."

A rustle went through the class. In the back, a readheaded girl bent over her notebook. It looked like she was drawing, not giving a fuck about the rest of the class, and I envied her.

"Okay." I waited to get my pass back, and for a second the teacher looked like she was going to keep it.

"I can't believe they didn't send anyone with you," she finally said, and tucked the pass inside a battered American History text-book with an eagle on the front and a broken spine, which she offered to me with both hands like it was a present.

I had to restrain the urge to accept it with a bow, as if we were in an Asian grocery. "I guess they were busy." *Duh.* On my way to the empty desk, I bent and picked up the Oscar kid's hat. My hair fell down on either side of my face, and someone whispered, *"Hippie."* Another titter went through the class.

Great.

I found out why that desk was empty, too. The seat was loose. I handed Oscar's blue baseball cap back and he didn't even look at me, just mumbled something and stared at his notebook. He didn't bother sharing his notes, and I didn't bother asking. It took almost the whole ten minutes until the lunch bell for Mrs Shieldman to pick up the thread of her lecture again, but at least I got the homework assignment.

And at least that kid Travis didn't show back up. So it wasn't bad for a first day.

7

THE SKINNY

OSCAR WAS ACTUALLY OZ, and he took pity on me while the room cleared out for first lunch, sticking out his hand. I shook it, only moderately surprised that his palm was moist. Some kids couldn't catch a break, and he had that look all *over* him.

"You one of the Harmony kids?" He stuffed his cap in his backpack, eyeing me warily. "They usually stick together."

"I don't even know who they are." Most of the class was already hell and gone, but I'd stayed put to wait for the crush at the door to subside. Mrs. Shieldman settled at her desk with a sigh that was halfway to a groan, and proceeded to ignore us. It was probably the only time during the day she actually liked her job.

"They're the ones singing all the time." He hitched his backpack onto his shoulder. His jeans were baggy, but not fashionably—they looked, instead, like hand-me-downs, worn at the knees right where they do a lot of work. "You know where the lunchroom is?"

I'd passed through it on my way to get here. "I think so." I longed to ask him who I should avoid, who was likely to think they could get something out of the new girl, who the worst of the bullies were. You can't just ask a guy that, though. Another girl would have known what I was talking about, and maybe given me the skinny. "Where do you go if you don't want to eat in the fishbowl?"

He shrugged. "Wherever you can. Most of Security's pretty cool. But the guy with the glasses likes to believe he's a hardass."

"Good to know." I buttoned my backpack up, rubbing my fingertips over the mandala on the flap. "Thanks."

"Hey." He glanced nervously at the door, a faint flush spreading up his neck. His hands kept moving a little, unable to contain themselves; I found out later he was in the marching band. "Some friends and I hang in the library. You can come along, if you want to roll a few dice."

Oh. He was a gamer. The first thing approaching a smile cracked my face that day. "Maybe, once I figure out where my other classes are."

His shoulders hunched a little, but he looked relieved that I wasn't latching on immediately. "Cool. We, uh, we don't have a lot of girls hanging out. But, you know, it'd be okay."

Great. "Thanks." Valley had a D&D club in the library at lunch, too. The pop-preppers mostly left them alone, but they were a closed group and I never did more than say hello to any of them. I was mostly with Tamara and the stoners at lunch. I wondered if Tamara was missing me. Probably not, she'd just started dating Johnny, and I was more a third wheel than a help, there. "See you."

He escaped and I trudged out, deciding I might as well just take a look at the lunchroom. Reconnoiter. Get the lay of the land, so to speak. Oz had already disappeared by the time I made it to the hallway.

The lunchroom was a three-ring circus, just like at Valley. They had a small outlet for a local sandwich shop shoehorned between the less appetizing options and of course the pop-preps clustered it, cutting in line, the girls flipping their hair, squeezing anyone else out. Rubbery overprocessed cardboard masquerading as food was handed out to everyone else, but at least the chocolate milk was free. I got a box of that, trying to look everywhere at once, and retreated to the margins.

The Harmony kids had their own table and packed lunches, too. One of them had chopsticks, and it made me think of Mom's bento boxes. She went through a real sushi craze when I was about thirteen; I ate wasabi, nori, and rice for a solid year. Fish is kind of nasty, but it's sea urchin I made a vow never to touch again. It tastes like the underside of a pier, and that's pretty much exactly what it is, too.

Thank God Mom went vegan right after that.

I studied the Harmony kids. They had a table not at the periphery or in the center, but in some middle orbit. They looked pretty serene, all things considered. The boys bracketed the girls, who elbowed each other and laughed and basically just glowed with health and security. A few tables over were a bunch of pop-preppers, including the blonde with the cork wedges *and* Travis the Bathroom Bro. The ponytails-and-thin-headbands were all over that table, and the guys mostly wore team jackets. There were a couple of outliers—a girl with a pixie cut, a slim guy with glasses and an honest-to-God neckscarf like an old Hollywood villain—thrown in for fun, but it was just the same as Valley. Only the skin colors were a little different. Valley had a lot more non-pale faces in the mix.

I couldn't find the stoners. So I just finished my chocolate milk, tossed the carton, and wandered off with the map to find out how to get from one damn class to the next for the afternoon. I didn't see a single security guard, which was all right by me.

8

BAD AIR

I HAD beef stew simmering when Dad came home, and the smell of it filled the entire apartment. I'd already started a fresh grocery list—he didn't even have flour, so I couldn't make biscuits or anything else. I had to check four or five times to make sure I locked the door when I got home, after he turned white and got all worried when I left it unlocked once before school started. It felt more like barricading myself *in* than other people *out*, and I'd gotten used to just letting the door go at the farmhouse.

You couldn't do that with straights around, though.

"Hello, dumplin'!" he sang out, and I snapped my French textbook closed. They were pretty remedial, way behind even Valley's second-year French classes, and *that* was going to be easy sailing if I had to take the final.

"I'm in here." I glanced over the list again, trying to guess what the total bill would be. I didn't know what he brought home every two weeks, but it had to be okay if he could afford this place *and* the Charger. Still, with me here eating and stuff, his take-home would get a hit. I couldn't help it, unless I got a job too.

The door-locks clicked as he threw them. "What you cookin'? It smells good. How was it today?"

A lot of questions all at once. Mom would have been more open-ended, gauging if I wanted to talk. "Stew, and it was fine."

"Wish I coulda picked you up, but we have every damn bay full at the garage."

"That's okay. I rode the bus home." The Harmony kids were on the bus, too. All of them, and they were still on when I got off, sitting halfway back and singing. Not loudly, because the bus driver turned some AM talk radio up, but enough that you could hear them over some inbred asshat talking about chemtrails. The driver, a graying man with a hard little pregnant potbelly, looked like an ex-Marine or something, and his mouth was a hard-set bitter line. I had to show him my bus slip twice—once when I got on, again when I got off in front of the apartments with a group consisting of two pop-prepper girls and a bunch of flotsam—some nerds, some geeks, four tight-knit goths with dark eyeliner and black canvas coats, a bigger group of nonstandards, and yours truly.

Any ecosystem needs a huge base to support the predators at the top, and high school's no different.

Dad came around the corner, big-shouldered, slightly slumped, his hands red and chapped from orange soap and his eyes a little under-smudged. Maybe he was working overtime at the garage because of me. I didn't want to ask, so all I could do was wonder.

I mean, I knew I cost Mom money and weighed her down. It was just a thing, like the funny bump on one of my back molars or the calluses on my heels in summer. I tried *not* to be so heavy, but it was impossible. Now I was weighing someone *else* down, and I felt like a overstaying guest. The bed in my room wasn't familiar yet, the walls in there were bare because I hadn't bothered to put up my collection of zodiac hangings and handkerchiefs from all the festivals we'd gone to. The dresser in there was sturdy enough, sure, but I never used one with Mom, especially once we got the same size. We just pulled whatever out of the clean laundry pile and went on with our lives.

"Already hitting the books? You're a smart girl. Like your mama." His smile held an edge of wincing, maybe because he didn't want to talk about her.

Smart's not everything. "They're starting for finals." At least I'd already done the year's crop of standardised tests back at Valley. I searched for something else to say. "How was work?"

"Busy." He rubbed at his eyes with his knuckles, and that was probably why they looked so bruised. Engine grease is pretty stiff eyeliner. "That smells awful good."

"It'll be ready soon. You want garlic toast?" At least he had garlic powder. And if I was cooking I was contributing, right?

"Sure thing. You, uh, you don't have to cook." He peered at me, blinking, and I suppressed a guilty start. "You got school."

"I should get a job." I darted a glance at his face to check the reaction. He just stood there, looking baffled, his wallet and car keys in one hand, about to be plopped in the big lumpy clay dish on the counter near the phone. I had a vague memory of making that dish in third grade, or something, and it was weird to see something I'd forgotten so completely.

"*School* is your job." Dad sounded shocked, and his eyebrows came together. "I know it's hard, with this being the end of the year and all, but you just do your best."

"Well, I mean..." I stacked my books together. French. American History. Pre-Cal. "I just, I know it's a hassle having me here, and all—"

"No, not a hassle, honey." He headed for the sleek white fridge. It never wheezed or got balky, and it was one of those frostless numbers. The shelves were clean. Even the ketchup and mustard were arranged neatly. "You're my dumplin'." And *that*, his tone said, was clearly *that*.

"Okay." I couldn't figure out if he really meant it, or if it was the kind of thing a grownup said because they knew they were supposed to. So I just carried my books back to my room, and came out to start the garlic toast. There would be enough stew for him to take in for lunch for a couple days, too. I was kind of happy to be cooking non-vegan again, too. It was just so much easier; Mom would get that pinched look if she knew I was eating mayo, let alone red meat.

My stomach flipped behind my ribs. She was never going to tell me how red meat decays in your colon and produces toxins ever again. She was never going to have me lay out the tarot cards and say, *tell me a story, tell me what you see*. Never going to sing off-key to the classic rock station in the truck, never going to roll her eyes at my craving for milkshakes, never going to tell me to *breathe deep and let the worries fly away, starchild*. Never going to call me *starchild* again, or proudly say, *my daughter does that for me*.

I burnt the first batch of garlic toast, but Dad said nothing. I made sure to give him the non-burned batch, and all that night while I lay in bed trying to sleep, I burped charcoaled garlic on wheat bread. It mixed uneasily with the Crest he bought me—Mom sometimes thought fluoride was okay, and sometimes didn't, according to what she'd read last.

Each time a pocket of bad air rose up my throat, it dislodged hot, stinging water from my eyes.

9

DECIDED TO CRASH

I MADE it through the first week of school without a major incident. The gym teacher didn't even make me dress out, which was a blessing, because as I sat on the bleachers and watched, I got an eyeful of the girl with the blonde ponytail, the perennial high heels, and the makeup so thick she looked flawless. Sandy flounced and eye-rolled her way through sixth period, doing her best not to work up anything that might have resembled a sweat. She had two henchwomen— another blonde, this one with bigger hips and a penchant for dressing in pink, and a redhead with wide, fresh blue eyes and wicked scarlet nails. They weren't her friends, necessarily, but they were proto-pop-preppers hungry for a little of her reflected glow. The henches dressed out, caught the dodgeballs, and covered for her.

Two of the Harmony girls were in fifth-period gym too—Ingrid and Gabrielle. They stuck together in the locker room and outside, often glancing at each other and cracking up in the middle of class like best friends. Occasionally one of them would sing a snatch of something, the other would catch up and harmonize, and then they'd dissolve into laughter when long, spare, sinewy Ms. Greeman looked at them despairingly. Even wearing the gray athletic T-shirts with the

Cold Ridge Crushers logo and baggy sweatpants, they looked different, somehow.

Friday the whole class got a break for a pep rally. I didn't yet know how to skip those, so I just helped set up the gym with Greeman's hectoring ringing off the fully extended bleachers, then tried to lurk near the doors to slip out. I had the bad luck to choose the doorset where they were herding everyone in; escape was impossible. I dug my mother's paperback *Complete Crystal Encyclopedia* out of my backpack and did my best to ignore the yells, the pounding on the bleachers, the jostling from every side, the blaring music over squealing speakers. The oily, sweaty, self-satisfied faces of the jocks swam across a polished wooden floor. I found out Travis the Bathroom Bro was on the wrestling team. Imagining him in one of those ridiculous unitards and hugging one of his besties was pretty amusing.

Unfortunately, about halfway through, someone above me tossed a half-full water bottle. It looped overhead and plummeted right onto a blonde head below, crushing Sandy's ponytail. I had no idea, because I was reading about chrysoprase, again. *Mother of Jade. Springtime. Good for clearing the heart chakra, restricts rheumatism—*

A change in the noise around me jerked my head up just as Sandy turned around, her face a picture of disgust and pain. It was by far the most human expression I'd ever seen on her, and I flat-out stared, my brain a blank as the water bottle bounced away, hitting one of her friends on a sticklike, orange-tanned arm. Mom always said chrysoprase was good for jewelry, but not for—

"*You bitch,*" Sandy mouthed, looking straight at me.

I shook my head and shrugged, trying to express it wasn't me. It did no good at all. By then, there were a lot of bottles flying, most half-empty but a few full ones dropping like rocks on the kids below. The music screeched to a halt, several teachers couldn't restore order, and when the chimes for the end of the day rang, they had to let us go get on the buses. Turned out some of the football kids had decided to crash a pep assembly that wasn't for them, and loaded their backpacks with used bottles left behind in the lunchroom for a week.

Of course none of them got into any serious trouble. But Sandy had already made up her mind, and maybe if I'd been there longer I would have suspected that trouble was coming.

10

OLD SOUL

I TRUDGED down the hall for Dad's apartment, my arms aching and my head giving them a run in the pain department. They hadn't given me a locker yet, so I had to carry every textbook around for every single goddamn class. The bus driver had turned his talk radio up, and we had to listen to some straight jabbering about how Muslims were dangerous and terrorists were everywhere. I couldn't wait to shut the door and have a few hours of blessed quiet to push all the noise and the idiocy away.

I had to pee like a firehose, too. I hate going in school bathrooms. Even an outhouse is better, unless it's below freezing outside. You just don't know what the straights have put on the seats, and having a straight listen to the trickle is the *worst*.

As soon as I turned the key in the deadbolt, though, I heard voices, and remembered Dad only had a half day this Friday for some reason. Maybe he'd invited Hooker home, but then I heard a woman laugh. I gritted my teeth and shouldered the door open. The carpet in here was finally sort-of-familiar, its pattern of light brown and slightly darker brown full of waves. The smell was familiar, too—a ghost of last night's chicken and pasta with red sauce from a jar.

He ate meat all the time. So far it hadn't rotted my colon, but I was uneasy. The apartment was full of a sudden, listening silence, and if I could around the corner fast enough I could get a glimpse at whoever was here *and* get to the bathroom without being flagged down.

"I'm home," I called, and hoped I could escape polite small talk.

"That's my daughter." The couch—a big leather thing, Dad's pride and joy—squeaked as he shifted his weight on it. "Val? You want to come in here a minute?"

"In a second, Dad." I almost yelled *I've gotta pee*, which I might have if it was Mom. She'd just laugh, or better, wouldn't ask me in the first place, just let me appear if I felt like it and be introduced.

The thing about peeing in an apartment bathroom is the persistent sense that everyone outside is listening to you. It's almost as bad as school. I stacked my books on the counter and put a few squares of paper in the ceramic bowl to muffle the sound, but it probably didn't work. Even if they didn't hear the song of my bladder they definitely heard the flush, and I took my time washing my hands, too. Maybe they'd leave and I'd only have Dad to deal with, and the awkward pauses between the conversational basketballs neither of us really knew how to lob at each other.

Or catch.

It was pretty useless, because they were still there when I trudged out into the living room holding my books like a shield in front of my chest.

The woman on the other end of the couch from Dad had long dark curly hair, and my heart lodged in my mouth before I saw it was just dark, not the blue-black of Mom's. She had wide dark eyes and a snub nose, and you might take her for early twenties from a distance. Up close, you'd realize it was more late-twenties, her mouth hovering between a soft smile and a sort of rueful kindness that had finally figured out the world isn't kind at all. Mom would have called her an old soul just on that smile alone. She had a long multicolored skirt and a pretty blue peasant blouse with the sleeves high up on her slim shoulders, her hair half-braided, and a gold cross glittered below the notch of her collarbones. In the easy chair where Dad sat to watch TV after dinner was a guy who looked a little older than her and had the same dark, curling hair wisping almost to his shoulders. He had a cross too, and a Mexican shirt with an embroidered yoke-pattern, broken-in jeans and motorcycle boots, and they looked like the Harmony kids.

"Val, honey. This is Clover and Leaf. They're, uh..." Was he blushing?

The guy looked familiar, but it took me a second. "You used to come into Enlightened Source all the time." I hugged my books even closer. The girl was familiar too, though I couldn't quite place her. "Did you know my mom? She read your cards."

"Shade?" The guy took a second look at me. "Oh, yeah, I thought you looked familiar. She was right-on, your mom."

So he did remember her. Relief and uneasiness mixed behind my throat chakra. "You brought in organic sage all the time, for the smudge sticks." I dug my toe into the carpet. "Good stuff." He *also* brought in organic not-sage, which was good stuff too. Coral swore it was better than Humboldt County weed, and she should know.

Maybe it was the wrong thing to say, because his face fell just a little. He didn't have a five-o'clock shadow, but his cheeks didn't look all scraped and raw like most guys' get. "We all gotta do what we can."

I wondered if he was Clover or Leaf. Probably Leaf, unless his parents were really way-out. I'd never known his name before, just his face. He used to wear a scuzzy black bandanna around his forehead, to go along with perpetually bloodshot eyes and a strong skunky scent of smoking-rope. It didn't look like he was blazing now, though. Maybe the lady had him on a short leash. They looked *awful* alike.

Cross-legged on the couch, the lady tucked a stray strand of hair behind her ear and beamed at me. "You must be Val. We've heard a lot about you—your dad's really proud."

47

I wasn't sure he knew enough about me to *be* proud, really. I still couldn't figure out where I'd seen *her* before. Had she come into the bookstore too? I tried to figure out what to say next. "Nice to meet you. Uh, Dad, I've got homework."

He was still wearing that dopey smile, and held himself carefully on the couch like he was afraid it would collapse under him at any moment. It was nice to see him in a T-shirt and jeans instead of his work overalls, even if the shirt was a pea-green Army number. "Okay, honey. I just wanted you to meet 'em."

"We should probably be on our way, right, Leaf?" Clover slithered off the couch and stood with a gentle rolling motion, stretching like a dancer. It was official, Dad *was* blushing. "Thanks for the tea, Earl."

"No problem." Dad gathered himself, rising slowly. "Listen, that van starts making that noise again, you just call."

"We'll see you Sunday?" Leaf said, and my ears perked. I retreated down the hall for my bedroom, first door on the left.

"Well, I gotta talk it over with Val." Dad was probably shaking Leaf's hand, the male goodbye ritual. "She, uh, she's had a rough time of it."

"I'm so sorry." Clover even sounded like she meant it. "Well, the invitation's open. There's plenty of room."

I closed my bedroom door and leaned against it for a few minutes, listening to the goodbyes and the small talk and crackling silence that falls after guests leave and everything in you takes a deep breath and congratulates you for not making an idiot out of yourself. I thumped my books down on the Sauder desk Dad had bought—he even got it new, at the big blue Shop-Mart, for God's sake, and put it together inside of an hour. It was amazing, he just knew where every piece went after giving it a thoughtful look. Mom hated putting together stuff like that, but she'd never have gone into a box store anyway. *The Universe will provide*, she'd say, and find furniture someone else didn't want or had thrown out, ready to be hauled home and petted like a rescued animal.

48

The moment the books hit the desk's pasteboard top, I remembered where I'd seen Clover. In the parking lot at the grocery store, singing as the wind teased at her hair. She looked a *lot* younger from a distance.

Harmony kids. Were there Harmony grownups, too? There had to be. All I heard was that they lived together off Cold Creek Road.

At dinner Dad told me, over pizza full of melted cheese and grease-waxy pepperoni, that they'd invited him out to their place on Sunday to take a look at another big white church-van that was having trouble.

"They're good people," he said, after he chewed a huge mouthful of too-hot sauce and cheese, probably burning his tongue, judging by the way his face squinched up. "Ouch. Pay cash, polite as you please, they run a soup kitchen out near Temberton Alley too."

"Mh." I didn't know where that was, and had carefully picked all the pepperoni off my slice so I could eat it all at once. Salty, full of processed chemicals, and delicious, it was sure to clog my arteries. But it was *pizza*. I didn't tell Dad it was my first time eating a slice since I was seven and went to someone's birthday party. I don't remember what it tasted like then, but now I knew for sure.

It was just as good as everyone said. That night, lying in bed and hearing the muffled sound of the television as Dad drank his usual single can of Pabst before turning it off and lumbering down the hall, I made up my mind not to forget again.

11

INDIGESTION CRYSTALS

THAT SUNDAY WAS bright and cloudless, warm in the sunshine but still chilly in any shade you could find. It wasn't freezing at night anymore and the apple blossoms were out in force, the cherries already shedding their pink petals when the breeze whisked by. It was that brief moment after the ice breaks for good but right before the mud really begins, when the grass poking up is pale but happy to be alive and you can see green threads on the tangle of deciduous branches. The evergreens look like adults right before they really wake up, in that half-hour or so where you can ask your mom *pleeeeeeease* and all you'll get is a noncommittal sound because no caffeine's been brewed yet, her eyelids shut and her cheek mashed against the pillow.

"I'm a pagan." I wished I could put my feet on the dashboard, settled for leaning against the car door as far as I could. "They'd better not try to convert me."

"Me either." Dad squinted at the road, blue eyes alive with banked excitement and his short hair almost standing up. "Don't think that's their style, though, dumplin'."

The Harmony people said that if Dad came out Sunday at

around noon to look at the van there would be lunch in the deal. I was pretty sure it wasn't food Dad was thinking about, because he blushed right up to his hairline when he said *Clover*. I didn't ask if he'd been seeing her for a while, or what. It wasn't my business, but still.

I mean, he and Mom had been split up for a long time, but...I don't know. I never felt that way about any of Mom's boyfriends, mostly because I knew none of them would last. I just tried not to notice Dad's excitement, rubbing at the turquoise under my WOOD-STOCK LIVES T-shirt. Along with ratty jeans and the combat boots, it was as close to armor as I could get. I'd gotten myself all set to ask him if we could go by the storage place again so I could dig in the boxes and find a thinner jacket, like a hoodie or something, but I lost my nerve when I saw him sitting at the table for breakfast all shaved and combed, a brand new lint roller still in its packaging right next to his plate.

It's got to be serious when a guy gets a lint roller. Even—maybe *especially*—if that guy is your dad.

It wasn't a long drive, especially since Dad's apartment was on the edge of town anyway. A funny, unsteady feeling settled in my heart chakra. It was kind of weird, how your stomach was all tangled up with that energy ball, one of the things I never understood and just took Mom's word for. I guess it made sense when you were sensitive to the energy, like she was. At least there was the turquoise, three flat rectangles in a heavy, jointed silver setting, its three thin chains sharing the weight. Mom even wore it to bed, so I did too, figuring sooner or later my hair wouldn't tangle in it anymore and I wouldn't get a wake-up headache from the pressure on my neck.

I stared out the window. Houses had drawn away from the road, gotten bigger, and instead of a paved shoulder there was gravel and a ditch full of winter-blasted grass. Subdivided fields swelled the further we drove; we crossed Cold Creek's likewise-swollen blue chuckling on an old bridge with decorative concrete flourishes on its side-rails. The *Est. 1963* carved into posts on either side was softened with moss that would dry up and turn brown in summer. I could almost pretend I was in the truck with Mom on one of her rambles.

Except it was a lot quieter than the truck, because the Charger's engine didn't rattle and neither did the doors. The windows were up, and there were little buttons to turn on heaters inside the seats. Not that we needed them, with all the sunshine. Dark circles under Dad's eyes matched the ones under mine. On the kitchen counter was a box of Celestial Seasoning teabags, Mom's favorite kind.

Instead, I'd poured myself a cup of bitter, overcooked coffee, and he hadn't said a word.

He didn't put the teabags back in the cupboard. Neither did I. I also hadn't washed the mugs Clover and Leaf had put, very mannerly, in the sink. They sat there, the used bags shriveled and drying.

Coffee-flavored acid boiled in my stomach. Maybe I didn't have a heart chakra, or I had a super-blocked one. Maybe it was just indigestion. What was good for indigestion? Citrine, maybe? Maybe azurite too. The Charger hugged the road, up and down, a nice smooth ride with brand-new shocks. When the hills with their green feathering reared and we plunged into branch-threaded shade as the road turned away from the creek and started climbing, I closed my eyes.

That was why, the first time we went to Harmony, I didn't see the neatly painted sign near the gate—*Harmony Home*—next to a faded red *No Trespassing* one almost hidden in clipped, winter-blackened blackberry vines. I got a confused impression of the long unpaved driveway under close-pressing trees, and the crunching of gravel under the tires scraped at my skin.

You don't want to look at that, dumplin'. I exhaled, hard, running my fingers over the biggest rectangle of turquoise. If you had a whole driveway full of turquoise, it would sound just the same. Pretty gravel, sitting on my chest.

The trees thinned, and we went on the dirt road for a while. Neat white-painted fences held back the fields, every third one lying fallow and the others dug up in long rows. You could grow a lot of food out here. There were pale buildings in the distance, too. One big fading-red barn, the only structure not freshly painted, and a couple smaller ones bright crimson, throbbing just-yanked teeth. A long low carport off to one side of a big white farmhouse with blue trim held long white vans and one powder-blue Corolla, and my heart wouldn't stop thumping in my throat.

Mom would like this place. And my chest squeezed in on itself, horribly. If I did have a heart chakra it was shrinking, turning black as tar and thick as rice noodles when you don't rinse them. They just turn into a glop.

There were goats and chickens, and a big orange-striped cat sunning himself on a fencepost—I never saw him again after that first day. Gardens in neat boxes, some of them with hinged covers made of old windows—probably for cabbage and starts too tender for a late freeze. A big churchy building—they called it the Pavilion—that I found out later was full of tables and a mismatched collection of chairs sat across a wide expanse of cracked paving from the big house. The Pavilion's windows and double doors were open, so you could see people moving around inside. Two restaurant-size cylindrical grills were going, and the guys standing behind them looked healthy and relaxed, all in T-shirts and jeans. The women were mostly in long skirts, but I saw a few with jeans on too.

Maybe I wouldn't stick out as much as I thought.

And the kids. There weren't a *whole* lot of them, just the amount you'd expect in a crowd that size. They were all in faded but well-fitting clothes, hair brushed neatly, faces scrubbed, the older ones helping carry plates and pots, the younger ones shepherded by adults who looked like teachers, if teachers wore hemp bracelets and laughed a lot. Long hair. Bright smiles. Everyone's mouths moving, because they were singing.

"Well, we're here." Dad parked behind the blue Corolla, and opening the car door let the music in. Massed voices harmonizing, tones rising and shifting as naturally as breathing, like the soundtrack to some kind of dramatic movie where someone gets a peek at heaven.

Even the kids sang, and if a baby—there were two, and four or five toddlers too— started to cry, the sound would gentle as someone scooped them up and comforted them. Or it would bubble with laughter if they were throwing a tantrum, folding around the edges of their outburst.

I stretched my way out of the car, listening. When the chickens or goats made noise, it fit into the music. Even the breeze in evergreens or greening branches fit too, like puzzle pieces.

Mom wouldn't have just liked it. She would have flat-out *loved* this. I stood there like an idiot, one arm over the door, listening with my mouth a little open. Dad, on the other side of the car, glanced around anxiously, maybe expecting someone to tell him to move his car or that he'd misunderstood.

Clover hurried out of the Pavilion, beaming a megawatt smile in the Charger's direction. Her blue-and-white skirt moved gracefully, and her yellow sweater was a splash of sunshine. The wind played with her curls, and when she broke off singing to talk, the rhythm rubbed through the words. "You're just in time! Come on, lunch is ready."

12

BIG BUTTON

I DON'T KNOW what I expected, but fried chicken and potato salad on heavy ceramic diner dishes wasn't it. The barbecues were doing slow-roast stuff for dinner. At one end of the Pavilion, stacks of wooden benches rested against the wall; at the other, a sort of platform, only about six inches high, put its back to the wall and curved gently in front. An electric piano sat to one side with a companionable drum set and a couple of guitars on those funny racks that look like they're holding up a fat-bellied drunk. The music retreated while we ate, string beans and flavorless store tomatoes next to melting, golden biscuits. I could have eaten twenty of the biscuits and gone back for more, but I was too busy looking around. I saw the kids that rode my bus, and wondered about it. Later I found out the bus stopped at the crossroads and they walked about a half a mile home. They were right on the edge between school districts so the bigger one took them because the smaller didn't have enough buses, or something.

Dad, wanting to be polite, sat next to Clover, and I sat next to him. There was a gap on my other side—maybe they were giving guests some kind of space, or maybe it was because we weren't

Harmony. At least, there was a gap until someone slithered into it, and I found out it was just a kid.

She was about eight, dishwater blonde with a long fringe across her forehead that fell and hid her eyes when she wanted it to. The rest of her hair was long and ruler-straight, surprisingly thick, and her cheeks were still a little babyfat-chubby. I learned later that her growing-out bangs simply couldn't be contained. They'd slip free of braids, work out of clips, and laughed at water or coconut oil used to slick them aside or make them behave. Behind them, a pair of dark eyes peered at me, with only a shade or two different between iris and pupil. It was kind of unsettling when she stared at you, because her eyes were deep-socketed, so even though they were big and thickly lashed she looked tired.

The rest of her was kind of...blurred. You know those young kids who look like clay, sort of? You can tell their body hasn't decided what it's going to do and they sort of run at the edges. A white dress and white patent-leather shoes shouted *church day*, except the shoes were dabbed with mud and the hem of the dress was torn a little over her left knee. Among all the other neat, clean children, she was the only one who looked a little dirty, like a kid should.

She blinked at me and I blinked back, just like with a cat. That's how they say they like you, with subtle eyelid moves.

You see kids like her at festivals sometimes, wandering around wide-eyed and drinking everything in. She had that same look, the world was still new and she liked it a lot. Mom would have called her an indigo child because of her eyes and the calm way she just looked me over. Dad was busy talking to Clover, awkwardly keeping up a string of *gee, this weather* and *so the sound the van's making, kind of a knocking?*

I slid my plate over a bit. The girl looked at the remaining biscuit, the remnants of string beans, the fried chicken I'd only taken a token nibble of. It's kind of weird to be chewing on chicken when you've just heard them clucking in one of the three pens Harmony Home had. It wasn't that I was going vegetarian, and I didn't know if they ate the egg-layers or just kept them until they got old or whatever, it was just...it kind of bothered me. The lump in my throat bothered me too, because everywhere I looked I saw something Mom would have liked. People all mixed together at tables, humming and talking and laughing and just being together. It *felt* good, like a festival or a faire where the drama hasn't started, the porta-potties aren't full, and the weather's still good.

The little girl kept her hands cupped in her lap. She shook her head a little, but her lips moved a little. You can tell when a kid that age is hungry, even when they're trying not to show it.

"You want the biscuit?" I hunched my shoulders, like Dad. Even if you can't make yourself smaller, kids can tell when you're really making the effort. They usually appreciate it. "I'm full."

She considered this. Her hands moved a little, long fine fingers on a chubby child's palm separating.

It was a tiny, bright blue egg. I had to lean in close to hear what she said.

"I have to keep it warm." A small, forlorn sentence.

Maybe she was shy. I knew how to handle this, though. "I can hold it while you eat. If you want."

There was a commotion at the far end of the Pavilion, but I didn't look. I cupped my hands, gently, and offered them like a dish. She examined me for another long moment, then, infinitely gently, put her hands in mine.

I think of that moment over and over again. I try to figure out if I felt something then—maybe I started to sweat, or a stray breeze would come in and lift my hair, just like in a movie. But it never happens that way outside of Hollywood.

Nothing ever does.

Her skin was warm, and she stared directly into my eyes like she wanted to see the back of my skull as she opened the bottom of her cupped palms and the egg touched my skin. "I'm Sarah." She folded my fingers over the egg. "Not too tight. Don't squeeze."

Of course not, jeez. "It's an egg, I won't squeeze it." I tried not to sound sarcastic.

She didn't even wipe her hands, just went straight for the fried chicken. It probably didn't occur to her that she was eating a cousin of whatever was in the egg. I thought it might be a robin's, because of the color, except it was pretty early for robins to be laying. It was heavier than I expected it to be, though, and she kept checking every few bites to make sure I wasn't squeezing it. She picked the drumstick clean and smeared a dollop of butter from the side of my plate on the biscuit, and the rustling of a crowd paying attention to something got my attention.

He was tall. Not as tall as Dad, but then, nobody is. He had surfer-streaked, shoulder-length wavy hair, broad shoulders, and a white dashiki with a single bar of red and blue embroidery along the neck plus a little bit down the chest. Square-jawed, clean-shaven, worn jeans and moccasins, he should have looked like every other guy there.

But he didn't. Part of it was the rings—big chunky ones, too. Onyx, turquoise, a couple thick silver ones. He didn't wear a cross, just a wooden medallion shaped like a spiral on a leather thong and a string of what I thought were small offwhite pooka beads. It was hard to tell how old he was. He looked awful young until he smiled and the fans of wrinkles at the outside of his eyes folded up. A single hemp bracelet on his right wrist, a leather strap with a buckle on his left, and he was the picture of a fashion-magazine hippie. It should have been ridiculous, but he owned it.

I mean, just the way he moved through the Pavilion, stopping every once in a while to talk to someone, touch a shoulder, grin, ruffle someone's hair or listen solemnly to what was obviously a problem someone had. It was like something warm leaked out of every inch of him, and everyone cuddled around it like Mom and me sleeping near the woodstove on a cold night.

Sarah chewed the biscuit so fast I had uncomfortable visions of her choking. It was kind of awkward to get my mug of apple juice slid over to her with my hands full of the egg, but as soon as she saw what I was doing she reached for the juice and dropped back down next to me. The man was working his way toward us. Behind him, a slight, willowy woman with a mop of reddish-brown hair glided, smiling, and though she stopped to listen and gave out hugs and bent to talk to the kids, it was different. Nothing leaked out of her but the usual mom-vibes.

"Who's that?" I figured it was a reasonable question.

Sarah finished all my apple juice. "Father Jim."

Oh. It hadn't occurred to me to ask how this place was organized. I guess in some fuzzy way I thought it was a commune. Mom was always talking about communes, how they were great in theory but people had too many hangups to really do it right.

She thought that about a lot of stuff.

I put my head down, opening my hands a little bit to peek at the egg. So blue, like the turquoise on Mom's necklace. Mine, now. What would she think of this guy? *Father Jim.* Huh.

"He's my dad," Sarah said, flatly, and scooted closer to me. "Look at how pretty it is."

"It really is. It's so blue." I felt kind of stupid, but maybe she could tell what I meant. Kids are good about that.

I wonder sometimes when it stops, probably sometime around middle school. The hormones kick in and the empathy takes a nosedive.

"Like a little piece of sky." She shook her bangs back and glared, as if daring me to disagree. "With a heartbeat inside. Do you hear it?"

I closed my eyes. *Feel through your hands,* Mom would say. *Let the energy flow, starchild. The earth says hello.*

She loved that song.

A rustle against my palms, a quivering too subtle to be real. You could fool yourself into thinking you felt things. *Fake it 'til you make it,* Donna was fond of saying. She was a reiki healer who thought crystals were crutches, and she and Mom had a frenemy thing going on. Low-key, of course, but still there. Nadine's wife Morgan didn't like Donna, thought she was too angry or something. But then, Morgan was a lawyer, and not one of Mom's favorite people though Nadine could have been her best friend. Nadine was *everyone's* friend, it just beamed out of her.

I didn't like the idea of faking it until you made it, even when I would have given anything to be sensitive like Mom. You either had it or you didn't; I didn't, and that was fine. Someone had to keep the electricity on and the woodstove full. Someone had to check the mail, sweep the floor, go to school, do the homework, remind Mom to have protein with every meal or she'd get funny-cranky.

"Well, hello!" A nice, rich voice. Like old wood, the kind that's been loved and polished for a long time until it glows a bit even in the dark because of all the caring poured in. "You must be the mechanic Clover's been telling us about." Father Jim stood on the other side of our table, leaning into a space that had magically opened up between two women, one with the half-braid the Harmony women liked to wear and the other with a feathery mess that had once been a pixie cut but was now growing out. Both of them smiled and made room for him, but not with the flinch that would say they were scared. The woman behind him tilted her head, looking at Sarah and me. Was she his wife? Secretary?

The little girl bent over my hands. "Okay, I can take it back now."

"Are you sure?" I kind of wanted to hold it for a few more minutes, to see if I could feel that tiny quiver again.

"I gotta go," she said, cupping her hands under mine now. There were traces of mud on her arms, too, and a green smudge that said she'd been climbing trees. Or trying to. "Do it careful...okay." When she had the egg again, she squirmed around in the seat and hopped down, and I thought she'd run off.

Father Jim's smooth, resonant voice kept going behind me. *Call me Jim,* he was saying, and *we surely appreciate you coming out* and *can we get you anything else,* like Dad was visiting royalty or something. Maybe they didn't have a mechanic.

"Hey." Sarah turned back and peered at me again, a fierce little owl under lank dishwater bangs. I didn't think eight-year-olds were usually that intense, but I barely remembered being that age. That was when Mom was living with the blacksmith dude, and that hadn't been fun. I mean, it started out nice, but it didn't stay. The guy—Monk, what a name—was fine until he started drinking again.

"What?" My hands lay empty in my lap, palms aching a little. Probably just from the tension of trying to hold something so lightly. Being gentle is always harder than you think.

"I pushed the button," the little girl said, all in a rush. "You had a big one, you know. You can do it now."

What? I opened my mouth but she was gone, skipping down the aisle, her long fine hair flying.

"—Val," Dad said.

"Huh?" I turned back around, like a well-trained dog that hears *treats* or its own name. There weren't any dogs at Harmony, but every once in a while you'd see a feral cat.

"I see you've met our Sarah." Father Jim's smile was wide and white. He held out his hand, like he wanted to shake. "Looks like she took a real shine to you."

I kept my hands in my lap, tried to match his smile. "How do you do." *How do I do what?* Mom would giggle sometimes, but she said that was the manners-game way of greeting someone. It popped out, and his easy smile didn't alter.

"How do *you* do." He dropped the maybe-shake-hands pose, and I found out his eyes were a piercing hazel. He looked at the person in front of them like they were the only human being left in the world, and it could be uncomfortable or super reassuring, depending. "Welcome to Harmony, Daughter Val. I hope you'll come back and visit us often."

Clover had her arm through Dad's, on the other side. "I knew you'd like them!" She beamed at Father Jim, just like a puppy bringing a newspaper up to the porch.

I turned back around to look for Sarah, but she was gone.

13

TOTAL STRANGER

DAD WAS HALF in the troublesome van's engine cavity. It was amazing how someone so big could fit into such a cramped space, but he managed. He also looked a lot less nervous. "Honey, you don't have to stay here. It's a one-butt job."

Mom said that sometimes too. When there was limited space in the kitchen and only one ass could fit, more just meant problems. "I just feel like I should help." I stood stupidly next to the stack of wooden produce boxes Dad's tools rested on, my hands throbbing. I kept shaking them out, wondering what I'd done.

"Nothin for you to do." He tensed, and muttered something too low for me to hear, probably a swear. "Go get some sunshine. There's kids your age here."

Yeah, I know. I see them on the bus. "I don't think I'm their type."

"They seem nice."

"Yeah." *Real clean-cut.* Everyone had scattered after lunch to do chores. Animals have to get fed even on Sundays, you know.

Some of the Harmony folks were at the barbecues, and the smoke was beginning to smell really good. Some cleaned out the Pavilion and took the dishes elsewhere for washing—even some of the guys. The kids got to run around, I guess, though some of the teenagers disappeared into the barns for hay or helped some of the adults weed the garden boxes. They didn't hurry, though, and their singing came back. Someone around the corner of the house was chopping wood, nice clean bright sounds, and the music gathered those beats up and moved on. Father Jim and a bunch of them were in the Pavilion, moving the benches back out. Maybe there would be some kind of service or something.

Metal clanged, and Dad cursed under his breath again. I tried not to smile. My mouth felt sticky, like it always does after apple juice. Where would Sarah put the egg? Back in the nest? Would the mama bird reject it? I read that if they smelled human on their chicks they'd abandon them. Mom said birds couldn't smell, but I wasn't so sure. Somehow flying didn't seem so great if you couldn't smell cut grass or pine or just the cold freshness of moving fast on a country day.

"Sweetheart?" Dad peered out from under the hood. "I dropped the wrench. Can you—"

The knot inside my chest eased up a bit. Maybe because I wasn't useless, I was actually going to help. "I'm on it." I got down carefully and peered under the van, gravel pressing sharp through my jeans, against my palms. "I don't see...oh, okay." There it was, glinting dully in the cold shade, pretty much under the middle of the engine. "I'll shimmy under and get it."

A shadow fell over me. "Lose something?"

I peered up. The sun was behind him, but I caught the glitter of that cross on the too-short leather thong at his neck. It was the dark-haired Harmony boy that seemed to lead their little group, if "lead" was the right word. "There's a wrench underneath."

He folded down easily, small sharp rocks grinding under his well-worn boots. "I'll get it." This close, he was cute enough, even though his mouth wasn't all bee-stung like was popular in the movies right now. Wide cheekbones, and his dark eyes were...I don't know. They seemed kind. It was funny, he had the same kind of almost-warmth that radiated from the Father Jim guy, but not nearly as strong. His shoulders were pretty broad, too. I would have pegged him for a jock, except he looked a lot more flexible. And jocks wouldn't ever wear their hair like his. It was an unwritten rule.

Still, *I* was the one helping Dad. "I don't think you'll fit."

He grinned like I'd just told a joke, bright white teeth, the front two only a tiny bit crowded together. It was a relief they weren't perfect. "Let me. There's rocks down there."

Was he being all chivalrous or something? We were on *gravel*, for Chrissake. "There's rocks everywhere."

"Yeah, but these are wicked sharp." He was already on his side, reaching under, all but pushing me out of the way. His arm was longer than mine, he hooked up the wrench and worked his way back out, bouncing lightly to his feet. "Here you go." He offered the wrench and also offered his other hand to help me up.

I took the wrench, and that's all. Which meant I had to flounder up, but I wasn't ever going to win anything in the grace department anyway, so yeah. I'd liked ballet classes, but after a couple years of pointe Mom tried to get me to switch to hip-hop or something because of what balancing on tippy-toes does to your feet.

The classes cost too much, anyway, so I just let it go.

"Thanks." Dad just held out his hand, the rest of him still buried in the engine. I gave him the stupid wrench and folded my arms defensively. Maybe he wanted a guy to help him instead. Another metallic clanging sound came from under the hood, and Dad swore under his breath again. I got the feeling he didn't say it louder either because I was standing right there, or because we were basically at a church.

The Harmony guy stood there, looking at me. It got awkward. Finally, he opened his mouth. "You must know a lot about cars."

It wasn't a bad conversational starter, but what was I going to do, lie about my mechanical capabilities? "Not really."

Another awkward silence. Then he stuck out his tanned, capable hand. "I'm Owen. Owen Harrison."

I still didn't take it. What was it with straights and wanting to grab at you all the time? "Hello, Owen-Owen Harrison. I'm Val Smith."

"Yeah. I know who you are. You go to Cold Ridge. New."

"We're on the same bus." I figured he probably hadn't seen me, though. I was invisible, and I liked it that way.

"Yeah." His gaze skittered over my face, touching my lips, sliding away, hurrying back up to my eyes, wandering again. "So, um, I can show you around. If you want."

"That's a good idea, dumplin'." Dad began extricating himself from the engine, a few careful inches at a time. "Val lived in a place like this."

Oh, God. He probably meant the farmhouse, but maybe the Harmony kid would think it meant another commune or something.

"Not like this," I began, but Owen-Owen's face lit up.

"Really? A lot of us didn't know anything really when we got here. Clover's been really great, she and Leaf grew up on a farm."

I didn't give a good goddamn where Clover grew up, but that wasn't the kind of thing you could say and still be polite. Hopefully they were paying Dad for this, but even if they weren't, well, we'd been fed. Mom was big on hospitality, when the hospitable didn't preach before you could chew. So I settled for something kind-of-diplomatic. "Where did you come from?"

"California. It was a lot different." His expression changed slightly, and I got the idea he wanted to say *better* instead and stopped himself just in time. "What about you?"

"Near Trillington." My boot-toes were scuffed. I examined them minutely, letting my hair fall down, hiding behind it. I wasn't about to explain about the farmhouse.

He waited, but that was all I felt like saying.

"Val, honey." Dad rubbed at his hands with an oil-stained rag.

"Why don't you let him show you around? I'm gonna be here awhile."

Christ, did that mean he was staying for dinner too? I tried not to heave a sigh. "I can help." I had to work not to dig my right toe into the gravel like a five-year-old. Anonymous little gray stones—monster teeth, like the trolls in the storybooks Mom used to read me.

"Aw, hell, go have a little fun, dumplin'." He stared at the engine like it had personally offended him. "I'll be on this bas—uh, this thing for a while."

Great. "Fine." I had to shake my hair back to look up at Owen. "Show me what you've got, Harmony boy."

I remember two things about the rest of that afternoon. There was a tiny, overgrown path on the north side of the paddocks, one I turned down while he was walking ahead of me, figuring I could "get lost" and relieve him of the responsibility of dragging around a heathen. It zigzagged down over rocks and bumps, still-naked trees and spiny bushes furring with light green at the end of their winter-dark branches both clutching from either side, and ended in a clearing. Even though it was only spring, some quirk of the hillside drenched a meadow in sunshine. It had been hacked free of the woods, and the stumps, like rotten teeth, still ached.

Right in the middle were four rectangular boxes. Tin or zinc or some shiny metal, they glittered, sharp and hurtful. They were taller than me, and wider than lockers. They *looked* like lockers, though. There were even little loops through flat metal pieces holding the doors closed, where you could clip a padlock. The middle one stood slightly open, and its interior was a slice of black in golden sunshine.

Weird. Maybe it was for smoking jerky or something? Drying vegetables? Holding shovels and stuff? Why would they put their shovels out *here*, though?

The other thing I remember is Owen behind me, spilling out of the bushes, and how he looked...pale. "What are you *doing*?" Two long angry strides out into the clearing, the sun catching his dark hair and filling with caramel highlights. "I turned around and you were gone."

"Sorry." I wasn't sorry at all. "What are those?"

"Those? They were here when we moved in." He ended up right next to me, and grabbed at my arm. "Come on."

I sidestepped, avoiding his hand. "What? There's something hip happening at the goat pen or something?"

His hand fell back to his side. He just *looked* at me, and I didn't want to, but I felt like a bitch. I wasn't being a good guest. It felt like someone had caught me going through their bathroom cabinet, and I didn't even have the looking-for-a-tampon excuse.

"You didn't want to come out here." Like it wasn't a surprise. His mouth tightened, but he didn't look mad, precisely. Just a little hurt. "I get it. We can go back to your dad."

I folded my arms again. "It's fine." It wasn't his fault I'd been dragged out here. And it was kind of cool. Mom would have loved this commune, or whatever. They hadn't even rung the Our-Lord-and-Savior-has-a-plan-for-you bell once. My hands itched and ached, and that wasn't this guy's fault either. "I'm just...things haven't been optimal, lately."

Well, that was a huge understatement. But maybe he understood. In any case, he stood there for a couple seconds, looking at me. "I guess not. Must be hard to switch schools this late in the year."

"Yeah." For a second the other words trembled in my mouth. *My mom. She was coming home. There was an accident.*

I swallowed them. No *way* did this total stranger need to know that about me.

Besides, if I said it...no. I didn't want to say it, and he couldn't make me.

My throat was full of something. My chakras were *all* blocked up. "Hey." I loosened my arms. "Look, let's...can we start over? Pretend I wasn't just—"

"Sure." He didn't even wait for me to finish. A smile lit him up, that kind-of-warmth intensifying all over me. "It's okay, you know. We're big on letting people do what they have to, here."

I followed him back up the hill, and when he reached the top, he turned and reached out, as if it was habitual for him. He probably helped little old ladies across the street, too. He just had that look.

I let him. His fingers were warm, and kind, but my hands ached so much I didn't hold his for long.

14

SHOCKED I TELL YOU

Monday came along full of pop quizzes and a French test so first-year I could have done it in my sleep. My hands didn't ache, they just felt warm and slightly too big for the rest of me. Owen Harrison smiled in my direction on the bus, but I just closed up inside myself and stared out the window, acutely aware that they probably didn't want someone new in their group, especially someone who'd only visited their place once. English was a total yawner. Travis the Bathroom Bro spent the entire American History period alternately belching and laughing, completely destroying whatever lecture Shieldman had planned. Pre-Calc was hopeless, I'd missed some earlier work and would be lucky to pull a D here at Cold River.

I mean, seriously, I could make change, find room in the budget for rice and beans, keep a running tab in my head and calculate the cut of the door Mom could expect from a festival organizer, what more did I fucking need? I also felt like I was coming down with something.

Not like the plague. Just, you know, a little sweaty, like running a fever.

The one bright spot in the day was Oz and his buddies in the library at lunch. I didn't expect him to *mean* his invitation, but apparently he did, so I sat there and listened to them roll characters and make inside jokes. They were kind of awkward since a girl was there, but it was only because they kept checking to see if I'd roll my eyes or leave in a huff. When I didn't, they forgot I was around. Oz told me he'd help me roll a character next time, and I pretended I didn't know how to do it. Shit, I went through my D&D phase when I was nine, when Mom had her serious RenFaire thing going on and was dating the guy who called her *my lady*.

He was nice, but it didn't last. I couldn't even remember his name, just his striped breeches.

Of course, even though my nose was stuffed and my head was pounding, I had to dress out for gym. I never liked that shit, and I liked it even less when curly-headed, rangy Ms Greeman tried to make me take off Mom's necklace. "No jewelry!" she barked, jabbing a chewed-down index fingernail at me. "Go on, put it in your locker!"

She didn't wait to see if I would, though, just headed out of the locker room with her red shorts twitching on her boy-thin behind. Long strings of muscle worked in her tanned legs; she probably ran marathons for fun. I tucked the turquoise back under my shirt and followed everyone else out, my head down and my arms crossed. *Just get through this,* I told myself. If it got really bad I could go and find out where the stoners had their lair. The fact that I hadn't yet was some kind of reverse miracle.

I kind of missed Tamara. Of course, there was that whole thing with Johnny, where she'd been hot for him since third grade but he had a thing for new girls. It could have been sticky, but I've learned to spot *those* in a hurry. Once the hormones hit there are guys who don't care who a girl is, only that she's a newcomer easy to cut out of the herd. It only takes singeing your fingers once to get a healthy reflex going.

"Stretching out!" Greeman yelled, clapping her hands like we were a bunch of third-graders. "Come on, ladies, let's go!"

I stuck near the back. It was kind of nice to stretch, but this bitch wouldn't know yoga if it walked up and bit her downward-facing dog. I followed along, not really thinking about much, and hung near the back when she herded us outside to the track. I hate running, it's the most pointless thing in the world unless the cops have shown up at the party some kid's rich parents didn't know he was hosting while they were in Bali or something.

Now *that* was an evening I wouldn't ever forget.

It was a chilly day, all the weekend sunshine gone, and it smelled like cold gray rain. I was glad I had ratty sweatpants instead of shorts.

Sandy with the blonde ponytail was in expensive blue Hopbrick exercise gear, and her nail polish had been repaired. That ponytail swing back and forth like a pendulum, and her legs were the same orange as Greeman's. I half-jogged, slowing to a walk whenever Greeman's head was turned, and lagged behind everyone. This was *bullshit*. I probably had enough PE credits to blow this class until the end of the year, didn't I? I'd have to look up the requirements again, but I was pretty sure I'd—

"Heads up!" A whisper-yell, a nasty high-pitched laugh, and a sudden shove between my shoulderblades. I went down hard, trying to catch myself instead of going limp, and spilled over onto my side as well, my cheek bashing the rubberized track service. It rang my chimes pretty good, and the nasty giggle was Sandy's. She'd lapped the damn track to come up behind me.

She bent over, as if she was apologizing or about to help me, but her face was a mask, lips skinned back and blue eyes burning. "*Bitch,*" she hissed, and swung one sneakered foot. They were a shiny blue pair of Nikes, top of the line. She hit me square in the thigh and I sucked in a high, shocked little breath, still half-dizzy, my head ringing. My cheek burned, I was going to have a good bruise there.

Sandy probably would have kicked me again, but she glanced over her shoulder just like any grade-school bully, checking to see where the teacher was.

I could have curled up and pushed out a leg to kick her back, I guess. Mom was pretty good about keeping me in dance lessons before the whole pointe thing blew up and if there's one thing you learn in ballet, it's how to take out a rival's knee. Before I could, though, more running footsteps thudded along the track, way too near for me to get away with it. I froze, staring up at her contorted face, watching the switch flip as she realized the running feet weren't her henchwomen. Magically, she smoothed out, right before Ingrid pounded up, dark curls flying and her long legs just like a gazelle's. The Harmony girl didn't slow down, just popped her shoulder against Sandy's and sent the blonde bitch-queen staggering.

"Ooops!" A long cheery drawn-out word, Ingrid's mouth a pantomime of wide surprise. Gabrielle, the blonde, loped along behind her, and for a second I thought *they* were in on it, instead of the henches. But Ingrid, a high flush in her velvety cheeks, hopped neatly to a stop between me and Sandy, while Gabrielle skidded a bit before she could bend down and offer me her hand.

Neither of *them* wore nail polish.

"Hey." Gabrielle's fair, freckled face was grave. "Ouch. You're going to bruise."

"We saw the whole thing," Ingrid added. It was kind of unfair, how some dark-haired girls had that beautiful skin, a natural tint to their lips, and those coal-black eyelashes. I got stuck with just being pale, and my eyelashes were nothing to write home about. "Assault. Probably aggravated, if we can prove premeditation."

Sandy's nose wrinkled. "Jesus, I just ran into her. It was an *accident.*"

"Uh-huh." The blonde Harmony girl grabbed my wrist, not waiting for me to take her hand. "Upsy-daisy. We're gonna tell Greeman."

"Suck it, hippie bitch." Sandy whipped her the finger. A thread of sweat cut the makeup on her temple, small golden hairs feathering down in the hollow and collecting moisture.

"Such language!" Ingrid mimicked fanning herself. Without the skirt and the cardigan, she looked just like any other high-school girl. Except her hair, and Gabrielle's, wasn't pulled back in ponytails but braided. "I'm shocked. Simply *shocked*, I tell you."

"Shit." Gabrielle case a worried, hazel-eyed glance over her shoulder. Her gray T-shirt was soft, the anonymous logo on front crinkled from many washings. "I think she's gonna pass out."

I found my voice. "I'm fine." I let her drag me upright. It took two tries, but I made it, and spotted Greeman coming across the field in the middle of the track, her short cap of curls bouncing aggressively. My cheek burned, already swelling. I'd be lucky to escape a black eye too. You'd think dance classes would have given me a little grace. "Thanks."

"You want us to tell Greeman?" Gabrielle steadied me. My knees ached, I'd barked the left one but good, and there was a sticky thread of something hot sliding down my shin.

Great.

I shook my head. That made the whole world spin. The green field and the iron sky wanted to change places. I blinked, several times, shutterclicks.

"...pass out," Gabrielle said again.

"Probably on drugs." This from Sandy, arms folded, her hair beginning to fray a little under the humidity. Looked like it was going to rain.

I came back to myself with a thump. Like I'd just been lifted outside my skin, shaken, and tossed back in.

"She's not on drugs," Ingrid weighed in. "You're just a bitch."

"Miss Smith? Val?" Ms Greeman tried to grab at my head, but I leaned back, almost knocking Gabrielle over. The blonde Harmony girl had her arm over my shoulders, and the rest of the class was starting to catch up. Greeman tried to catch my head again, her silver whistle bouncing against her chest.

"*Val*." Sandy sniggered. "What kind of a name is that?"

"Be quiet," Greeman snapped at her. "Val? Look at me, honey."

"I'm *fine*," I repeated, glad I'd talked Mom into shortening my first name for school registrations. Everything came back into focus, clear and sharp. There was a slither inside my shirt, a metallic shifting. Mom's necklace. "She just knocked me over, that's all."

"Do you have an icepack?" A thin thread of patchouli drifted through the smell of Gabrielle's shampoo. Her hair was pretty amazing, thick and buttery, and some of it touched my cheek. "It's going to swell pretty bad."

"What happened?" Greeman actually looked concerned. Of course, sending the new girl home with a face full of road rash was probably bad for the performance reports. Did teachers even get those? They had to, they were union, right? Mom was really pro-union, though she'd never join one when she worked for the straights.

The bitch had knocked my mom's necklace right off me. Its hook-and-eye closure was really old, and I wanted to dig in my shirt to get it out and figure out if it'd been damaged.

"Sandy ran into her." Ingrid's earrings—silver leaves on long fluttering strands, really pretty—chimed gently as she moved. No jewelry my *ass*. "Just ran right up and pasted her."

Greeman squinted at me. "Is that true?"

Sandy's eyeroll and huffy sigh all but echoed. She was playing to the gallery—not Greeman, but the other girls in class. "She was in the *way*. God, it was an *accident*."

The gym teacher's cheek twitched, once. Maybe it was irritation. "I'm sure it was. Valerie? Is it Valerie? What happened?"

"It's *Val*." A thin hot thread also touched my upper lip. *I already told you that the first day, and no, it's not fucking Valerie.* "I don't know. I was just going along, and next thing I knew I was on the ground."

"It was an *accident*," Sandy insisted.

My hands cramped, like they'd fallen asleep and were now waking up, the really hideous part of pins-and-needles where it hurts so bad you'd gladly force a limb back to numbness. The rest of the class began to crowd around, and for the rest of the period Greeman had them running relays in the gym while I sat on the bleachers, an icepack clamped to my throbbing face and a tissue half up my nose to stop the bleeding. Mom's necklace was fine, I put it back on. The girls ran, and sweated, and ran some more; if they hadn't hated me before then, they certainly did now.

At least, Sandy did.

15

AS HARD AS YOU GOTTA

DAD WAS EARLY. He dropped his keys in the dish on the kitchen counter, flicking the overhead light on. His short black hair was messed up, and his shoulders were set and tense. He glanced into the attached dining room at me, and did a double-take. "Holy hell, dumplin'. You been in a fight?"

I wish. I hunched over my American History textbook. "Gym class." The bus ride home had been a misery, but at least the icepack had the swelling down. My face throbbed a little, that was all. I'd scrubbed the dried blood gingerly out of my nose. Ingrid and Gabrielle sat with the other Harmony kids, and maybe they would have let me sit with them too but I didn't ask, just leaned against the window and ignored everything going on around me. A time-tested method, one I wished worked at home too.

Mom would have already been fussing at me with arnica and a compress, and a rose quartz or two to draw the swelling out and fix the vibrations. She wouldn't ask what happened, leaving it up to me to decide what to tell her. Boundaries, she called it. *You'll talk when you want to, starchild.*

My chest gave a funny, flickering quiver, like the big smooth egg

76

inside my heart chakra was shifting again. As long as I kept that egg nice and solid, none of this mattered. I'd been doing pretty good so far; I'd even mostly figured out what Shieldman had been trying to teach third period.

"Gym class?" Dad's hand's twitched, like he wanted to touch me, fell back to his side. "You get hit with a basketball?"

"It was on the track." I shrugged, and decided I'd studied as much as I was going to for the time being. I could do more after dinner. "How was work?"

"Busy." He carried a paper grocery bag, and I smelled roasted chicken. "Stopped at the store for dinner."

"I could have cooked." Pre-made stuff was always too expensive.

"Your job is *school*, dumplin'." He set the bag on the counter. His right-hand knuckles were scrape-skinned; it looked painful. "You get some Tylenol or something? Ibuprofen? There's some in the bathroom."

"It'll be fine." Mom always said masking the body's natural pain response was a bad thing. Aspirin was okay, because it came from willow bark, but ibuprofen was bad for your liver and Tylenol was a pharmaceutical con job. "What happened to your hand?"

"Got bit by a Chevy." He grinned, the same lopsided smile I remembered from when I was five. It was different than just hearing him on the phone when I could call. I mean, I'd known he was there, but Mom and I were tight. We had to be. Sometimes I wondered what it was like to be shared by your parents, have two bedrooms and two adults fighting over you like a chew toy. I never wondered very long, though, because Mom always had a new adventure planned and I could call Dad anytime.

He stepped into the dining-room area and peered at me, bright blue eyes and the shadow of stubble on his face. *Have to shave twice a day*, he said. *Just to keep on top of it.*

"Gym class?" His eyebrows went up, anxiously. "You want to tell me more?"

"Not really." I marked my place in the textbook with an expired fabric store coupon, pushing my chair back. "Nothing to tell."

He still looked worried. I hoped my face wasn't giving anything away. Rotisserie chicken, pre-made garlic bread, packaged salad. It wasn't bad, but I wished he'd just let me cook. Maybe he would once he got used to me being around. "Do *you* need ibuprofen? That looks really gnarly, Dad."

"Kids still say that? Gnarly?"

I scooped up my books. If everything stayed this boring I might start assigning myself my own homework. "I do. Mom does." My throat closed up. "Did."

"She did." He nodded, his gaze skittering away. Another uncomfortable silence, this one swelling between us, full of sharp edges. "Wash up, honey. This'll get cold."

He even had paper napkins, like in a restaurant. The chicken was a bit mealy and the outside dripped with grease, but it was okay and I was hungry. There was a packet of dried cranberries to go in with the salad, too. He poured me a monster glass of milk, gave me all the Caesar dressing packets, and kept watching my face, anxiously.

"How's school?" He tucked into his own chicken, dabbing at his mouth every once in a while. The napkin rubbed against his stubble. He'd left the TV on in the living room during most of our dinners, but stopped the one night he got home late and I mentioned how nice and quiet it was.

"Stupid." I washed down a mouthful of garlic bread. They used margarine in the spread, I could just taste it, but at least it wasn't burned. "But that's usual. Every school is stupid."

"Always knew you were smart. What about those, you know, the special classes? For the smart kids?"

"Advanced placement? I guess. They were fun at Valley." AP English with Griffin was pretty good, and Integrated Math was full of sarcasm and a friendly kind of cutthroat competition. Cold Ridge's math classes were all taught purely by sadists, as far as I could tell.

I could do the work, sure. But I didn't *like* it, and I wasn't about to kill myself catching up on damn Pre-Calc.

"Well, what about here?" Dad persisted.

What about it? "They didn't put me in them, since it's so late in the year. Maybe next year, unless you move."

"Move? Why would I?" The idea pushed his eyebrows up. They were pretty ferocious, I was glad I'd gotten Mom's.

"I don't know. It's just, you know. Mom never liked to stay in one place very long." Except the farmhouse. *I'm going to drive in roots,* she said. *Wandering's fun, but maybe it's time.*

"Yeah." He lifted his glass of tomato juice, stopped it halfway to his mouth. "How long were you living there? That, uh, house, with your mom."

"Year and a half-ish." The cranberries were good. I usually didn't like them, no matter *how* good Mom said they were for the bladder. The tartness cut the grease and margarine, and my body gave that happy little feeling it gets when you eat something you've been craving but don't know why.

"Must have gotten cold." Excessively casual, like he wasn't sure just what he could ask.

I shrugged again. There didn't seem much else to do. "It was okay." With the woodstove going, it really was. Leftover firewood along the north side of the farmhouse had been just enough. I hadn't even thought about *next* winter, and now I kind of wondered. Of course it wouldn't occur to Mom that we needed to plan. The Universe would provide, right? "We closed up most of the house and slept near the stove. It was like camping."

"Well, the property's yours." He took a few gulps of tomato juice. "Your mom went to a lawyer. She's got a will."

Oh, God. "Wow." My stomach flipped twice. Did we have to talk about this at dinner? I was *hungry.* A hot bite of shame crunched all the way up the inside of my ribs. Here I was, sitting and eating. Again. And Mom never would.

She made a will. When had she done *that?*

The egg in my chest quivered. Its shell was thinning, and something was tapping from the inside, a sharp, pointy, poking bone-beak. My cheek throbbed, hot as the woodstove when we kept it going all day and night, too. At Christmas we'd turned out all the lights and left a candle in a dish near one of the windows to light the wandering souls home. She broke veganism for Christmas, but not vegetarianism. Tofurkey was okay, though.

With enough seasoning, you could eat anything.

"It's in a trust." Dad examined his plate like it held a universal secret or two. "And there's...well, an inheritance, too. Left over from your grandma Stella."

That was Mom's mom. I had vague hazy memories of gingersnaps and a mouth pulled down bitterly, pinkish-red lipstick feathering at its edges. A smell like talcum powder, and bright sunshine. "She had a lot of doilies." It was all I could think of to say.

"That she did." Dad's mouth twitched, like he wasn't quite sure if he should laugh. "There's enough to help with college. It's in the trust too."

"Oh." *I don't want it.* I stared at the food on my plate. A clump of muscle fiber and bone, a bird dead and rotting. The salad—lettuce slowly dying, cranberries yanked from the branch and already deceased, garlic bread with all the millions of yeast in it dead too, of overheating. Dead, dead, dead.

Not Mom. Nuh-uh. I shook my head. Shook it again. My eyes were full.

"Oh, honey." Dad reached across the table. I grabbed his hand, because it helped to smash together the edges of the egg in my chest. He winced, and I realized I was squeezing the scrapes on his knuckles.

"Oh, crap. I'm sorry." My throat was full of hot, slick, nasty weight.

"No." Dad shook his big, graying head. "Squeeze as hard as you gotta, dumplin'."

I didn't want to, I really didn't, but my fingers wouldn't come loose. Dad patted my hand, gently, before reaching to grab a white paper napkin. "You're leaking a bit. It's okay, Val. It's all right to cry."

It was *not* all right. None of this was all right, even though both of us were trying. "I don't *want* to."

"Sooner or later, you've gotta get it out." Dad said it like he was certain, and maybe I believed him. "Take your time."

I didn't end up eating much, and neither did he. But the pressure around the egg in my chest loosened fractionally, just a little. Just enough.

Dad washed the dishes, I dried, and by the time the soapy water gurgled down the drain, his right hand was water-wrinkled, red from the heat, and raw. It was funny, though. His knuckles didn't look nearly as bad.

When everything was put away he hugged me, and that helped loosen things up even more. He said the same thing then, too.

Squeeze as hard as you gotta, dumplin'. Just as hard as you gotta.

16

PLACE TO BE ALONE

GREY AND NASTY, the sky squatted over hills and trees and roads and buildings. I found out where the stoners hung out—at a forgotten quad tucked behind the Performing Arts building, right where I should've checked first—but I didn't join them just yet. Instead, I slipped out of the 500 building and headed for the track. You weren't supposed to at lunchtime, but *fuck* that. My head hurt and I had some thinking to do, so I carried my paper sack out into a wind too cold to be springtime. The blossoms were all falling, but the deciduous branches hadn't put out any more green and the evergreens looked dusty and tired. There was thin, fragmentary ice at the edge of every puddle in the morning. Just the edges, sharp and lacy with the chill.

A single stand of bleachers reared up on the far side of the track, a concrete pad underneath starred with broken glass. It wasn't raining just yet, so I climbed to the middle row and settled with my lunch in my lap, my tapestry backpack slumped obediently next to me, and looked at the school.

From out here I could pretend I was an alien, sent undercover to gather information about humans. *They lock their young in these*

*funny buildings and force them to fight for places in the social hier-
archy. Law of the jungle, except built of steel and brick and concrete.
Very few escape the clutches of the System.*

It was the kind of idea Mom would have liked. Aliens, outlaws,
opting out.

Dad's old houndstooth suit jacket was long enough that my ass
wasn't numb from cold, cheap metal, or soaking up the damp. He
didn't know why I wanted to wear it and neither did I, but he let me.
It argued with my long gray skirt with pink flowers in the weave, but
neither would win as long as my pink sweater was there to keep the
peace.

I lost myself in imagining something strange inside my skin, a
different body forced to look like a human's, its face a mask. I chewed
mechanically, trying to taste the atoms instead of just bread and
peanut butter. No chocolate milk, I didn't want to risk the
lunchroom.

The only real question, of course, was what I was going to do
sixth period. My face wasn't bad; the bruise looked a week old
instead of a day. The swelling was gone. Still, everyone looked at me
like...

I don't care. I could imagine I was taking notes on them. *All* of
them. Marking time until my assignment was over and the mothership came back.

Marking time. Funny. And *Mothership.* Maybe it meant a big
ship, carrying a bunch of smaller ones like ducklings on a broad feathered back. Had Mom ever felt like a stranger, watching the weird
things the straights did to each other? Did she ever get...well, lonely? I
mean, she'd had *me,* though.

Right?

I examined my hands while I chewed the last of the sandwich.
My palms and fingers were flushed, probably from the cold. I imagined the bones buried inside, muscles moving in straps, blood vessels
pushing their way through, treelike, riverlike. Hands are weird when

you think about it, but if you look at anything close enough, long enough, you can see the strangeness.

Footsteps. I jolted out of alien space when a pair of boots hit bleacher stairs. What was *he* doing here?

"Hey." Owen-Owen hopped up the steps. A plain, unlined denim jacket stretched over his shoulders; tiny gems of moisture clung to his dark hair. He'd reddened up a little from the chill, and if he wasn't shaving yet he'd start soon. "What are you doing out here?"

"I could ask you the same thing." I hunched up, protectively. His boots were brushed and polished, unless I missed my guess. Who did that anymore?

"Hard to find a place to be alone, you know?" He did the same kind of skittering-glance thing when looking at me again, like his eyes couldn't quite find a place to rest.

I wasn't alone since *he* was here, which kind of defeated the whole purpose of being outside in nasty drizzle-weather. I decided not to point out the logical inconsistency, and went for tact instead. For once. "What about your friends?"

"The others?" He shifted a little, all his weight on one foot, then another. "They're in the lunchroom, I guess. Hey."

I waited. The track was a wet black ribbon, the grass in the middle violently green despite the cold. They probably soaked it with chemicals to make it that way. The goalposts on either end of of the field stretched their hard, unforgiving arms, stabbing the pressing-down sky. Finally, he spoke again. "What happened?" He didn't point at my face. Instead, he used all his fingers, his hand not flat but cupped a little. It was a strange movement, almost like ballet. I kind of appreciated him not jabbing a finger at me, too.

I suppose it was nice Ingrid and Gabrielle hadn't mentioned the big event. It probably wasn't worth talking about when there was that singing of theirs to do. "Some bitch in gym class."

"Oh." Did he sound disappointed? Wary? Disbelieving?

I couldn't tell. "Blonde. Ponytail. Lots of makeup."

"Wears blue all the time?" He waited for my nod. "Yeah, that's Sandy. Not quite head cheerleader, but she'd like to be."

Usually guys weren't capable of figuring out the fine gradations of ambition on the girl social scale. I decided it was a cautious mark in his favor. "Yeah, well."

"Her last victim moved away. Homeschooling, I heard." He clicked his tongue, and sat down on the other side of my backpack, carefully out of my personal space.

So Sandy had been on the lookout for a new target, and I was nominated. Great. Still, it made me feel a little bit better that there was a *reason*, at least. "Aren't you cold?"

"Father says if you breathe right, you don't get cold."

It sounded funny and old-fashioned. *Father.* "Your dad?" Then I put it together. "Oh, you're the preacher's kid. You're probably trouble."

"*Preacher's kid.* Haven't heard that one in a while." He stretched out his legs. You can tell when a pair of jeans has been broken in the right way with work, instead of bought pre-softened. Probably lots of heavy lifting out on the farm-commune-thing, in winter.

"Well, that's what it is, right? You guys are a church." I folded up my empty paper lunchbag, slipping it inside my backpack. Wished I'd been able to grab some chocolate milk. Mom would have told me not to drink it—full of hormones, probably oversweetened, and the syrup in it wasn't likely to be *real* chocolate.

But it was good.

"Not precisely." He hunched his shoulders and stared at the field, his throat moving as he swallowed. Like he had something sticking in there.

Probably just insulted his entire family. Way to go, Val. "Well, I mean, I'd call it a commune but you all wear crosses."

His hand jumped up, fingertips almost touching his. "Commune's closer. You can't say that around here, though. People get funny about it."

That was one way to put it. "They get funny about all sorts of things." Like the tangle-haired tartan-skirt-wearing woman who came into Enlightened Source every once in a while and started yelling about abortion. Mom called her Fetus Lady, and it cracked both of us up.

"Yeah." He didn't sneak a sideways glance, which was fine by me. I studied his profile; he stared at the school, stuffing his hands in his jacket pockets. "It's camouflage, kind of. So why are *you* out here?"

"Hard to find a place to be alone." My teeth wanted to chatter, but if you keep your jaw a little relaxed, they can't. It's when you tense up that the shaking starts. "I wish the sun would come back."

His cheeks were too red, it wasn't just the breeze. Was he blushing? He nodded, once, chin dipping and jerking back up. His hair flopped into his eyes. "Me too."

That about finished up all the conversation I felt like having. The chimes for the end of lunch drifted across the field, faint and tinny.

"What do you have next?" He stretched, turned it into a rising motion, and the movement sang though the bleachers. Thin metal, rusting bolts, the entire thing would probably collapse if it filled up with tubby parents.

"Math. You?"

"Spanish." *His* tan wasn't orange, it was the burnish of someone who spent a lot of time outside. "I'll walk you."

Oh, man. So *he* thought he was going to get up on the new girl. It was a good thing my heart chakra was closed up tight, or I might have felt a twinge. Disappointment, that's all—if that's all you feel, it never gets any worse. "That's okay." I made it to standing, hitched my backpack onto my shoulder, and in order to get off the bleachers I'd have to push past him. Or I could turn around and walk for the other end of the big metal structure. Decisions, decisions.

"I'd like to." He backed up a step, though. Again, carefully not invading my personal space. Which wasn't usual. The guys who'll try for the new girl stand close and lean closer, breathing on you like they want to drug you with pheromones or halitosis, whichever's stronger.

Maybe it was just the fact that he did that, respecting my aura.

Maybe it was that kind-of-warmth radiating from him, or the damp clinging to his hair. Or the way my face hurt, a residual ache echoed by my right elbow and my stupid chest. At least if he was walking with me, I wouldn't have to think about the egg inside my ribs and how hard it was to keep the shell nice and thick. It would just keep itself that way because someone else was around. That's one thing being around other people is good for.

One of the only things, maybe.

"Okay." I stuffed my reddened hands in my pockets. "Hey, I've got a question."

"Yeah?" He headed for the stairs on the right, looking back every couple of steps to check on me.

"Yeah." I almost slipped on slick metal, caught myself, and the damp began to hold spatters of actual rain. "Where's the best place to skip sixth period?"

17

JUST LIVE WITH IT

TUESDAY WAS chicken soup with the leftover supermarket rotisserie. Wednesday was chili. Thursday it was leftover chili, and Dad brought home tortilla chips. Friday I got home to find him already there, sitting straight-faced at the table, obviously waiting. His face told me he knew, of course.

He didn't draw it out, either. "You been skippin' school, dumplin'."

"Just gym class." I had to pee, and I was hungry, and the steady drip of spring rain outside was stupid to slog through. Mud everywhere, all soft and squishy since it wasn't freezing at night anymore, raindrops tiptapping every window, gutters holding thin steady streams, the slow steady nasal drip from an overturned bowl of cloud intensifying around four in the afternoon without fail as a fresh wave of moisture moved in. Sometimes in the mornings, forlorn little golden gleams would peek through, but they were always gone by noon. After a solid week of that, no wonder everyone looked disgusted and damp all the time. The entire school smelled like floor wax and wet socks, except for when you brushed against one of Travis the Bathroom Bro's buddies or copycats, drenched in body spray, "quality" and knockoff colognes both scouring the inside of your nose the same. Some of the girls moved in a wave of perfume too, but at least theirs didn't have the acrid under-edge of nasty oily testosterone.

I'd managed to stay entirely out of Sandy's way for the week. Which was pretty much worth whatever Dad was going to dish out, in my book. It wasn't that I was afraid of her, I just didn't want to deal. I spent lunchtime in the library, but not with Oz and his friends. Instead, I settled on the floor at the end of one of the long shelves in the Nonfiction section, propping my feet against the heater under a window that looked out on a paved area kids probably hung out in when the weather was better, between the library and the front of the Performing Arts building.

I had to hand it to the preacher's kid, the spot he showed me near the Home Ec classrooms made skipping sixth easier than I expected. Plus, sometimes they were cooking, and it smelled good. "They called you?" I guessed, dangling my heavy backpack from one hand. It was damp, too, and my textbooks would need to be set out overnight to dry.

"Been calling me all week. I was waiting for you to say something about it."

"What, report skipping school? To you?" I was honestly baffled but it came out sounding sarcastic, I guess, because his face changed. The lines on either side of his mouth got a little deeper, and he looked, I dunno. Disappointed. "I got all my PE credits to graduate out of the way early. Besides, Mom never cared."

It was out of my mouth and hung there, heavy and bitter. My heart gave a funny sideways jerktwist. It was like getting pinched over a fresh bruise, saying the M-word.

"She let you skip?" Those lines got deeper, highways on either side of his lips. His big hands lay on the table; they weren't tense, but the rest of him was.

"When I needed to, yeah."

Was he feeling the same pinch in his chest when someone

mentioned Mom? I couldn't tell. My cheeks were hot. The bruise had vanished a lot quicker than I expected. Maybe it hadn't been that bad, or maybe your face healed faster. My heart thudded, filling my ears, and the egg in my chest shifted a little.

No. I focused on Dad's mouth moving. He was talking.

"You could have told me."

Well, yeah, I suppose he was right. Technically I *could* have. "I'm sorry." The noise in my ears kept going, and I was grateful for it because it blocked everything else out. That was good. I squeezed my legs together. I had to *pee*, goddammit, after holding it all damn day. "I just..." What could I say? *Look, can I just go to the bathroom and then we can do this?* "You're mad at me." If I said it that way—flatly, just talking about the weather, just remarking on something everyone knew, making conversation—maybe it would help. Or maybe he would *get* mad, like fathers on TV. Or like the fathers a lot of Mom's tarot clients muttered darkly about.

You're so lucky, they told her. *My ex was furious.* They all had stories that would give you nightmares. Even though Dad had never, ever been like that, even though Mom always said, *at least he never hit me*, it was enough to make you wonder.

Enough to make you think twice.

But Dad just lifted his right hand slowly, scratched at his cheek. "I'm thinkin' this has to do with getting hit in the face, and if someone is whaling on you at school, I need to know."

What? I stared at him for a couple seconds, just hearing that *thumpthumpthump* in my ears. "Why?" If he kept me here much longer, I was going to piss my jeans. "It's not like you can do anything."

"The hell I can't. Did your mom just let kids beat up on you?"

"She's a pacifist." *Was a pacifist.* "She kind of let me sort things out on my own. I'm a big girl, Dad." I'd done it myself, using the M-word, it was an invitation for him to say it too. If I wanted to keep my alien chest-egg nice and thick, I couldn't fucking open my stupid mouth.

"Oh, yeah." His fingers curved a little, like he wanted to push them into the tabletop. "You're *sixteen*, Valentine."

I winced inwardly. "I know." I really, *really* had to go. "Look, I've got to use the bathroom. Then you can punish me, or whatever." I set off down the hall, swinging my heavy, sodden backpack. At least I'd wiped my feet before stepping inside the building; my boots weren't too bad. I wished the pounding in my ears would turn to static, or get loud enough to drown everything else out. Maybe it was my heart chakra, backing up just like a bad drain.

"I could have sent you with a note," he called after me. "Or gotten you into a different class."

Christ. Why not just let me skip? I shut the bathroom door, and for a few minutes, sheer relief drove everything else out of my head. Maybe that was why I didn't want to pee at school. Something might creep into your brain while you were relaxed. Some sound from the other girls, some invisible floating thing looking to latch itself onto someone who wasn't guarded. Bad energy. There's so much floating around in middle and high schools. I couldn't remember using the lavatory in elementary, but I suppose I must have.

I even washed my hands afterward, putting off going out and finding out what he was going to do. My stomach revolved; I wasn't hungry anymore. Just sick, and shaky, and sweaty under my arms, at the small of my back, the crease at the top of my thighs, inside my elbows and behind my knees.

When I did come back out, he was standing in the kitchen, in front of the sink, looking at the garbage disposal like there was some kind of answer to be found in its rubber-lidded eye. Maybe he *was* angry, because he gripped the edge of the sink, his knuckles standing up white. Big hands. I could never remember them being hard, or anything other than gentle.

But still, you heard the stories. They soaked in, and so did the way the air changed in a group of women when something male showed up.

"I'm sorry." I held onto the edge of the kitchen doorway. Both of us grasping different things, like there was a current and we were swept up in it. "It's not a huge thing. I just don't want to be in that class. It's easier to just skip it."

He nodded, slowly. Maybe he was so mad he had to wait before talking, because it took him a little while. "If it wasn't a huge thing, you wouldn't be skipping. You're a smart girl, Val."

God. Just let it go. "It's bullshit. All of it."

"Well, yeah." Like he was surprised I hadn't figured it out by now. "That's life. Getting along with the bullshit is part of it. Your mom hated that."

Stop talking about her. I'd started it, sure, but I just wanted it to stop now. "What about you?"

He sighed, still staring at the disposal. The sound was a big heavy one, lifting him up before deflating him like a punctured beach ball. "I guess I just always figured that it's not going to change, so I might as well just live with it."

As philosophies went, it wasn't a bad one. But he was a grown-up, and he had *power*. He could walk away from a fucking gym teacher or a Sandy without any problems at all. Had he forgotten what it was *like* to be trapped in a building with people who didn't understand or just plain hated you, day after day?

Maybe that's what grown-ups did. They forgot. Some iron curtain dropped in their heads once they could buy smokes or drink, or they forgot about being helpless because really, who would want to remember that shit? "That's a cop-out."

"Could be." He straightened. "What'll skipping do to your grades?"

Oh, my God, I could care less. "Nothing. But fine. I'll go to stupid gym class." So he wasn't going to get mad. That was a relief, right? I just wouldn't push it. He might decide I was too expensive to keep. What would happen then?

Did I really want to know?

"You could tell me when you want to skip."

I stared at his back. "No, that's fine. I'll just live with it." Rubberkneed, I backed up and headed for my room. He didn't say anything else. I grabbed my backpack from outside the bathroom and made it past my own door, shutting it quietly. Not slamming.

Strictly speaking, it wasn't really *my* room, though, was it? Even though he'd got this place on the off chance I'd come visit, I wasn't just visiting any more. Sooner or later he'd get tired of me just like Mom sometimes got tired of being tied down to a kid. A big heavy bowling ball weight she'd carried around in her belly and then had to feed, clothe, take to classes when she should have been dancing, reading, doing fun adult things.

I fell onto the bed, curled around my backpack, and stared at the wall until the scratchy, hot, welling feeling in my eyes could be shoved down, bottled up, pushed away.

I didn't come out for dinner. He just knocked once at the door, and left it at that. I couldn't tell if I was grateful.

Maybe he was.

18

SOLO CAREER

I TOSSED and turned all night, and waited until he left for work Saturday morning to creep out and eat. He left a note on the *Hebler Mechanics* pad on my place at the table, careful awkward printing. *Working half day. Be home at two. Love you. Dad.*

Did he really still love me, or was it just what he had to say? I couldn't figure it out, and felt too stuffed-head and hungry-stupid to try. I choked down some breakfast and started cleaning the apartment. I'd already decided that I needed to be useful just in case. It wasn't like he was messy or anything, but one person doesn't make the same kind of gunk buildup two does. I vacuumed with his ancient machine, swept, mopped, made the dinner menu for the week, made a grocery list. What little homework I had only took about an hour.

When he came home, he had a huge bake-yourself pepperoni pizza and gave me a peck on the cheek, as if he wasn't even upset about Friday. He didn't ask anything, just said he was happy to see me. The pizza was nice, but I would've felt better if I could have cooked him dinner. It wasn't until afterward that he asked if I wanted to go back to Harmony.

"I want to check on that van, now that I've got the parts." He pushed at his water-glass with one blunt fingertip. His hands weren't all scratched up now. "I'm heading out tomorrow, same time as last week."

"The van?" I couldn't help it, my eyebrows went up. "*That's* what you're checking on?"

His mouth opened, closed. Finally, he shrugged, a teenage-worthy movement that would have been fine if he was my age. As it was, it looked kind of weird on him.

But it felt familiar. I used to talk over Mom's dates with her. She hadn't had one in a while. *I'm pursuing a solo career*, she'd say, pursing her lips and blowing a kiss to imaginary men lining up to talk to her, to stand near her, to feel her smile all over them like a warm bath.

I didn't blame them, really. When Mom paid attention to you, the whole world was sunshine. "Well, do you like her?" I persisted. "Clover. She looks a little young."

"Five years younger than me." Dad shook his head, sharply, twice. His eyes weren't bloodshot anymore, but his chin and cheeks were scratchy. "Now why would you say a thing like that, Val?"

"Because you like her, right?" It was different than talking to Mom, I decided. She thought it was healthy to show the full range of human emotion to your child, to let them know everything was okay and feelings were all right. "I mean, it's okay. I'm not five, Dad, I know what it's like."

He had a particular way of looking at me sometimes. Blue eyes dark and a little worried, his chin down and his shoulders up, like he couldn't quite believe the Universe had stuck him with me instead of with a boy he could grunt baseball and talk gonads with.

Maybe him-and-Mom would have lasted longer that way. Mom was always happier with guys around than other girls.

"Val." His plate was bare. He even ate the crusts, and would eat mine too in a little bit. I just liked the sauce and cheese. "I'm your dad first, and everything else second."

It was a nice thought. Really it was. If he wanted me to believe it, maybe he should have, I don't know, *done* something. Insisted on the visits the courts said he could have. Come out to the farmhouse before Mom...

Well, you know, he always paid monthly. Mom said *that*, too. He never hit her, and he always paid the child support. He just didn't push anything, which was probably the best way to handle Mom.

I didn't even know what else I wanted, or why I was irritated.

"It's okay, Dad." I also don't know why I did it, but I put my left hand over his right. My fingers looked really spidery and small next to his big callused paws. "I don't mind. It's okay."

He looked up at me, changing and softening in that heartbeat of time, and later I would kick myself for it. I would pinch myself and rock back and forth and scream inside.

Because maybe, if I'd said something else, we wouldn't have gone back.

19

DO YOU SING

Up the hills. Down a little, not all the way, always ending a little higher than we started. The rise and fall, like breathing. You could imagine Cold Creek Road was drawing you along with no effort on your part, the dips and slopes a conveyor belt under the Charger's tires. A thick mist—sort of a fog with pretensions rather than actual rain—spattered the windshield with little tiptap feet. Dad had to wait for it to build up before he flicked the wipers. Evergreens bent, hushed and dripping. When we turned up the ridge, I caught a glance of Cold Creek at the bottom, a foaming, burbling hurry under the slender gray bridge. It was a nice day for curling up near a wood-stove and reading, maybe getting up with a blanket still around your shoulders to go make tea. A long lazy afternoon spent just being with yourself, maybe not even reading, just enjoying the fact of a damp and chilly outside when you're warm and dry.

Dad had classic rock on the radio; Jefferson Airplane was singing about a white rabbit. Mom never really liked that song. I said nothing, watching the green and the brown blur by, listening to the guitar wail played so soft we could have been in an elevator.

At least Dad hadn't broken out the lint roller this time.

That was when I saw the sign, *Harmony Home*. The *No Tres-passing* sign too, near enough to be a warning but a polite one, the blackberries and scrub brush clipped back along the fence. With the windows closed I didn't hear the gravel under the tires as much, but I touched Mom's necklace just the same. Now that I'd had it on for a while, I could see why she liked it. A comforting, metallic warmth, like armor. A knight in metal sheathing, flat pieces hammered into tubes to protect the soft, round, squishy stuff under-neath. The egg in my chest was a cold hard weight—something hard inside of soft, the rest of me safe inside a layer of *don't-touch*, just like those dolls with smaller ones nesting inside. How many layers could you have before you started to rattle around inside them?

Dad parked behind the blue Corolla again. This time I saw the license plate—*LUVSNGS*. Love snuggles? Love songs, or love sings? It was like one of those Sunday newspaper puzzles.

The Pavilion doors were all open, and music came out. Not just singing, but piano too. Someone strummed a guitar. There was no electrical whine on the guitar though the pinao had to be plugged in. It sounded a little gospel, but not much.

"I'm gonna get to work." He didn't even glance at the building, though the set of his shoulders said maybe he wanted to. "Sounds like they've got something going on in there."

"Holy rolling." I slammed my car door, not overly hard. "I'd rather help you."

He popped the trunk, ready to grab his toolbox and get started. We were being so careful with each other. Tiptoeing, just like the fog-plus, which had turned to a light drizzle. The vans were under a carport roof, but it was still going to be chilly. The ground was prob-ably wet. All the gravel looked slick and clean. There weren't a lot of weeds except at the edges. Did everyone come out and sing while they grubbed up dandelions and thistles?

That mental image was silly, and was the reason I was smiling when there was a soft commotion at the nearest pavilion door. "It *is!*"

Ingrid, the dark-haired girl with the beautiful skin and blue cardigan, yelled over her shoulder. "It's them!"

Jesus. Had they been waiting for us or something?

The piano stopped, though the guitar kept going. Ingrid bounced out, followed closely by Gabrielle; Clover trailed in their wake. Dad didn't glance at her, already heading for the troublesome van, and for a moment she looked almost worried before she shook her long, loose, curling dark hair and turned that megawatt smile onto me. Did they treat all their visitors this way?

"Hey!" Ingrid put on the brakes, scuffing a line in the gravel with a crunch and a swing of her arms, a pink skirt floating and flowing under the blue cardigan but it worked for her. She really did move just like a gazelle, like gravity could only manage to keep her down half the time. "I was scared we weren't going to see you. What happened? Greeman's been asking us, we didn't know what to say."

There was really no need for them to say anything. It wasn't like they were my buddies. Still, they saw me get on the bus in the morning, and ride it home in the afternoon. "I decided to skip for a bit. Gym's a drag."

"Wow." Gabrielle arrived, snub-nosed and scrubbed until she glowed. Her lashes were blonde at the tips, giving her eyes a wide, childlike look, especially since she didn't wear makeup. "The whole week?"

They were looking at me like I'd just eaten a live frog. I shrugged. "Yeah."

"How did you—" Ingrid hunched her shoulders, swallowing the rest of the question when Clover arrived.

Clover, in a long red-and-white broomstick skirt, pushed up the sleeves of her black sweater before she beamed at me and held out her hand. "You're a little early! We were just singing."

I searched for something polite to say. "Didn't mean to interrupt the, uh, the service."

"Oh, today's just a thanksgiving. We're really excited, Father Jim has been working very hard." Clover's dark eyes sparkled. She had good skin too, not as great as Ingrid's but nice and clear. Healthy living, maybe. "We've got a real feast for you, too."

Well, that was kind of awkward. Or did they do it for every after-church guest? I wondered what it was like out here during the week. Did they have jobs and turn their paychecks over? I mean, you can only sell so many vegetables, or so many eggs.

The Pavilion began to lose people, trickling from the open doors like yeast had been added to a pile. People-froth, bubbling free. A familiar dark head and jean jacket filled the closest door, and how stupid was it that I figured out just then *that's* what I'd been waiting for? I was going to have to smash that stupidity, bury it really deep. *Don't get attached* was a good rule, and it saved me a lot of grief.

"Dad just came out to check," I managed, almost numbly. My hands and feet all of a sudden didn't know what to do with themselves, and I focused on the tip of Clover's nose. She really didn't look nearly as old as Dad, except for those fine soft lines when she smiled. "You don't have—"

"Oh, you guys are so *polite!*" She grabbed my hand, shook it once and *dropped* it, pulling back as if I'd stung her. Her prettily arched eyebrows shot up. I did a hurried mental check—yeah, I'd washed that morning. I wasn't sweaty or anything. "Sorry, I was afraid you wouldn't make it, with the rain, but Father said your dad is *reliable*. It's a really big thing around here, you know. A lot of people outside, well, they don't do what they say they will."

Don't I know it. I restrained the urge to wipe my hand on my jeans, wondering what the hell. Maybe they had rules about touching, like massage practitioners. "I know." I might have asked if she was really happy to see Dad, but she looked up over my shoulder and her entire face lit up. There was my answer. She brushed past me, and her cry of greeting sent a weird shiver down my back.

Ingrid rolled her eyes. "Queen Clover," she muttered.

Gabrielle elbowed her, cupping a hand over her mouth. "Don't," she whispered behind it, but her eyes were wide and avid. All of a sudden I felt a little better.

Sweetness and light is okay, don't get me wrong. You even get points for effort if you're just trying too hard. But it gets weird when people don't act, well, *human.*

Tiny, cold little kisses touched my cheeks, drifted along the top of my head. Looked like the mist-with-pretensions was about to turn into real rain. A rooster crowed somewhere, near the barns, and Owen the Preacher's Son walked up like we were friends, his jacket damp and dark at the shoulders. Looked like he'd been outside more than a little today. "Hey." The cross, on its too-short leather cord, winked at me.

"Hey, yourself." I rocked back on my heels. The girls were all in skirts, and here I was in jeans and a Grateful Dead T-shirt. It was vintage, though, and Mom had got it what she called the old-fashioned way at a Dead concert. She used to tell me I was conceived at one, too, until I figured out Dad probably wouldn't be caught dead or alive at a venue like that.

He just wasn't the type. It was a great story, though.

"Bleachers got too cold?" One side of his lips lifted, a crooked and very charming smile.

Did you look for me out there? "Maybe." I tried to figure out why he was grinning at me, and decided he was just doing his social duty as the preacher's kid.

It was a relief. Well, mostly a relief, mixed with a strange, toothache disappointment.

"Well, praise and blessings, they *are* here!" Father Jim showed up in the door, too, and the rest glommed behind him, following like raindrops running down a window. His smile was *really* wide, and that almost-warmth coming off him was...it felt stronger, maybe? Or maybe I just hadn't noticed it before. Some people just look like they're plugged into a cosmic outlet, and the glow makes everyone around them seem a little transparent. No, not transparent exactly.

Just a little less, you know, *there.*

"You skipped the whole week?" Ingrid shook her dark head, pushing her cardigan sleeves up. "Does your dad know?"

I made a vague face, slightly uncomfortable. "Yeah."

"Wow. If mine caught me skipping it would be full Meeting Circle." Ingrid's eyes widened, if that were possible.

I didn't ask, partly because it sounded dire, and partly because a familiar brownish-blonde head bobbed out of the Pavilion doors and headed straight for me. Sarah, in a red sweater just a little too big for her and a fluffy pink skirt, broke into a gallop past Father Jim, and when she skidded to a stop she grabbed at Owen's leg, peering shyly at me.

"Hey, monkey." He ruffled her hair with his free hand. "This is Val."

"I know." The little girl leaned into him. "She's nice."

That was vote of confidence, and it brightened me up a little. "Hi, Sarah. Did it hatch?"

She shook her head, a solemn waif. Her pink rainboots were dabbed with thick black mud, and her hair had that funny wavy texture that said it had been rained on, dried, and was now crinkling up under fresh moisture. "The mama's sitting on them."

"Wow. She must like you if she told you about her birds." Owen's grin got deeper and more genuine, if that was possible. Father Jim reached us, and I was beginning to feel a little crowded.

"Well, hello, Daughter Val. We were afraid the rain would keep you away." Today the preacher—I couldn't think of anything else to call him—wore a long black coat, severe and straight, and it meshed uneasily with his surfer-streaked hair.

"Nosir." I put my hands behind my back, so he wouldn't try to shake with me. "Dad got the parts for the van. He said we'd only be a little while."

"No, that won't do at all. You should stay for lunch. I'll go talk to him. Owen, why don't you show her into the Pavilion?" He bent down a little, peering at my face like he needed to see up-close. His eyes, hazel with threads of green, were kind enough, but they had...I don't know, a sort of wall far behind them. He could look out, sure, but you weren't gonna look in. "Do you like music, Daughter Val?"

Buddy, I am not your daughter. "Uh, yeah." I supposed everyone's got a wall or two they don't want strangers peering behind, though. "Doesn't everyone?"

"Good answer. Have Owen play for you. Everyone, why don't we break for lunch a little early?" He said it like it was just an idea, a suggestion, but the adults all nodded and scattered as he ambled away towards the long carport. Clover was already there, looking up at Dad and talking very rapidly, in a low confiding tone. He hunched his shoulders, trying not to loom over her so much. What was it like for him, super-size in a regular world? He was always so careful.

"Cloooooo-ver," Ingrid said, low and drawn-out. A faint flush stained her velvety cheeks. "There she goes."

"Where's her brother?" I didn't see Leaf, and I wasn't sure if I'd seen him last time, either. A small, embarrassed silence bloomed, and I tried to break it. "I kind of wanted to talk to him about a place we both used to go to."

"You know him?" Owen pulled Sarah closer in, and she didn't look fazed in the least. Instead, she shifted from foot to foot, tugging away, the picture of a kid who had business elsewhere when the olders were finished doing their boring things.

"Not really. I just saw him there a lot." I hadn't asked Dad to take me to Enlightened Source. I could have figured out how to get there by bus. Why hadn't I?

Well, maybe I didn't want to talk to anyone there. Since they hadn't come to...the funeral. That was the wrong thing to be thinking about, my face probably showed as much. That embarrassed silence just got a little deeper. *Ooooookay. Good one, Val.*

Sarah wriggled free of Owen's hand. "Come on." She grabbed my left wrist, thin hot fingers surprisingly strong. "I want to show you."

"Aw, come on, Sarah. She doesn't want to play dolls." Gabrielle ruffled the girl's hair. It wasn't cruel, really. Just casual, dismissive.

Sarah dropped my hand. "Fine." She glowered at the older girl, turned on her rainboot heel, and ran back for the Pavilion.

"Nice," Owen drawled. "Now I'll have to listen to her complain."

"Poor you." Ingrid grinned. "Hey, Val. Do you sing?"

I shook my head, but they were already pulling me for the Pavilion, too. They introduced me all around—Rob, Kellan, Amy, Ben, all the kids who rode the bus. That was when I found out Owen played the piano, and they all sang with the rippling music he produced. I just listened, though they kept trying to make me open my mouth. It was all I could do to keep the egg inside my chest good and strong. I watched Owen's hands against the keys, and I had no idea what Dad did in the hour before they began setting up the tables. After eating he went back to work on the van for a long two hours.

Later, of course, I suspected what had happened before lunch.

Maybe I should have stayed with him.

20

ROTTING WOOD

THAT NIGHT, Dad paused in my open bedroom door, tapping his knuckles on the frame. A tentative little one-two, and I looked up from the bed, my back against blank white wall and my French textbook open in my lap. It wouldn't do any harm to work ahead, seeing as how the class was so far behind me I could finish the homework in my sleep. I had a chunk of calcite I was playing with while I memorized, rubbing it gently against my palms.

Mom said it was good for memory.

"Hey, dumplin'. Can I come in?"

I could kind of tell what was coming. "If you want."

He took a couple of steps in and stood, slump-shouldered and familiar, a big blue-eyed bear. Once, when I was little, he held me up over his head, near the ceiling. I squawked with delight, and he grinned up at me, his face the whole world for that brief, tiny instant of memory. His thumbs stuck in his jeans pockets, and with his chambray work shirt's sleeves rolled up, the muscle in his forearm showed. He had to shop big-and-tall, and I was pretty sure that was expensive.

Everything was expensive. Kids cost money; I tried not to.

"I was talking to Clover." A slow sullen flush worked up his cheeks, died away. "You know, I'm no good with girls. Never was. So, I kind of asked her about you."

Oh, boy. "What about me?" My fingers turned white, gripping the textbook cover, digging in. So much for knowing what was coming—I thought he was going to give me the *I'm-dating-her* talk. Not the *we-have-discussed-a-kid* talk.

"Just, you know." He sighed, heavily. "About your mother."

"You discussed Mom with *her?*" I didn't mean to sound screechy, really I didn't. It just came out. The days were getting longer, and the sky outside my bedroom window was indigo instead of black.

Relax, starchild. Go with the flow. I wanted to, but the flow was full of rocks.

"Discussed you, Val. How you're dealing, how you might feel. What I can do."

"Do?" It was hard to keep the egg solid inside my chest. Keeping myself tense and ready all the time was fucking exhausting. All I wanted was to wake up in the farmhouse with cold feet and the tip of my nose frozen, hearing Mom breathe on the other camp cot, smelling woodsmoke and the faint tarnish of mildew. I would stretch and think *what an awful dream* and get up to make some tea. And I would never, ever complain about the balky stove or the sagging floorboards or all the weeding in summer. Not even to myself. I would never, ever mutter about Mom spending bill money on a chunk of lazarite she gave away a few days later, or when she didn't show up for parent-teacher meetings, or when she didn't go to the doctor like she said she would, or any of a hundred other things. I would never roll my eyes and heave a sigh about an open jar of kimchi on the counter or the reek of a dead sourdough starter.

"Well...it's a big change, with your mom gone." His breath hitched a little right before *gone*, then he rushed through the rest of it, running for the finish line. "A whole new school. Everything."

"I'm fine." I looked down at the textbook. A whole page about *quelque chose*. A bright illustration of a red dress a French woman would probably never be caught dead in. It had *shoulderpads*, for God's sake. "Really."

He spread his hands a little. "Maybe you could talk to someone?"

Did he have to sound so worried? I was dealing, I wasn't going to be a problem for him. I mean, I already *was*, but I wasn't going to be *more* of a problem. "I'm not talking to Clover, Dad." A shiver went down my back, just a small one. *Queen Clover.* The thin brunette woman who followed Father Jim around probably had a couple names for her, too. The Harmony kids called Father Jim's wife *Mother*, just like they called him *Father*, but she'd never even said two words to me. Just beamed from a distance, following him around, a planet tugged along after a sun.

Dad just stood there, steady and stolid. "No, I mean...someone professional."

I stared at the red dress on the page. Man, it was ugly, neckline to hem. You had to admire the commitment. "A therapist?" Those cost money. And I didn't need a straight with a degree poking around inside my head and asking about my mother. *Totally Freudian*, Mom would say, and laugh.

"Maybe. Whoever you got to talk to, dumplin'. Grief is hard for kids—"

"No. I mean, thanks, but no." *I'm not a kid.* Well, I was, but I wasn't five anymore. Sixteen was practically grown-up. I could live on my own if I had to, if I didn't mind working dead-end jobs for the rest of my life. Money for college—when had Mom thought about that? A will, too? Had she *known*, somehow? "I'm fine." A faint edge of orange crept up in my window—the lights in the parking lot were coming on. Back at the farmhouse we'd be building up the fire, Mom would do some meditating or tuning, or she'd get out her cards while I studied. "I promise, Dad."

"Val—"

"I'm *fine*. Just don't talk to Clover about me, all right?"

That rocked him back on his sock heels a bit. Black tube socks, bought by the bag. His feet were huge. They had to be, to carry him around. "You don't like her?"

"She's okay." What else was I going to say? "I just don't want you to talk to her about me."

"All right." Still, he just stood there. "Val. Honey."

"What?" I turned the page. *Common Grammar Mistakes.* Thankfully, no red dress on this page. Pictures of people eating, shaking hands, red underlining errors, green with a little gold star showing the correct terms.

"It's all right to be sad."

"I'm not sad." That was a lie, but I didn't want to try to explain anything right now. It wouldn't do any good.

"Honey..."

"Dad." I took a deep breath, pressed my shoulders against the wall behind me. Nice and clean and white. "Please." You could paint over anything, really. Even the farmhouse might have looked better with a good coating or two of something pretty. Underneath, though, there were still the rotting floorboards.

There was rotting wood under everything. You stepped too hard, made too much noise, and it could break.

He persisted, of course. "It's okay to miss her. I miss her too."

As if he'd spoken to her in the last eleven years, beyond a *hi* or *here's the money* or *can I talk to Val?* "Then why did you divorce her?"

"Kiddo, she divorced *me*." He actually took a step back. In the farmhouse, shifting your weight like that would get a groan from underfoot. Here, nothing happened. Little box-houses, stacked on top of each other. A warren full of straights, and I was hiding in the middle of it. "I'd've taken her back in a heartbeat. She was my wife, and you're my girl."

And Clover's gunning for one position or another. But maybe you don't see it, or don't care. "Okay." I closed the textbook with a snap, almost stinging my own fingers. "I know you're trying to help, Dad.

Really. When I feel like talking to someone, I'll let you know." I decided right then and there to keep my mouth shut, and shut *hard*.

"Okay." He waited another few moments, obviously expecting something else, but I said nothing. Just unfocused my eyes and pretended I was like Mom, that I could see what he was feeling, see the glow around him that would tell me what he really wanted. What I really wanted. *Auras never lie*, she said.

Well, they might not, but the people inside them, what about them? I never asked.

"School tomorrow," he finally said, awkwardly. "You need a note for gym class?"

I shook my head, my hair whispering against white paint. What other conversations had this room seen before Dad moved in? What was painted over in here? Did I even want to know? Maybe Mom could have told me. "I'll deal."

"I love you, dumplin'." His thumbs were out of his pockets now, his big chapped hands dangling loosely.

"I love you too, Dad."

I meant it. But all the same, I was glad when he retreated and closed the door, gently, as if I was already asleep.

2 1

ORBITING PARTICLE

Travis the Bathroom Bro was quiet during American History, for once. I caught him looking at me a couple times, his arms folded and a smirk plastered on his wide, greasy face, but I managed to ignore it. Shieldman looked nervous, probably because she sensed the calm before some kind of storm. I was too busy trying to breathe through the fog of body spray and sweat Travis put out. When the chimes rang for lunch I almost startled clean out of my chair, as Mom would say.

I'd been expecting...what?

Oz kept sneaking glances at me too, but he didn't say a word. If he would've asked, I probably would've fallen into spending lunch with his friends. It would be just too awkward to show up like a stray looking for a handout, though. I could hear them in the library at lunch, a low murmur of male voices and the rattle of dice on the table. Sometimes there was shared laughter. I sat in my hidden little space, chewing my peanut-butter-and-apple sandwich, and tried not to strain my ears.

I really did mean to give gym my best try. Well, at least, I'd told Dad I wouldn't skip. There was a whole world's worth of difference between the two. It didn't help that the gym floor had been redone, and you could smell it from the locker room.

"No jewelry!" Greeman barked, pointing at my mother's necklace again. I said nothing, just folded my arms and stood there, the locker room full of echoes and the high slamming squeaks of lockers champing. Mouths, all of them, flapping open and crunching closed.

"Then you'll have to tell Sandy to take her big old earrings off." Gabrielle slung an arm over my shoulders and hustled me past, and Greeman didn't say anything else. "Don't worry," the blonde girl said, her breath hot against my ear. "She's got the attention span of a goldfish. I love that necklace, by the way. Where did you get it?"

"My mom's." I let her pull me out into the hall. Ingrid bounced along right behind us; both of them smelling faintly of patchouli and fresh air.

"Cool." Gabrielle tightened her arm, almost as if she was afraid I was going to get away. "She and your dad divorced?"

"Yeah." I hunched and said nothing else, just let her pull me along. Her hip bumped mine. It was kind of nice to be close to someone who wasn't parental, even if we were both in grubby-ass sweats.

"It's turquoise, right? That's a good stone. Cleansing. Indigenous people use it for all sorts of stuff."

"You know about stones?" And bonus for *indigenous*, that was the Right Word. You don't say *Indian* unless you mean the subcontinent, goddammit.

"Oh, yeah. Father says it's all energy." She grinned, letting go of me to reach for the gym doors.

"My mom said that too." I was cautiously revising my opinion of Father Jim. "Your dad's at Harmony, right?"

"Yeah, he and my mom split a while ago." Studiously casual, as only a teenage girl can be. "It was grim."

"Oh boy." Ingrid bounded past us, stopped dead, and turned in a circle, her mouth pulled down in mock-dismay. "Guess what the Greem's got on tap for us today!"

"What?" All I could see where some manky old yoga mats on the floor.

"Oh, *fuck*," Gabrielle moaned. "It's *aerobics*."

Greeman jerked and panted her way through things I'd only seen in falling-apart exercise books about Jane Fonda and super fitness from the eighties. What was even worse was the music. It wasn't even *disco*, it went from some chick yelling about how girls just wanted to have fun to one yodeling about bang-bang being a warrior. Ingrid bounced along, every once in a while glancing at Gabrielle, who did, like me, the absolute minimum. Sandy and her henches, of course, didn't even do that, lagging behind and complaining at each other. Greeman obviously expected us to use the mats for stretching and cooldown, which meant you were faced with the chemicals on the revarnished floor, fumes coming off fit to burn your lungs, or a mat that had been sweated on by God knows who and was probably full of microbes.

And not the beneficial kind.

Stretching is always good, but I was woozy by the time it was over. A single sandwich was not enough to get through the day on, even if the apples were organic. Mom always said organic stuff had more nutrients, kept you full for longer. She would have had a fit over all the chemicals in the flooring. Maybe she'd even talk to the principal about it. I didn't even know who the principal *was*, I tuned out the morning announcements in favor of concentrating on the egg in my chest.

The egg that was cracking, right now.

I wiped at my cheek, straightening from a forward bend. Greeman's form would have gotten her gently encouraged in a yoga class. Nadine would have clucked her tongue and said, *let's loosen you up, my friend.*

Rolling up the mat, all of a sudden I wanted to see Nadine's studio again. The mellow wood floor, the silk meditation pillows in the corner, the mirrors on one wall and the ballet barre because she believed yoga was Ballet 2.0, really. The big Buddha statue at one end, with soy candles and fresh flowers laid out daily. The warm sunlight when it came through the high windows, and Nadine's calm, happy voice. *Let's try Child's Pose for a bit. I like to call it wisdom pose. Let's reconnect.*

Why didn't she show up for the funeral? Did she not *know*? How could any of them not feel it when my mother wasn't wearing her seat belt and...

You don't want to see that, dumplin'.

"Oh, my God." Sandy sounded disgusted. She loomed over me, holding her blue mat—it looked the newest out of all of them, of course—by one corner, tweezed between index finger and thumb. Her makeup was just as thick and flawless as always, but a single eyelash, carrying a heavy cargo of mascara, stuck high up on her left cheek. "Are you *crying*?"

Maybe I would have said something, but I was saved the trouble because Gabrielle on my right, bending to pick her own rolled mat up, grabbed it and whipped around, nailing Sandy with a tube of slightly sticky plastic across her bare, orange-tanned shins. It made a thin cracking sound, lost in the music Greeman still had going at top volume—a watered-down instrumental version of a Bob Dylan song.

Mom would have been furious.

"*Ow!*" Sandy skipped back, dropping her mat. Her Nikes squeaked against the varnish.

"Whoops." Gabrielle, unrepentant, narrowed her hazel eyes. A smattering of golden freckles across her nose looked planned for maximum effect. "Next one goes on your face, slutgirl."

Wow. My jaw dropped.

"Painted up like a ho," Ingrid added. "Still trying to spread your legs to the top of the pyramid, Gibson?"

So that was her last name. Later, I found out Sandy's big dream was head of the cheerleading squad, and supposedly she'd slept with one of the football players to make it. I had no idea if she even thought that had a shot of working, or whatever, but when I heard it, I all of a sudden understood the flash of something harsh but kind of vulnerable, too, that passed across her contoured, powdered face.

Even if it wasn't true, everyone at Cold Ridge probably *thought* it was.

"Bitch," Sandy hissed at Gabrielle, and backed up. It hadn't been hard enough to really hurt her, which was kind of a shame, and you could barely see the red mark on her shins through the weird I-lay-in-a-broiler shade she had going on.

"Yo mama," Ingrid chirped back, and that broke her and Gabrielle out in giggles. My mouth stretched, and the pressure inside my chest eased all at once.

"All right, ladies," Greeman yelled over the music. "Let's hustle!"

"Don't worry, Val." Ingrid leaned down, offering me her hand. "We've got you."

Neither of them mentioned the dampness on my cheeks. That afternoon, on the bus, I sat across the aisle from them, the window seat on my other side empty, and the Harmony kids acted like it was no big deal. Not really one of the constellation, just an orbiting particle.

That was fine by me.

22

HOME EARLY

ALL WEEK, Ingrid and Gabby flanked me during gym and I sat on the periphery of the Harmony kids going home on the bus. It was workable, if not ideal. Owen kept leaning over the back of what was now my habitual seat, asking me questions about my classes. The only bad bits were in American History, where Travis the Bathroom Bro had decided to go back to his old self after staring at me Monday and Tuesday. He gave Shieldman hell; he tormented Oz, too. Poking, prodding, sometimes flicking staples at him, even though that sort of thing could really hurt someone.

Assholes like Travis don't care. There wasn't a single thing I could do, even though Oz was the first kid who'd been even *sort* of kind to me here.

But all that was over, and I was free for a whole glorious weekend. I was looking forward to pizza. I mean, I was hopeful, not expecting or thinking I was entitled to it or anything, it had just become the Friday thing. I raced through a few lonely pages of stupid homework, congratulated myself on making it through another school week, and filled the new kettle. I have to say, the well at the farmhouse might have been better than city water, but not having to hand-pump it in the kitchen was pretty sweet.

I dropped a teabag into a big red Mechanic's Union mug and waited while the water chirped in the kettle, marveling again at how *easy* his stove was. You just turned the dial, it heated up, and it *stayed* heated, like a miracle. All Mom's kitchens were makeshift and make-do, it was the price of being a free spirit.

The doorknob rattled, and I probably had forgotten to lock the front again. I bounced into the hall, ready to grin and yell *welcome home!* He was early, and that was great, I was feeling good, and—

"Just come on in," Dad said over his shoulder. His short hair was combed back, and his hands had been scrubbed with that orange goop-soap mechanics like, I could smell it all the way from the end of the hall.

Clover trailed behind him, small and dainty in a long skirt patterned with blue flowers, a cotton peasant top showing straps of what definitely wasn't a bra but just a camisole underneath, a blue kerchief over braided hair. She smiled at me, her eyes twinkling, as if we shared a secret.

"Hello, dumplin'!" Dad grinned, carrying a couple of those you-bake-them pizzas and a paper grocery bag. Clover cradled a wine bottle in her soft pale hands, and I was suddenly very sure she didn't fork hay or do any of the heavy work in the gardens out at Harmony Home.

Girls like her never did.

The kettle made a high-pitched rumble, the song right before it drops into almost-silence and the bubbles get bigger right on the edge of boiling. "You're home early," I managed, through a dry throat.

"Well, I couldn't wait to see my favorite girl. Ran into Clover at the grocery store, and invited her to dinner."

"If you don't mind," Clover supplied helpfully. She stood just two steps inside, that most polite of distances. "I know Friday's probably your time with your dad, Val."

Oh, that's really nice of you. Except she probably didn't mean it.

What was she going to do, take her bottle of wine back to the compound? Leave it here? Mom got a good bottle of French red every once in a while, especially when the Wiccans came out to the farmhouse to do their circle stuff.

Where were they holding circle now, I wonder? Would they go out to the farmhouse and find it abandoned? They'd want to celebrate spring returning.

I spun and marched back into the kitchen. Flipped the burner under the kettle off, set it on the back of the stove, and shoved my cup with its sentinel teabag back into the cupboard for good measure. Dad murmured something that sounded like *let me talk to her* and when he came into the kitchen, all the air left the room.

Great. I was going to be *talked to*.

"Val?" Anxious, his bushy black eyebrows raised, his mouth soft but also pained. "Dumplin', I got pizza, I thought..."

It was like Mom with one of the boyfriends even *I* could tell was bad news. Hair in short ponytails, throwing around words like *tantra* and *consciousness* and *meditating a lot, you know* and *poetry*. They hung around occult shops and open mics and drum circles, thinking any woman into crystals or tarot was easy prey. It didn't help that they were often right. And each time, Mom would think she'd found something worth having, and she'd look at me hopefully, just like Dad was doing now.

"It's fine." My throat had turned to a pinhole. My tone said it was obviously *not* fine, but he looked relieved and happy. He lit up, and I felt like a shit for not liking her. It wasn't her fault, right? Mom and Dad had been split up forever, over ten years.

The realization gave me a funny feeling in the pit of my stomach. Right down near the navel chakra, right where you're supposed to center yourself when doing breathwork.

It wasn't like it mattered, either. Mom was gone, and Clover wasn't that bad. I couldn't see why she wasn't dating closer to home, but maybe she didn't want to? And if she made Dad happy, fine.

So I pasted on a smile. "Actually, well, I got invited to dinner. At Jenny's." I didn't know a Jenny. "She lives in the complex. Can I go?"

That brought him up short. It was a big old super-huge lie, but it came out naturally. It wouldn't have flown with Mom. Her own beautifully arched eyebrows would have drawn together and she would have tilted her head just a little, daring me to tell another one, until we both broke up laughing and she asked me what the real problem was.

Dad just stood there, his arms full of groceries. "Where does she live, now?"

"In the building on the other side of the pond." Lying again. I did know a girl who lived in that building—a shy bookish one with dishwater hair and glasses so thick her dark eyes swam behind them. She wore sweater vests and frumpy old-lady skirts, and hunched her shoulders when the boys on the bus yelled. Just another noncomforming kid at the bottom of the food chain. I knew her by *sight*, at least, and maybe her name was Jenny, so it wasn't a complete lie.

He glanced at the clock. "You sure you want to? I mean, I got pizza. I got a lot of it."

"One of those can go in the fridge for later. It's fine if you don't want me to go." Did I feel guilty, or just relieved? I couldn't tell. I hadn't taken my boots off, though that was usually the first thing I did when I got home. Maybe I'd known somehow, or maybe my feet were just cold.

"No, no." A shadow of relief warred with uneasiness on his broad, familiar face. "That's okay. I mean, I'm glad you're making friends. She in any of your classes, this Jenny?"

Keep it simple, Val. "No, just on the bus."

"All right. You be back by..." He left it open, which was kind of what I wanted.

"After dinner. Can I?" I tried to put just the right amount of wheedle into it, without going overboard.

"All right, dumplin'." He just stood there, stolid, blinking. The entire apartment, cozy and roomy just a few minutes ago, shrank and filled with an uncomfortable crackling hush, too. "Go ahead."

I ran to grab my backpack, not too heavy without the textbooks. On the way out the door I had to slide past Clover, who stood three not two, feet inside now. She didn't move, and I tried not to touch her, but her skirt brushed my knee. She watched me, and I couldn't tell if her face was set with embarrassment or something else. Close-up, the fine lines around her eyes and mouth broke the illusion.

"Val..." Softly, her glossy lips shaped my name. I bet her lip balm had petroleum products in it instead of good old honest beeswax which Mom said was better and more humane.

"See you," I mumbled, and escaped.

I didn't know where I was going, but that was what Mom would have called a secondary consideration. I just knew I had to get *out* for a while. Maybe I should have stayed, but I didn't want to sit there and watch them making goo-goo eyes at each other.

Half of me felt like a total bitch. The other half didn't care. All the second half could think was just this: *You just be good to my Dad, Clover.*

Or I'll fix you.

23

SOLD

Across Parkington Street from the Swallows Mill complex were duplexes, cars parked on either side. On the other side, a neighborhood with rundown rentals, cars parked thick along every available curb. At the top was the small stream that fed the pond, surrounded by a bit of raggedy park that had a jogging loop and a small paved area with swings and a slide. There were a couple other playgrounds in the complex, but I took off for the opposite edge, where the bus let me off every day. Across the four lanes of 173rd was one of those chain pharmacy-drugstores that sells overpriced sunscreen, hair ties, and gum along with oxycontin and penicillin. The type of place with a machine that will squeeze your arm in a manky plastic cuff and tell you about your blood pressure, give or take a few decimals. I don't know quite why I ended up there, dashing across four lanes, two shoulders, and a bit of fresh new sidewalk in the cold gray almost-evening. There was a crosswalk a couple blocks up, but the worn-down places at the roadside and in the weed-choked meridian told me pretty much everyone in the complex took their chances here.

Maybe I wanted a candy bar or something, since I wouldn't be eating dinner. If I went back to Dad's after a couple shivering hours outside and dug in the fridge, he'd ask questions, wouldn't he? Unless he and Clover didn't notice. If they were busy, you know. Doing...stuff.

That thought skeeved me right out. I kicked at a pebble at the edge of the parking lot, hunched my shoulders, and scuttled across pavement striped with faded lines. There weren't many cars, everyone was probably hitting the freeway for the end of rush hour. Dad had left work a full two hours early, on a Friday. Again.

Was he in love? It was kinda soon to tell, wasn't it? How long had he known her? I had no idea.

The automatic doors whooshed open. Preservative-laced candy bars, full of high-fructose corn syrup, were high on the list of *don't evers* Mom had in her head. Other kids knew what kind of candy they liked, I knew what kind of gluten-free flour made bread dough that might not turn into a rock. I could buy gum full of aspartame that would turn into formaldehyde inside my body. I could do anything I fucking wanted, except go back to Dad's apartment for a while.

Enough time for me to think up a good story. I gave a small embarrassed smile to the old woman at the counter who wheezed out a *Welcome to Wesgreens* in my general direction.

Fictional Jenny, I decided as I blinked against the fluorescents and read aisle signs, was a *total* straight. Her mom worked part-time as a secretary and her dad was a...oh, he worked in an office too. He sold *insurance* or something. Their TV was on all the time and Jenny was up on all the latest shows, and I decided dinner for them tonight was spaghetti and meatballs. Fictional Jenny had a B+ in every class and listened to the Top Forty station, or streamed her music through her phone. She knew all the shows and some of the internet memes.

Above all, Fictional Jenny was normal. Her parents fought but stayed married, and sooner or later they would move into a small rundown house in the other neighborhood when her dad got a promotion. She already had her mid-grade college picked out, and she didn't worry about pesticides in her food or synthetic fibers against her skin.

Her parents didn't agonize over vaccination, or gluten, and they certainly didn't drive without seatbelts.

How could anyone decide what kind of candy to buy? There was so *much* of it, all brightly colored and over-wrapped. Snickers, Reese's, Payday, M&Ms, Almond Joy, circus peanuts, Swedish fish, Red Hots, Jujubes, Good'n'Plenty, Junior Mints, Three Musketeers— even the smell of the candy aisle, slightly waxy with its undertone of sugar, was enough to make you dizzy. I wandered through the greeting cards right next door—saccharine paper condolences, little flaps of pressed, dead trees to make your conscience feel better rather than express anything *real*.

The middle of the drugstore was taken up with "seasonal" stuff. Easter stuff was on clearance, more sugary marshmallows and hollow chocolate bunnies already showing a pale feathering of age inside their cellophane. Some of the shelves were empty, but there was a rack of cheapass windchimes and a couple boxes on the floor full of small, useless gardening tools, obviously in the process of being put on the shelves.

A red wire rack near the end of the aisle caught my eye. It was also full of clearance, but they were...cactuses?

Half of them looked dying. They were a dollar apiece. Thirteen of them, a lucky number.

A *powerful* number.

Mom would have stopped to look at them. We probably couldn't keep them alive at the farmhouse, it just got too cold in the windows. She would purse her lips and three tiny lines would appear between her eyebrows, her head tilted just a bit as if she could hear them calling. Her braid would hang over her shoulder, black hair shining. *Poor things,* she would say.

I had money left over from the last month in the farmhouse, and Dad sometimes handed me the change from groceries or something else. *Kid needs a pocket dollar or two,* he said, gruffly, almost each time.

Was he gazing into Clover's eyes, smiling like he couldn't believe his luck? Were they drinking the wine?

"Can I help you?" It was the arthritic lady from the front, shuffling up with that faintly sour expression of every adult who suspects Kids These Days of doing awful things. Her faded blue eyes were almost lost in pouches of flesh, her cheeks swollen too.

That was all it took to make up my mind. "I'll take them." The rock in my throat had magically eased.

"What?" She had a little trouble catching up. It looked like an ongoing condition.

"I'll take them." I pointed at the rack of cactuses.

She all but rolled her eyes. "Which one?"

The thought that I was probably looking at Sandy Gibson in about another forty years was sharp and nastily hilarious at the same time. What had this woman been when she was young? She was *definitely* a straight now. Did you have to fight it, growing on you like a snail's shell?

"All of them." I hitched my backpack on my shoulder. Where was I going to put them? I'd have to haul them across the street and back to Dad's apartment. They'd probably die of the cold before I got there. I could say I'd misunderstood or that Fictional Jenny's parents had gone out for the night. "Does the rack come with?"

She eyed me up and down, leaning a little, all her weight on her left hip. Her right shoe-sole was much thicker than the other; it looked painful. So did the rest of her. Her joints probably throbbed, especially when it rained. My knees tweaked and twinged just thinking about it, and my hips. Either that, or I'd done something to myself during Greeman's enthusiastic but not very ergonomic aerobics.

"Honey." A weary smile lit her swollen face, and for a second, something gleamed underneath. It looked an awful lot like kindness. "You take those off my hands, you can *have* the damn rack."

No, I decided, she wasn't an old Sandy. She was probably an old *me*. "Sold," I said, and began digging for my wallet.

24

LITTLE GREEN GLOWS

THAT NIGHT I lay in bed, heavy American History textbook propped on my chest, and listened to the sound of quiet conversation from the living room. Once in a while Clover laughed, a warm, genuine sound. Neither of them seemed upset I'd come back carrying a rack of cactuses. Cacti? What was the right plural?

I said Jenny'd given them to me because her parents wanted them out of her room. Anyway, the rack stood right where the afternoon sun would come through the window and give the spiny things a good shine. I didn't know anything about them except they didn't freeze well and didn't need a lot of water, but I had the school library and the internet there, too. I could figure it out. At least they wouldn't freeze, Dad's apartment had good heat.

The voices paused. I closed my eyes, trying not to imagine what was happening on the couch. At least they hadn't opened the wine with me sitting right there. Mom would have asked if I wanted a half a glass. *You should know how to drink for the taste of it, not for the buzz*, she would say. *Though the buzz is nice.*

My eyes squeezed shut, blobs of color moving in the darkness. My eyelids must have been super-squeezy, because the blobs had clear shapes off to my left. Soft greenish stars—I opened my eyelids and peered over at the rack. Closed my eyes again.

The greenish stars stayed put, even when I moved. They hung out right where they should be when I shook my head, as if my eyelids were transparent. I could even count them. Three groups of four, and one on top.

The cacti. Some of the stars were weak, struggling. It wasn't the ones you'd think, looking at them with your eyes open. Maybe I could talk to them.

Mom always said plants heard you, and knew when you cared.

Wow. I tried it a couple more times, trying to tell myself it was just imagination. I was tricking myself into seeing them. *Mom* would have been able to see them, and hear them. Even with all her patient coaching, though, I was still her hard-headed, practical little starchild. *Everyone's a little sensitive,* she told me. *Your talents will come, honey.*

Movement in the hall. The voices came back. Dad's a little raspy, Clover's very soft. After a little while, the front door opened.

Huh. I turned off the bedside lamp and lay there, snuggling into sheets that had begun to smell like me. At least the bed was comfortable, much better than a camp cot. And there were all the blankets. Even a down comforter, I'd've liked that back in the farmhouse.

The front door closed. A single pair of heavy footsteps tick-tocked into the kitchen. He tried to step softly all the time, but he was just so *big*.

Once I turned the light out, my room was full of those strange phantom colors and the little green glows. I blew out a long, soft sigh. Imagination. Had to be. *Mom* was the talented one, not me. The lights didn't go away, just glimmered softly.

After a little bit of moving around, Dad's footsteps came down the bedroom hall, even softer. He paused outside my door.

I held my breath. Clover was gone. They hadn't had time to do anything more than swap spit. Gross, but much better than the alternative, right? Thinking about one of your parental units involved in the alternative had to be super-high on any list of ewww-worthy things, even for someone with no patriarchal hangups.

Dad stood for at least sixty seconds, right outside my door. If my light had been on, would he have come in? I don't know. Finally, he shuffled away, towards his own bedroom.

I fell asleep, smiling.

25

SHEBA

SATURDAY THE SUN finally came back, high and bright, forne of those spring days where everything has burst out green all at once, daffodils and hyacinths and fresh grass, new leaves, the trees not winter-brittle but elastic, the mud no longer icy and lifeless but thick and squelchy and wonderful. Everything *smelled* sweet, too, with the raw under-edge of growing things waking after a long sleep. Birds showed up—robins, jays, crows sleek and shiny blue-black instead of dull matte blots. Stray cats poked their heads out of hiding, and insects buzzed.

It was, in short, a fantastic morning. Except Dad had taken the day off instead of half and was on his way to the Harmony soup kitchen to help out. Clover was probably going to be there, and I wasn't entirely sure he should be unsupervised around her, so to speak. So I was in the Charger, wishing I was anywhere else.

He had the radio on, but not the oldies station. Instead, it was some country wavelength, and he hummed along, his big hands sure and gentle on the wheel. I would never have figured him for a ten-gallon-hat and fake-Western-accent guy, but I guess he was. Singing about whiskey and hearts gone wrong—Mom would have grimaced and spun the knob in the truck to get something different out of the speakers. In her opinion, every single country singer was from New York, sham-drawling to make money from the stupid cornfed straights who thought they were being spoken to directly. If it wasn't folk music or Summer of Love, she wasn't interested. She didn't even like the New Age CDs at Enlightened Source. *Muzak cash machines*, she called them.

She would have been going a mile a minute on a day like today, butterfly-bright with her bracelets jangling, heading to Nadine's studio or to the bookstore, intent on whatever project had gotten into her head, enjoying the sun. I stared out the window, trying not to listen to Dad's off-key humming and a song about thunder rolling.

At least he hadn't slicked his hair back or patted on any after-shave. The lint roller was tucked in a drawer somewhere.

The soup kitchen was in an old storefront in Temberton. You could call that part of town a bedroom community, but it wasn't a nice bedroom. Its heart was the Alley, a strip of road crowded with pawnshops, motels that rented hourly, liquor stores, and apartment buildings with boarded-up windows and crumbling brick walls, empty lots behind sagging chainlink fencing, stars and glitters of broken glass on cracked pavement. It was the kind of place you drive through to get somewhere else, and its tentacles spread past a bowling alley I knew since Mom had briefly dated a guy who worked there. I wondered if Sal was still behind the counter, with ranks of manky shoes frowning behind him, until we turned onto Smohausen Way and I saw it had burned down. Only a blackened shell remained, its unburned patches tangled and starred with graffiti.

"Oh, man." I couldn't help myself. "It burned down."

"What?" Dad, startled out of his humming, snapped a quick glance to the right. "The bowling alley?"

"Yeah. We used to...man, it burned *down*." I didn't even like bowling, but I'd liked Sal well enough. Of course, I'd never bowled before, but he put bumpers on one of the lanes for me and gave me all the French fries I could eat, which Mom didn't appreciate but was totally the way to a fourteen-year-old's heart.

"When were you ever out here?" Dad frowned a little.

"Long time ago." I decided not to tell him *when Mom was dating that one guy*. It just wasn't—

It happened so fast. One moment I was debating whether or not Dad might be upset to hear about some guy Mom had dated for all of two or three months, the next I was jerked forward and there was an awful squealing sound. The brown Audi in front of us had snapped its brakes on too late, and the dog darting out into the road was hit with a crunch and a snap.

Dad cussed. I let out a short yelp. The Charger's fender didn't touch the Audi's back end, but it was *damn* close, and behind us there were more rubbery squeals as traffic reacted.

A big padded hammer hit me from the side, and I couldn't *breathe*. I thought it was the seatbelt too tight across my chest not letting my ribs expand, and I actually blacked out for a second. It *hurt*, and when I could finally whoop in a breath I found the seatbelt wasn't tight at all, but Dad was swearing in a fierce low tone at the Audi's presumably illegitimate-born driver.

The dog, a golden retriever, had bolted from the sidewalk. Its owner, a gangly dude in a parka too heavy for the weather and tightly-belted jeans, stood staring in shock, half a broken leash in his hand. He had dirty brown hair, standing out from his head in those dreads white boys think are cool but just look infested.

Seriously, Caucasians just need to step *away* from the dreadlocks. It never ends well. Right at that moment, though, I was trying to get air into me. It wasn't working too well either.

"Val?" Dad's voice was very small, faraway. "Val honey what is it Val—"

I grabbed for the doorhandle. The dog, staggering out into the oncoming lane, fell and lay there, twitching. Bright red blood, bright white bone, matted-down fur, its head jerking up and slamming down on the concrete as it had some sort of seizure. My other hand, dreamlike, fumbled with the seatbelt catch.

I don't remember getting out of the car. I don't remember horns blaring, or Dad yelling, or how I got around the Charger or the Audi or anything else. All I remember is the pain. My head jerked aside like I'd been punched, again and again, and I couldn't tell if I was walking because it hurt so much. I don't remember going to my knees in the road, or my hands clamping themselves to the thrashing, strangle-yelping dog's side.

One second I was in the car trying to breathe, not understanding what the fuck had just happened, and the next there was a giant confusion, my body full of all sorts of pain it couldn't find the source of, every inch of me jumping and thrashing and hitting my head on something hard, and the *fear*.

I mean, I've been afraid before; to be a kid is to be in a constant state of high energy or absolute terror, right? But this...it wasn't even *fear*, it was terror so huge it swallowed me. I wasn't *me* anymore, and later I thought—

But that was later. I found myself on aching knees in the middle of the road, the dog looking sidelong at me, a rim of white showing around its pupil, its fur still gluey with blood but everything underneath...well, just fine, actually. Maybe it had just been stunned.

No, it wasn't. You know it wasn't.

Dad was shouting; I heard him from very far away. The dog just lay there, looking up at me. She whined a little, way far back in her throat, a *sorry, what just happened* sound.

I was still on my knees, looking down at her, when the thin, dread-headed guy arrived. "*Sheba!*" he yelled, and went down on his knees too with a jolt that knocked my teeth together. I felt it even through the pavement. "Oh shit *Sheba!*"

Shit Sheba. That's pretty funny. "I think she's okay," I managed. All of me was sore, and I couldn't figure out how I'd gotten here.

The worst noise was from a grumbling truck engine. I looked up at the front of a heavy Chevy pickup, blue as a summer sky or a robin's egg, sitting in the left lane. Which is to say, less than four feet from me. For a single, weird, heartstopping second I was convinced it was Mom, that there had been a mistake somehow and she'd found me, that the casket had been closed because they hadn't had her at all, that it was just some sort of practical joke. My heart exploded inside my chest, Dreadlocks Guy all but picked the dog up, hugging her like she was a kid while she wriggled and tried to lick his face.

She was just fine. Even the blood didn't look bad, like she'd rolled around in bright red paint.

Dad grabbed my shoulder. "*Val!*" he shouted, and I flinched. "God *damn*, dumplin', you scared the *shit* out of me!"

I wanted to say I'd just scared the shit out of *myself*, too, but I was too busy looking at the blue truck and breathing, praying, springsweet air full of exhaust and a weird coppery smell that was all the blood, plus a straw-yellow smell of doggy pee. Cigarette smoke, too, plus a breath of body-odor funk from Dreadlocks Guy.

Dad bent down. Someone blasted their horn a ways back, and the Audi that had caused this whole mess dropped into gear. It took off while I was still swaying, barely daring to look at the windshield of the blue Chevy.

It wasn't Mom. My heart crashed into my stomach; I sagged in Dad's hands. It looked like he wanted to shake me, I guess, because Dreadlocks Guy began to babble something about how I'd saved his dog Sheba just like a superhero, and a couple other drivers leaned on their horns.

Behind the wheel of the blue Chevy was an old man with a scraggly white beard, a red bandanna around his forehead, and a faded checked shirt. He stared at me, his cheeks pale and his old, big-knuckled hands quivering a bit on the wheel, and I realized he'd probably almost run *me* over, too. He looked like he'd seen a ghost.

"I don't know," I mumbled to Dad. "I don't know."

"Man, thank you." Dreadlocks Man blinked at me, tears standing in his dark, bloodshot eyes. "I thought she was a goner. You saved her. Sheba's my only friend, man. My only friend."

"Damn lucky dog, sir." Dad all but lifted me out of my boots. "Come on, Val." He got me back into the Charger, the Audi was long vanished, and all the while, the guy behind the wheel of the blue Chevy stared at me like he knew some secret but we didn't stick around for him to share. I fumbled for my seatbelt, repeating that I didn't know, I didn't know, I didn't *know* until I heard myself and snapped my mouth shit, almost biting my tongue in half.

26

AS USUAL, LIKE ALWAYS

THE STOREFRONT HAD a small parking lot choked with white Harmony vans and other cars. Dad parked and cut the engine, and a tense quiet full of ticking, cooling metal filled up the Charger's interior.

Finally, the muscle along his jaw stopped twitching. "You could have been hit," Dad said, again.

I hugged myself even tighter. "So what?" I didn't mean it like it sounded, I swear. What I meant was, something had happened, something weirder than being hit by a car, something....Jesus. I didn't even know *what* to call it, other than freaky as shit. Why wasn't he talking about *that*?

Mom would have been delighted. She would have called it *manifestation*. Or pure energy.

But she wasn't here. Mom was in a box under a blanket of wet dirt. Somehow seeing the old man in the truck convinced me. Or maybe it was just the hideous, heart-swelling, absolutely crushed hope draining out of every part of me, fingers and toes and cracks behind my eyeballs letting it escape like air from a slashed tire.

"Don't do that again." Dad exhaled, hard. His wrists had little black hairs, sliding down from his forearms. I noticed because his hands were shaking on the wheel. "You may not care if you get run over, dumplin', but *I* do."

Well, didn't that make me feel like an asshole. I opened my mouth, closed it. What could I say? Had he seen it? He was right there, he *had* to have seen it.

Like a superhero.

"Hope he takes that dog to a vet," he continued, mopping at his forehead.. "Damn. Lucky dog."

"Dad..." I hoped he'd heard me, because my throat could only push out a tired little whisper. "Dad?" A little louder.

"And you, you scared the everloving *shit* out of me. What on earth were you thinking?"

"The dog," I managed. *Tell me you saw that. Tell me you saw something weird happen, and I'm not just going nuts.* "The dog, Dad, you..." *You saw it. Tell me you saw it.*

"Fucker in that Audi should be shot," he said. "Driving off like that. Jesus."

Say something. Tell me you noticed it. "Dad..."

"Reminds me of your mother." He stared out the windshield, still wiping his forehead. "Bail out of a moving car on the interstate to rescue a got-damn turtle. Jesus Christ."

"Did she?" She would have told me if she could do anything like this, though, right? I would have *seen* her do it. But no, she was more the aura-healing kind. The knowing-things kind. Her necklace was heavy against my skin, and I wondered where her bangles were. Which ones had she been wearing that day? The good-luck *semanario*? The gold ones? I couldn't remember.

"Oh, yeah." He dropped his hand into his lap. "She was a sucker for the needy. Never quite figured out what to do with the ones that weren't broken."

Which was pretty perceptive, really. Then again, he'd been married to her, so of course he'd know. What would *she* do in this situation? Deep breathing, probably. I would have to face the fact that Dad had not noticed a single goddamn thing. Which meant either I was a giant bag of mixed nutbar, or Mom was right about energy and healing and a talent showing up for me one day.

Why did it have to happen *now*?

Deep breath. Let it out. Took another. It felt good. I was a little shaky, muscles and bones carrying the deep unsteady relief right after you throw up really hard and you know more is coming but just for a few minutes, there's a glorious, feverish lightness.

"Were you broken?" The question popped out, surprising both of us. At least, I was surprised, and Dad's hands twitched a little, as if he'd been slapped and his whole body wasn't quite sure what had happened.

"Nah." He shook his big head, slowly. "Think that's why she left. Couldn't believe I would stay with her anyway." He gave me a funny sidelong glance, one that actually saw *me*. Or at least, I thought it did, and it was a relief. "Shouldn't have said that, dumplin'. Sorry."

Yeah, well, we both say things we shouldn't. Maybe I got that from you. It was a good thought, a *normal* thought, and I grabbed at it. "It's okay. I...I always wondered."

"About what?"

It was heating up in the car, since the windows were closed and the sun was grinning down on the earth like it knew a great joke and couldn't wait to share. "About why she left. She said you never hit her, or anything."

"I never did." His jaw loosened up a little, as if I'd said the opposite and he couldn't quite believe it.

"She told me you never did, yeah." Raw needlepoints of sweat pinpricked cold all over me. "Dad..." *Tell me something. Anything.* I don't know what I wanted. It was like I was underwater, the egg in my chest threatening to crack under the pressure. There was so much to keep *inside* me, and everything pressing from outside wasn't helping to keep it contained like it should. One pushing in, the other pushing out, and I was a balloon skin caught between them. Tissue paper. Cheesecloth.

The dog...her ribs had been broken, puncturing her lungs. *Seizures,* that's what her jerking around was called. I'd put my hands down, and something happened. It hurt like fire, and nobody had noticed a thing.

Well, okay, fine. So I was going full crystal-crazy healing nutbar, and Dad was no help. Mom really wasn't any help for daily living either, and definitely not with the bills or with school.

I was on my own, as usual and like always.

"I'm gonna take you home," Dad said, finally. It was really heating up inside the Charger, a locked car gathering heat. You weren't supposed to leave kids in cars on sunny days.

Or dogs.

The back of my neck was damp, my hair sticking to skin; I should have braided it or done a ponytail. I reached for the door, flipped the locks. *Electric* locks, power locks. "I'm fine." I popped the door, too, before he could reach for the keys still in the ignition. "Really. I just... I'm sorry I ran out there. I didn't think."

"Val—"

"It's okay." I was sick of dealing. I was sick of being on my own. It didn't matter, it never mattered, and I supposed that's what being a grownup was all about. Nothing matters, oh-fucking-well, nothing to see here, move along. "You said we'd help. Come on, let's go."

It didn't take much to move him along. Just like Mom, once I started bossing in that particular way, he gave in and went with it. I don't know how other kids did it, really. They acted like savages in grade school while I was learning how to talk a landlord out of locking our trailer until the rent was caught up, they were busy playing little social games in middle school while I was trying to keep the lights on and Mom was giving away her paychecks to festival people, and high school? Don't even get me started.

Everything happens for a reason, Mom said. *There's a lesson in everything.*

And her in a box made of synthetics, under however-many feet of wet dirt, didn't change anything. I suppose that was the lesson.

27

A CREDIT TO MY AGE GROUP

I SPENT most of that afternoon smiling until my face hurt behind the long counter of the Harmony soup kitchen. There were at least two hours of ladling out chicken-vegetable stew to kids and homeless women—that's something they don't show on the news; most of the homeless aren't druggies or anything, they're just single mothers. The drunk guys might be more aggressive, but in soup kitchens, food banks, and shelters it's mostly kids and moms. I have to say, it was a little weird being on the serving side rather than the receiving, but I liked it. Feeding people is just...good. Especially when you do it without yelling at them about your imaginary sky-fairy and his habit of looking in your bedroom windows to see what you were doing at night.

I even went back into the kitchens with Dad and did some chopping and cleaning and prepping the vegetables while he carried in stuff arriving from the white vans. One or two vans went out at a time, coming back pretty loaded. A lot of the veggies were a little off-color, and that was where I learned they often went around to supermarkets and took the damaged but still good stuff for the soup kitchen. What they couldn't get on sale they got from wastage.

They called it Hope, Harmony Hope. And they sang the whole time. The whole place, from busted yellow linoleum to scavenged school-cafeteria tables, from dying fluorescent tubes buzzing and their neighbors outright dead to the smell of steam tables and Sterno cans, was drenched in music. When they didn't sing, they hummed, and when they had to say something it wove into the melody. I kept trying to figure out what they were singing, because it sounded kind of, you know, gospel. But it wasn't. There wasn't the driving beat. It was...you know, in movies, where you hear choirs and the light comes from above? Like that.

Mom hated those kind of soundtracks. *Gregorian hip-hop,* she called it, and I once set out ask her about Gregorian but came across the word in a book about the Middle Ages. Monks meant Catholic, and Catholic meant super-historical straights, not to mention witch-burnings.

Mom never identified as Wiccan, really, but the way she talked about the Burning Times, it was like she'd been through them personally. One or two of the Wiccans looked a little pained when she got going about it, especially Maya. I sometimes wondered what had happened to short, slight, dark-haired Maya. I never knew her last name and she just sort of vanished after hanging around for about half a year. A while later some blond guy in a long black coat showed up at Enlightened Source looking for her, but we all clammed up.

I don't know exactly why, we just did.

Anyway, none of the other teenagers were there. Just most of the adults. No Father Jim, but plenty of Clover in a yellow sweater, adjusting, managing, smiling, patting someone on the shoulder. She often crouched when she talked to the kids, looking at them eye-level instead of looming.

That's something nobody ever realizes about Harmony when it's mentioned in the papers or on documentaries. They treated the kids, even toddlers, like they were *people.* Not how adults usually do, like anyone undersized is a small bipedal appliance instead of a human being, but like they understood kids were actual human beings.

That wasn't the weirdest thing I saw that day, though. Not even the dog was, but I probably wouldn't have seen the weird if I hadn't been shaky and feeling like a huge bag of cray.

"Hey, honey. How's school going?" Clover went around the long counter to greet what must have been a couple of regulars, a solemn dark-eyed little boy clinging to his rail-thin mother's hip. There were fading bruises on the inside of the mom's arms, but her skin was clearing up and the whites of her eyes weren't yellow. And I knew about the bruises even though the mom had a winter jacket on, buttoned all the way up even though it was almost hot in here with the kitchen and the steam-tables going.

I knew because I *knew*, I can't say how. I can say it was just there, a chunk of knowledge plopped into my head like the aches and pains of everyone who shuffled into the line. Whatever happened with the dog did something else to me, I guessed, because they were all in pain, every single one.

The smile pasted on my face hurt, too. I was pretty much wishing I'd said okay when Dad offered to take me home.

Clover swept the unbraided part of her hair back, glanced smiling up at the mother. I swear I saw...*something*, while I was ladling soup into big bowls with a stir to get all the good stuff off the bottom of the tureen and into the spoon. Something like the shimmer over pavement on a dry summer day, one where even thinking about moving makes the sweat pop out on your skin.

"Better," the kid whispered. He even produced a ghost of a smile. "I got a sticker for good behavior."

"That's great!" Clover's grin looked genuine, and she reached forward to touch the boy's shoulder; her fingernails bitten all the way down. The kid's mother, a fringe of lank hair across her forehead, made a restless movement. I handed the mom a big bowl of soup and an extra slice of crusty sourdough bread, a day past fresh but still okay. "I'm proud of you." Clover dug in the pocket of her sunflower-yellow cardigan, and what came out was a grape Tootsie Pop. "Here you go. I know you'll keep it up, Mikey." When she straightened, she looked at the mother, who stood holding the big bowl of soup while I ladled for the kid. A goofy, dopey smile that reminded me of Dad spread across the little boy's face. "Hannah? How you doing?"

"Fine," the mom said, but the look on her pinched face said something different. She glanced at the kid, who held his small hands out for his own soup bowl. "It's just, you know..."

Clover's hand shot forward, closed around her elbow. "You're going to be okay." She leaned in, her nose an inch from the other woman's, and I almost dropped the ladle. Dad was in the back, hauling bags of pinto beans and pallets-worth of almost-expired canned goods, and if he was here, he probably wouldn't see the heat-shimmer coming off her either. "You're stronger than *it*, Hannah."

The mom nodded. "Thank you." For a second her eyes looked black before her pupils shrank to normal size, and her face eased. Even the itching and deep ache in her arms went down, and my own arms relaxed a little.

"See you next week." Clover straightened and stretched a little, both hands at her lower back. Her sweater glowed, and for a moment she looked...well, I didn't feel any pain from her. Nothing but a hazy humming, like standing next to a power transformer on a hot, thunderstormy day. Her dark irises looked velvety; she really was pretty. Not like Mom but in a wholesome, girl-next-door, sporty-mom way. Sort of.

Clover darted me a glance. I looked down at the soup. Agneta, a tall bony woman with a pacific smile, was the cook, and she could make *anything* taste good, I bet. She was Ingrid's mom, with the same velvet skin and barely-contained energy.

"It's good of you to come and help." She stepped around the end of the counter. There was a break in the line. For the moment, everyone had been fed. "A lot of people your age wouldn't want to."

And you'd know? "Guess I'm a credit to my age group."

For a second she almost looked surprised. Mom would have gotten the reference and known I was being sarcastic as fuck. She probably would have smiled, that particular smile she used when she suspected I was about to start handing an adult a serving of truth. *My practical girl can take care of herself,* she always said.

Well, there was really no choice about that, was there. Especially now. My shoulders tightened, as if I had a heavy backpack on.

"I didn't mean it like that." Clover stopped just inside my personal space, just a fraction past the line no stranger or acquaintance should cross. "I'd like to be friends, Val. I like your dad a lot."

There were other things I could have said. *Leave my dad alone,* or *there's something weird about you.* I could've gotten personal. Something like *don't women your age go to bars for this?* Instead, I looked at the soup again. It was hot, thin curls of steam rising from its rich, oil-sheened surface, and the thought of filling the ladle, whipping it up, and giving her a faceful of almost-boiling liquid was momentarily so intense I was kind of surprised I didn't do it. It smelled good, and I realized the eggs and toast I had for breakfast weren't enough to get me through the rest of the day.

Bodies are funny. You're going along, dealing, and all of a sudden they wallop you with *I'm hungry!* Or *You've got to pee, and Ma Nature is one woman you can't put on hold.* Or you wake up with cramps and your mom has to be talked out of throwing a menarche party.

God. Thinking about Mom again. And the guy in the blue truck, gripping the wheel with his old knotted hands and staring at me. The egg inside my chest shifted, turning restlessly and scraping.

It wasn't a mistake. The Universe wasn't going to correct itself. My mother was gone. Really, truly gone.

"Val?" Clover leaned towards me, just a little more, just a few fractions more over that line. "I know your parents are split up. I don't want to take your mother's place."

I dropped the ladle. It clanged against the side of the stock pot. My chin came up, and I was probably wearing what Mom called the madface—dead pale, red patches high up on our cheeks, blue eyes narrowed. Hers were fierce enough to spit sparks, sometimes, and when she had the red spots I always felt two things: a thrill of cold awe that my mother had turned into a hurricane and the terror of seeing a goddess in unpredictable motion. You know your mom would never hurt you, *never*, but when she's that angry, it's like the world will end anyway. I had the same red spots, and I hoped, good God did I ever hope, that I looked as fearsome as my mother ever did.

As Mom *had*.

"Good," I said, numb-lipped. "Because she's dead."

Clover's jaw dropped a little. Her dark eyes widened. The funny thing was, she honestly looked even younger than me, now. Like a little girl whose birthday party was interrupted by a pony with diarrhea. I left her standing there while a fresh group of people shuffled up to be fed, and when I found Dad in the kitchen I said I was getting dizzy and I wanted to go home.

So we left, but he stopped to say something to Clover on the way out.

He also leaned down, careful as a bull who knows he's in a china shop so is doing his best not to brush against any shelves, and kissed Clover's cheek.

28

FOR VALOR

SUNDAY WAS JUST AS BRIGHT, just as sunny, and about eight degrees warmer. I slept so hard my neck froze when I woke up blinking and confused at the thin threads of daylight sliding through the venetian blinds. They were at the wrong angle because it was eleven-thirty already. That brought me out of bed with a jolt, my neck aching until I cracked it the way football players do—one of Mom's boyfriends taught me how, after he'd dropped out of chiropractor school. I think he ended up selling real estate or something, a reedy blond guy with a nervous smile and gentle paddlefish hands. He was nice, I guess, but he was always cracking every joint of his he could.

The noise got to you after a while.

The apartment was empty. I stood in the doorway of Dad's bedroom for a little bit, my mouth tasting like iron and morning.

In the summer, Mom and I used bedrooms on the second floor of the farmhouse. Wintertime we closed everything up and slept in the same room with the woodstove and the cots, but summer was for upstairs. She liked the north room with its windbreak of firs, always a cool, green cave even on the hottest afternoons. I preferred the smaller bedroom up front, with the gnarled branches of a maple turning the window to an underwater shimmer. It was gasping-hot sometimes, but still, I lay on the floor and watched the shadows of leaves trace over walls, floor, ceiling, feeling like I was floating, cradled.

Dad's bedroom wasn't anywhere as comforting. Boxspring and mattress on a metal frame, probably too small for him. I wondered if his feet hung off the edge, and why he didn't have a bigger bed. He had ugly orange and yellow plaid curtains as well as the venetians, and a dresser of dark wood with a crowded top. One wall had pictures in cheap metal frames, but they were grouped precisely, and I just knew he'd used a ruler and a level putting them up. Above the bed a plain wooden cross hung on a single nail. Not a crucifix, which was a good thing—it's always disconcerting to see a corpse hung on the wall. But still, it was kind of weird.

I crept into the room, as if he was asleep instead of just gone. He was probably out at the compound, pretending to fix one of their vans. Or maybe sitting at lunch with Clover, their heads bent together like a couple in the school caf. He was handsome, I suppose, and lots of girls like tall guys.

There was Mom in the pictures, so young in a white dress edged with eyelet lace, Dad beside her in a sky-blue suit. They were both grinning like idiots, and Mom had a wreath of baby's breath nestled on her cloud of black curls. She leaned on Dad's arm like he was a raft after a shipwreck. Even with the faded colors, you could see their eyes, Dad's a shade or two lighter.

They looked good together. She never really said why she left him and it wasn't something you could ask, you know? He had his own ideas why, and maybe he was right. I traced the line of her cheek in that photo, my fingernail against glass. The pictures weren't dusty at all. There was another one of Mom at a beach, barefoot on sand, her hands full of tangled kelp and the wind in her hair. Her earrings were big silver hoops. Her bare shoulders were a little tanned, her skirt was whipping in the wind and the turquoise necklace was full of sea and sunshine against her collarbone. You could see the clean line of her jaw, the curve of her cheekbone, everything working together.

She was really beautiful, and I could tell she'd just finished laughing.

The rest of the pictures were of me. There was one of Dad holding me, against a window that had dark firs outside. My baby face was squinched up tight, and I was red and bawling. But Dad's disbelieving, goofy grin hadn't changed an inch. There was a picture of Christmas, a tree with tinsel and red ornaments. Little three-year old me clutched a plastic dumptruck and glared into the camera. School photos, then. Kindergarten, first, second—Christ, it looked like he had every single one up there. Except seventh grade.

That had been a bad month or two, and we just didn't have the money. Dad sent the child support, but Mom lost the check somehow. I don't know exactly what happened, just that I got home from school one day and found her sitting at the kitchen table pale and red-eyed.

Now I wondered why she just hadn't asked Dad to give her a replacement.

Anyway, he even had this year's picture, in a newer frame. I met my months-ago self as she looked blankly into a camera's eye, unaware of what was coming. I'd smiled in my elementary school ones, but by middle school they were lucky not to get a scowl out of me. Mom put more stock in aura photos, but she always filled out the form each year, carefully reserving a 5x7 for Dad.

They hung right where he could lie in bed and look at them.

The jumbled top of his dresser wasn't dusty, either, and it only looked messy from a distance. There were a few pictures of elderly people that were probably related to us somehow and another picture of me, this one in a heavy silver frame. I was five, standing in a pile of autumn leaves, wearing a red cardigan and grinning up at whoever was holding the camera. I had handfuls of crimson and orange leaves, my arms flung out like I knew I could fly. A little brass dish with a cover sat right there, and I picked up the lid.

"Oh, ew," I whispered, as if I might be overheard. They were *teeth*. Tiny baby teeth.

My baby teeth.

There was a pink-and-white rattle, too, a plastic thing, pretty well-chewed. A funny flat case that I opened up to find some sort of medal—a brass eagle over a cross, on a purple ribbon with white and red edging. The eagle clutched a scrap that said *For Valor*. "Huh." Now that I'd said something out loud, it felt less like he was in here sleeping and more like I was, well, snooping around.

There were two other things on top of the dresser. First, a kid's sweater. A red cardigan, pretty familiar. Kid Me was wearing it in the picture.

The other thing, tucked underneath, was a folder with paperwork in it. I was tempted, so I slid the corner out out from under the sweater.

Kasparov, Ellen S. Mom's maiden name, on a sticker on the tab. I went hot all over, then cold. The iron taste in my mouth got a little more awful, and my skin crawled. I slid it out the rest of the way, carefully. It looked official. There was red thread keeping it closed, wrapped around a plastic-looking tab on the front. I unwrapped the thread, flipped it open, and stared.

ACCIDENT REPORT. Typed across the top in big, bold letters. *Oh, God.*

There was something else. Pictures. Of the...the scene.

The accident scene.

Now I knew. She wasn't wearing her seatbelt. The semi had almost gone straight through the old truck and she'd been thrown clear. Waxman Hill Road—what had she been doing out there? She'd just gone to the store that morning, right? I fuzzily remembered her saying something about almond milk while I was in bed, still half-asleep.

If there was one thing about Mom, it was that things happened. She could get it into her head to visit someone she hadn't seen in months or decide to take a drive, or be following a robin or something.

The mangled thing lying crumpled on Waxman Hill Road didn't even look like her.

You don't want to see that, dumplin'. Well, now I had.

The key rattled in the lock. I hurried to shove the file back under the kid's cardigan and made it into the bathroom before Dad got the door open. I sagged against the bathroom door, staring at myself in the mirror. Yeah, the two bright red patches high up on my cheeks were just like hers. My nose was hers too, and the special little spot underneath my bottom lip was shaped just like hers too. Black hair. Blue eyes. Turquoise glowed blue in the harsh electric light. One of my hands tangled in the necklace, metal edges digging in, the hook biting my nape. I didn't look beautifully angry like she could, though.

I just looked like a scared, sleep-headed kid.

"Val? You up?" Dad headed for the kitchen. Plastic rustled. He hadn't gone to Harmony after all, just to the grocery store. In a few moments he was at the bathroom door, tapping gently. "Sweetheart? You awake yet?"

I made some sort of garbled sound. It must have sounded like a normal morning *don't-ask-me-questions* noise to him, because he chuckled.

"All right then. I went and got donuts. The good kind. I'll put your tea on. Hurry up, I gotta use the bathroom too."

It took two tries before I could clear my throat enough to talk. "Okay." I sounded a little gravelly. Just-woke-up. Not like my cheeks were wet and bright red, not like my nose was full and my legs were a little too shaky to hold me up straight. "Be out in a sec."

It took more than a sec. It took a lot of cold water splashed on my face before I made it out into the kitchen, but if Dad noticed, he didn't say anything. He just sat down at the kitchen table and opened the blue-and-white Mercy's Doughnuts box. They really were the good kind, Mercy's was famous. "I didn't know which ones you liked, so I got a dozen. Can't get every kind." He looked at me, anxiously, and the kettle began to chirp. The coffeeemaker was going, too.

"I thought you went out to visit Clover." I found my mug, right on the counter with a teabag already in it.

"I'm not gonna see her if you don't like her, dumplin'." He peered at the donuts like there was something written on them.

Jeez, I wasn't his dating guardian or anything. "It doesn't matter."

"It *does* matter." Now he fixed me with a piercing, very parental stare, his eyebrows two thick black bars and his just-shaved, blue-shadowed jaw set. "You're my baby girl. The most important thing in my life ever since your mom told me she was carrying cargo."

Well, that was one way to put it. "I mean, it's fine." God, this was an awkward conversation. Mom's version of this talk was more *try to get along, give him a chance.* I didn't know how to handle this one. "I don't mind Clover, I guess. I just..." Maybe I should have some coffee instead. That might jump-start my brain enough to get through this minefield. It wasn't really like I had any control over who Dad dated.

Dad nodded. "I know you preferred your mom." His chair squeaked a little against the linoleum. Everything in here was so... whole. Nothing was broken. You didn't have to jiggle handles or skip stairs that might break. "But I'm all there is now."

"It's not a preference thing." The water was boiling, I poured steadily. "I always used to wish you guys would get back together."

"So did I." If it bothered him to talk this way, he didn't show it. I kept sneaking glances at him, but there was no hint of anger on his broad face. "Maybe I should've pushed it, I don't know. I was afraid she'd take you and disappear again. You're the best thing in my life, dumplin'."

Disappear again? I didn't remember us *disappearing,* but... Jesus. Now I *really* felt like an asshole. Clover wasn't so bad, really. What had she done? Just tried to help out, and been nice to Dad. The Harmony people were kind of weird, and I didn't really like Father Jim, but...well, they weren't *bad.* Ingrid and Gabrielle had even helped a total stranger, risking Sandy Gibson's bad side. A popular bitch could make your life hell, but they didn't seem to care. That was worth a little leeway, I figured.

Besides...there was Clover's hand on the woman's arm, yesterday. And the dog. Something weird was happening to me, and if Clover could do things too...well, maybe I could learn something, figure this whole thing out. I was pretty sure I wasn't totally crazy, but starting to see plants glow and the whole thing with the dog wasn't anything a straight would have any information on, so to speak. I could go back to Enlightened Source, or to Nadine's studio, but they didn't even show up for Mom's funeral, so why would I bother?

"Clover's okay," I said, finally. "Really. I just don't want you getting hurt." It sounded lame, probably because it was.

"You let me worry about that, Val." A quizzical look drifted over his face, but his shoulders relaxed. "You don't have to take care of me. That's not how this goes."

It's always how this goes. Still, it was nice. I wrapped the teabag's string around the mug handle. "Okay." The coffeemaker finished gurgling. "You want a cup of coffee, Dad?"

"Sure. But I'll get it, you sit down. These donuts aren't gonna eat themselves."

2 9

SEE RED

"HEY." Travis the Bathroom Bro leaned pretty much out of his seat. "Hey. New girl."

I didn't answer, just stared straight ahead at the chart Shieldman had put up about the domestic impact of the Korean War. I'd already taken all the notes I needed to, but I kept doodling. Henna patterns, mostly. Mom and I used to get them done sometimes, and if you can stand sitting still long enough, it's actually kind of pleasant. You can meditate while they do it, but most of the painters like to talk.

It's a social experience. Nobody can just sit there and let you think or be quiet, they always have to *talk*. It's not just girls, either, though that's what all the movies and the magazines tell you. Guys have to know you're paying attention, like they'll vanish if you stop looking.

"New girl." He whisper-yelled it, as if something was wrong with my hearing. Probably didn't think anyone could be ignoring *him*. Why, he was the center of the universe, right?

Mehndi patterns are fun to draw, even if you're only a halfass artist and would never show them to anyone, they're small and finicky enough to get your mind off anything. Especially secrets burning behind your breastbone.

All those times Mom swore I'd someday get *abilities* like her. Now she was pretty much right, but it was too late. I could have gone with her that day, if I'd bothered to get up out of my camp cot. If I had, would the thing—whatever it was, the energy transfer or whatever all the books would call it—have helped her? I'd never, ever felt it before.

And Mom would have seen it, wouldn't she? She knew about all this sort of stuff.

"Neeeeeew giiiiiirl." He was getting louder, but up at the front of the room, Shieldman probably didn't hear him.

Or she didn't *want* to.

One or two of the kids around me shifted uneasily. I glanced at the clock without moving my head, a quick flicker of eyeballs. Almost lunchtime, and then he'd leave me alone. He probably went on the hunt for kids to shove in the cafeteria. His cologne was sickening. It pulsed out of him in little waves, probably in time to his heartbeat.

The seat was uncomfortable, and I had to balance just right or it would slide off its base. The tiny desk surface wasn't big enough for any serious work, but at least it was its own little world. I could have been stuck at a table, instead of Travis leaning out of his seat two back and one to the side, its legs scratching the floor a little as he shifted.

Shieldman was wearing a pastel pink sweater, the wool full of fluffy bits, and a black skirt which had the unfortunate effect of making her top half look even bigger than it was, and there was a slight run in the pantyhose on her left shin. Mom told me pantyhose used to be something you *had* to wear, and some straights still did it. *Like turning your legs into sausages*, she said. *Awful. Just awful. Never again.*

I colored in a series of small triangles, listening about the 38th Parallel. *Not* listening to Travis, who decided he just wasn't being annoying enough.

"New girl. Hey." Something hit my shoulder. "*Val.*"

Well, he'd graduated to my name. My teeth hurt; I was grinding them. A pencil.

He'd thrown a fucking *pencil* at me.

"Val. Vaaaaaaaaal." He drew it out, and he wasn't bothering to keep it down much anymore. Shieldman blinked myopically, the lenses of her glasses full of reflected glow from the projector. Maybe she didn't care as long as he was leaving *her* alone. I touched Mom's necklace with my left hand, concentrating on filling in the triangles with my right. Then I'd do the scallops, until half the page was a solid sheet of ink.

"I heard about you, Vaaaaaal." He snort-laughed, quietly. "They say you're a *leeeeeezzzzzie.*"

Was it possible to shatter your teeth if you ground them hard enough? The clock wouldn't speed up, no matter how often I looked at it. I tapped the biggest turquoise on the necklace. What would Mom do in this situation? *I hated high school,* she told me often enough.

"That means *lesbian,*" Travis said, and something else hit my shoulder. I couldn't tell what he'd thrown this time.

I imagined getting up, a sharp turn on my heel, taking two steps, and punching him in the face. He'd probably duck, but my boots were steel-toed. Those never go out of fashion, and Mom got them for my sixteenth birthday. Dad got me new socks so I could wear them without slipping around. I could kick Travis's leg—he'd have it stuck out into the aisle, of course, taking up all the space because he thought it was *owed* to him. I probably couldn't break his nose, but I could give his shin a wallop. It might not shut him up for good, but it would at least make Shieldman do something, right?

Of course he was picking on me because I was new. I was thinking Oz used to be his victim, by the half-guilty looks he'd sneak me every once in a while. I knew all about the grim relief of finding out an asshole had chosen a fresh target. It was kind of strange that Oz looked so broken up about it, but then, maybe he was a nice guy.

Third period was an endurance contest and so far I was winning, but not by much. I had an idea that Sandy, who hung out with a whole group of pop-preps that included him in the morning, had pointed me out recently. The pop-preppers sometimes congregated off the buses, near a senior history teacher's room the AP kids were always going on about.

I suspected half of them, boy and girl alike, had a crush on Mr. Pale. He was tall, and skinny, and biked in to work.

Anyway, you had to go past the glossies to get from the buses to any of the other buildings, and they were loud. Sandy wasn't the *biggest* queen bee, but you got the sense she was the one none of the others didn't really want to fuck with, so they acted like they liked her.

"Hey, Val. Come on, just tell me. You a lesbian?"

The kids around us were *really* shifting uncomfortably now. Shieldman started talking about Russia and North Korea.

"'Cause I am too." Travis whisper-laughed again. "I'm a big ol' lesbo, and so are you. Lesbo."

Something else hit my shoulder.

"Shut *up*," a girl hissed from behind us. Travis's desk squeaked. He was probably looking back to find out who said it, but everyone would be straight-faced.

My right hand clamped down on the pen. For a second I saw red, and I don't mean figuratively. A sheet of crimson slid over everything, like when you close your eyes in a really bright light and it shines through the blood in your lids. I imagined slapping him. A good, hard, ringing one, right on the cheek.

I was imagining it so hard I wasn't sure, for a moment, what that cracking sound was. A collective gasp went through the classroom.

"—in 1954." Mrs Shieldman blinked again, staring past me, her mouth slowly opening. She said nothing else, and there was a general rustle as everyone turned to look. I resisted the urge for about a second and a half, and when I twisted in my seat, I couldn't understand what I was seeing for a second.

That's when Travis let out a short, strangled, gurgling yell.

It looked like one of the legs of his chair had suddenly given out, and since he was spread out to take up all sorts of space, the entire thing collapsed with him. And by *entire thing* I mean chair, desk, and the metal bars holding one to the other. Somehow in there his nose had broken, and blood gushed all down his front. I heard later they had to call the fire department to get him out of the tangle, but I didn't see it because the bell rang and I escaped while Shieldman waved her hands and began giving ineffectual orders to the kids crowding to see what the hell the noise was. I also heard later one or two of them managed to kick Travis while he was howling, bloody-faced, and thrashing.

I hoped like hell Oz had, at least.

30

SAME SHOES

ONE THING about Cold Ridge High, the chocolate milk was rarely frozen. Some schools, you get ice in the bottom of your milk and forget the chocolate, the prep-poppers always get there first. I grabbed a carton and was about to make a fast getaway to the library when Owen appeared right out of thin air and reached past me o nab a carton of regular milk. "Hey." He bumped against my backpack, and I skipped sideways to get away. "Sorry. Didn't see you Sunday. Where were you?"

"Having donuts." I could have sworn I felt a warm trickle of something on my upper lip, and the thought that I was snotting myself in the lunch line sent a hot embarrassed flush up my cheeks. I swiped at my nose with my free hand, and it came away dry. Nothing there. "With Dad." I wanted to add, *a hot date, right?* But I didn't know how he'd take it.

"We missed you." Owen grinned. The cross at his throat gleamed, and his hair looked just mussed enough to be planned that way. "Sarah keeps asking when you're coming back."

"Oh." Something about that nagged at me. My ribs hurt, too.

Maybe I'd pulled something getting out of Shieldman's room. Everything inside me was whirling. "I don't know. It's up to Dad."

"Yeah, well, she's dying to see you again."

"Move it!" A pop-prepper girl, one of Sandy's crew, shoved past me. "Don't stand in the fucking line, morons!" Her smooth brown ponytail switched like a horse's as she stamped away on a pair of cork wedges just like Sandy's, too. She didn't quite have the makeup, or the color-coordination, but her jeans looked like she'd been poured into them and there were rhinestones across the ass. A slice of spray-tanned skin showed on her back; her crop top had ridden up a bit.

Owen stepped neatly aside and somehow he had my elbow, so I had to go with him. I don't know how he did it, he made it seem like the most natural thing in the world. I didn't even realize he was steering me, because the headache and the persistent pressure in my chest both vanished at once and I was too busy trying to figure out *why*. "God, I hate that," I muttered.

"What?" He stopped, once we were both out of the lunch line and next to an empty table. Nobody wanted to sit here, it was too close to a door one of the security guards liked to lurk near. He was a heavyset older man with restless hands and an ingratiating grin, and none of the kids liked him. It was his lips, mostly, greasy and quivering just a little when he looked at the girls. Even the boys felt it.

"Ponytail bitches shoving everyone around." I hitched my backpack higher on my shoulder. The straps were beginning to give under textbook load; I was hoping it would last or I could repair it. The sewing machine was in storage, along with everything else from the farmhouse. I could ask Dad to drive me out there.

The brunette pop-prepper got to the prime real estate—tables near the bank of windows looking out on a concrete area they called, with forlorn hope, the park. When the weather got nicer it would probably be jammed with kids during lunchtime, but for right now it was spindly bushes in big pebbly containers, tougher bushes planted in triangular slices of packed dirt, all of them full of fresh green that probably wouldn't survive the habit of teenage creatures to pluck, crush, kick, or scatter trash. The glossies brightened at the brunette bitch's approach, and Sandy was heading for the same table, swinging a plastic bag that had her custom-made sandwich from the little shop in the lunchroom.

"God," I said. "They're even wearing the same shoes."

"Yeah. And they all think they're unique." Owen's hand still cupped my elbow. He made no move to let go, and I didn't feel like pulling away. I kept looking at Sandy and the preppers, though, as if I didn't notice him touching me, or standing so close. Like I didn't feel the healthy boy-heat from him, like it didn't make my heart chakra— and the egg under it, that blockage—unsteady. "I hear Gibson's got it in for you."

News travels fast in the high school jungle. I wiggled my toes inside my boots, grateful my head had stopped spinning and that there wasn't snot on my face. It's the little things, Mom always said. "I guess."

Owen's hand fell away. "You want to see something?"

Really, what I wanted was to sit down somewhere quiet and think about all sorts of things. But my mouth fell open, and what came out instead was, "Sure."

He grinned, one of his front teeth slightly crowding the other. A little bit of thin stubble was already roughing his cheeks and chin, and his chestnut hair glowed under the fluorescents. It was a nasty gray day outside, but he brought his own sunshine. Maybe it was that faint warmth, the same as his preacher dad's, or maybe it was just that his tan wasn't fake and his dark eyes were full of a kind of amusement.

"Watch Gibson." He shook out his left hand, flicked his fingers.

She was moving at a good clip, one foot directly in front of the other like she was on her own personal runway and the rest of us were an adoring crowd. Maybe that's what it was like inside her head, I don't know. Owen exhaled next to me, softly, and a sort of shimmer —that heat-haze over pavement, that's *exactly* what it looked like— rippled in my peripheral vision. A soft subliminal hiss filled my head.

It could have been a coincidence, I suppose. A wet patch on the linoleum, someone had spilled something, or just one of those things that happens when you're wearing heels. A momentary weakness in the ankle, or a wobble in the knee. Happens all the time, what *doesn't* happen is something invisible tipping a shoe sideways, right?

Wrong.

One second she was striding along, top of the heap, on display like a big fan of peacock feathers. I swear I heard a cracking noise as her ankle buckled, the same sound I heard just before I looked back to see Travis trapped in his chair. Sandy's sandwich flew, a high arc ending with its fluttering plastic splatting in the middle of a table of medium-prep gothy girls who let out shrieks of fake or real surprise. Sandy went down hard, and her own yell pierced the ocean-noise of the cafeteria, a bone needle like the ones Bert got in a shipment from Tibet that once. My jaw flat-out dropped and I pitched to the side as well, almost falling into Owen. He grabbed my elbow again, and the swift flash of pain in my own ankle vanished.

"Don't say anything." His grin had fled, and he looked at me like *I'd* somehow made her fall. "Okay?"

Jesus Christ, what *could* I say? *Hi, I've been dialed over into the weird, too.* Was it just him? Well, no, there was Clover, too. That little heat-ripple...I was seeing it. I was *seeing* things, just like Mom. They were happening in *school*, for Chrissake. I mean, there was the world of energy and healing and crystals and tarot, and then there was school, and the overlap made an unpleasant feeling travel down my back and grab at my knees.

I didn't like it at all.

"Okay." My lips were numb. "I won't. If you don't."

He studied me, and I was abruptly aware we were standing too close. Nobody was watching, really, they had all clustered Sandy—including a couple of the lunch ladies—or they were looking in that direction, hungry for gossip. I shut my mouth with a snap, tugged my elbow out of his grip, and got out of there. He didn't try to stop me, and neither did the creepy security guard on his busy-hurrying way to boss everyone. I headed for the library and walked around in the nonfiction section, everything inside me slipping first one direction, then the other. I didn't realize I was still clutching my chocolate milk until the bell rang for fourth.

In sixth, while Greeman had us puffing and jumping through aerobics again, Ingrid told me Sandy Gibson had broken her ankle in the cafeteria. "Serves her right," she added with a single brisk nod. "Wearing those slut-shoes every day."

"She won't be messing around with us for a while," Gabrielle added. "Hey, you coming to the compound on Sunday?"

I said something, I don't know what, and neither of them looked at me funny so it must have been all right. I even sat near them on the bus home, listening to them sing, and Owen kept glancing at me. It wasn't until the bus lumbered away on a cloud of diesel fumes and the knot of kids scattered to go to their separate apartments that I finally figured out what had been nagging at me. Well, at least, one of the things.

Sarah. What had she said, holding a robin egg and watching me?

I pushed a button.

No, not that. The other thing she'd said.

You can do it now.

HYPOTHESIS, EXPERIMENT

INSTEAD OF FRENCH HOMEWORK, I flipped to a fresh page in my five-subject notebook and grubbed my lucky green pen out of my backpack. When things get fruity, Mom's solution was to meditate until an answer appeared, or go for a drive.

Me? I prefer a list.

I tapped the pen against my teeth, staring into the kitchen. The clouds had thickened, and by the look of it we were going to have a thunderstorm. I was glad to be home before it hit, and even gladder to be somewhere I could turn up the heat and not worry about setting out pots and pans to catch leaks from above. Every window here shut tight, and I checked twice to make sure the front door was locked. It was like waiting for a bill collector to show up, sitting in the dark with my heart in my throat and pretending not to jump at every noise.

Except there were no bill collectors knocking at the door. Dad hadn't said anything worried about rent, either. Was it just not a problem for him?

I decided to worry about that later. First I listed all of them.

Clover. Owen. Sarah, almost definitely. Father Jim? I put a question mark next to his name, because he had that invisible warmth, but

I wasn't sure if that was natural or something else. Charisma, Mom would have called it.

Man, why hadn't *she* met the Harmony people? I mean, people with those sort of talents were supposed to find each other, right? But then, only Leaf had come to Enlightened Source. I hadn't seen him at the soup kitchen *or* at the compound the last time.

Then I listed the weird things. The green glow of the cactuses on the rack. I'd have to figure out if the plants outside had it, too, and if it had to be dark for me to see. That went on the lower right-hand bit of the paper, where I put things I could *do*.

The dog in the road. That one went in capitals and underlined. I put question marks around Travis's collapsing desk, even though I was having trouble figuring out where his sudden nosebleed came from, and I listed Sandy's broken ankle.

I hate to say it, but it was the last thing that bothered me most. Broken bones were *serious shit*, even if I hadn't done anything. Or had I? Why had Owen done it? Could he tell by looking at me that something weird was happening? Or had Sarah told him something? Was she just going around turning people into...I don't know, making them different? But I didn't think it was all of the Harmony people. I'd have to watch carefully, if we went back there.

I wasn't sure I *wanted* to, now. Even if...oh, *hell*.

There was something else. I chewed at my lower lip, concentrating. A list forces you to think, makes connections visible. Mom laughed at my habit of writing things down like this, putting them in neat columns. She preferred a life without boundaries, she said. Without shoving things in boxes, distorting them to fit.

I pushed the thought away. It was too distracting. Instead, I pursued the tickle of down into the back of my brain, taking a few deep breaths and shifting a little in the faintly wobbly sunflower chair each time. It was more comfortable than the school chairs, but not by much.

The dog. I'd felt its pain. The cactuses, they hurt too, when they needed water or had too much of it. I'd *felt* Sandy's ankle give. And

Travis's nose, how had *that* happened? I'd felt it bleeding, too, on my own upper lip.

Sympathy pains, to go along with...what? If I walked up to someone and put my hands on a broken bone, would it be just fine? Was it worth it, to test the hypothesis?

Which brought up a better question. Did I even want to?

Well, that was a big no, I did *not*. Mom was always very clear about not showing the straights anything you could do. But she also read tarot cards for money, and...God. This was fucking confusing. It got darker and darker as I sat there, staring at the list and thinking. Tapping the green pen first on one name, then on another. Drawing little lines between them, maybe-connections.

By the time the rain started, I hadn't arrived at any solution. I wasn't even really sure there was a problem. I made tea, glancing at the open notebook on the table again and again as if it might twitch.

Scientific experimentation wasn't just for straights. I carried the ticking, cooling, still half-full kettle to the sink, steeled myself, and spread my left hand.

I upended the kettle.

"*Shit!*"

The French door in the living room lit with a glare of lightning, startling me, and the crash of thunder a few seconds afterward rattled the windows. Fat, driving droplets smacked down; I peered at my left hand, swearing. The skin was already angry red and puffing up; the water had to be boiling when it hit the teabag.

Mom taught me that. Real tea was close to a religion, she always said.

I dropped the red enamel kettle, and the hollow *bong* it made in the sink might have been funny if my hand didn't hurt so goddamn much. I turned the cold water on full blast with a vicious twist, thankful I didn't have to pump it.

It was awful to think this was better than the farmhouse, really, or most of the places we lived before. It was also awful to think that, somewhere way down deep, I was...grateful?

Oh, God. Maybe the lightning would hit the apartments, dig through the roof, and find me. It would be what I deserved for being even a little happy about doors that closed all the way, windows that weren't broken or warping, solid floors, a stove that worked. My own bedroom. Heat at night. Extra blankets. An electric bill that was just paid with no trouble, because Dad had a steady job.

I snatched my hand from cool water. Pain, immediate. It was a bad burn, and the thought that I could heat the kettle again and pour even more hot water over it rose like a black bubble inside my head. It would hurt, and that was all right, because anyone who might be even the teensiest bit grateful something awful had happened *should* hurt, right?

Another flash of lightning. The thunder was more than a few seconds behind, and the space in-between stole all the air from my lungs and squeezed tears out of my eyes. Burns hurt like *fuck.* I shut the water off, making a small sound as my left hand curled up. Hot water blurred my vision. It was *really* dark outside, I just hadn't noticed because it had happened by degrees.

You can get used to anything in increments, I guess.

I made a fist. The pain was a splotch of red in the black behind my lids, a low punky glow like the fire in the woodstove at around 4am. That's the worst time, because you have to get up while it's still cold to shuffle over to the stove and poke the flames back into life. Those were the times I heard Mom breathing softly in her sleep and wondered, sometimes angrily, if we could just settle down somewhere and be a little more normal. Not straights, but just...a little less *something.* Whatever it was we were.

I sucked in a short sharp breath as the pain crested, that same weird heat-shimmer settling over the reddish smear. I couldn't see where it was coming from but I *felt* it, somewhere between my eyes and the middle of my brain. Deeper, too, in some space that wasn't quite me but was still inside me a patch of previously unexplored territory.

Maybe it was Mom's necklace? I hadn't thought of that. There was a way to find out.

By the time the next rattle-boom of thunder went off, I'd turned the kitchen light on. Probably not the best move with the lightning outside, but I needed to see.

The deep crimson burn on my hand faded, shrinking as I watched. That weird heat-shimmer settled above it, and if I looked hard I could see the red pain-smear shrinking too as the sensation drained away. It was easier to see in the dark; I wondered why Mom had never told me that. Maybe you got better at it and forgot how it started out?

Oh, come on, Val.

There was another horrible thought lingering, refusing to be shoved out and away where all the rest of the uncomfortable stuff had to go if you wanted to keep moving instead of breaking down. My knees were pretty gooshy, but there was the counter to lean against. It was strong and solid, and I watched the last trace of the burn fade. My left hand was just fine. I stared, turning it over, examining my palm, my knuckles, my bitten-down fingernails. Mom said nail polish was full of formaldehyde and toulene and those were bad poisons, but sometimes I wished I could paint them like other girls.

There was nothing stopping me now. Dad wouldn't care. Hell, it might even make him proud that I was doing normal girl things. Could I tell him about this?

How would I even begin? Would he believe me? I wasn't imagining things. I *wasn't.*

I rinsed the kettle off and put it back on the stove. My cooling tea sat on the counter, the liquid rippling when thunder boomed again. I sat down at the table, picked up the green pen, and stared at my left hand some more. Stretching out my fingers, not long and elegant like Mom's. My knuckles, not big like Dad's. Just a kid's hand. There wasn't a trace of redness, or swelling.

"I'm gonna need a razor blade." My own voice almost startled me, but not as much as the next thunder-boom. "Cotton balls too."

I made another short list of supplies, then closed my notebook and sat there, watching the window light up as the storm raged, volleys of rain splattering everything in sight. It was moving away, the time between flash and rattle getting longer. Dad wasn't due home until after seven; I had to think about dinner, too.

Homework could wait. I stacked my books to one side as if I'd already done it, and went looking in the bathroom cabinets while the storm rattled and howled and gushed outside.

32

MENTAL HEALTH DAY

I stared at my plate, drawing my fork through mashed potatoes. He liked them with butter—real dairy, not soy. "Dad?"

Mom would have been appalled at the sheer amount of cow-squeezings I was consuming. Butter. Milk. Cream cheese on bagels. Other kinds of cheese. There were so many, and a lot of them delicious. Soy just didn't compare, although it's okay in a pinch, I guess.

"Yeah?" He glanced up from cutting steak into strips. Red meat, another no-no for Mom. "Sure you don't want some?"

It smelled good, but I'd probably had all the changes in my diet I could handle for the time being. "I'm sure." I stabbed my mashed potatoes again. More spring rain splashed the windows on an uncertain, flirting evening breeze, but the thunder was gone. "I need a mental health day."

"A what now?" He laid his knife down and reached for the pepper, but his bright-blue gaze was all on me. He didn't look at something else when I talked to him, mostly. That was nice, except when I wanted to slide something by him.

Like now. "A mental health day. Mom and I..." I had to stop for a second, clear my throat, and try again. "Sometimes Mom would call me in sick to school, and let me take a day off to do stuff. Even just to stay home. She called them mental health days. Said everyone needs them."

He peppered his potatoes with a few quick shakes. The pepper shaker was shaped like an onion, a ceramic dealie that looked grandparent-old. "Okay."

Well, that was simple. "Can I have it tomorrow?"

"Looking for a three-day weekend, huh? Can't blame you. I'd want one too." Dad nodded, forked up a bit of steak and mashed, and chewed slowly. His undershirt, white cotton, had a small hole near the collar. Three of his work jumpsuits was in the plastic laundry basket by the front door, I'd take it down after dinner and plug quarters from the kitchen jar into the washer. "Okay. You need some pocket money?"

I wasn't prepared for him to agree just like that. It took a second to shift mental gears. "I've got enough."

"Should get you a phone this weekend. Just in case."

"Nope." I shook my head. Made another set of lines on my mashed potatoes. "Those are expensive."

"I got a job, dumplin'." At least he didn't sound irritated. Just slightly baffled, and that was probably reasonable when faced with a weird-ass kid like me.

"I could get one, too." I kept looking at my left hand. There was no trace of scalding; it felt just fine.

"*School* is your job." He laid his fork down, reached for a napkin. "Did your mom make you work?"

"No." At least, not the way he was probably thinking. Dinner smelled really good, I'd put enough garlic powder in the potatoes to kill a vampire at thirty paces. "I wanted to, though." I also wanted to explain more, tell him about handling the money for her tarot readings, the conventions and fairs, the rest of it. I mean, he knew we traveled, and now I wondered if he'd worried when I called him from different states, if he was relieved when Mom circled the city and finally settled at the farmhouse. It might sound like I was complaining, so I didn't.

"Well, don't worry." Dad said it like it was possible not to, like that was an *option*. "So what are you gonna do tomorrow?"

"Hang out. Read." *Get something really sharp and see if I'm nuts.* "Maybe take the bus to the library on Carcoa." It was time for a little internet searching, I figured. I'd probably read all the books that could be useful, hanging out with Mom at Enlightened Source, but I'd look for more at the library, too. "Just, you know, it's been really..." I tried to find a word. *Busy* didn't cover it. *Terrifying* was close, but then I'd have to explain, or he'd think I meant Mom...which I did, but that wasn't all of it, and God I could not seem to find anything that applied for the *life* of me.

Then, probably the second he opened his mouth to help me out, I found the right word. "Stressful," I finished. My own napkin, set demurely in my lap, shifted a little.

"Yeah." He looked at his plate like he was feeling the same lump in the throat I was. "I know."

There wasn't much to say after that, but my stomach settled and I could eat. I kept wanting to tell him, but how do you even begin? *I boiled my hand, but that's okay because I can fix it. Want to see?*

Maybe Mom had wanted to tell him things too? I tried not to think about it, and mostly succeeded. He asked me about school, I made up something about a French quiz and some math homework. Mom would have suspected something, but he didn't. The rain fell off, in dribs and drabs, no longer pounding on our little strip of balcony overlooking the parking lot. The pond at the edge of Swallow Mills was swollen, its surface trembling and edges blurring, streetlamp light dancing on its skin.

I washed, he dried, and when the dishes were done, he gave me a hug and cracked a beer, heading for the living room and the television. I took laundry down, retreated to my room, and sat on my bed looking at the cactuses. When I concentrated, their small green auras showed up even with the overhead light on.

God, Mom would be so happy I was finally *sensitive*. Wouldn't she? There were so many things to try not to think about.

Top of that list was the ancient package of rust-pitted razor blades I'd found below the bathroom sink. It was a choice between them, and whatever tetanus they were carrying, or a paring knife from the kitchen. Or walking across the highway to the box pharmacy.

Did they even have just-plain-razorblades for sale anymore? Everyone used disposables now, right? And did I honestly think I wasn't a big chicken when it came to slicing myself up?

Yeah. Tomorrow was going to be fun.

33

NOT LEGAL, BUT RIGHT

THE STORM HAD WASHED everything clean. It was too warm for a jacket, but not warm enough to go without one, so you either sweated or shivered unless you were inside. Still, the sidewalks were full and the downtown library branch hummed like a well-mannered beehive. Thankfully, I got there between waves of people and—total bonus—got a computer near the windows. The first quarter hour of searching didn't tell me anything I didn't already know. Energy healing, meditation, seeing auras around plants—pretty standard stuff. Typing in *psychokinesis* didn't get me much beyond a bunch of skeptics debunking things and sites promising to teach you how to move matchsticks with your mind for a "small" fee. I sat there for a few minutes thinking about Owen, wondering what he'd actually done. With someone wearing heels, you didn't have to do much to push them off balance. Could I could get him to explain it?

Owen seemed like an easier target than Clover in that department. What were the chances of the two of them with special abilities living in the same commune? Statistics classes would have a field day with *that* problem, but I needed to know other things, too.

So I tried *Harmony*. Nope, wrong search term. *Harmony Home*, then.

Bingo. And *wow*, the straights did not like Father Jim Harrison. So *that* was his last name. Owen had told me, but I'd forgotten.

Owen had also mentioned California; apparently they'd moved away from there after some elderly church members died and left all their stuff to Father Jim. The families had sued, and some of the headlines were grudgingly admiring because Father Jim had simply signed everything back over to the families, who now looked like assholes because he said *We don't need the money, the Lord provides. But if they need it that bad, well, let 'em have it.* It was pretty great, even though a lot of the news stories called Harmony a cult. There were "allegations of drug use" and former members refusing to talk to the press.

Well, I wouldn't talk to the straights either.

There was also something about a custody battle. Sarah wasn't Father Jim's biological kid. She was a foster child he and his wife took in—his wife's name was Carole, I found out—after a bad car accident with Sarah's mom. There was all sorts of stuff about the accident, how it was a DUI, how Sarah had to be resuscitated, things about the mom's "lifestyle." When Sarah's mom went to the state to get her back, the Harrisons refused to give her up. Sounded like the mom was a junkie, and again like the Church of Full and Righteous Harmony—what a mouthful, wow—was on the right side.

Maybe not the exactly *legal* side, but certainly the *right* one. There was a grainy picture of a younger Owen holding a younger Sarah's hand, both of them dressed like straights and Sarah leaning into him like she was trying to hide. There was even a shot of a dark-haired woman who had to be Clover, with her arm over Carole Harrison's shoulders. The older woman was leaning into her, too.

Maybe Clover wasn't that bad.

There were news stories about their soup kitchen, and a couple old ones on Father Jim. He'd been a preacher all his life, apparently, but broke away from his church after a car accident.

The way they put it sounded like a near-death experience. Those made people weird sometimes. There was a woman who came into Enlightened Source who wanted you to push on her arm while she asked herself questions, on the principle that her body knew subconsciously what she needed to be reading or buying next. She was harmless, really, but she wouldn't stop talking about how she'd almost died and the angels had rescued her.

I checked the clock. My time was almost up. I had to get home and test whether or not it was Mom's necklace that was making me—no, giving me...abilities.

That was the right word, I decided. The only drawback was if I looked too hard at anyone, or was around an injury, I was feeling it too. I could have been just feeling sympathy pains, but I'd never really been that empathic.

Not like Mom.

Clover's brother had come into Enlightened Source more than once. Did he have abilities too? Had he been interested in Mom because of hers? Although Mom had never mentioned anything like this.

The aura never lies. It was like *the cards never lie*, but her reading of them was sometimes incomplete. She always figured it out too late. And Clover's brother hadn't been overly interested in her, not like men usually were. He was way more interested in unloading his ganja for a good price.

I reached for my collarbone, but Mom's necklace was at home on my nightstand. I figured I'd keep it off for a while and see if I still noticed things.

Well, I did. Every time I glanced away from the screen, there were smears of color before my eyes adjusted. It was distracting, and the weird sensations when I looked at people—the woman who had a backache, the tired cranky toddler, the man sitting at one of the tables rubbed at his throbbing head—were, too.

Empathy is great, really, but I needed some way to turn it off if I was going to deal.

I probably should have been looking *that* up instead of the Harmony church. There were people waiting to use the computers, their irritation rasping against the back of my head, so I went to go check dear old Dewey Decimal 130-140. I found—big surprise— nothing there I hadn't read or decided wasn't useless, and it was already near lunchtime. I should've known people would have pretty much stolen anything really useful from the library, it was just how things went. You couldn't keep occult books on the shelves in public places, if the Jesus freaks didn't take them for burning the kids were always taking them to giggle over.

All the way home on the bus my stomach kept twisting and lurch- ing. Some of it was hunger, sure, but I kept feeling like I was missing something important, something nagging, something huge. It got to where I rocked back and forth on the seat like I had to pee, every once in a while looking around to see where the feeling was coming from. Nobody on the bus looked like they were going to toss their cookies, but a few gave me strange glances because I probably looked drugged or something. I got off a stop early so I could check the box pharmacy, and headed home with an new X-Acto knife, a fresh container of Band-Aids, and my stomach fighting with the quiet, hard little egg in my chest. It wasn't big and pulsing today, but that could be because I had other things to worry about.

It took a while for traffic to clear enough so I could dart across the four lanes into the complex, and I plunged into a band of saplings a little taller than me, following the path worn by apartment people who headed for the bus stop or the pharmacy without bothering to go all the way around.

I don't know what made me stop behind a screen of bushes and look at one of the small playgrounds dotting the grounds. This one had a metal slide and two swings, its sandy floor probably a litterbox for every feral cat in a five-mile radius. The slide glittered sharply under a flood of butter-yellow sunshine, and I blinked a couple times before I realized what I was seeing.

It was Leaf, Clover's brother. Same dark wisp-curl hair to his shoulders, same brightly embroidered Mexican shirt he'd worn visiting Dad, same jeans and engineer boots. The fringed leather jacket was new, and so was the way he leaned against the side of the slide, his cheeks bright red and his eyes glazed, breathing hard. Colorless ripples wavered all around him, and I almost, *almost* stepped out of the bushes. The *oh my God are you okay* was on the tip of my tongue, but I hesitated.

I don't know why.

Leaf flinched as if he felt me looking, hunched his shoulders, and peeled himself away from the slide. He staggered in the opposite direction, and the hesitation turned definite. What was he doing here? Did he live in the complex? I hadn't seen him at Harmony Home, *or* at the soup kitchen.

Maybe I would have followed him, but that's when the sirens began out on the highway, and some irresistible instinct turned my head. A pillar of greasy black smoke billowed, faint sweet spring breeze smudging its edges, and when I looked back Leaf was gone.

PART III
HARMONY

3 4

OUR OWN

"Val! *Val!*" Dad sounded frantic. Maybe someone had called him at work. The Charger was parked across two spaces, its door open, engine still running, and Dad forced his way through the crowd. His hair was a mess, his hands were black with engine grease, and he was in his work coveralls. They were covered with goop, too, like he'd been rolling in it. Then he yelled my full name, like I was in trouble.

"Over here!" I waved my arm. Neighbors I didn't know were all of a sudden shouting Dad's name, too. I had no idea he was so popular.

He shouldered aside an older woman still in her bathrobe—at two PM on a Friday, wow—and the next thing I knew, he had me in a bear hug and picked me up off the pavement. He damn near crushed me, too. "Jesus Christ," Dad said into my hair. "Oh, thank you, God. Thank you."

"I was at the library." I could barely get the words out, he was squeezing so hard. My ribs ached. "I'm okay. I'm okay."

Behind festoons of yellow caution tape, fat canvas snakes of fire hoses, and the big red bricks of firetrucks, our building belched smoke. They were pretty sure everyone was out, but they were going room by room. The firemen yelled things at each other, and the crowd cheered a bit when one of them brought out a limp tabbycat, cradling it tenderly as if it was still alive. I knew it wasn't because it had no glow, and the shivers and shakes were all through me. Dad hugged me, and said *thank you* a few more times, like I'd done something awesome by not being inside when the fire started.

The was when I started shaking. Just a little bit, tiny earthquakes running up and down my arms and legs. He was here, and I didn't have to stand rigid, listening to neighbors ooh and aaah while I wondered if the fire was in Dad's apartment, and what the *fuck* was going on. It was the first time I ever felt like someone else could possibly take care of a disaster, which was strange. But Dad was so big, he blocked out the smoke and the noise and the feeling that somehow, some way, this was my fault.

Maybe I shouldn't have felt comforted. But I did.

It wasn't Dad's apartment, but there was smoke everywhere and Dad's door was in splinters. It was the floor right below, something electrical. A curling iron left on, a fuse not behaving the way it should, or a bathroom fan deciding now was a good time to protest being taken for granted—at least, that's what one of the neighbors said, and it was repeated all around so it felt true. Nobody could go in, even to get underwear, until the firemen said it was safe. So we just stood in the sunlight, everyone grouped up according to who they knew, and a few people going from group to group full of "news" and big balloon-feelings of special responsibility just like when something happened at school; everyone retreated to their cliques except for the drama-llamas.

I didn't let go of Dad even when he made a restless movement. A minute later, though, I found out why he'd twitched.

"Oh, blessed Heaven," a familiar voice said. "Are you all right? We heard on the news at the kitchen—"

It was Clover, her almost-black hair messed up, her denim jacket askew, and her dark eyes wide and frightened. She threw her arms around me, and around as much of Dad as she could reach. A breath of patchouli, a faint hint of peppermint Castile soap, her chest pressing softly against my shoulder and the heat-haze of the soup kitchen—cooking for a huge amount of people has a certain smell, you can't wash it out that easily—surrounding me. "Blessed Heaven," she repeated. "Oh, thank God, thank God, praise be." Behind her trailed Rebecca in a long skirt and a chunky yellow sweater, her black skin glowing, and Paul in engineer boots and worn jeans, his mop of soft brown hair threaded with gray, stood shoulder to shoulder. They looked different from everyone else in the crowd. More finished, or maybe just calmer.

You could tell a Harmony adult at a single glance, really. They didn't wear their clothes the same way straights did. They were just, I don't know, *easier* in them.

I buried my face in Dad's chest. It was weird, I couldn't *feel* anything from Clover except that heatshimmer and a dim staticky sense of someone breathing and thinking a long way away. You know how you can tell someone else is in a house, even if they're in a room on the the whole other side? A sense of *presence*, between the outside of your ear and the place where your brain turns electricity into sound.

They talked to each other, but the heatshimmer coming off her didn't flex and ripple. I figured Clover wasn't doing...whatever it was she did. At least, not to Dad.

Good.

It was decided that she'd take me back to the compound, they had extras of everything I'd need. Dad would stay here until he could go in and get clothes and my textbooks, and there was an empty place at Harmony for us. "Don't worry," Clover kept saying. "We'll talk to Father. He'll be glad to help, I know he will."

Paul and Rebecca nodded and chimed in that of course Father Jim would help. Everything would be taken care of.

"Val?" Dad bent back a little, tucking his chin and peering down at the top of my head. "Sweetheart, does that sound okay?"

Clover's arms loosened. She stepped away a little bit, to give us privacy I guess. Stood with her head tilted back, looking at the blackened hole in the side of the building. The fire had eaten right through wall, insulation, and siding. Nobody was hurt, except that one cat. Clover's eyebrows drew together, a vertical line between them, and I couldn't figure out what her expression meant. I needed to, though. It was really important.

"Val?" Dad jostled me a little. Not rudely, just getting my attention.

"My cactuses." My throat was too dry. "And Mom's necklace, it's up there too."

He looked relieved that I'd finally said something, I guess. "Don't worry, dumplin'. I'll take care of it. You wanna go with Clover, and stay with the folks out there? I'll bring everything I can, soon's they let me in there."

I nodded. "Yeah. Sure." My head hurt, all the people around me were loud and scraping against me with thinky-feely-glowy crap, and my feet hurt from standing in the parking lot for a while. I'd've probably agreed to move to Peru if it just meant I could sit down for a bit somewhere quiet.

Dad persisted. "I could call Hooker. We could stay with them, or go to a motel—"

I shuddered. "Dad, it's fine. It's just for a couple days, right?"

"Well, yeah, hope so." He scratched at his cheek with his filthy free hand. He must have raced here from work. "We'll figure it out. You go on with them, then. If you're okay with that."

I wasn't really okay with any of this. But what else could I do? Dad hugged me again, like he didn't want to let go. Finally, though, we had to. Rebecca put a motherly arm around me; she and Paul ushered me away through the growing crowd in the parking lot. Everyone coming out to see the disaster, to crane their necks and feel glad it wasn't them. Rebecca was taller than me, and she hummed as she walked. They'd parked in the C building lot, and it wasn't until they bundled me into the middle seat of the van that I realized Clover had stayed behind with Dad.

Rebecca tucked a multicolored wool shawl around me, examining my face. "Clo'll help him get things arranged. Don't worry about anything, Daughter Val. We take care of our own."

Which was weird, right? We weren't *their own*. At least, not then.

Paul turned the key, and the van sputtered a bit before catching. "It's gonna be okay." He smiled encouragingly, half-turning in his seat. He had those cold blue eyes and narrow nose you see on men who think the world should be fully organized, but he seemed pretty okay, especially since his hair was always so messy. "Ingrid'll be thrilled to see you, she and Gabby talk about you a lot."

Is that a good thing? I couldn't say it, of course. That's right, he was Ingrid's dad. Rebecca clambered in the front passenger seat, and the radio crackled softly. The fire had made the news, because of that big plume of greasy black smoke. After a few minutes, Rebecca turned it off, and by the time the van was waved out of the apartment complex's entrance onto the highway by a bored-looking cop who glared at the Channel 5 van blocking half the driveway, she and Paul were singing softly about an apple tree. It was a lilting melody, and it wasn't until we got free of the traffic jam and the van worked up Clostermann Avenue to drop onto 138th and approach the tangle leading to Cold Creek Road that I realized none of them had said a word about Leaf.

Of course, I hadn't either. But it made me think, while I sat there clutching my backpack and my plastic box pharmacy bag.

The trouble was, I didn't know *what* to think. Everything inside me was whirling, even the smooth stone egg inside my chest. The egg was growing spikes, and they prickled insistently. I couldn't breathe deeply without the jabbing.

So I just sat there, hugging my backpack, and wondered.

35

RELIEF, TOO LATE

I HADN'T REALIZED how large the compound was. They had tiny prefabricated houses—a studio space, small bathroom with just a sink and a toilet, the bigger ones with a stamp-size bedroom and a door you could close. They weren't *trailers*, since they were on foundations and you couldn't ever put them on wheels, but they were about as teensy. They called them mods, for "modulars". The showers were in a low brick building that also held a nurse's station, where Carole Harrison, Pam, and Cass ran the medical division. They called it the dispensary, but it was more like a school nurse's office. About the only thing they couldn't do was X-rays and surgery, but between Pam and Cass, both ramrod-straight and no-nonsense, I bet they could have done open-heart if they really wanted to.

Anyway, there was a new modular at the end of a row, each of its neighbors with a little patch of turned earth in front for flowers. Plenty of the tiny gardens were already greening with seedlings, and one of them, painted red, had purple hyacinths bruise-blooming on either side of the narrow steps to its door. In California they lived in yurts, Rebecca told me, and they'd brought some of them up here too, but the modulars were more permanent. "We have a place to rest, now," she said, unlocking the door. "We just put this one up, Father's been saying all winter we need more."

I was busy trying to keep her shawl from falling off me and keep my backpack in my arms. The plastic bag was securely inside. Each time it shifted I jumped a little. I followed Rebecca up the two steps and found myself in a small, wood-floored space full of disturbed dust, paint, and the smell of a place closed up for a while, like a singed feather brushing inside your nose.

The bedroom had a plain wooden bed with a bare blue mattress, and the windows had thin blue curtains made of leftover sheets. For all that, the bathroom was clean, the wooden floor was solid, and the windows were vinyl instead of metal. No kitchen, because they ate all their meals together and the big kitchen was always open for snacking.

I paced around the wooden box, the shawl slipping off my shoulders, and looked out the window. There was a long patch of open ground before the line of the woods, and there were more concrete pads with weird pipes and stuff thrusting up, for more of the "mods". Marching along, a parallel line of pads to the right carried on toward the trees. Did they really expect that many people to show up out here?

"I know it looks bare." Rebecca sounded a little nervous. Her afro was really pretty, especially in the sun when the ends were lined with gold. "But don't worry. Paul went to go see Father. Everything will be all right."

She looked so...I don't know, sort of forlorn, maybe? "It's nice." What did you say in a situation like this? "It's cozy."

"When it gets really cold in winter we all sleep in the Pavilion. It's like a slumber party." Her narrow dark face eased, and the sweater against her soft buttery skin was a nice contrast. "Here, lay your stuff down. Are you hungry? I'll bet you're hungry."

"I'm fine." I wasn't, I was starving, but it was like visiting a straight's house for the first time. Be cautious, keep looking for what they really mean under all the politeness, and never let your guard down. "Just, you know." What sounded really good was going into the postage-stamp bedroom, pushing the wooden bedframe up against the door, and sitting down. Just...sitting, for a bit.

"Oh, honey." Hands on her soft motherhips, she examined me from top to toe. The door, open behind her, was full of spring sunshine, but you could tell the day was getting older. Dust danced in the gold, whirling lazily. "Your *house* just burned down. You don't have to be polite."

It wasn't a house. It was an apartment. And it wasn't home. Home was the farmhouse and its stupid rotting floors and its cold damp in the winter and Mom in every room. At least all her stuff was in storage, untouched.

She was gone, and Dad's apartment was gone. And here I was, in Harmony Home. You have to go along when they have you, straights or anyone else. All of a sudden I was just so tired.

No, that's a stupid word for it. I was *exhausted*. Like I hadn't slept since the farmhouse, that afternoon with cars grinding on gravel still lingering. Everything since then pressed down on me, like water at the bottom of the deep end. I couldn't hold the whole world up on my own. I mean, I was used to trying, sure, but how long could I keep trying before I folded up like used tinfoil?

"I'm fine." I tried to say it like I really was. "Really. It's, you know, really nice. I'm sorry for all the trouble." There was nothing but trouble, following me around like a bad spirit in one of the fairytale books Mom read to me.

"Rebecca?" Someone was at the door. I almost jumped out of my skin, *and* her nice shawl. It was a lean Hispanic man in coveralls, his proud nose the biggest thing on his face under a thatch of messy dark hair. He looked right off a Mayan codex, and the long brown feather tied to a lock on the right side of his head with red thread added a finishing touch. "Heard we're opening up this mod! Oh, hi, you're the mechanic's girl. Listen, we're going to get some furniture in here for you guys. What kind of colors do you like?"

What? I hugged my backpack tighter. "Um. Hi." I'd seen him at the Sunday meals, of course, but all of them started to blur together. Except Ingrid, maybe, and Gabby.

And Owen.

"What's your favorite color?" he persisted. "Everyone'll bring something by, but it's nice to know what you like so we can make you comfortable." He grinned, strong white teeth, and leaned on the side of the door.

"She's a little stunned, I think." Rebecca stepped close to me, and with two quick efficient movements had the shawl wrapped around me just fine and now magically staying in place. "We'll take care of everything, Daughter Val. Just tell us your favorite color."

I *had* one, but I didn't want to tell them. How dumb was that? There wasn't any escape, though, I had to be polite. "It's already got blue in here," I managed. "Blue's fine."

"There are a *lot* of blues. Dark? Light?" He seemed really, really set on finding out. "I'm Rob, by the way. Brother Rob V."

"Pleased to meet you," I mumbled. *How do you do* didn't seem appropriate.

Rebecca visibly decided I was out of my depth, and she didn't let me keep trying to swim. "Let's get you something to eat." It was the no-nonsense tone a mom uses when she has *decided*, and Heaven help the hindmost as Dad sometimes said. "We'll leave it in your capable hands, Rob." She ushered me towards the door, little movements of her graceful hands. Her nails were painted pale pink, another contrast against her skin. "By the time you come back, you won't recognize the place."

"Blue." Rob hopped off the steps so we could leave, stepping back into sunshine that had come down on the back slope of the afternoon. "I've got a comforter that'll work. Pretty sure Sister Nina's got a few ideas too." He actually *clapped*, like an excited little kid. "Oh, man, it's great to have you! Go on, go eat. Mother Carole's in there with apples, and you know what that means."

I didn't, but I plastered a smile on my face and followed Rebecca's fluttering skirt and decisive step. She was a big bossy tugboat dragging a tired, tiny dinghy in her wake, and all of a sudden warm reassurance swamped me so hard I staggered on the gravel path. Behind us, Rob burst out in a rousing chorus of something in Spanish, a nice clear deep voice rising to the innocent baby-blue sky.

"Whoops, careful there." Rebecca put a slim ebony hand on my arm. The feeling was still there, and it made me dizzy all over again. I didn't even mind that I saw heat-ripples around her. Weak ones, sure, but they were there.

I gave up, and let her do the deciding. It was a gigantic goddamn relief. Now, I think that was the last moment I could have left, escaped, run away.

But you never know that until it's too late, do you.

36

PUSH YOU OVER

FINGERS IN MY HAIR, deft and sure. Little tugs back and forth, while I stared at my empty hands in my lap. The big echoing space inside the Pavilion was full of voices. There was the warmth of hot food, of so many human bodies together giving off heat, and the soft singing. Behind me, Ingrid hummed. It was her hands tugging and braiding, and behind her, Gabrielle sat, braiding Ingrid's dark curls. The girls all did each other's hair, and it was kind of soothing. There were pillows on this corner of the rise where Father Jim stood to give talks while the band played. Owen was at the piano, fingers sure and deft on the keys, his wrists soft and his expression halfway between thoughtful and worried.

"We are going to have so much fun," Ingrid said. "We'll show you the pond. And the bridge. Oh, and the Powells let us ride their horses sometimes. You ever ridden a horse?"

"One summer." My face felt strange because I was smiling, a tiny unwilling movement. "My mom met a guy. He lived in Montana."

"What's it like there?" Gabrielle leaned forward to ask over Ingrid's shoulder. I felt the movement by the way Ingrid's hands changed on my hair. Funny how you can sense those tiny shifts. Like ice right before it cracks.

"Big." The wind comes across miles and miles of nothing, and it has its own song. In spring it's a soft mouthing even when the storms sweep through, in the crackglaze-dry heat of summer when the creeks vanish it's a sandy brush stealing moisture from every crack. Fall veered between grass rippling like the sea and sharp, jagged spikes of frost, the mountains stabbing at a distance.

We left in the middle of winter, Mom driving through the night in the pickup we had before the blue Chevy. I thought the wind was getting to her, and if it wasn't, the snow certainly was. It wasn't until I was older that I remembered the voices in the middle of the night, Mom wincing as she got out of the truck to pay for a motel room on the outskirts of Butte. A few days later, she came out of the shower in a towel, and the bruises glare-blue and yellow up and down her legs and back.

"He had a ranch," I finished. "It was nice." *While it lasted.* "There were mountains in the distance, and all the grass. The sky's huge. My mom said it could drive someone mad."

Some of the kids were running around and shrieking, playing a kind of tag-game. There were adults coming in and out, doing setup for dinner, clearing dishes from after-school snack, seeing what remained to be done. Whatever Ingrid was doing to my hair felt complicated.

"Your mom?" Ingrid, naturally curious. "Where is she?"

I waited for it, but the jab in my chest didn't come. There was a hazy feeling instead, like the moment after thunder rattles the house and you stop what you're doing, just waiting to see if anything will fall.

Maybe I stayed quiet too long. Ingrid sucked in a breath. "Sorry." Her fingers were so gentle. "Never mind."

"She had an accident." *Didn't Clover tell you?* But that wasn't fair. Why would Clover tell *anyone* that, especially a kid? It wasn't anything that would come up in normal conversation.

"Oh, man. I'm sorry." She smoothed my shoulder, her left hand still caught in my hair, holding things steady. It felt really good. The last time anyone messed with my hair...God, it had to be when the Wiccans were out at the farmhouse. Maya had braided lavender into my hair along with dry, reddish leaves, a crown for fall. Mom used to put my hair up when I was little, but I liked doing my own.

I wished I'd let Mom do it more. I kept staring at my hands. Especially the left one. It didn't look like I'd boiled the fuck out of it yesterday. A shadow fell over me, and I had to crane my neck a little weird to look up.

It was Sarah, in a blue sweatshirt and slightly too-big jeans. Her fine, thin bangs fell in her eyes. Between brown and blonde, her hair was still deciding what it wanted to be just like the rest of her. She shifted from foot to foot in brand-new red sneakers, staring at me. I don't know what she was looking for, but she must have decided my face held it, because she dropped down and wormed her way into my lap.

I've never been one of those girls who likes kids. You know the type, they squeal whenever they see babies and talk about when they'll get married and spawn, like it's the biggest thing to look forward to. I mean, small humans are fine, and most of them are way lower bullshit than adults, but I heard enough from Mom about sleep deprivation and changing diapers to make me wary. I always used to feel bad I was such a drag on her when I was little.

I can't remember when I didn't.

Sarah was a little too big to fit, but she folded herself up and snuggled against me. I let out an involuntary sound, partly because her elbow hit my stomach and partly because...well, I didn't *feel* all the people around me anymore. The confusing silent clamor of little aches and pains, bigger ones, spikes of momentary annoyance or a pleasant sense of community, all fell away and I was myself again.

"Well, hello, Sarah-monkey," Ingrid said over my shoulder. Sarah smiled, a sleepy, heavy expression, and I wondered if she felt the

189

same way. Could I ask her with everyone around? What if I was wrong, and she was just a normal kid?

"Hi, Ingrid." Sarah examined my face some more. "Hi, Val."

"Hi." My throat was too dry, I croaked.

"It's nice, isn't it?" She rested her head on my shoulder. My legs were going to go numb if she stayed there for any length of time, but it was so good not to feel all of them crowding me. "The quiet."

She knows. "Yeah," I said, cautiously. "I'm trying to figure out how to do it myself."

"Ask Owen." She scooted her skinny little butt, and she was hiding sharp bones in there, to judge by the way my thighs began to feel bruised. "He likes you."

Oh, boy. Awkward. "He likes everyone." *Except preppers, maybe.*

"Nope. He just acts like he does." She smelled like fresh air and pencil shavings; I wondered what her classmates thought of her. I wondered if Father Jim showed up for parent-teacher conferences. What did teachers make of him? Or did his wife go?

"I guess he has to." *Don't we all.* I could *think* again, and it was a gigantic relief. Not nearly as relieving as it would be to have Dad show up and say *good news, kiddo, we're going home,* but close.

"You don't." Sarah wriggled a little more. Her feet hung off to the side, those red sneakers mini-sized. "You're comfy."

"Well, great. Jeez, go easy, okay?" I thought about the machines that made the shoes, and wondered if they had different settings for different sizes. They probably had to; you couldn't have a machine for every single size.

She finished wiggling around, finding a position that suited her. "What happened? You're sad."

"There was a fire."

She froze. For a second I thought it was because of me, but the buzzing at the Pavilion door proved me wrong.

Father Jim, his blond-streaked surfer 'do haloed in sunshine, stood at the threshold. Adults clustered him, speaking in low voices, some of them reaching out, almost touching. He spread his hands and beamed, the smoked lenses of his sunglasses eerie on his tanned face, and the hemp bracelet on his right wrist slid against a thin leather one.

Some guys wear bracelets and they look stupid. For some reason, Father Jim didn't. They made his wrists look strong. He stepped fully inside and pushed the sunglasses up, settling them in his hair like he'd planned the motion and practiced it to get it right.

Owen's playing at the piano softened, wound down. Ingrid shifted behind me. I could tell she was looking over her shoulder, and all of a sudden, I knew *why*, too. It's always useful to figure out who has a crush on someone, especially in a small group when you can be locked out in an instant. Moving around with Mom taught me all about that. So I looked down at Sarah's red shoes again, trying to move so one particular point in her bony ass wasn't cutting off an artery on the inside of my leg.

"Hey." Owen loomed over us both briefly before he crouched, easily, his hands dangling inside his jean-clad knees and that too-short scrap of leather around his neck for the cross. "You okay, Sarah-bear?"

She nodded, her cheek moving against my shoulder. "Here comes Father."

"Yeah." It was hard to tell whether he was commiserating, agreeing, or both. "How was school?"

"Boring." Sarah didn't bother twisting around to look at him. They seemed pretty tight. I wondered what that was like—having a brother. A sister. Mom would never have agreed to get pregnant again, I was all she could handle. Maybe *that* was why they split up. I could see Dad liking the idea of another kid, maybe thinking it would make her stay. *Your dad will be in my life forever,* she sometimes told me. *That's what happens when you have a child. So don't do anything stupid, Val.*

Ingrid finished with my hair. "There you go. You're a Harmony girl now, Val."

Something hot rose in my scratchy throat. I didn't know quite what to call it. "Thanks." I tried to look over my shoulder, but with a lapful of kid, it was kind of hard. "I mean it, Ingrid. Thanks."

She laughed, a soft sound almost as smooth as her skin. "No problem. Everything belongs to everyone, here. You done, Gabby?"

Gabby had to raise her voice to be heard over the shuffle and buzz as Father Jim moved through the crowd, stopping to talk to one person, then another. "Yeah. I did the fishtail braid. You want to work your magic on mine?"

"Sure thing." Movement behind me, and I was left with Owen settling himself crosslegged in front of me and Sarah in my lap, nailing me in place. Father Jim's gaze was on us whenever I looked, and it was a little...well, it was moderately unsettling. Was he coming to tell me Dad had come back and I had to go?

I didn't know how to feel about that. Was the apartment home now? I didn't think it was, had refused to call it *home* even to myself. Was something only home when it was gone? A person could go crazy thinking about that, worrying and working, fraying all their internal edges.

"Hey," Owen said, soft and low and fast. "Sarah said something about you."

That brought my head around so hard the half-braid bumped against my back and my chin almost whapped Sarah in the nose.

"It's okay," he continued. "Just...don't let Father push you over, okay?"

Push me over? And oh, God, would today *ever* end? I was getting to the end of my ability to just keep on moving through without breaking down sobbing or screaming.

"Okay." I decided to just agree with him and figure it out later. Mom would be proud. Her practical, hardheaded kid, the one she despaired of ever "loosening up," finally going with the flow.

Owen nodded, and reached over to ruffle Sarah's hair. "Don't you want braids, monkey?"

"Nah. Makes my head feel funny." She curled more tightly against me as Father Jim approached, finally breaking free of a knot of women asking questions about dinner. It looked like he could barely move without being mobbed. Did it get old after a while? It would drive me right up the wall, I decided.

"Hard for my head to feel any stranger nowadays." I didn't realize I'd said it out loud until Owen laughed, slapping his hand over his mouth like it was an embarrassing bodily noise or something. "What?"

He shook his head, still laughing, and Sarah grinned. It turned her solemn little face into something else for a second—just a kid, eyes dancing and cheeks flushing, an infectious bubble of happiness. The singing, bouncing off the walls, went up a notch, like Father Jim's presence meant everyone had to breathe a little harder while they hummed.

"Daughter Val." He was *right there* all of a sudden, and Sarah's grin faded inch by inch. "Our little Sarah-spark's taken a liking to you."

"Looks like it, sir." I shifted a little uncomfortably.

Father Jim glanced at Owen. "Son, you made sure these ladies are taken care of?"

"Yessir." Owen's shoulders hunched a little. "Val had snack with us, and Sarah—"

"I got Jello," she piped up. "I like Val. She's nice."

"Well, it looks like she'll be with us for a while. We're happy to have you, daughter. If you need anything at all, just ask anybody. We believe in helping out here."

It was on the tip of my tongue to ask just what else they believed in, but I didn't. I knew pretty much how Mom would have reacted if I did, but I didn't know about Dad and the last thing *he* needed was me making problems. "Thank you." Sarah wriggled again, and I don't know if she meant it, but I took it as a warning anyway. "Sir."

"You just call me Father, honey." He grinned, wide and white and forgiving. Maybe he wasn't all that bad. He certainly seemed to be patient, what with everyone clustering around so it took him a long time to get across the Pavilion. "God brought you to us. You're a gift, and we believe in treating God's gifts with the respect they deserve." His smile widened. "There'll be a special dinner tonight, for you. And Brother Earl."

Brother whosis? Then I realized he meant Dad. "Oh. Okay. Thank you, that's really kind."

He nodded, and reached down a big tanned hand, as if he was going to pat me on the shoulder. Sitting on the dais put me at about that height, and I was just glad he wasn't going to touch my head like some kind of mall Santa or middle-school teacher who thought he was cool with the kids.

I leaned away, just a fraction of an inch. Teenagers don't like to be touched, right? It occurred to me that it was rude, especially when they were being all nice and all, and I opened my mouth to apologize.

Father Jim's grin stayed steady, but his hand stopped, dropped back to his side. "Welcome home, then."

What could I say to that? I already felt like an asshole. "Thank you."

He swung away, and they mobbed him again. A big-shouldered teenager in overalls—his name was Wolf, I learned later, he had just graduated—was saying something about boxes in a low, hurried rush.

Owen let out a long breath that wasn't quite a sigh. Sarah had gone tense on my lap, a stiff little doll instead of a wriggling kid. She relaxed again, bit by bit, and maybe I should have wondered about it. I should have wondered about *everything*.

I was just so tired inside. Owen didn't say a word. I was grateful, and even though my legs had already gone numb I sat there and held Sarah for about twenty minutes before Dad showed up, still covered in engine grease and with dark circles under his eyes, and waved at me from the Pavilion door.

37

CAME TO HARMONY

FATHER JIM and Dad walked in front, Sarah held my hand, and Owen trailed behind us. I got the feeling he'd rather be elsewhere, but maybe greeting the new people or even just looking after Sarah was a Family Duty.

When we got to the mod, the first surprise was Owen's mother in the door, beaming at us. She was flushed, stray wavy bits of her dark hair sticking to her forehead and cheeks, like she'd been moving things around. Her thin hands clasped in front of her, she bounced a little on her toes like Ingrid. "Oh, bless us, we're not ready." Those were the first words I heard her say, and she had a nice voice. Some of the news articles said she'd been trained at Julliard. "Brother Robbie said you liked blue, right?"

The little mod now had a couple bright Navajo-patterned throw rugs, and there were neatly mended sky-blue towels in the small bathroom. The postage-stamp bedroom was full, because the bedstead had been moved to the wall and a white-painted dresser carted in. A futon couch sat in the bigger room, next to a small rickety endtable and an amber glass lamp from the sixties with dangling glass beads all over its shade. I figured out later everything had come from someone else, because everything Harmony owned belonged to everyone. There was another dresser in the bigger room, this one painted a pale greenish with recycled glass knobs. A small wicker cabinet hung on one wall, and it looked like people actually *lived* here.

"Oh, wow." I couldn't help myself. "It was completely empty when I saw it."

"This is mighty kind of you," Dad repeated. "We coulda just gone to a motel—"

"Now why waste money on a motel?" Father Jim laughed, rich and deep, bouncing off the walls. "Especially when you've done us such a good turn keeping those vans running."

"Hey." Gabrielle stuck her head in the door. It was getting crowded in here. "Paul and Big Tom are bringing your suitcases. Dinner's almost started."

It was like swimming and all of a sudden realizing the current has you, but not in the terrifying way. Instead, it's bringing you in to shore, and you don't have to struggle quite as hard. The wicker cabinet had sheets for the futon, and a neat stack of mismatched blankets. Paul showed up, carefully carrying the rack of cactuses, and that was when I started to snivel and sniff like a little kid. Because Dad had gone up and gotten them out, and he also pressed Mom's necklace into my sweating hands. He hugged me tight, and I didn't care where the hell we were, just that I didn't have to *deal* anymore.

They told us to come to dinner soon and closed the door, so it was Dad, and me, and this strange, small place without any kitchen.

∼

AND THAT WAS how we came to Harmony.

3 8

FIRST SERVICE

SATURDAY PASSED IN A BLUR. Learning where the laundry was, what to do if you slept through breakfast, how the kitchen worked, watching the big blue seeders work freshly plowed fields. Helping with the cleanup in garden boxes that had been fallow last year—they believed in crop rotation. They really were more like hippies than Baptists, which is where Father Jim started out, I guess. Cabbages were harvested from cold frames, and though I'm not a huge fan of them, Mother Carole took over the kitchen and made a soup—*borscht* —with a dollop of sour cream in each bowl and it was really good.

Sunday morning, the cars started showing up at 6am. I didn't know quite what to expect, and even though I wasn't *required* to go— Father Jim was clear on that—I was curious.

The Harmonies went into the Pavilion for a while, and strangers waited outside. At first it was only four or five, but a steady stream kept arriving. They were parking up and down Cold Creek Road for a ways, choking the long driveway, and when Carole Harrison slipped out of the Pavilion's big double doors they all turned still and expectant in the gray misty hush. I wondered what they did in the winter—wait in the cold?

They were mostly families, either with really young kids or past the age of dragging the little ones around. I guessed, looking at the crowd, most teenagers didn't want to drive out to a country church and had dug in their heels. The singles were usually women, older ones with a faraway look I recognized. They were the type that would come to Mom for tarot readings, and they generally only asked one question. They already knew the answer, too, and more often than not they got mad at her when she told them they knew already, why were they asking her?

You have no right, they would huff. *You asked,* was Mom's inevitable reply.

That was why I took the money *first.* Cash up front, the only way to make sure the straights won't cheat you.

Anyway, Mother Carole smiled, wrapping her pink sweater-coat more firmly. No wonder, she was so thin she probably felt cold even in summer. Cords on her neck stood out. I wondered if she was just naturally skinny or if she hated eating.

"Welcome, dear guests." Arms folded, head high, silvery leaf earrings fluttering, she had no trouble pushing her voice through the crowd. I knew those earrings—I'd seen Ingrid wearing them. "We're so glad to have you with us today, on this blessed day." A pause, just like a teacher in front of a rowdy class, waiting for everyone to settle. "Come in, come in." A couple Harmony teens—Ingrid and Ben— pushed the doors wide and popped down the little rubber-bottomed feet to hold them there, and just inside was Father Jim, smiling and beckoning.

All the Harmonies were already humming, spread along the sides of the Pavilion. Owen hit a chord on the piano, and they began to sing, layers of wordless harmony like the movie version of angels. A thin, nervous-looking guy—Brother Tim G, distinct from Brother Tim S—was on the drums, a soft hazy beat like a heart pumping. Owen's hands moved dreamily on the keys, liquid rippling notes mixing with the heatshimmer.

Because it was there, hanging above the chairs, that weird trembling. I blinked several times, slipping in with the tail end of the crowd to avoid the handshaking and hugging. The Pavilion was almost to capacity, and it was a *lot* of people. I rubbed at my eyes, but it didn't go away. The feeling of so many people gathered, all their aches and pains and the chitter-chatter inside their heads, turned into a type of static. It was an unexpected relief.

Father Jim headed for the stage while everyone settled. The music softened even further. I wondered what Dad would think of this—he was asleep on the futon, probably still worn out from working a double shift Saturday to make up for leaving early Friday. His boss hadn't asked him to, he just *did* it. I mean, a fire at home was a reasonable excuse for dropping everything and running, but Dad felt responsible I guess.

I folded my arms and stayed at the back, near the doors. Father Jim reached the stage, turned around, and made a wide, welcoming gesture. Owen's fingers slowed, halted on the piano, and the drumbeat stopped. The singing went on, a hushed hum, and...how can I explain?

I mean, I know Father Jim gave a sermon. I know it wasn't like any other church-talk I'd heard Mom dismiss while she scrubbed dishes or leaned against the counter at Enlightened Source. I even know what he said—that there were three nails holding us down, just like there were three nails holding Jesus on the cross. Take those nails out, and we're free, we're divine, we're just like God, created in his image—and I wondered what the Wiccans would say about that one.

At the top of my brain I know that, like you know that the Gettysburg Address exists and that Argentina exports beef. But underneath, it's just...blank. It's like I was there, but I wasn't. Like something else happened, and Father Jim's words were only a tablecloth laid over it. I know everyone in the audience sang—*Amazing Grace*, how cliché is that? There were other hymns, but I touched Mom's necklace and kept my mouth shut though my throat hurt with wanting to follow along.

I do remember other bits and pieces. A woman in a red coat

jumping up, arms waving, and outright screaming, a sharp spike through the enfolding music. I flinched, but she didn't seem *hurt*, just...happy? A heavyset, balding man who'd hobbled in next to his wife, leaning heavily on her, standing up and yelling too, something about his back. A dark-haired woman lifting her carefully wrapped baby, tears running down her face. A little girl with arm braces, carried up to Father Jim by her husky, wet-faced dad in a striped rugby shirt, dropped the braces with a clatter and taking two unsteady steps on her own. The dad hovered, a disbelieving goofy grin spreading over his face, and I saw Clover, her hands clasped tightly and her mouth open as she sang, her dark eyes blank.

The only person who didn't look into it was Sarah. I caught a glimpse of her, paper-faced, sitting cross-legged near Owen's piano bench. He was hunched over, his hands not moving on the keys, and he looked a little green too. Sarah stared across the people in the chairs popping up like jack-in-the-boxes when the singing hit a peak, and her big dark eyes met mine.

I grabbed Mom's necklace at my collarbone, edges biting into my palm, and I don't remember much else after that. Just a whirling sensation, and Sarah's thin face suddenly easing. I could tell because somehow, suddenly, I was in the front row, shoulders and hips bumping me from either side, everything narrowing to Sarah's gaze locked to mine.

I pushed a button.

The heatshimmer poured out of me. After that, it was just a confusion, a feeling like something *draining*, a bathtub emptying through my middle, sucking me dry. It pulled and pulled and pulled, and if it wasn't for the people jammed together on both sides of me I probably would have collapsed. As it was, I just...went away, inside, for a while.

That was my first Harmony service.

∾

I CAME BACK in a folding chair, gripping the sides of the seat so hard my knuckles were white, my hair knocked free of the yesterday's braid and my stomach chugging like a washing machine. Sarah crouched in front of me, her elbows on my knees, peering into my face. She didn't look worried, or scared. Instead, her cheeks were flushed, her eyes sparkled, and her bangs stuck to her damp forehead. Around us, the Pavilion echoed. There was a crush at the door where Father Jim and Mother Carole were shaking hands, smiling; the Harmonies were there too, moving among the visitors. Their humming faded but never quite died, moving from place to place in the crowd.

What the fuck did you do to me? I couldn't say it, my throat was too dry. Even the egg inside my chest was empty.

Maybe she heard it. Or maybe I just looked like I needed explanation.

"You helped." When she tilted her head like that, you could see what she'd look like when she was older. Sharp nose, a full lower lip, a thin upper one, big eyes. "It's easier when we're together."

I stared at her. She shifted from side to side, joggling my knees.

It took two tries before I could talk. "What..." There was so much to ask. A million questions, and I couldn't find the first one I wanted. Or the second. I settled on the obvious. "Does everyone have...have a button?"

She shook her head. "Just some people. It's different shapes." A dimpled smile. It was the happiest-looking I'd ever seen the kid, really. "Father thinks—"

"Val?" Someone touched my shoulder. "You okay?"

I couldn't leap out of the chair because Sarah had her arms on my knees, but god *damn* if I didn't almost try. I also let out a thin little noise, like a stupid-ass pop-prepper girl in a horror movie jump scare. It was Owen, and he yanked his hand back like I'd burned him.

"It's okay," Sarah said. "She knows."

He glanced nervously for the front of the Pavilion. "Of course she knows, I..." His mouth shut with a snap, and he glared at me like I'd done something wrong.

Sarah snorted out the type of laugh only a sarcastic eight-year-old can manage. It turned her into a grinning imp, digging her sharp elbows in, her sneaker soles squeaking a little. She was the only one of the Harmonies not dressed up for church; I mean, as far as this was a church and as far as "dressed up" went.

Owen crossed his arms, still glaring. "She tell you?"

Sarah shook her head. "You're gonna be in trouble."

I decided some yoga breathing was in order, but did I really want to blow an exhale over her face? I couldn't remember if I'd brushed my teeth or not this morning.

"Not if you keep quiet," Owen hissed. "Damn, Sarah, what did you do to her?"

"She wanted to help. And you just said a swear." Her elbows dug into my thighs. "There are big buttons and little ones. Owen's is big. So's yours."

"Great," I muttered. I didn't want to know the *size* of anyone's button, for God's sake. It sounded like highly personal information. I found one of the things that worried me in the soup my brain had become. "Can you turn it off?"

That managed to kill her smile, and I felt bad about it. Sarah shook her head. "Nope." She peered at me, eyes slit and dimples gone. "Why?"

"I dunno." But I did. It meant it couldn't be taken away; it meant, after all this time, I finally *had* something, just like Mom. My chest hurt, a swift spike of something red and raw. God, she'd be so proud, wouldn't she? "I just wanted to know."

"Did Father guess?" Owen bent over, like he was comforting me or something. He rested his hand on the back of the folding chair. He smelled like Ivory soap, fresh air, and cut firewood. "Forget it, he *has* to. Shit."

Well, that didn't sound promising. My stomach was beginning to settle down. I hadn't even had breakfast, for God's sake.

"I like it," I managed to say. "My mom...she was like, you know. Like this."

That brightened Sarah back up. "What did she do?"

She had a lot of talents. Tarot cards. Picking mean boyfriends. Seeing auras. "Just stuff." My head bobbled unsteadily—I remembered, I *had* brushed my teeth, thank God. Deep breathing was sounding better and better.

"Shit," Owen said again. "Here comes Clover."

"You said a swear *again*." Sarah bounced upright, almost cracking me in the face with her forehead. "Let's go to the barn. Or the pond."

"You guys go ahead." I tried loosening up on the sides of the chair. My hands wouldn't do it, probably because I'd spill out of the chair and onto the floor.

"You don't look good." Owen kept leaning over me. His thumb on the back of the chair touched me, a small, hot candleflame right near my spine.

"Hey. Is she all right? Val?" Yes, there was Clover. "Oh, honey. You're pale. Did you even have breakfast?"

I shook my head, and let her take over. Sarah vanished. Owen trudged back to the stage and the piano, stopping once to look back at me. I couldn't tell what his expression was, but by then Clover had me upright and pointed both of us for the kitchen, which was just getting into gear for lunch. She didn't ask any questions, just got me a bowl of oatmeal and brown sugar, patted my back, and went off to find some orange juice.

I could still feel Owen's thumb pressing against my back.

39

A LITTLE ADVICE

I⊤'s a lot different to walk into school with a group. When that group is girls who have braided your hair like theirs that morning and shared their vintage sweaters and broomstick skirts because all their laundry gets done together along with yours, when they obviously don't give a shit about anyone looking at them, when the guys have farm-muscle shoulders and walk easily, protectively—it's night and day. Even sitting on the bus, not on the periphery but squeezed between Ingrid and Gabby, surrounded by soft singing...a wall had gone up. A nice high one the straights couldn't get through. A blanket, like the guided visualizations Mom used to do. *Imagine yourself surrounded by a bright white light.*

I even caught myself humming along with them, trying to find the notes they all seemed to know by heart. Mom was the musical one, singing along with the radio all the time. I mostly just listened. I didn't have a good voice anyway. But they didn't say anything about me humming along or not, except Gabby. "I was like that too," she said on the bus. "It's okay. It takes a while."

Cold Ridge High looked more familiar now. Even when the bell rang and everyone scattered to get to their first period, it still felt...

almost welcoming. I didn't scuttle along with my head down and my backpack straps cutting my shoulders. Dad had brought all my books from the now-waterlogged desk; today he was going to find out about the apartment. At least I'd finished my Pre-Calc homework. If I pulled better than a C in that class for the end of the year I'd be grateful. Generally I like math, but the teacher here was a cranky rotund straight who kept talking about how "you kids these days" did everything wrong. I never thought anyone actually said it, just that it was a cliche, but Mr Edgitt was full of gems like that.

Second period English, one of the Harmony boys—Kellan— motioned me over to the desk next to him while everyone was milling around. The guy who usually sat there—a stoner with greasy hair and perpetually bloodshot eyes—just shrugged and moved over one.

"Hey." Kellan grinned, shaking his blond hair back. He was the easygoing one, even among the generally laid-back Harmony kids. "I should warn you, I'm no good at this."

"At what?" I thumped my math and French textbooks down on the desk.

"English. I hate writing papers."

"Don't worry." It felt good to say it. "I've got it covered. You any good at math?" I mean, I didn't need any help, but boys like feeling good at numbers, right? I wasn't hopeless, I knew *that* much, at least.

"I knew I liked you." He grinned, stretching his legs out. "Which math?"

"Integrated. Pre-Calc."

He whistled, a long low note, and the tone for class beginning harmonized with it. Even without trying, he was musical. "Wow. I'll do my best."

Mrs Jackson rapped on her desk with her bony knuckles and I sank into my seat, a funny light feeling in my chest. I realized, as Jackson turned on the projector and began droning about literary devices in *Hamlet*, I hadn't thought about Mom all morning.

And that felt guiltily, shamefully *great*.

THE SUNSHINE WAS GLORIOUS, and the pop-preppers were out in the small quad. They boys were larking around except for Travis the Bathroom Bro, who had raccoon-eyed bruising, a taped nose, and wrapped ribs. I knew because I'd had to sit through third with him staring at the back of my head and the haze of his painkillers filling the inside of my head with cotton.

Thankfully, he didn't say a damn thing to me. Or to Oz, who snuck glances back all through class but didn't stick around when the bell rang.

I stood for a few minutes at the end of that bookshelf in the library, watching the pop-preppers in the sunshine. Maybe the Harmony kids were in the lunchroom, but I didn't want to push it too far. Just because they had to be nice to me on the bus didn't mean I was really a part of their group.

Travis sat on a concrete bench, with one of Sandy's standard henchwomen—the girl with the ink-black pixie cut—right beside him. I'd've liked it if my hair was as straight as hers, or if it had all Mom's stubborn curl, but I was stuck with watered-down waves.

The pixie girl stuck a straw in his Capri Sun and handed it to him, and he nodded over it. Moving stiffly and with his face all banged up, he kind of looked...Well, he looked like a kid.

Just a stupid, injured kid.

I spread my hand against the plate glass window, glancing over my shoulder. Nothing but the faint noise of Oz and his friends at their usual table. Some beeping from the big desk where the librarian was checking in books, or whatever it was they did all day. I might as well have been on the moon, for all anyone knew. Usually, that's comforting.

Especially when you have a secret.

I closed my eyes. *Breathe deep*, Mom would say, so I did. *Focus*, the books all said, so I did, feeling around for the colored smear that was Travis the Bathroom Bro and his busted nose, his aching ribs, his swollen eyelids.

He was a dirty yellow, a smear of snot. Not the clear kind that a cold day forces out of your nose, or the thickening, opaque hot slickness when you're coming down with something. No, he was old grungy stuff from a sinus infection, clotted and dried to a hard paste. Everything in me cringed away from touching it, even mentally.

Cold glass against my palm, warming by increments. My fingers tensed, digging at the hard slickness. There was a way to do it, I could *feel* it, just like you can feel furniture in a dark room if you go quiet and slow enough. Groping around, getting closer, still closer, the dirty smear that was a kid who...

—staring at Sheila's tits while he sucked at the Capri Sun, sugar-water tart on his tongue and the buzz from the pills swiped from dad's cabinet a pleasant burn all down his back shitty-ass chairs dad gonna sue them that's sweet make 'em pay dad—

My back hit the bookcase and I sagged, sliding down. *Ugh. Ew.* My ass hit the floor and my teeth clicked together, and I was glad I'd put my backpack off to the side because collapsing on it would *not* have been a good time. Shivers raced through me, my teeth chattering. My face hurt, my chest hurt, everything hurt.

That was either amazing or a really bad idea. I couldn't figure out which. I grabbed for my backpack, dragged it over, and managed to fish out the tin box that had been sitting on the wooden counter in the Harmony kitchen just that morning, with my name neatly written on a strip of tape on the lid.

Inside were two peanut-butter-jelly sandwiches on fragrant homemade wheat bread. A small reusable plastic tub full of homemade yogurt. A dense, chewy, homemade granola bar. Nothing to drink, because there was milk at school. And a slip of paper, folded neatly into a butterfly shape.

I was ravenous. My stomach twisted, turned. It made a kind of sense —I was probably burning physical energy trying to do some of this stuff, and food was always a good way to come back down after a drum circle or anything else. That was why the Wiccans always brought a ton of munchies for after their circles and stuff. *Got to feed the magic,* Maya would say with a twinkle in her dark eyes, and Mom would hurry to agree.

Mom loved the Wiccans, she really did, but I often thought she didn't like Maya very much. Which was weird, because they were both pretty, both dark-haired, both graceful, both with invisible talents. It occurred to me now, stuffing half the granola bar in my mouth to quiet the roaring in my stomach, that maybe, just maybe, Mom hadn't liked Maya for the simplest reason of all.

I barely tasted the granola. There was even a little bamboo spoon for the thick, soursweet yogurt. Maybe I was supposed to dip the granola in it, that would have been good. But I chowed down, barely tasting, and realized I didn't know if I'd done any good or not.

That could wait. I was *hungry*. I'd never felt this hole in my insides before, not even when there were bad months and Mom and I were down to rice and beans. It *hurt*.

The paper butterfly was a note. I almost choked on granola, wished I had something more liquid to wash it down with, and tried swallowing again. God, I could not chew fast enough.

Dear Val, it said, in blue ink, nice looping letters. *It may not be what you're used to, but I tried to pack what I thought you'd like. Hope your day goes well.*

It was signed, *Clover.* The 'o' was a little heart.

The shivers went down. I spooned some yogurt, brushed away the granola crumbs from the front of my shirt. Jesus, I'd pigged it. I started feeling warm again. Later in the day the sun would move and come through these windows, and honestly, I didn't really want to move until it did.

I almost licked the container clean. Did I want the sandwiches? I probably did, but now I felt queasy. I made it up to my knees, clutching the small round container in one hand and the bamboo spoon in the other like a cartoon kid caught in the middle of stolen ice cream.

The pop-preppers were still in the quad. Golden light drenched them, lined the girls' ponytails and glinted off the boys' baggy Adidas jackets, super-in this year because some rapper had worn one in a video.

Travis was on the same concrete bench; the pixie-cut girl—Sheila, I knew her name was Sheila now—was gone. He sucked on his empty Capri Sun pouch, pulling in his cheeks, and now that I knew what he thought about soft sticky little fingers of disgust crawled down my back.

His eyelids weren't swollen anymore. He looked a lot better, and while I watched, he stretched a little, wincing as if he expected it to hurt, then looking confused when it didn't.

Was I just imagining it? What had I expected, to look out and see him turning cartwheels? But the bruising on his face had *definitely* gone down, and his nose didn't hurt me to look at anymore.

I collapsed against the bookshelf again, sliding down and pulling my knees up. I tucked the yogurt container back in the tin box and got out one of the sandwiches. My hands shook like branches when a small animal runs up a tree trunk.

Jesus. What did I just do?

If using this...power, whatever it was, came with having to look inside other people's heads, I wasn't so sure I wanted it.

That was a lie. I wanted it badly, and I wasn't giving it up.

I smoothed Clover's note over my knee. Maybe she wasn't so bad. Maybe, just maybe, she could even give me a little advice.

40

BACK FROM THE DEAD

"WE LOOKED ALL OVER FOR YOU." Ingrid's lower lip pooched out as she pulled her shorts up, settling them at her hips with a practiced wiggle.

I slammed my gym locker, spun the dial on my padlock. "Sorry. I just, you know. Didn't want to intrude."

"Intrude?" Gabby, perplexed, squinched up her face as she struggled into her sweatshirt. "What?"

"You're a *Harmony*. Father Jim said so." Ingrid rolled her eyes. "You *can't* intrude."

That was nice of them to say, but we were just staying in that mod until Dad found out about the apartment, right? When we moved out, things would change again. Everything kept changing, and I was having trouble keeping up. If things would just *stop* for a while, I could...what? Go back to eating alone, putting my head down, sitting in my room at night while Dad had his one beer?

They didn't have televisions at Harmony Home. *Or* alcohol. Dad wasn't a heavy drinker, but it was nice to know there wasn't any choice. Not that I thought he ever would, but—God, there I went again, worrying.

"Owen kept wondering if something happened." Gabby shook her hair free. Blonde curls framed her face. "I think he's getting a *thing*."

Maybe she didn't know. But I'd seen Ingrid's face around Owen. He might be nice enough, sure, but Ingrid was—at least provisionally, for the moment—my friend. "Preacher's kids are always trouble." There, that was the right tone. Light, careless, but underneath it, the signal. *I know he's taken.*

They exchanged a look, both of them wearing identical expressions, and I wondered if I'd said it the wrong way.

"Father's not a *preacher*," Gabby said, scandalized.

"She doesn't know." Ingrid's legs, bare and smooth, were just as pale as the rest of her. Her skin looked soft enough to dip a finger into, like whipped cream.

"Priest?" I hazarded, tucking Mom's necklace under my T-shirt collar. "I mean, *Father* and all. Isn't that the right word?"

"The right word is *Father*." Ingrid's smile was forgiving, though. My signal must have been decoded. She propped her foot on the squeaky, shuddering wooden bench and bent to tie her sneaker. Locker doors slammed all around us, the noise reaching a feverish pitch rivaled only by a stadium crowd. "He used to be in a church, but he left when he found out they were all full of shit."

"That's not all." Gabby shut the locker she shared with Ingrid, carefully instead of slamming. "He came back from the dead."

The car accident. Huh. I played dumb. "Seriously?"

"Yeah. There was an accident. He was dead for, I don't know, five minutes."

"Three," Ingrid corrected. "And there was no brain damage or anything. They shocked him but he didn't come back, and they were about to shock him again when his heart started on its own."

"Really?" That wasn't *quite* what the news report said. *Resuscitated* was the word used, in black-and-white ink. There weren't any details, though. The Harmonies probably knew the whole story better than a newspaper would. "That's kind of amazing."

"Yeah, and when he went back to his church to tell them what he saw while he was, you know, *dead*, they told him he was crazy." Ingrid's dark eyes glittered hotly at the insult. "Church people. They're always like that."

"Her dad used to be a Jehovah's Witness," Gabby chimed in. Everyone was draining from the locker room. "She didn't even have a birthday party until they came to the old place in California."

I could believe it. Her dad looked downright military except for his hair, and from what I heard of the Witnesses, they were pretty thou-shalt-obey. Whenever they came to the door, Mom liked to walk around without her shirt on, and encouraged me to do the same.

It worked, more often than not.

Greeman was at the locker room door, chanting her usual *Come on ladies, pick it up, let's go.*

"Mom threatened to leave Dad, so he came with her." Ingrid slipped her arm through mine. "He says it was the best decision ever. Because really, nobody else would marry him, he's so gummed-up."

"Gummed up?" I let Ingrid pull me along. Greeman waved us through the door, for once not saying a word about my mother's necklace. Maybe she was just too harried to notice.

"He *thinks* about things. Father says if you do too much, you end up paralyzed and you sink like rotten fish food." She made a face. "Look, there's Gibson."

Sandy was about halfway through the gym doors, balanced precariously on crutches. Her right foot was in a cast, and her friends had decorated it with glitter and scribbles. There wasn't a clear spot on it, but right now, she was all alone while she tried to hip-check one of the heavy doors to keep it open.

"Serves her right," Gabby muttered.

I could have sped up, maybe. Pulled free of Ingrid and gone to hold open the door for Sandy's painted, ponytailed self. Her blue fingernail polish was more chipped than usual, and just looking at her made my armpits ache as if something had been jammed into them like the crutches she wobbled on. My back twinged too, and my ankle. I took a deep breath.

She finally made it through the doors. Gabby giggled, a short nasty sound.

I let Gabby take my other arm, and Ingrid set our pace. She began to hum, so did Gabby, and I didn't have to do anything but go along. Greeman let Sandy sit on the bleachers while we played volleyball, and every time I glanced over, I couldn't help but think she looked a little lonely.

Later that night, on the bed in the tiny bedroom because Dad told me outright he wanted the futon in the mod, it kind of bothered me.

But I turned over, thinking of how she'd pushed me out on the track, and went to sleep.

41

HIS RELIEF OR MINE

THE STRAP on my embroidered Tibetan backpack finally gave out on a Wednesday afternoon, right as I was jumping off the last bus step. One second the weight was there, the next it was gone, and I might have staggered sideways from the sudden release if Owen hadn't grabbed my arm with one hand and my backpack with the other. He made a sort of trilling sound while he did it, too, not quite a whistle but not a note either. He pulled me out of the way and Kellan grabbed my French book, which had hit the steps with a dull thud. Ben hopped lithely down after him, shaking his dark hair back, and grinned at me.

"Oh, no." Ingrid was immediately there too, concern floating off her in waves. "You okay?"

The bus door shut—I got the idea the driver, with his talk radio and his buzzcut, didn't like the Harmony kids—and it chugged away on a cloud of diesel, spewing roadside gravel. He didn't even wait for us to cross Cold Creek Road like he should have. Harmony was the last stop, of course, but he always spun out like he had somewhere important to be.

"Shit." I grabbed my backpack, staring at the damage. It was only a matter of time, sure, it wasn't built to handle the textbook load I'd been putting it under. It wasn't even the stitching coming loose, which I could fix with a little luck and a sewing machine. Instead, the left strap had broken clean through, and I hadn't even noticed it was fraying, I'd been so worried about the seam. "Sonofabitching shit*fuck.*"

"Wow." Ben's eyebrows were all the way up, his chocolate skin gleaming. "Don't hold back, Val. Tell us how you *really* feel."

It shouldn't have irritated me. And yeah, I'd just cussed in front of a bunch of *church* kids, even if Ingrid and Gabby said it wasn't really like that. If they got together on Sundays, it was church, goddammit, and why the fuck had I kept using this backpack anyway? It wasn't fair, I'd been stupid, I should have gotten another bag or something, and now it was ruined.

Redheaded Amy grabbed my French book, and tapped Ben lightly on the shoulder. "Like *you* don't have a filthy mouth, *Benjamin.*"

"Fuck if I do." Ben's hair bobbed as he shook his head. He was developing dreads, and they looked good. He had the right face for them, and the new silver cross at his breastbone glittered high and sharp in the spring sunshine.

I stared at the strap, cradling the rest of the backpack like a baby. God *damn* it. I could maybe patch it, but it would be fragile afterward. The bright colors blurred, and I took a deep breath. Another one.

It didn't work. For some reason, the egg in my chest was picking now to get unstable. Cracking like a thin blue shell, a sharp, awful beak poking from the inside, taptaptap. Right in time to my heartbeat, and a hot droplet slid down my cheek.

"Oh, shit," Ingrid breathed. "Oh, honey, what's wrong?"

Everything, I wanted to say. *Every single fucking thing in the whole wide world.*

"Jesus." Owen's shoulder hit mine. "She just changed schools and her house burned down, that's what's wrong."

"I'm fine," I croaked, but nobody listened. They crowded around me, so tight I could barely breathe. Another hot droplet slid down my *other* cheek, and it was official: I was crying like a stupid kid on the side of a country road with a bunch of church kids all around.

Ingrid hugged me. Owen put his arms over hers. The others group-hugged, putting me at the center of a breathing lump of kids. I should have been kicking and biting to get out from underneath, I should have jabbed Owen with one elbow, Ingrid with the other, and started screaming at them to leave me the fuck alone.

Someone began to hum. My chin dropped forward, I couldn't get my arms up to bury my face in my backpack. A gulping, shuddering sob rocked me sideways into Owen. His arms tightened, and he rested his chin atop my head. On my other side, Ingrid's breath was warm in my ear. *Let it out*, she crooned, and *it's okay, we're here*, and *shhhh, it's all right.*

I cried until I was a limp rag, and nobody got impatient or told me to loosen up or anything. They just stood there, on the side of the road, arms interlaced and that music of theirs, voices rising and falling in lullaby cadence, somehow dissolving the jagged edges of the stony shell in my chest.

"You don't have to." I was light-headed, and whoever had produced tissues from their backpack was *not* going to get any of them back. The sunshine was butter-yellow, and it lay over Harmony Home like a gift. Someone was laughing in a mod two doors down, and there were kids playing near the garden boxes. High thin sounds of glee, like elementary recess bursting out of school doors, punctuated the drowsy humming of bees awake after cold winter, pollen packed around every leg. Doors and windows were open everywhere, and the breeze was too warm for a jacket.

"What if I want to?" Owen's arms were full of my backpack and my French textbook. *I'll walk you home*, he'd said, and I tried to tell him no, especially with Ingrid right there.

He didn't listen. And she trudged away towards the kitchen with her head down, Gabby, Amy, and Beth trailing mystified in her wake.

"You shouldn't." My cheeks were hot. I'd just had a fucking breakdown in front of all those kids. God. *Way to go, Val.* Plus I'd probably pissed Ingrid off, and I didn't want to. "Look, you should go to the kitchen."

"I'll drop by there later." He had to lengthen his stride to keep up with me. "Jesus, did I do something wrong?"

Oh, for God's sake. "Look, I just had a crying meltdown in front of total strangers, and Ingrid *likes* you, okay?" As if he didn't know. He *had* to know. "Don't blow her off. She's nice."

"We're not strangers." His mouth pulled down at the corners, and chestnut streaks in his dark hair caught the light. Guys like him always have the best hair, just a little bit of a wave so it doesn't lay flat. Mine just tangled all over everything, snarling into a mess even with the Harmony braids doing their best. "And Ingrid's not—"

"She's nice, and she was here before me, and I don't want her upset." I grabbed for my backpack. Really, it wasn't his fault, and I was being a bitch, but I didn't care. There wasn't a whole lot I cared about at the moment, other than splashing some cold water on my face and closing a door against the rest of the world.

"She's not interested in *me*, she's interested in—" Owen began, and I yanked on my backpack. He didn't let go, so that was how Dad opened the mod's door and found us.

He loomed at the top of the steps, bright blue eyes narrowing and turning paler at the same time. His cheeks were rough with stubble.

I tugged on my backpack again, and Owen let it go. He kept my French textbook, though, and smiled tentatively. "Hi, Mr Smith."

At least he didn't call Dad *Brother Earl.*

"Owen, right?" Dad didn't return the smile. His broad, friendly face stayed stony, even when he looked at me. "Hey, dumplin'. You all right?"

No. "Yeah." I was pretty sure I didn't *look* all right, not by a long shot. "My backpack broke, that's all. It's been a day."

"Oh." Dad studied me, and I had the uncomfortable thought that he was probably guessing a lot more than I wanted, though probably not about me feeling other people's injuries and fixing them. No, he was probably seeing the awkward way Owen held my backpack, and the way my eyes and nose were red, and the discomfort pouring off two kids in front of a big adult.

Dad nodded, pursing his lips slightly. "Your mom got you that backpack, didn't she." It wasn't a question.

I winced. "Yeah." *Awkward.* "Thanks, Owen. I've got it."

He let go of bright Tibetan embroidery, and the backpack fell into my hands. "Sure." The cross at his throat gleamed. "I'll bring you snack from the kitchen."

"No, that's okay, I—" I was too late, he'd already stepped away, still holding my French book.

"If that's okay?" he said, and for some reason, that made Dad's expression soften.

I am standing right here. Why was he asking *Dad*, for God's sake? "You don't have to—"

"That'll be fine," Dad said, and Owen headed back down the gravel path, head up, his step long and loose. "Well, dumplin'. Come on in."

Nobody was going to listen to me, so I stamped up the steps. The mod smelled better now, lived in. Like someone had been breathing there for a while. "Dammit." I toed the door to the small bedroom open, threw my stupid backpack on the bed, and leaned against the doorway to catch my breath.

"Nice boy." Dad closed the front door. "I think he likes you."

"I think he's got a case of new girl." I closed my eyes. My cheeks were chapped, my nose was raw, used tissues were balled up in my fist and shoved into the top of my backpack, and the stupidest thing of all was that I felt like fucking crying *again.* I'd been doing so well keeping everything buckled down. "It's the same every school, some guys think the fresh meat's the best."

Silence. Total, utter, electric silence, as if I'd shouted at him. *Crap. Did I just say that?*

When Dad finally said something, it was quiet, like talking to himself. "I keep forgetting you're not little anymore."

"I wish I was." My throat was full. "Everything's wrong. No, not everything. Just mostly everything."

"Dumplin'..." The floor creaked as he moved. Why was he even home? Didn't he have work today? "Valentine." Did he have something in his throat too? "You know why we named you that?"

Jesus. "No." *What the fuck does it matter?* Val was good enough, it was unisex, and it kept me from getting teased *too* badly.

His big hands closed around my shoulders. He pulled me into a hug, and it was what I'd been needing all damn day without knowing it. For a few seconds I was five years old again, and the entire world could just go away because a parent had me and they were big enough to make everything, even God, back off. He even *smelled* the same—his aftershave in the funny bottle with the sailing ship on front, the slightly oily tinge of a guy who liked fried food, the warm breath of *Dad* and *safe* and *it's okay.*

"Because you were a big old red-heart present." His voice rumbled against my cheekbone. "Our baby girl."

It should have been corny. It should have made me roll my eyes. Instead, it hurt my chest, but in a good way. Not like something sharp-clawed trying to tap its way out, but a sort of relief like popping a zit or a blister. We stood like that for a little while, Dad stroking my hair, and afterward, when I washed my face and sat down on the futon, he told me that he'd talked to Father Jim.

"Figure I can save up for a house if we stay here a while," he said, diffidently. "Even if I shift to part time to be home for you. I'll work on their vans, too. Damn things need it."

It sounded good to me. A real house, with windows and doors

that stayed shut. Still, part-time? That was a serious move. I opened my mouth to say so, but he wasn't finished.

But, Dad said, he didn't want to stay here if I didn't like it. "They're good people. But a little funny."

Oh, man, you don't even know. I absorbed this, and heard the kids playing outside. There were footsteps on the gravel path, and I'd already made up my mind by the time Owen knocked on our door with a plate of brownies, my French book, and Ingrid right behind him.

"It's okay with me." My face felt funny after all the crying, and if I looked hard, I could see the cactuses in their rack under the window —they didn't seem to have suffered from smoke or firehose—glowing green in the sun, and Dad's slow bluish whirl of worry, heavy responsibility, and a heaping helping of a big, clear, clean feeling I didn't know what to name. "As long as we're together."

I couldn't tell whether it was his relief, or mine, but it sure felt better than the rest of that day. So I figured it didn't matter.

42

LIGHTS GOING ON

ANY RESPITE from the Bathroom Bros of the world is short-lived. I knew that, I'd grown up knowing it. Somehow I thought it wouldn't apply now that I belonged somewhere. Not with the stoners, where I hung out but wasn't part of the pack, or the gamers, who were all over stuff you needed an internet connection to play nowadays, or the *other* gamers, D&D or cardboys you had to spend a whole school year with before they opened up. I walked in with the Harmony kids, I sat with them at lunch, but there were whole chunks of the day none of them were in my classes.

Like, for example, Shieldman's.

I bent my head over the textbook while she droned on about the Vietnam War. Her cardigan today was pretty cool, an orange-yellow-red yarn, autumn flame. Wrong season, but maybe she liked it. I wondered how she'd gotten into teaching. How did *anyone* end up thinking it was a good idea to spend any more time in a high school than was absolutely necessary? Elementary teachers seemed to like little kids, but somewhere in middle school kids became teenagers, and that means a pile of hormones, rage, and Bathroom Bros just when the school schedule loosens up. You could get away with a lot when you were changing classes several times a day. The whole thing was a horrible shitshow from the beginning, and teachers like Shieldman actually *chose* to plunge into it.

Weird.

I stared at a map in the textbook. Vietnam. Some of the old hippies at fairs and gatherings still talked about it. Protests and scars, helicopters and jellied gasoline—

Something hit my shoulder. "Hey." A whisper. "Hey, Vaaaaaaal."

It was a paperclip. Again. Where was he *finding* them, for God's sake? And why the fuck was he fixated on me?

For a second I'd thought he suspected I'd done something to make his chair collapse last week, but then I figured out, it wasn't that. It was just that he'd been embarrassed, though I wondered how far that word could go for any pop-prepper. They didn't seem to have a hell of a lot of shame.

But no, I decided, he was pissed because the last time he'd been trying to get my attention, he looked like an idiot. Even if he knew I had nothing to do with it, *especially* if he knew I had nothing to do with it, he had a wounded pride.

The fact that I *had* done something was hilarious but not really applicable, and didn't help when he was tossing shit at me.

"Vaaaaaal. Lesbo hippie giiiiiirl."

The next paperclip hit my hair. I thought about turning around again, trying to make something happen. Collapse his chair, again? I didn't even know how I'd done it the first time. And there was the attendant risk of getting a blast of what he was thinking, if thinking was the right word.

I shuddered, trying to keep the movement to a minimum so he didn't think he'd gotten a reaction. I could hold out until lunch. I'd done it before.

A slight scraping. The desks in here had all been rearranged, and he'd gotten a squeaky one. Figured. I glanced at the clock over the door. God, lunch was right around the corner. Why wouldn't the bell ring? Tick, tock, tick, tock. Stealthy movement behind me. I didn't even want to look at him, it would only make it worse, but my back crawled with the idea that he was sneaking up on me.

"Travis," Shieldman snapped. "What are you doing?"

It was such a change from her usual sleepy delivery I jumped, and half the class did too. I know Oz jerked in his seat, probably because he was writing furiously on a D&D character sheet instead of taking notes.

"I uh—" Yeah, he was *right* behind me, the creeper. I twisted in my seat and glared at him. The ghost-remains of bruises puffed out his face, and he actually took a step back. "I, uh, it's time for lunch."

"When the bell rings, and not a moment before. Sit *down*." Her hands knotted up, knuckles pressing through papery skin. Even an old woman can get pissed off, I guess.

Good for you. I wished I could say it. But just then the chimes sounded, and Shieldman's assertion of authority subsided in a few giggles from the pop-prepper girls who maybe found Travis's troglodyte ass charming or something. Or they just didn't want him to start picking on *them*. Nervous laughter's one way to defuse a ticking male; every woman, straight or not, knows that.

I jammed my textbook into the new backpack—a red Eastpak with plenty of room and more pockets than I'd ever need. It was heavy, but the straps were padded, and it had just appeared in our mod after dinner the evening my Tibetan one broke. It was like the school supplies fairy had visited. One of the older Harmony women —Anne, who had a ferocious gray braid hanging down her back, wicked sparkling eyes, and a high proud nose—said she could patch the strap on the old one for me, too. Things just got *done* there. If you saw someone needed something, or there was something that needed doing and you were passing by, you just helped out. Going from that to the feeding frenzy of school was...weird.

Maybe that's why they sang, moving through the halls. To cushion the shock.

There's a fine art to moving with a crowd to get out of a classroom, and I almost made it, especially since Shieldman hissed, "Travis, you're staying after."

I got out into the hall and sighed with relief, joining the flow to the right. The shortest way to the lunchroom, and maybe I'd even duck into a bathroom. I mean, normally I don't pee at school, but maybe it was time.

"Hey, lesbo girl." Travis skidded to a stop next to me. He got too close, and I flinched aside into the lockers, banging my shoulder a good one. "Where you goin'?"

Jesus fucking Christ, leave me alone. He'd just ignored Shieldman bigtime. "Leave me alone." It was probably the worst thing to say, because he laughed. A couple kids glanced nervously at us, but everyone was too intent on lunch, and everything inside me shrank down to the size of a pin. Roaring filled my ears, and I didn't hear what he said because he *smelled*. Some kind of body spray, he'd damn near bathed in it, and it reminded me of muffled sounds behind thin walls in so many places Mom and I lived. First there was the itchy sense of a thunderstorm, then came the yelling, and sooner or later there were the other sounds, an openhanded smack against a cheek, a punch sinking into flesh, and Mom would hug me so tight but nothing blocked it out.

All of that filled my head in milliseconds. My foot came up on its own; I kicked him in the shin.

Hard.

"Ow!" He barked, a surprised dog, and my shoulder hit the lockers again because I felt the blow in my own left leg. Steel toes are nothing to mess with. "Bitch!"

I slid to the side, figuring I could wriggle away, and hit someone else. They didn't move, just stood there, and all the noise and the static fell away. It was *quiet* all of a sudden.

The pain vanished, too.

"Hi, Val." Owen's boots planted themselves solidly against blue-flecked, scuffed linoleum. He looked down at Travis, almost a full head taller, and his faint smile wasn't an expression I'd seen on him before. "Miller."

Travis straightened. He'd gone cheese-colored, and the ghost-bruises on his face stood out starkly. "Harrison."

"*TRAVIS MILLER!*" Mrs Shieldman was in her classroom door, and she did *not* look happy. "I've called Security, and you *are busted*."

"Wow." The word just fell out of my mouth.

Owen's arm was somehow over my shoulders. "I thought I'd walk you to lunch." That tiny smile didn't change. "See you, Miller."

"Anytime, Harrison," Travis sneered.

Owen didn't let go of me all the way down the hall. We passed the heavyset Security guy, the one with glasses and an attitude, and Owen's muffled laugh turned clearly audible once we hit the door and the hallway between all the science classrooms. "What an asshole. *Anytime.* Jesus."

The world put itself solidly underneath me again. Why had I frozen like that? Jesus. I tried to shake away from his arm. "Great. Now he'll be even *more* of an asshole during class."

"Has he been messing with you?" Owen's hand was right where I'd banged into the lockers. I could already feel the bruise rising. "Val?"

"Why do you care?" There was a better question, though. "Hey. Wait a minute. Stop."

I stepped aside, he followed, and again I had the lockers on one side and a boy on the other. This time, though, it didn't feel like being trapped, probably because Owen let go of me. He wasn't quite out of my personal space, but at least that awful, devouring noise in my ears didn't come back.

"Why do you think I care?" He stared at a point just over my head, and his Adam's apple bobbed as he swallowed. Today his chambray shirt was a little big on him, but with the sleeves rolled up and his tanned forearms exposed, it looked like planned looseness. "Am I not allowed to like you, or something? Ingrid's not my type."

"You have a type?" Not like I wanted to know, but it got the conversation moving, right?

"Non-tattletales." His forehead knotted up. "She tells Father everything, all right? So stop it. I'm allowed to like who I like."

"Good for you." I didn't bother explaining that maybe *I* wasn't, not if I wanted the Harmony girls to like *me*. But there were other fish to fry, like Mom would have said. "Listen. I've noticed that when you..." *How do I say this without sounding like an idiot?* "When you're right there, it hurts less."

"What hurts..." Realization spread over his face. He was more than passably cute, I decided. Even though it didn't do me any good, I could still appreciate. Artistically, and all that. "Oh, yeah, that. Sarah says that too."

"She does?" Finally, I was getting some answers. "So she does the same thing I do?"

"I guess so? She says yours is bigger, though." He glanced down at me, fixed his gaze back up above my head as if there was something stuck up there. "She fixes things. Mostly small animals. Father wants her to practice, but she says it hurts to try larger stuff."

I'd gone from being harassed to talking about weird psychic powers. My knees were a little gooshy. At the same time, the relief was so deep it filled up my head with helium or something.

I wasn't crazy.

I mean, I'd pretty much known I wasn't, but it was so good to get independent verification. Even if I'd seen him break Sandy Gibson's ankle, that still could have been coincidence. You could convince yourself of a lot when you *wanted* to believe, even something cuckoo crazypants.

"Did she push your button?" What a thing to ask someone. "Is that what it's called?"

"It's what she calls it." Owen kept looking up over my head. That leather thong was really too short for his neck, it looked like it choked him. "Sort of. It was there, but she made it stronger. All the way down, instead of a quarter or less."

"Did it hurt?" The flood of kids going to lunch had slowed to a trickle. The hall filled with the rustling hush of school, classroom doors closed like disapproving mouths.

"Nope." He still kept his gaze fixed at some point over my head, like he couldn't quite believe he was talking about weirdo psychic stuff in a school hallway either. "Just felt funny, like lights going on inside me."

"Cool." My arm hurt. I rubbed at it. Maybe I could fix it? That would be a good experiment.

"Val." His chin tipped back down, and he fixed me with a glare. "Has Miller been messing with you?"

Miller? Oh yeah, Travis. "Just petty shit. It's nothing."

"He'll stop." Owen's eyes lightened a little. "Come on, let's get to lunch. The others will think we're making out."

Great. "Owen, for God's sake—"

Maddeningly, he turned away and set off. I had to hurry to keep up. Go figure, when he was dragging me I wanted to get away, but now I had so many other questions to ask him, he didn't even slow down.

He was quiet all during lunch, and the Harmony kids were quieter than usual on the bus without him participating, just humming instead of singing. Ingrid kept giving me funny sideways looks, but she didn't say anything.

43

WHAT THEY SHOULD

"IT MUST BE ROUGH." Clover tipped her head back while I ran the comb through half her hair, gathering it up as gently as I could. "Everything's all new for you."

I wasn't sure I'd be able to do some of the more complex Harmony braids but she said it didn't matter, she just wanted two and she could wrap them up. I could do a French braid in my sleep, they're super easy. Cross-legged on the futon, I went to work with a comb. Her hair was less thick than Mom's, and less curly, more wavy like mine. Mom wouldn't have wanted me fidgeting with her head, but Clover seemed content to sit on the mod's floor, humming a little while I worked.

"Yeah," I said, finally. "New school, new house, new everything." Even though it technically wasn't a house. A real house had a kitchen, right?

"Your father's a little worried." She said it very softly, an open invitation. Something about the way the sentence lifted at the end, almost questioning, told me she was ready to drop it if I didn't want to talk about it.

I appreciated the space. And I also appreciated that there was none of that heatshimmer on her right now. She wasn't trying to push. I'd been kind of an asshole to her, I guess. Maybe it was time to change that. "He thinks I need a therapist."

"Do you?" She had her knees up, her skirt spread over them, her back against the futon frame.

It was kind of gratifying to have an adult actually ask my opinion, really. "Just one more person to keep secrets from." I began braiding on her right side, carefully. The mod door was open; sunshine, fresh air, distant singing stepped in to take a peek every now and again, but mostly just leaving us in peace.

Clover left a little space in front of her reply, too. "We all have secrets." Giving me room.

No shit. "Not like this." Would she catch my drift? She had to know, really. If she came clean about it, maybe I could trust her.

Maybe.

"You mean about your gifts."

I decided she didn't mean my ability to tap dance, so to speak. "Gifts." Well, that was an opening. "Like yours, right?"

"Yes." She didn't try to act surprised. I liked that, adults who don't treat you like you're stupid are super rare.

"Have you always had...that thing you do?" I took a deep breath. Kept going, making sure the hair was nice and smooth. It's harder with curls, they have their own damn idea where they're going to go, and you don't want to manhandle where you can just politely corral. "Like, you made that woman at the soup kitchen stop using. Right?"

"You're really observant." She made a little movement, stopping the nod halfway, realizing I was holding her hair. "I haven't always, no. Father Jim says it's a gift from God, a blessing." Her back touched my knees—the futon, folded up, was pretty much the only place to sit other than the floor.

So Father Jim knew about all this, too. I'd guessed, but it was kind of nice to get confirmation. "What do you think?"

She shrugged. I kept braiding in bits from each side. It looked nice. "I don't think *blessing* is the word I'd use. But if Father Jim says it, it must be so."

"Do you really think that? About him?" I'd just gotten to the part where I had to be careful to pull the sides just right, so it wouldn't floof out and look ridiculous.

"He's been right about everything else so far." She pulled her knees up a little further, carefully not moving the rest of her body, and folded her arms atop them. "I didn't believe in anything, really. We grew up in a commune, but nobody there was...well, it was just like everywhere else."

Now *that* was fascinating. I'd pretty much suspected, though. "So all this, living together and stuff, you've done it before."

"My mother was always looking for something." Clover sighed. "Some new thing that would make everything else make sense."

"Mine too." It didn't hurt to say it. It was just uncomfortable, like a scratch-scabbed mosquito bite, but inside me instead of on the skin. Then it occurred to me that it might be totally awkward for Clover to hear about Mom, seeing as how she was interested in my dad. "She was really special, but the straights wouldn't leave her alone."

"Every mom is special."

A fucking cliché. A sudden, vengeful thought of kicking her roared through me. Instead, I kept braiding, steadily. She was just being *nice*, goddammit. Why was I such a bitch? "No, I mean, she could do things. Like you, and...like Owen."

"So you know about Owen." She didn't sound surprised.

Relief filled my chest, sharp and precise. "I can see it."

"What does it look like?"

"Like air over pavement on a hot day."

"Oh, ripples. That's so cool." She really did sound impressed. "What did your mother do?"

"Well, she could see auras. And she read tarot cards." Put like that, it seemed pretty tame next to moving things with your *mind*, you know. Or getting someone to stop taking drugs. "She called me her starchild."

"That's beautiful." A smile filled Clover's voice. Maybe being around people singing all the time made you sensitive to tone and inflection, let you hear the lilt of a bright feeling. "She must have known you were special."

Not really. "I didn't get any of it, though. I handled the money at the fairs and stuff, and at the bookstore. She wasn't good with that sort of stuff. I'm the practical one."

"Huh." Clover made a thoughtful sound. "You took care of her."

"Yeah." *Well, what else could I do?*

"My mom was like that too." Clover spaced her words out carefully. "It's not how it's supposed to work. They're supposed to take care of *us*, not the other way 'round."

Getting down to the bottom, where it's just braiding and you don't have to gather in little bits from the sides anymore, makes it easier. I used a blue elastic to tie it off—she didn't even have split ends. She tilted her head slightly so I could do the left side. I said nothing. Half of me was shaking with the urge to yank on her hair and say *don't talk about my mother that way.*

The other half was guiltily glad someone had said it. Another *adult* had said it. Articulated, that was the word. You could use it for saying a word out loud or for a joint moving the way it should, and I remembered being happy in a deeply specific way seeing it on an English quiz in ninth grade. It was good to find the right word, the right number, the right anything.

When I was sure I could talk without my voice shaking like a little kid's, I focused on the braid on her other side, shaping up nice and even. "So what do you do? With your...gift, thing, whatever."

"I help people do what they know they should." She scratched at her elbow through her thin green cardigan, carefully not moving her head. Like a ballet dancer. "Like Hannah. She knows she should leave the needle alone. I just...you know, help her."

"Huh." The only problem I could see with that was, who really knows what they *should* do all the time? "Do you ever make people do what they don't want to?"

"I just make them do what they know they should." Her shoulders had tensed up a bit. "That's the easiest way to explain it. What do *you* do?"

Now I felt like an idiot, because it was hard to put into words. "I, uh, see colors around things. Auras. I feel where people are hurting. It sucks." It was a huge relief; she wasn't going to call me crazy or start laughing at me. I took a deep breath. Some of the weight on me, pressing down on shoulders and everything else, slid away, and for a few seconds even the sunshine felt brighter. "Plus, there's this thing. I put my hands on them and they get better."

"Faith healing." She began to nod, then froze again. "Whoops, sorry."

"Maybe just healing." My fingers had their rhythm now, and went on without me. "I was thinking of getting some crystals and seeing if that helps make it less, you know. It hurts when I'm around hurt people." Doing the nervous-talking thing again. I picked up the comb instead, got everything nice and straightened out.

"That's smart." No hint of patronizing in the words. "And you haven't told anyone else, have you."

"What, and get called crazy?"

"You're not crazy." She even sounded like she knew from crazy, as Mom would have said. "You're special. There's a difference."

I didn't know quite what to say to that, so I shut up and finished braiding. When it was done, I watched from the door of the teensy bathroom as she pinned the braids up in back, and smiled at me in the mirror. It looked nice on her, I had to admit. A little less trying-to-be-young. More like a crown, and the *Queen Clover* joke made sense. It was in the way she held her herself, the way her shoulders stayed back and her toes pointed slightly outward like a dancer's but not, you know, *planned.*

Natural grace. I wondered if I could copy it.

"Not quite Harmony style," I said, then felt like an idiot. "I mean, it looks good." I ran my fingers over the comb's plastic teeth. One was snagged. Not quite broken, but not like the others.

"And all thanks to you." She grinned, her dark gaze meeting mine in the mirror. Her eyes weren't blue, but for a second she almost, *almost* looked like Mom. "Two beautiful ladies in one mirror. You want to help in the kitchen a bit?"

Funny thing, I did.

4 4

COLORS

Inside the Pavilion, with the doors closed and people waiting out in the rosy hush just after Sunday dawn, Father Jim spread his arms slightly and smiled down at everyone in the chairs. "A bright blessed Sunday to you, brothers, sisters, children."

"Amen," a couple of the older Harmonies murmured. Some in the back hummed, softly, a layered counterpoint to Father Jim's deep round voice.

Normally that would have made me crack a smile. But I was sitting in the front row next to Dad, and that close to the stage, with that warmth Father Jim put out, it didn't seem funny at all. Expectant, and agreeing, instead.

"Now, today's a joyous day. It's always a joyous day when we add more voices to the chorus." It didn't look like Father Jim felt the chill. He must have had more than one of those embroidered dashikis. No black coat today, but the same worn jeans and boots.

The humming hushed. I pulled my hands up inside the sleeves of Mom's old velvet coat. My fingers curled in, cold and prickling, fingernails digging. I wasn't biting them all the way down anymore. The Harmony girls generally didn't wear nail polish. I wondered if

I even wanted to; I used to think red would be a wicked good choice.

"Amen." This time more of them said it.

Owen sat on my right. His chair was too close, and his elbow kept touching my arm. Ingrid was a few rows back, and I wished Clover hadn't pointed me to this plain-backed wooden chair. It was like sitting in the front of class—nowhere else to look, nothing to do, a pair of eyes and ears pointed inescapably at authority. Sarah slumped on Owen's other side, swinging her scuffed maryjanes under a yellow-flowered skirt she probably had to be talked into wearing and looking monumentally bored as only an eight-year-old can manage.

Father Jim went on for a little bit, about how Harmony was a chorus and we all had our parts. Behind him on the stage, a cafeteria table stood in front of the drums, next to Owen's piano. Mother Carole busy behind it. Little paper cups, and a tray holding sugar cubes. She dropped a cube in each cup, with methodical grace and a pair of tiny tongs. *Sweet with the bitter*, Father Jim said, *to remind us we're made in the image.*

That was probably the beginning of the religious bit, so I quit listening, trying to count the cups instead. There were a lot of them. It was a pretty tame way to take Communion, but sugar was definitely better than Catholic crackers. I knew all about the host and the wine and shit; Mom called herself a recovering Catholic.

Had called herself that. I sank down a little in my chair. I kept getting those little jolts. I'd see something I knew she'd like, or think something I had to tell her, and inside me everything would jump a little bit and thud down, landing brick-heavy. Little internal earthquakes, the hole inside me where she used to be getting wider and deeper.

"—Brother Earl," Father Jim said, and I blinked, everything coming into focus. "Sister Clover, will you bring him forward?"

Dad looked even taller next to her. If I squinted, with her long dark hair and her subdued green-and-grey skirt, Clover looked a bit like Mom. Just a little, though. Dad took short steps so she didn't have to hurry, and Owen's elbow touched mine again. Father Jim beamed down at Dad; Mother Carole shuffled up behind her husband with a wooden tray full of those little paper cups.

Did they recycle them afterward? Did Mother Carole count out how many they'd need? Organizing something like that was a job and a half, especially at five a.m.

Father Jim took one of the paper cups. "Welcome to Harmony, Brother Earl. We hope you'll stay and sing awhile with us."

"Yessir, Father Jim." Dad ducked his head a little, his hand rising like he was going to touch a hatbrim. There was a general movement —people getting up, moving for the two aisles between arcs of chairs.

Father Jim said something, too low for me to hear. Dad nodded, and Father Jim took two tiny paper cups, lifted them up, then tipped the contents of one into Clover's mouth. He tipped the other into Dad's, and Owen leaned over to whisper.

"It's *soma*." His breath touched my hair, my ear, my cheek. "Fruit of good and evil. Like in Eden."

It's sugar. Jeez. I didn't know any better though, not then. The Catholics called their crackers-and-wine bits of an actual body, which was revolting when you thought about it but made perfect sense to them; this was, at least, a little less gross.

All the adults and the older kids lined up. Each time it was the same, Father Jim lifting the cup briefly, tipping it into a Harmony member's mouth.

"Should I get up?" I whispered.

Owen shook his head. "Not this time, Father said."

So they'd talked about me, even briefly. Another jolt went through me. I was shaking all the time these days, on the inside where nobody could see.

After they got their sugar cube, they stepped to the sides and went back to their seats. The kids got just the same as the adults, except the few toddlers and Sarah. Ingrid's sister Astrid, a thin, nervous middle-school version of Ingrid with a defiant set to her black-lipsticked mouth, almost didn't take hers, but her parents prodded her from either side, and Father Jim just kept smiling. I heard Astrid snuck in makeup and sometimes tried to get out of the compound at night.

Where would she go, really? Hitchhike into town?

Clover settled next to me with a sigh and a slow, quiet smile. She reached over and took my left hand, squeezed it gently.

I let her. She began to hum, and the rest of them too.

At first I thought it was just the body heat, everyone up and moving around. It got warm, but not in the prickle-steaming sweaty way of everyone breathing. Instead, it was like a bath, I guess? A heavy liquid, just the right temperature to work into aching muscles, warm enough you can't tell where your skin ends and the water begins. Clover's humming became singing, rising and falling while she breathed; I peered around her at Dad, who wore a set, determined expression. His eyes looked too dark, because his pupils had expanded, and he stared at Father Jim. His big hands closed gently around Clover's small left hand, and while I watched, a smile flickered across her face and spread to his.

Weird.

Owen's fingers brushed the back of my hand. More music, angels harmonizing, men's voices low and insistent, women's lapping like waves, occasionally soaring to make the entire pavilion vibrate.

That's when they started to glow.

Father Jim, up on the stage, spread his arms. Mother Carole perched on a stool a little to one side, swaying slightly with the music. I couldn't tell if she was humming or not, and a low reddish glow lit up her edges. I craned my neck, staring in wonder as the Harmony people lit up like the cactuses. Bigger smears of color—orange, blue, yellow, greenish, tomato-red, some swirling with two colors not fighting for dominance but just sharing, swirling back and forth like food coloring dropped into water. Most of them were low-watt, just barely there. But a few...

Clover was bright deep yellow like sunshine, a strong steady glow. Owen was a slow-moving vortex of red, gold, orange—fire colors, but no smoke. Sarah glittered, a blue gleam ragged at the edges. Tom—Gabby's dad—was yellow too, but a different shade, banana instead of sun. Cass was blue, a regimented box instead of a smear. Amy was green, a light springtime new-leaf color. Kellan and Wolf had the same color, a dusky purple like the end of long hot summer day. Lana, Kellan's mom, was a bar of russet light, weak but concentrated at the same time. Big Tom, with the scars running down half his face and his shoulders as wide as Dad's, was a bright deep sonorous purple; Rebecca was a gleaming column the color of rosewood. Nina was pinkish, a stinging rose.

Most of the others were just pale gleams. Owen's fingers slipped through mine. I could see him perfectly well with my eyes, but the smears...it was like tasting a sound, hearing a painting, information coming in such weird shapes my brain just had to throw up its hands and put into color because it didn't know what else to do.

While they sang, they all mixed together. Dad's glow was the last to merge, and it was *almost* bright, almost cohesive enough to be one of the shining ones.

I tipped my head back, stared at the pavilion ceiling. It had a high peak and exposed beams, and they vibrated like they were breathing each time the music rose.

It felt like a long, long time before my chin drifted down again. Owen still held my hand. It felt nice. I wanted to see the pattern our fingers made together and if the colors mixed, but instead, I saw Father Jim on the stage. His arms were still out and his expression dead level, looking out over the singing crowd. Mother Carole's eyes had closed.

Father Jim's were open, and they were dark. Maybe it was his pupils swelling, or...I don't know. He didn't really have a color. Instead, the colors and the music bent *towards* him, falling in, spiraling down. The longer it went, the brighter the warmth coming out of him got.

Owen's hand tensed. He squeezed, and I looked down. It was hard, I was moving through syrup, and the hazy, dreamy, disconnected thought that something wasn't quite right, that I was missing something important, fled as the music crested again, every soul in the Pavilion now open-mouthed and holding a long sustained note.

Even me.

I hadn't even noticed I was singing. I don't remember the service afterward, either, but there were whispers in the compound that a blind man had been brought, and started yelling in the middle of it.

Screaming, of course, that he could *see*.

45

CALLED CONFORMITY

"Two weeks," Ingrid said. "I'm not gonna make it."

"Me neither." Gabby sighed, her head resting on my belly. It was a good thing my bladder wasn't full. The south meadow was a good place to take your after-school snack—today it was carrot sticks, homemade peanut butter, trail mix, and apple juice in big mugs to wash it all down. It was warm and the grass wasn't damp in the really sunny parts of the field. We'd grabbed blankets from the pavilion cupboards but barely needed them.

I lay with my arm over my eyes, soaking up the sun. It smelled good, fresh air and juicy grass. There was singing in the distance, and Amy, hunched over her Spanish textbook, mumbled every once in a while as she memorized. We were supposed to be helping in the garden, or in the kitchen built onto the side of the Big House where Father Jim and Mother Carole lived, or any of a hundred other chores.

Instead, we'd snuck off to hang out in the sunshine. Technically, I suppose we were doing homework, since both Amy and I had our books. My French textbook was firmly under my head, a hard pillow but not bad with the grass and blanket underneath.

"Do they send all the grades to the Big House?" It was comforting-dark under my arm, but I could still *see* them, kind of. Just their colors. I never wore jeans anymore, all the Harmony girls were in skirts all the time, and it just felt right to have the material swishing around my legs. I didn't care if it was what Mom would call *conformity*. I was just glad to finally fit in with a group of non-straights.

"Oh, sure." Ingrid laughed. "But it's not like it matters. The guys have to keep theirs up, we don't."

That didn't sound promising. "Why not?"

"Father Jim's not a feminist," Gabby chimed in.

"He's just older." Ingrid shifted uneasily. "Mother Carole talks to us if our grades bail, that's all."

"Huh." I might have asked something else, but a shadow fell over us, and I knew who it was before I peeled my arm away and squinted up at Ben. "Hey."

He grinned, settling down next to Ingrid, dark skin gleaming. "Look who got out of mucking the barn."

"Sneaky you." Ingrid leaned over, her shoulder bumping his. "Just imagine, in two weeks you can do it all day instead of going to school."

"Big fun." He almost blushed every time she talked to him. It was kind of cute to see, except for when she spent her time staring at Owen. "Sarah's looking for you, Val."

"When *isn't* she?" Gabrielle turned her head slightly, peering up at me. "Did you see her copying you at dinner?"

I hadn't. "What was she doing?"

"Every time you took a bite, she did too." Gabby blinked, slowly. "Funny kid."

"Your biggest fan." Ingrid snort-laughed. "Hey, what's paparazzi in French, Val?"

"*C'est Italienne, soeur* Ingrid." Her name sounded strange with a French accent, and that cracked us all up for a little while.

Laughing. In sunshine. With other kids. It was really nice, I could see why people liked it.

I closed my eyes again, the light through my lids turning everything crimson. Seeing through blood. Where was the button Sarah pushed? Inside the brain somewhere, a collection of electrical impulses? Somewhere else in the body's energy or branching nerves? Now was a fine time to wish I'd spent more time finding, you know, *practical* books. I'd never really went digging because Mom was the gifted one, not me.

How was it she'd been wrong about people so often, though? Mostly men, but really, there had been some lulus.

"Here she comes." Ingrid sighed. "Always tagging along."

"She's a sweet kid." Amy snapped her Spanish book closed, and the sound was a mini-thunderclap. "You know the frogs down at the pond? She has names for all of them."

"Hey," Ben called. "Owen, man, hurry up, they'll catch you."

"Nice." Owen, the sun filling his hair with chestnut and honey highlights, had Sarah on his broad shoulders, big brother playing horse. "Wolf is gonna kick your ass, leaving us with the mucking."

"If you don't tell him, there won't be a problem, right?" Ben's voice dropped, imitating Father Jim's. "What he cannot see, will not harm him."

That cracked us up for a while too, and for a bit, there in the sunshine, everything was all right until Wolf showed up, rolling his eyes and chasing everyone toward chores. Sarah grabbed my hand and pulled me away for the woods, and it wasn't until we were lost in the tangle that I realized I'd left my French book behind.

And Owen had followed us.

46

SAME REASON

HE CAUGHT MY ELBOW. "Careful, it's slippery."

Mud squelched underfoot even though it was sunny above the trees. The branches were full of leaves now, soaking in all the light they could get, and their shade wasn't quite chilly, just damp. Sarah ran ahead, her red sweater and shoes bobbing as she hopped hummocks, roots, and puddles. Out here, her hair was a forest-colored banner, and when she stopped to look back at us—older, slower, less interesting—it was a fan, hanging behind her until she bolted again, always staying just in sight.

My mud-slicked boot shot out from under me and Owen grabbed my waist, his fingers sinking in. He set me on my feet, I shook him away. "Thanks."

"No problem." He didn't seem offended by my need for personal space. I almost wished he would *get* offended, though, so we could hash it out and it would be done.

"You guys, come *on!*" Sarah hopped from foot to red-sneakered foot under a maple sapling twice as tall as Dad.

"Was he really blind?" It burst out of me, just as Sarah turned away and ran further down the path. "That guy, on Sunday. Or am I nuts?"

"So you do remember." Owne set off down the approximation of a path. "I wasn't sure."

It wasn't a yes, but it wasn't a no, either. There were other questions to ask while the breeze rattled the leaves and ruffled the puddles. "It was in the sugar. Right?"

"You're a bright girl." He hunched his broad shoulders. You could almost mistake him for a jock, except he wasn't all stiff like they get. Weightlifting's fine, but it's no substitute for actual *work*.

I wasn't sure he wasn't being patronizing, but I didn't care. "That's why you didn't want me to—"

"Father said." He gave me a sidelong look, dark eyes almost hazel today, lit with a splash of gleam from leaf-dappled light. "You're, uh, taking this really well."

What am I going to do, call the cops? "I like it here." I followed carefully, holding my skirt up a little. Jeans were better for this kind of rambling, but I didn't mind.

"Really?" Another one of those sneaking looks, like he suspected I was lying or something. "I thought, you know, you hated Clover." *And me*, he was probably adding.

"She's not so bad." Each day there was a little origami note in my lunchbox. Mostly they were simple things, like *have a good day* or *you have a beautiful smile*. I figured she had what she wanted, so now she wasn't being nice to buy something from me. Maybe it was just who she was, and I'd been wrong about her.

Owen wasn't so bad, either. If I could just get him to pay some attention to Ingrid it would be better, so I wouldn't have to worry she'd take it into her head to cut me out of the group.

"Yeah, well, just don't get on her bad side." He hopped a puddle, turned around, and held out his arms.

"Everyone's got a bad side." I just looked at him, over the teensy earth-cavity full of water. Like a tooth socket, or the space inside my chest where the egg had been. It had cracked for good, and now I was bracing myself for pinches, pokes, and spears whenever I had to think about Mom.

"I'm not gonna drop you. *Jesus*." He did drop his hands, though. His boots were muddy too, and splashes of damp came up to his knees. "What do I have to do, Val?"

"I told you." I folded my arms, dropping my skirt. Sarah could wait. "Ingrid's the one you should be after. She likes you."

"Yeah, well, she had her chance." His chin set a little, like he smelled something bad.

Now *that* was interesting. I filed it away to ask Gabby about later, if I could find a subtle way. "Is it because of the things, you know? Sarah's button-pushing? Is that why? Or just that I'm the new girl?"

"God, no. I just *like* you, for Chrissake, is that so hard to believe?" He shut his mouth so quickly I almost heard the snap.

"Pretty much." But something inside me relaxed. "We traveled a lot, me and my mom. I've seen...stuff."

"You *guys!*" Sarah yelled from down the path, a bird's insistent piping. "Come *on!*"

Owen's chin jerked to the side, instinctively, a quick movement that said he was used to looking out for her. "I didn't know that. Where is your mom? Does your dad just have you for the summer?"

My face felt stiff, all at once. "They broke up when I was five." I waited for the stab in my chest, but it didn't show up. It was waiting for me, though; I could tell as much. Somewhere later in the day, it would hit. "Owen?"

"Yeah?" Tentative. He probably thought I was a huge bitch.

Well, he was right. I *felt* like one, and what you feel you are. Mom always said that.

"You gonna catch me?" The pain would hit me back at the mod, I decided. When the door was closed and nobody could see. I could put it off until then. Right? I could save it up and pay off later, just like layaway. I just had to keep myself busy until I was alone.

"You gonna jump?" Half his mouth turned up, a slow, sweet smile. It was a nice one, I decided.

"Tell me why, and I will." Now why did I go and say that? Was I curious? There was no way playing with this wouldn't burn me. It was like the firewalks Mom told me about, where if you got in the zone you could walk over the coals without it hurting.

I never had the urge to try, but Mom swore it was a rush.

"Why *what*?" Owen's eyebrows drew together.

God. Was he being dense, or did he just not know? I shook my head, pulled up my skirt, and hopped to the side; the convenient root I planned to use slid underfoot but I still made it, landing right next to him with a squelch. "Never mind."

"Oh. You mean why I like you." He turned as I slid past him, and his heatshimmer added to that sense of warmth, like Father Jim's.

Like radiation. Or sunlight through a window, warming a patch of farmhouse floor. "No, I mean why the earth goes around the sun."

"Probably the same reason." His tone plainly said, *fine, be snarky.*

Mine wasn't much better. "What?"

"Gravity." His hand darted out, and before I knew it, he had mine. His fingers were warm. "Quit trying to hook me up with Ingrid. She's not what you think."

I didn't know what I was *supposed* to think. "Then what is she?"

"She talks to Father, all right?" He swung my hand, tentatively, like he was deciding how it felt. "I like to make my own decisions."

Must be nice. I opened my mouth to say as much, but Sarah pelted back up the path.

"You *guys*." She hopped from foot to foot again, her cheeks flushed. Out here, she didn't look pinched, and she didn't try to attach herself like a barnacle. "Stop being slowpokes." Now you could see she'd be pretty when she was older, her hair moving with the wind, and her heatshimmer was full of a deep rippling joy I hadn't felt since I was ten.

Or even before, when I thought about it. I couldn't remember ever being that happy, though I knew I had to have been with Mom, right?

Right?

"We're *coming*, jeez. Go on." But Owen said it kindly.

I didn't pull my hand away. Another few minutes of trudging along later, I caught a glimpse of something red to my left through moving branches. For a second I thought it was Sarah, going off into the woods, but I realized it was the wrong shade. "What's that?"

Owen halted, looked, and hunched his shoulders before pulling me onward. "The Red House." You could *hear* the capital letters. "Don't go there."

"Huh." Really, I thought, he must have known that was the best way to get someone thinking about doing just that. If I needed things to keep from chewing myself up inside, exploring was at the top of the list.

We spent the rest of that afternoon watching the frogs swim in a small pond, the water dancing with ripples and sunshine. Birds flicked over the water, and dragonflies danced. I was thinking there would be mosquitoes, but I didn't get a single bite. There were tadpoles to watch, and a tree with a long low trunk out over the water, just right for sitting on while Sarah crooned at the frogs from the bank. Plenty of them answered, and she played with them, hopping when they did and whistling when they dove. Insects danced and shimmered as she did, and the frog-tongues flicked. Every once in a while the shimmer over Owen would get concentrated, and a small stone would lift from the bank, flicking lazily across the water.

We didn't say a lot. Halfway through the afternoon, just for a few minutes, I rested my head against Owen's shoulder, and the humming around us felt good. Safe, and warm, and quiet.

I liked it.

On the way back, I caught another glimpse of that red through the trees.

There was more than one thing I was curious about, here at Harmony Home. That night, curled up in the small bedroom in the mod, I heard Clover's soft voice from the main room and Dad's reply. I squeezed my eyes shut, and to keep myself busy until I could finally sleep, I thought about skipping school.

47

SPONTANEITY

MONDAY I sort of chickened out, because Owen walked me to first period. He also showed up to walk me to second, though it would make him late. And to third, though it would make him late again. Magically, Travis didn't say a goddamn thing to me all through class. Fourth and fifth, it was the same.

Tuesday, though, I decided enough was enough, and paused right outside the Integrated Math door. "You're gonna be late again if you keep this up."

"Two weeks left." He shrugged, moving aside out of the flow of kids scurrying to class, but keeping himself upstream so nobody bumped me. Awful nice of him. "Might as well."

"Don't for today, all right? And don't look for me at lunch." I wished I was carrying a book or two, because it would have been nice to have something in my hands. I couldn't tell where to put my fingers, my palms, even my legs, when he kept doing things like this. "I'll show up for the bus."

"Huh." He raised his chin a little, looking down at me. From that angle, he resembled Father Jim more than a little. But younger, and a little less...I don't know. A little less harsh, maybe? "What are you up to, Sister Val? And what's that short for?"

Harsh was the wrong word, because Father Jim wasn't. I just had the idea that he could be, if he wanted to. "None of your beeswax, Brother Owen." I was smiling, I couldn't help it. A goofy-ass grin, like Dad's when Clover showed up. It felt good to stand there with his attention on me, all that warmth. It was a losing battle to worry about what Ingrid would do if she caught on. Maybe I'd cross that bridge when I came to it. Maybe she'd decide Ben wasn't so bad. Who knew?

"Okay." But his own smile didn't waver. "Where are we going?"

Time was ticking away. There was a bus stop across the street, I knew that much. I figured I'd get a look at the map there and make a few decisions. "What's this *we*, white man?"

"Come on, Val." He leaned in, just crossing the border of my personal space. Just a *little*. "Live a little."

It was the sort of thing Mom would say. I pushed that thought away, knowing I'd pay for it later. It occurred to me that with Dad happy and everything taken care of at the compound—dinners, laundry, *everything*—maybe I could be even more like her. A free spirit. Planned spontaneity, because I'd intended to go today anyway, but spontaneity all the same if I took Owen with me.

"Okay," I said. "But we've got to go now, and you need to not ask any questions. All right?"

"Done." He leaned forward even more, but I turned my head just slightly and he backed off. The bell-chimes jangled for the start of first, and he grabbed my hand. "I know a way off-campus. Come on."

A JINGLE-JANGLE as the door opened, a burst of of nag champa with tangs of skunky weed and intense patchouli, married to the good dusty vanilla smell of books. My throat blocked up, my heart pounding, and Owen was behind me so I had to keep going, stepping past the big solid brass Buddha holding loose change and the torn-up remains of bounced checks from bad customers. *Karma's a bitch*, Bert always said while ceremonially ripping them.

"Well, look what the universe dragged in!" A familiar voice, and Coral hurried from behind the register, her arms wide. She was in the same sloppy orangish sweater I'd seen her in a million times before over acid-washed jeans, Doc Marten sandals clip-clopping on her large feet with painted-green toenails, her hair a wide henna frizz and her smile electric as Mom's. Bracelets jangled, her rings flashed, and she wore the biggest necklace I'd seen on her yet, masses of tiny carnelian beads holding an amber chunk almost the size of her palm. "Bert! *Bert, come down, Val's here!*"

She even *smelled* the same, faintly sourish because she believed in the body's natural ability to clean itself. Her arms were around me, and she hugged tight enough to make me lose my breath. "It's so good to see you! We were worried, where is your mom? All her clients have been asking. We have Pammy in to do the readings, but she doesn't have your mom's *way*, you know?"

"Holy hell!" Bert yelled from the top of the stairs to their apartment overhead. "Val! Where's your mom?"

You mean you don't know? I couldn't talk. Everything bunched up inside me. I breathed into Coral's ample tatas, closed my hot, prickling eyes, and tried to swallow. Tried again.

"Oh, honey. What's wrong? You in trouble? Bert, get some tea. Or coffee, she likes coffee. Who are you?" Rapid-fire, Coral took over. Mostly, Bert ambled through life and she bounced. The only time that reversed was when there were cops around, or someone with bad energy. Then Bert got attack-dog nervous and Coral, well, she got really, scarily calm.

"Owen Harrison, ma'am." Trapped between me, Coral, and the door, he didn't sound worried.

"A boyfriend now? Well, never mind. Val, honey, where have you *been*?" She held me at arm's length. "Honey? What's wrong?"

That did it. My eyes were full, and a hot fat drop slid down my cheek. So they didn't know. They hadn't come to the funeral, *Nadine* hadn't come, because they didn't know. There was no reason why they would, I hadn't called or anything, and Mom wasn't one for keeping in touch. Dad, of course, wouldn't know if I didn't tell him.

So it was my fault. Of course.

"There was an accident," I managed, thickly. "I'm with my dad now."

"An acci..." The word trailed off. Coral's lips, glossed with all-natural peppermint beeswax balm, pursed a little. "Oh. Oh, honey. You come on in, now. Come on."

The store was the same, tucked in a big old building that had once been a library but was now offices upstairs along with Bert and Coral's apartment, with the bottom split between Enlightened Source and a meandering, stuffed-full antiques dealer next door. There was a new display of Shiva stones and the incense rack had been rearranged, but the old-fashioned wooden cart with its boxes and baskets of semiprecious or other stones for everything was the same. Turquoise, carnelian, selenite wands, beach glass eggs, rose quartz, plain quartz, agate, hematite, obsidian, opal, moonstone and more. Jasper. Petrified wood.

There was the spinning rack with packets of herbs, too. Sage wands. Mugwort, horehound, stinky wormwood, chamomile. Dragonsblood incense in tiny plastic bags. White copal. The jewelry in a glassed-in counter on one side, and the bookshelves, each as individual as a person, collected from roadsides and thrift stores. The books, a wonderland of knowledge and special hidden strategies, each section's name on a hand-lettered sign.

It was all just the same. And Coral, Coral who could feel someone's aura and did energy healings, Bert who led the drum circles and talked about peyote being the path to God, looked just the same. There was no heatshimmer on either of them. Nothing, nada, zip, not a thing, zilch, zero.

I'd meant to play it cool, act like it didn't matter that they hadn't come. I don't even know why I told them about the accident, Mom not wearing her seat belt, the semi crossing the double yellow line. I *meant* to go down there and do some research, find some books that would help me figure out a way to practice what I now had. Pick everything up casually, and get out the door.

Instead, I got an awkward half-hour of trying not to cry even more while Coral fluttered at me and Bert went downstairs whenever the door-bell jangled, Owen mostly silent and his expression set, and Coral trying to reach Nadine but only getting her voicemail. I promised to call, left with a string of jet beads Bert pressed on me for free because it was what widows wore in Victorian times and it was very healing for grief, a care package of incense and rose quartz, and a list of phone numbers for Mom's friends Coral pressed into my palm before we were outside, blinking in the sunshine. I'd also snagged a better length of leather for Owen's cross, and insisted on paying for it and the rose quartz even though Coral looked like she might tear up when she took the cash.

I set off for the bus stop with my head down, my cheeks aflame, and my nose full. It was just past lunchtime, and we had to get back to school if we were going to go home with the other Harmony kids.

I didn't say a word on the way back. Neither did Owen, but on the heaving, lurching silver bus, he put his arm around me while I took great gulping breaths and tried to keep my cheeks dry. And I was secretly, shamefully glad he was there, because outside his little bubble of heatshimmer everyone around me was aching with something, and I couldn't handle any more.

I just couldn't.

48

BETTER OFF ALONE

"WHERE WERE YOU?" Gabby looked worried, fine strands of buttery hair floating free of her braid. The schoolbus's motion was about to make me sick. I huddled between Owen and the window, rubbing at my nose, wishing I had some tissues. Anything other than my sleeve.

"Val had some business." Owen shook his head, his arm still around me. Even if I tried to pull away his fingers would bite down, and I'd give up. "I said I'd go with."

"So you both skipped? Oh, man." Ben ran his hands back through curling, wooly hair, lifting nascent dreads and dropping them. He didn't have stubble yet, but when he did, he'd have to beat off the interested parties with a stick, he was that gorgeous. "They'll call the Big House. You'll be boxed for sure."

"Shut up." Kellan elbowed him. Amy wasn't even humming, just looking at whoever spoke with her wide, liquid eyes. Her Peter Pan collar was flipped up on one side, and she chewed on her lower lip a little, too.

"He did the right thing." Ingrid's dark eyes were wide, and there were two spots of color high on her cheeks. "Father says we shouldn't go alone."

"But..." Gabby's tongue flickered, nervously, wetting her lips. "I dunno. Maybe we can say he was here, the school just missed him?"

"Yeah, five teachers in a day, they'll believe that." Kellan blew out a long frustrated breath. "What kind of business did you have, Val?"

I couldn't even begin to explain, and I was saved the trouble.

"Personal," Owen said. "Don't worry. If I get boxed, I get boxed."

That shut all of them up for a good few minutes. The driver smacked the doors shut, the schoolbus started with a deep rumble, and it was weird to hear the talk radio crackle into life without the Harmony kids singing over it. I wanted to ask what "boxing" was. It didn't sound fun or happy. If I opened my mouth, though, I'd start leaking again, and I'd done enough of that for a day. Or a week. Or a whole fucking *year*.

"It will be fine," Ingrid said, suddenly. "It will all be fine." She leaned over the back of the seat, her dark hair swaying as we jolted into motion. "Father will forgive you, right? I mean, all you have to say is you were with *her*." She smiled, a bright wholesome grin. "Right? New Harmonies are a little, you know."

"Ingrid..." Amy finally spoke up, all in one breath. "Come on, you guys. Let's sing."

Owen didn't agree. He fixed Ingrid with a hot stare and that same faint smile he'd used on Travis. "What does that mean?"

"You guys..." Kellan shifted nervously. "Amy's right. Let's sing."

"Oh, come on, Owen." Ingrid blinked, sleepily, stretching out her arms. The color had died out of her cheeks. "When Dad first brought me and Astrid, you were supposed to help us...adjust, right? It's your job. We all know."

I closed my eyes. Owen had gone stiff. Especially his arm, his hand digging in, pressing me against his side. Hard.

The silence was heavy among us. The other kids on the bus whispered or chattered. A pop-prepper girl near the front laughed, a nasty, bright little sound.

"Sure," Owen said finally. "We all have jobs. Harmony relies on everyone doing their part, right, Ingrid?"

"You guys." Ben cleared his throat. "We should sing. It's, uh, yeah. We should sing."

Amy began, a thin trembling sound. Ingrid joined in, and Gabrielle after her. Kellan and Ben joined within seconds, and Owen hummed along, still clutching at me. We swayed with each bump like we were one person, but I kept my mouth closed and my eyelids firmly shut the whole time.

All I felt was a deep unsteady quiver in my stomach, low down. Like the fumes over a lake of gasoline before you drop a match, plus a kind of wonder that I hadn't been wrong. Eventually, wherever I landed, I would fuck things up royally.

I was always better off alone when it came to other kids. I shouldn't have forgotten.

49

LET ME HELP

I HAD to open my eyes to trudge back for Harmony Home, lingering in the pariah's spot at the back of the group. Owen walked right in the middle, back where he belonged, and Ingrid only turned once to glance at me, her expression unreadable at that distance. Gabby kept sneaking little looks over her shoulder, and all I could see was how perfect they all were. How balanced, healthy, how much of a unit. Even the power, the gift, whatever it was, didn't change that I wasn't any of that.

Not even close.

The yellow Charger wasn't parked near the carport with the vans and Father Jim's Christmobile—that's what Gabby called it, her hand cupped over her mouth as if to catch the words before she said them and her eyes dancing. I made it to our mod, banged the door open, and wild thoughts of convincing Dad to move out of here, that I hated it here, rolled through me along with the acid slosh of Bert's instant coffee—he ate the crystals *dry*, for God's sake, *just like we did in Iraq* —in my stomach. I'd skipped the lunch Clover had handed me this morning, and that was probably a good thing, because—

"Heavens!" Clover leapt up, wide-eyed, her skirt flaring. She'd

256

been on the neatly folded futon-couch in the big room, and I stopped like I'd run into a wall. "Val? Oh, sweetheart, what's wrong? What is it?"

Her hair was braided up like I'd done it before, and pinned, too, Queen Clover with her crown. Her arms spread, and though I tried to lunge past her for the tiny bedroom and its door I could shut and the bed I could collapse on while screaming into a pillow or two, I ran straight into her.

Maybe I didn't try too hard to struggle. Maybe I was just so tired, again. Broken down, my windows fogged and my engine wheezing.

"Shhh," she kept saying, into my tangled, half-braided hair. "Let it out, sweetheart. Let it all out."

And, God help me, I did. I sobbed and yelled, mostly yelled. About Mom, broken sentences pouring out of me. How much I missed her, how much I hated the farmhouse and its rotten floors and the cold in winter and how much I wanted to be back at my old school nevertheless. How Ingrid hated me because Owen didn't like her, but he was only being nice because I had this thing now, and it wasn't even *mine*, Sarah had done it, and as soon as everyone found out I was going to be right back where I used to be, and Mom was gone. Mom was *gone*, she was rotting in a coffin and I knew she didn't want to be because she was scared of the dark and this time there was no landlord to talk to, no utility company to plead with, there was nothing but me and I was so *tired*, I didn't know what the fuck to do next.

"Oh, sweetheart," Clover kept saying. "Oh, heavens bless, baby girl."

I didn't even care that the heatshimmer over her got sharper and clearer. I didn't care that I was pouring out everything I wanted to keep locked up. Because she said something else that afternoon, too.

"Oh, Val, Val. Sweetheart." She kept stroking my hair whenever there was a break in me ranting, wonderful soothing fingers. "Don't worry. Don't worry, I'll take care of it. We'll find a way. You don't have to do it all yourself. I want to help, I *want* to. Let me help."

God, how long I'd waited for an adult, someone, *anyone*, to finally say that. This was too big for me. All of it was.

She kept repeating it, that she wanted to help. That she wanted me to *let* her help.

So I did. And things got fuzzy. Hazy. Out of focus.

For the first time since tires crunched on cold morning gravel outside a neglected farmhouse, I rested.

50

BACK TO TRUE

I DIDN'T WANT to go to the pavilion for dinner. Clover pointed out Dad would meet us there, and after a few cold, wet washcloths pressed against my face I just looked like I'd been rudely awakened from a nap instead of sobbing my eyes out and vomiting word salad all over her. "I'm going to go talk to Father," she said, cupping my face in her hands for a moment. "You just take a few deep breaths, and you can come to the Pavilion when it's dinnertime."

"Can I come with you?" I immediately regretted it, it was a five-year-old's thing to say. "Please?"

"There'll be a lot of people at the Big House." Her forehead furrowed, and she stepped away, leaving my cheeks cold and the rest of me a little less steady. "If you're okay with that...?"

I shuddered at the notion; I was raw all over. Maybe staying here and just chilling for a little bit was a better idea. I could soak the washcloth again. Eat some of the lunch she'd packed me, though it would mean I'd be too full for dinner. I could curl up on the bed and really nap instead of just looking like a mess. "No. No, that's fine. I just, I don't want Owen to get in trouble. Maybe if I explain..."

"It sounds like it's Ingrid who has explaining to do." Clover sighed. "I remember being that age, though. Poor girl."

"Do you?" I twisted the washcloth in my fingers. "I mean, do you really remember? I thought grownups, you know, didn't. Like you hit eighteen and a curtain drops, you don't remember what it was like."

"Don't I wish." Her expression turned wistful, a kind of pained smile. A few strands of dark hair had come loose, framing her face. Today her skirt was yellow and orange, a golden sunshiny fabric I remembered last seeing on Rebecca. "I think a lot of grownups spend their time *trying* to forget. We're all looking for the same thing, all the time."

It was, again, a pleasure to hear someone—an adult, no less—articulate something I couldn't quite. "What's that?"

"Somewhere to belong. I'm lucky." She straightened with unconscious pride, pulling the shoulder of her chambray button-down a little, settling it. "I've found mine."

That sounded really good. "Was it hard?"

"Not so much as you might think." She smiled, gently, and stroked a few curls back from my flushed, damp face.

"What about your brother?" It seemed weird that he wasn't around. Had he left Harmony? "I mean, he was here once, right?"

"Leaf? Well." Her mouth pursed a little and she dropped her hands, moving for the door. "He's got his own demons to fight. I keep hoping for him."

I nodded. It was on the tip of my tongue to tell her I'd seen him the day of the fire. She even looked expectant, like she could see me wanting to say something. I don't even know why I decided not to.

Maybe I just didn't want to give her any bad news. Maybe I wasn't even sure I'd seen him after all, if I was nutbar or if I'd just misunderstood something. Maybe he'd been living in the Swallows Mill complex, it was a big place.

All I knew was that she wanted to help, she was a grownup, and maybe, if she liked me, I could find a safe niche here that didn't depend on Ingrid and Gabrielle. So I just twisted the washcloth a little harder. "Clover?"

"Hm?" Thoughtful now, she paused at the window. A few thin tendrils of dark hair had come free of her braids, but that only made her prettier.

"Thank you. I really mean it. I, uh. I wasn't nice to you, and you're...really great. I mean it. Thank you."

"Oh, honey." Her smile wasn't as beautiful as Mom's, but it was steady, and she didn't skimp when she poured it over me. "I lost my mother when I was a little younger than you are now."

Earlier, I might have been furious that she was trying to make it like we were in the same boat. But it wasn't like that now. Instead, a deep red throb of relief went all the way from my head to my toes. "You did?"

"I did." Her shoulders slumped momentarily. "I know nothing can replace her, ever. But I'm here, and I promise, I am going to do my very best to take care of you."

Oh, thank God, was all I thought, because I sure as shit wasn't doing too hot on my own. Maybe I should have thought about Dad, but really, he was kind of as helpless as Mom, in his own slow methodical way. I mean, I loved him, and he was always there, but he wasn't about to fight. I suppose, being so big, he'd learned not to, so he wouldn't be a bully.

But Clover, well. She seemed like a fighter.

I had no idea, then, how right I was.

WHEN I STEPPED into the pavilion, anyone could tell something was going on. There was food, all right, and plenty of it. Tonight it was smoky-juicy barbecue, smelling so good I almost regretted wolfing my packed lunch in the mod. Barbecue was for special events; scarred, diffident Big Tom, called that because he was almost Dad's size, had a special recipe for the sauce. I can close my eyes and taste it even now, tangy and full of burning wood, rich mouth-filling salt, a complex bite of vinegar and a deep caramel sweetness. I can also feel the sick thump under my solar plexus—not my heart chakra, for once, but the one below it—when I realized Father Jim and Carole were at their usual table, and Ingrid was sitting with them. Owen was at the end of another table, and there was a space around him like they could smell he was in trouble. Gabrielle, hunching her shoulders, didn't look happy sitting with her dad, and kept craning her neck to look at Owen all alone. I saw Amy, who was busy eating, with Kellan right next to her. It occurred to me that they were a *thing*, but they kept it really quiet, and I wondered about that. Amy's mom sat next to Kellan's, and they were chattering away while Amy's dad applied himself to a mound of barbecue and potato salad.

I was scraped clean, hollowed out. So I didn't get a tray, or a plate. Clover was nowhere in sight. Had she talked to Father Jim?

When I slid onto the end of the bench, Owen didn't move. He sat and stared at his plate, where a single dab of potato salad with a scattering of paprika sat exactly in the middle. He barely turned his head to speak. "You shouldn't sit here."

"Some law against it?" I put my elbows on the table, leaned forward.

"You don't know." His back hurt. I felt it, throbbing through my own skin. "It's not safe."

I took a deep breath and the feeling faded, a stripe below my shoulderblades twitching like my bra strap had been snapped by some asshole kid. Only wider. Like...a belt.

A leather belt. Now why would I think of that?

"I don't care." I rested my chin in my hands. Clover said she'd talk to Father Jim. How could I ask without giving anything away? Was it possible? "Owen..."

"It's not true." He said it low, and fierce, under the crowd noise. It was like being in the cafeteria, except we weren't in the middle of the Harmony kids. We were on our own, a bubble of space around us like he had something contagious. "Okay? Whatever Ingrid told you, it's not true."

Do you really like me? Ridiculous, and selfish, that I wanted to ask at all, that I even cared about something like that when there were so many bigger things to worry about. "I want to know something."

"What?" He pushed a fork for his potato salad, gave up before touching it.

"Did you tell your dad? Where we went?" *About my mom?*

That earned me a single, contemptuous, sideways look. A fierce scowl darkened his entire face. "Of course not."

"Why not?" I had the leather for his cross coiled up in the pocket on my own button-down chambray shirt over a tank top with scratchy lace edging its neckline. Could I give the cord to him now, maybe fix up that cross of his?

"It seemed private." His scowl deepened, if that were possible. "But if you want me to—"

"No. God, no." I scooted so close my hip touched his. The contact was immediate relief, everything around us fading. "You're in trouble. Because of me."

"No, *Val*." He pushed his plate away. "I chose to skip school. My mistake."

My cheeks began to burn. Well, I'd been a total dick to him and now he was in deep shit, so I couldn't blame him. "Okay." I watched the door all the way across the pavilion. Nobody would come in that way unless they were late from the fields, but it helped to have something to look at. If you look above everyone's head, they can't make eye contact and smirk at you. "For what it's worth, I'm sorry."

"You should get away from me." Evenly, quietly. "Before you get hurt."

"Too late." *I'm already hurt, I guess.* "But if you've changed your mind about me, fine."

"You don't change your mind about gravity, Val." He rose, the bench rocking while he did, and scooped up his plate with its lonely scoop of potato salad. "Not even if you can fly."

Can you? It was a stupid thought. Lifting pebbles wasn't like lifting a whole human body. What were the limits to this stuff? If I'd had this power, this energy before, God, I could have helped Mom in so many ways, right? I could have…maybe I even would have been in the truck with her, instead of left at home like a disappointment.

Because if I was being honest, that's what I was. Practical instead of gifted, but Dad didn't know what to do with me either. He had a nice apartment and a good job, then I showed up and everything burned down. I was mean to Clover and hurt Ingrid, hurt Owen too. About the only person I hadn't pissed off was Sarah, and she was just a kid. It wasn't her fault I was having trouble with what she did.

Maybe she'd even thought she was bringing me a present. That tiny robin's egg—had there been an actual baby inside? A tiny little thing, curled up tight and protected, kept warm by her tiny, gifted hands?

"Hey, dumplin'." Dad settled next to me. "Sittin' all alone, you all right?"

"It's been a day." I was so glad to see him I threw my arms awkwardly around him, and he looked abashed and pleased all at once. "Dad, I skipped school."

He nodded, thoughtfully. His hands were raw from scrubbing, grime worked under his nails, and he had a plate with a small mountain of barbecue and another peak of potato salad as well as a healthy helping of pickled cabbage. "Did you now. You need a note?"

Wow, he was taking it really well. "I don't know. Maybe. I went to this place Mom used to work. They didn't know about her." What else could I say? "I should have called them when it happened, but I didn't."

"Oh." He spread a napkin in his lap. It was to small, but he did it anyway, carefully, his fingers surprisingly delicate for their size. His eyes weren't bloodshot, but he blinked like they hurt. "Honey, that wasn't your job."

"I should have." I decided he was probably hungry and pulled myself away. My hands ached like his, a fresh scrape across his knuckles smarting. Someone in the crowd had back pain, a nagging feeling. Someone else had a scratchy throat, a summer cold coming on. I hunched my shoulders. "Uh, how was work?"

"Two trucks and a goddamn Subaru with a little bitty engine, burning rice to keep up." He began digging in, his fork almost lost in his big paw. "Someday they'll have computers and robots doing all the fixing, and then where will I be?"

I elbowed him, but gently. "By then I'll be out of college, and taking care of you."

"Hm." His smile was a warm balm. "My smart dumplin'. College. Your mom always said you'd go."

Well, she went, didn't she? And Dad said there was money for school. If there was, why hadn't Mom spent it to, I don't know, fix some of the farmhouse? Could she have done it?

Or did she know something was going to happen?

A hush fell over the Pavilion. I flinched, but it was Father Jim stepping up onto the stage, ponderously. Mother Carole drifted to the steps, and Owen, helping to scrape dishes like everyone who finished early had to, stiffened. I could feel that, all the way across the building. His tension invaded me, and I didn't want it.

"Now settle down, people, settle down," Father Jim said, raising his hands.

"Hope he doesn't start preaching." Dad took a giant mouthful of potato salad. A traitorous, nervous little laugh bubbled in my throat, I swallowed it and the squashed peanut-butter-and-strawberry-jelly I'd carried around in my backpack all day. Nothing could come out because my mouth was glued shut.

Owen turned, slowly. He watched his father, his face set and deadly pale.

Father Jim smiled slightly, but his eyes crinkled at the corners and it was the expression of a grownup who had bad news to give as politely as possible. He wasn't wearing his sunglasses, but his hair was perfect in its streaked, curling glory. His embroidered dashiki— red and green, Christmas colors in summertime—glowed under the

265

lights. "Thank you, brothers, sisters, children." Even the humming in the background faded.

He spread his hands slightly, and began. "I'm sad tonight, children. Just a little." He waited for the swell of sound to die down, everyone making a soft noise of assent at his pain. "We're a chorus, but sometimes, you know, your voice might be a little off. You might have a sore throat. You might just not be feeling it on a particular day." A rueful echo of laughter, but there was an edge underneath it.

Clover arrived on my other side, bumping me from the end of the bench. "Hi," she whispered, and patted my shoulder. Dad looked pleased to see her, and kept eating. I wanted to ask if she'd had a chance to talk to Father Jim, if Owen would be all right, but that blockage in my throat wouldn't let me.

"But that's all right, because we have a way to bring everyone's voice back to true, and it's called *apology*." Father Jim's smile widened, less pained and more genuine. "We get together in a big circle, and we apologize for all our little bad notes or out-of-tune, now don't we? But sometimes, someone just can't rest until they make it right, and that's when they come up here and tell us all about it."

Oh, boy. That sounded about as fun as sitting through an entire class period between Travis the Bathroom Bro *and* Sandy Gibson, and all their pop-prepper friends as well. I twisted again to look at Owen, and Clover grabbed my hand. She didn't squeeze, just held it, and Owen's entire body was an iron bar. His jaw was set. Everyone kept sneaking little glances at him. Gabby's eyes were wide. She'd pushed her plate away, too.

Dad had stopped eating. He had a thoughtful line between his eyebrows, and his fork rested gently against his potato salad.

Father Jim let the silence hang on for a long moment before he spoke again. "Someone has something to tell us." A long pause. "Daughter Ingrid, please come forth."

51

PLAYING MEAN

"I'm not sure I like that," Dad said again. He eased himself down on the futon couch and began working at his bootlaces. "Poor girl, she was shaking."

Clover sank, a slow, graceful movement, and started picking at his laces too. The yellow-orange sun skirt pooled around her. "Well, now it's out in the open." A few more strands of her dark hair had come free, and she brushed impatiently at them as she tweezed at the heavy strings. "Which means it can start healing. Heavens, these are tight."

"Got to make sure they won't come off." Dad looked at her, then glanced at me. I leaned against the door to the tiny bedroom, wishing for a hot shower; I felt grody all over. "You all right, dumplin'?"

"Fine. Just, you know, tired." I watched as Clover patiently loosened the double knot. Dad's head was right next to hers. His hair was darker, with a blue undertint instead of the rich reddish brown of hers. They looked all right together, I decided. "Crap. I forgot the laundry today."

"I took care of it," Clover said, absently. "There. I'm surprised your feet don't hurt."

"Can't tell until I get them out." Dad's fingers, blunt and callused, worked on the other boot until she gently pushed them away. "Clo..."

"I like it." The knot unraveled under her fingers. "You're so methodical. It's nice." She tilted her head a little, and he must have been brave, because he pecked her on the cheek.

A needle jabbed at my chest. A big one. It didn't really *hurt*, I suppose. For a second I caught myself wondering what it would be like. Another apartment, probably, a nice one, with two bedrooms and good carpet. Clover humming while she cooked dinner, all of us sitting at the table. Maybe Clover working at Enlightened Source, reading tarot cards, and her origami notes in my lunches. Coming home after school to milk and cookies at the table, all that stuff. Christmases, birthdays, bringing home my report cards. Going to the same school for more than a six months or a year or even two.

Dad happy, me happy, Clover happy too. Or would she be? Mom wasn't. Mom preferred the falling-down farmhouse or the fleabag motels or the tiny trailers. She must have, because Dad would have taken her back, right?

Your dad is in my life forever because of you.

It looked nice inside my head, but Clover had her place to belong, and Dad was saving up for a house. A *real* house. Would it make any difference? That was a lot of money. College was a lot of money too. At least here, I'd know he was being taken care of.

I turned around so sharply my skirt hit the side of the doorway, but it was only to get the metal lunchbox off my bed. "I forgot to take this to the kitchen and clean it out. I'm gonna do that now."

"I can take it later—" Clover began, as Dad straightened and began to work his feet out of the boots.

"Nah, I've got it. I want to walk, anyway, and I should help clean up." I made it to the front door, and whirled again. Jesus, I couldn't even settle to one thing at a time. "Clover?"

"Hm?" She brushed those stray strands out of her face again, and she didn't look too young anymore. She didn't really look *old*, either. Just...capable. And pretty in her own way.

She just seemed so much more grownup now.

"Thanks." I restrained the urge to dig my toe into the floor like a grade-school kid. "For everything."

Dad couldn't have looked more perplexed, but something eased in Clover's face. "You're very welcome, Val."

"What was that about?" Dad said as I banged out the door and into the thickening dusk.

"Girl talk," she replied, with a light, lovely, lilting laugh.

Girl talk. Could it be that simple? I swung the lunchbox as I walked, crunching on the gravel path. Mod doors were open to catch the breeze, everything cooling off after a day of simmering sunshine. Laughter came from one mod, singing from the next; a little boy named David, his arms outstretched, ran up and down porch stairs while his dad—lean pale-eyed Brother Steve, not married to Sister Luna but with her all the same—hovered, making sure he didn't fall. Steve nodded at me, his five o'clock shadow turning his cheeks hollow. Despite that, his entire body shouted that he was relaxed after a hard day's work, and inside their mod Luna's voice lifted singing about how Jesus loved them, this she knew.

The breeze from the fields was full of warm earth and green growth. Summer was just around the corner, everything was all the way awake, not still spring-drowsy. Out of school soon, and the days would be full of what? Helping out around the compound. Getting books from the library or thrift stores like I did every summer, every place we lived. Long lazy afternoons, heat and sweat, the woods to cool off in. Time slowing down and speeding up at once. A whole summer could be over before you were ready, full of infinitely long days that ran through your fingers.

Harmony Home was a thrumming beehive, and I was just one more tiny part of it, humming along while the sky turned that deep blue-green Mom called "peacock eye." Things were fine, but I still felt...unsteady.

Ingrid, her big eyes wet with tears. *I have to apologize,* she'd stuttered. *I've been jealous, and mean, to my friends. I've been selfish. I know I was wrong. This is Harmony. Everyone belongs to everyone else.*

The crowd murmured, repeating the last sentence.

I hope you can forgive me. Her chin up, her cheeks dead white, staring at Owen. Then Father Jim put his arm around her, and everyone started to sing something they all knew the words to, but Dad and I didn't. Ingrid sang along, and afterward, everyone went back to eating. Including Ingrid, who still sat next to Father Jim and Mother Carole.

Owen kept scraping dishes. I don't know if he sang or not, and when dinner was over he disappeared.

Dad was right, it was weird. I wasn't sure how *I* felt about it, either, standing up in front of everyone, all the *embarrassment.*

And that stinging, smarting welt across Owen's back.

The kitchen, a long low building fastened to the Big House, was alight even at this hour. I stepped inside, still chewing over everything inside my tired, aching head. Maybe laying down on the bed with some rose quartz and doing some breathing was a good idea. Mom would have approved.

I heard them before I saw them.

"Don't." Owen, a low angry tone I hadn't heard from him before. "I didn't do a goddamn thing."

"I did it for you!" Ingrid, her voice breaking. "Don't you *get* it? Your dad—"

"Like you didn't go running to him knowing I'd probably get boxed? Yeah." There was a clatter. "Back *off.*"

"You don't even like her! You just have to keep her here because Clover—"

"Ingrid." Through gritted teeth. "Fuck. Off."

Smack. My head jerked aside, and for a second I thought someone had found me behind the racks holding pots, pans, and big bags of dry stuff like rice and pasta. Looked like the supermarket runs were paying off. The kids didn't go along on Food Days, probably because of the dumpster-diving parts.

My cheek burned, and I lifted a hand to touch it, gingerly.

Owen actually laughed. "You're lucky I won't hit a girl."

"You'll be sorry." Ingrid sounded like she meant it, too. "You will be so fucking sorry."

"Sure." A splash, a contemptuous snort. "Go away. I'm washing dishes."

Jesus, Val. Get out of here. I stayed, nailed in place.

Ingrid sucked in a small, hurt breath. "Father's gonna change his mind. I'll make *sure* he does."

Owen made another bitter little derisive sound. "Go *away*, Ingrid."

"You think *she'd* like being boxed?" Venom, now, just like a pop-prepper's voice. Did Ingrid guess how much she sounded like Sandy? It was an uncomfortable thought. "Sooner or later she's not gonna be the special new girl anymore."

"Go ahead. Try to get her into trouble. See what happens." Another clatter, and Ingrid made a soft sound of pain. "You'd better hope Val likes you. Because if I hear one single word from her about you being a bitch, I'll start playing mean. You got that?"

My wrist twitched and ached, sharply—Ingrid's pain. Owen's cheek was throbbing, too. The two of them, in hushed whispers, were having the kind of fight that only happens when you've known someone a while, when you've got History with a capital H. My entire body turned hot with shame at eavesdropping, and cold with wondering what would happen if they caught me just inside the open door.

A charged, staticky quiet descended, broken by quick slapping footsteps. Fortunately, Ingrid chose the other door. It slammed open and she plunged outside. I stayed where I was, frozen, my cheek and wrist both twinging.

Wet splashing sounds. Water running. Someone else came in, a slower, heavier stride. It was Seamus, with his deep basso voice. "Owen? You okay?"

I decided my lunchbox still had enough homemade hummus and

crushed pita chips for tomorrow. The three remaining carrot sticks would have to do, and I'd get chocolate milk at school.

I fled.

5 2

GOOD OFFICER

THAT SUNDAY—THE last before school got out—was warm even before dawn. The private Harmony service ended the same way all the others did, with me sitting cross-legged near the piano. With Sarah's warm bony weight in my lap and Owen at the piano bench, I didn't end up feeling so...weird. Father Jim didn't hand me any of the sugarcube soma, and I couldn't tell if Dad noticed they were spiked or not. I figured it probably did him some good to relax, and with Clover right next to him maybe he didn't feel it. The crowd waiting to get in the doors had gotten bigger, and their aches and pains poked at me through a thick warm veil of the music and Father Jim's words. Newcomers caught on pretty quickly to the responses when he said certain things.

I never heard so much *amen* or *praise be* or *heaven bless* in my *life*.

Ingrid and Gabby sat together, just like on the bus. They didn't cut me out during gym class, but with Sandy's ankle still in a cast even her stand-in henchwomen left me alone. Owen walked me to class each day, and it was sort of accepted that we were, you know, a thing. I tried not to make a big deal out of it, so Ingrid wouldn't have to see him putting his nose in my hair or leaning over me all the time. I finally arrived at the conclusion that he liked shutting the rest of the world out too, in our own bubble of heatshimmer. Maybe it was just a relief. I was like a bottle of ibuprofen or something.

Mom hated ibuprofen. The body needed pain to tell you when things weren't going so well. What would she say about feeling everyone *else's* pain, I wondered?

Well, I only wondered sometimes. When I had nothing else to do and couldn't avoid thinking about it.

Sarah's head was heavy on my shoulder, her eyes half-closed. I always ended up with both my legs numb, but after a few seconds of *ugh-that-hurts* they worked just fine. As unexpected effects went, that was an okay one—I hate it when a limb goes to sleep and you have to hop around waiting for feeling to come back while the nerves keep screaming something that isn't quite pain but hurts all the same.

I never thought I'd miss that feeling, but sometimes I do.

The doors opened for the non-Harmonies, and they crowded in. Today Father Jim and Mother Carole weren't at the doors, it was standing room only, and Sarah got heavier in my lap. Her eyes got big, though, and she scanned the Pavilion, her head turning clockwork-slow.

I saw him too. Sports coat and tie, but it was really the shoes and the hair that gave him away. The dishwater high-and-tight was mean, the way only a straight with a grudge and a stick shoved somewhere personal would wear it, and his shoes were shiny, but they had rubbery bottoms in case someone ran. Not particularly lean, not particularly stout, he still had the aggressive gut that comes from a lot of processed food and a backlog of what Bert would call *bad karma, man.*

For Bert, karma was digestive as well as energetic.

Everything about this guy screamed *cop.* Owen glanced over, and his fingers flicked on the piano keys. A couple minor chords threaded through the music, real horror-movie style, as the guy walked right up the right-hand aisle. Father Jim kept going, his usual welcome ringing cheerily through the pavilion, but several Harmonies started to notice something wasn't right. Mother Carole's hands moved slightly at her sides, little bird-flutters.

Father Jim made a shushing movement, and the Harmonies quieted. "Children," he announced, "you may have noticed, we have a special visitor today. Let's all welcome the good police officer, shall we? He's come on a blessed day, a holy Sunday."

The cop reached the stage, stood looking up at Father Jim. Because I was there and the piano hushed, I heard what he said, low and snappy, a man used to saying things like *perps* and *interrogation* and *discharged my firearm.* "Can the act, Harrison."

"Well, hello, sir." Father Jim pitched it loud enough to be heard by everyone. He had that gift of pushing his voice out to every corner without yelling; he probably learned it from Mother Carole. "Have you come to sing with us, or just to listen?"

"You can come with me now, quietly, or I can bring in a couple buncos and clap you in handcuffs in front of everyone." The cop's lips peeled back. It wasn't a smile, but it probably fooled his cop buddies. Or anyone who thought the cops were *friendly*, like they used to try to tell us in elementary school. I mean, sure, sometimes they helped out, but that was only when they had no other option and no power trip to pull off.

"Harper, isn't it?" Father Jim's smile didn't waver, and neither did his tone. "I'd be happy to come with you. May we finish our service?" Perfectly polite, but you could see the amusement dancing behind his eyes.

There's not a lot that stick-up-the-rump straights, especially ones with shiny badges, hate more than being laughed at.

Owen's hands stilled. Every Harmony in the Pavilion stopped between one breath and the next, the music dying.

"*Now*, goddamn you," the cop said, clearly audible in the hush. His head immediately turtled between his big soft shoulders, because a murmur went up.

There's another thing straights with shiny badges hate: looking like the assholes they are in front of other straights.

Anyway, Father Jim spread his arms again. It took a second before I realized how he was posing, just like he was nailed up. He only held it for a few seconds, but it was enough. "Certainly, Officer Harper. I'd be happy to come with you."

"No..." Mother Carole drew out the syllable, her hands fluttering. "No, you can't."

"It's all right, Mother." Father Jim turned back to her, and the piano bench scraped as Owen pushed it back. "Hush now."

"Mom." Owen got there, catching at her hands. "*Mom.*"

"Hold on a second," someone called from the crowd. "What's he doing? What's going on?"

Sarah cuddled closer into me. I sat there, frozen and useless, sudden anxiety rocketing through my stomach. It was *their* panic, *their* pain, and it churned up my stomach, an elephant trying to fit through a dog door.

The cop turned on his heel, reaching into his breast pocket and whipping out a small black leather badge holder. Everyone in front of him flinched, and maybe it was that small movement that made him realize just what kind of impression he was making, because he flipped the holder open and flashed the badge with a wild, sweeping motion. "Detective Harper, CRCSD. Everyone just *calm down!*"

"You're the one yelling," someone piped up. It sounded like Seamus. I could have cheered, but Sarah was trembling.

"Bad man," she whispered. "Bad, *bad* man."

Was she thinking of the cops who tried to take her back to her mother? "It's okay," I whispered back, and hugged her tighter.

"Sir." This was Clover, stepping forward smoothly. "Do you have some kind of warrant? This is private property."

Jesus. Mom would have already been out the door and slipping away from a bad scene. If the cops were occupied with someone else, that was your chance to hope they didn't notice you and flee while you could.

"Is it now?" He sucked his cheeks in, holding the badge out stiffly, as if the gleam on it would keep her away. "You got a lot of guests here, missy."

"That's not against the law. And it's *Ms.*" Clover folded her arms, and behind her Dad loomed. He looked uncomfortable, but someone who didn't know him might read menace just in his size alone. "If you don't have a warrant, we're going to have to ask you to leave."

"I can come back with one—" The cop was used to people who cowered, obviously. I could have told him Clover wasn't that type. I also wondered what would happen if she used her heatshimmer on him.

"Now, now," Father Jim cut in, smoothly. "I'm sure the good officer—"

"*Detective,*" Harper spat.

"I'm sure the good *officer* has his reasons." Mischief danced in Father Jim's eyes. "Must be something important for him to come here on a Sunday and interrupt our meeting." Father Jim made that curious arms-outstretched movement again. "Children, would you mind very much if Clover and Mother Carole led your singing today? I'm sure I'll be back soon, isn't that right, Officer Harper?"

"*Detective* Harper," the cop said, stiffly. There was a embarrassment in the set of his shoulders now, and the consciousness that he looked like a garden-variety bully. "Just a couple questions."

"Well, then." Father Jim stepped down once, twice. He didn't take the third step, though, which meant he could look over the cop's head at the whole Pavilion. White-faced Harmonies, confused visitors, Dad behind Clover, Clover's dark eyes blazing and her chin up. "Come on up to the house, Officer, and we'll have some coffee. Children, will you sing with Clover and Mother, now?"

"Yes, Father," the Harmonies chorused.

Sarah buried her face in my shoulder. I made us as small as I could, hoping nobody would notice. My mouth was a dry cave, my tongue too big and furry. Owen hugged his mother, glaring at the cop, and the heatshimmer over him intensified.

"You sonofabitch," the cop mouthed, and I thought desperately at Owen, *no, don't.*

Father Jim's smile didn't waver but Owen's head snapped aside and he looked at me. A curious expression drifted over his face, his eyes going dark and his mouth turning down a little. Thoughtful, and intent.

"Language, Officer. This is a place of worship." Father finally took the last step, brushing by the cop as if he'd invited him and was leading him back down the aisle. "Sing, my children. I'll be back soon."

The crowd rumbled. I think things could have tipped either way, really, but Clover climbed the steps and was at Mother Carole's side in a few long strides, her skirt snapping and her braided hair—early this morning I'd done it half-braided, Harmony style, finally learning some of their little tricks—bouncing. Owen just stood there while his mom was subtracted from under his arm, and the Harmonies began to sing, a low mournful hymn everyone else in the audience seemed to know too, because they joined right in.

They sang hymns and prayed for an hour and a half, Mother Carole's voice lifting like a white seagull over the chorus below, Clover gesturing with her soft, pretty hands, two thin silver bracelets chiming on her left wrist as she directed the music. Owen went back to the piano, his back tense but his fingers coaxing melody free, and Sarah relaxed, bit by bit until Father appeared in the door, a black shape silhouetted by the sunlight, and everyone cheered with relief. His sermon was all about forgiving those who had done you wrong, and it didn't take a genius to figure out he was winging it.

But it sounded really good, or so the non-Harmonies agreed.

Not a single one of them had left.

53

RUMORS

By the time we finished clearing the pavilion for lunch, rumors were already flying.

"Cops just hate people who're different." Clover took one end of a bench, I took the other, and we carried it to its allotted table. Buzzing and soft consternation echoed under the soft chorus of Harmony's Sunday.

Dad followed, hefting a long wooden bench all on his own. "You sound like Shade."

Hearing him say Mom's name was...weird. She hated to be called *Ellen*, it was always her middle name or nothing. "She was right." My voice sounded a little funny, probably because I was breathless. We were moving fast. Everyone was hungry, I guess, and relieved. "They're mean."

Dad shook his head. "Just people with jobs, that's all. Your own grandfather was a cop, dumplin'."

"Yeah, well, maybe that was why Mom knew." I straightened from setting the bench down, realizing Clover was standing right there too. "Clover?" Trying not to sound anxious. "What's going to happen? What did he want, did you hear?"

Clover shrugged. "I'd have to talk to Father. I *do* know they didn't like us in California, and that's part of why we moved."

"What was the other part?" Nobody talked about it, really. Sometimes they mentioned little things about California, like *remember the old place and where we used to*, but as for what made them move, all I had was the hints in the newspapers.

"Well, we got this property, and Father Jim said maybe it was a good idea to go somewhere we weren't paying rent on the land, and where there were actual seasons too." She stretched, her fists pressed into her lower back, leaning and pressing like it felt good. I didn't feel any pain from her, though. "He was right, of course."

Maybe I could find out some more, if I just knew the right questions to ask. "Do you miss California?"

"Not much. This is home." She pointed. "Over there, Earl. Heavens, you're strong."

Dad hefted another bench like it weighed nothing. "Comes from healthy living." The line between his eyebrows was getting deeper, though. "Val takes after her mama, though. Teensy as a baby bird."

"I could still get taller," I objected, the way I did every time he said that.

"Sure you could." His big booming laugh was cut in half by the bench hitting the floor precisely where it needed to be. "And I could shi—I mean, I could poop roses."

It was funnier with the *shit*, but I guess it was hilarious enough for Clover, who also laughed, cupping her hand over her mouth like she was afraid of getting caught. Maybe she was, because Father was up at the stage, his arm around a blinking, much calmer Mother Carole. Owen wasn't at the piano, and Sarah had disappeared too. I heard little snatches while going around to straighten tables and get the silverware containers on each one, the benches and chairs pushed in just so, each table surface checked and wiped so Harmony could eat neat and mannerly.

Something about drugs. No, it was from California. I heard some guy saying he used to be blind. No, no, the cop has a kid with some sort of disease and he wants Father to...Detective means someone's dead, doesn't it? No, it could be something else. Drugs. No, it can't be, they're all organic. If the cop had anything, he would have arrested him, right? He's helping out with an investigation. Drugs. It's all right, Father will tell us. It's just like California, they won't leave us alone. Father will tell us. I don't know about you, but he's a good preacher. They sure don't look like druggies, except their hair...

We had Sunday lunch as usual, cleaned up like usual, but nervousness settled and smoked through the air. There was going to be a Meeting Circle when the visitors went home. There wasn't going to be a circle, just a talk. Father was considering moving us again. Poor Father. Someone had Done Something and Father had to turn them over to the authorities.

The last gave me a shiver. I wasn't quite sure what I was thinking, but it wasn't pleasant, and it had to do with smoke and a bright shiny metal slide.

"Hey." Ben caught my arm, stepping out from between two cafeteria tables with dark wooden tops. His skin almost matched their shine, a gloss-healthy deepness. "I have to talk to you."

"I'm kind of busy—" I began, his his face changed just a little, and I braced myself. "Okay. What?"

"Come on." He tugged my arm; I followed to one of the side doors, propped open. Outside, it was so bright it seemed bleached after the electric light inside. Sunshine makes things look different than electricity can. It gilded the edges of Ben's fuzzy hair and brought out the highlights in his skin. Smooth and gleaming, he was just like a statue. With that nose and his carved mouth, big shoulders over a back narrowing perfectly to his hips, he could model if he wanted to.

He dropped my arm, and I jerked down the hem of my T-shirt. It was too short, especially if I was going to be moving fast and bending to put things away or clean them, but it was what I'd grabbed from the laundry this morning and that was that.

Ben glanced around, making sure we were alone. Or at least, as alone as you could be with a crowd of people milling around the Pavilion, the Harmonies doing tasks and the visitors chatting, breaking up into groups, chasing children, whispering about what they'd seen, or felt, or heard.

"Look," he began, "it wasn't right, okay? I know it wasn't, but that's just how she is."

I stared at him for about five seconds, trying to catch up. "Who?"

"Ingrid." He folded his arms, his own blue T-shirt straining over muscles. "She's got it rough, with that sister of hers, and her dad being boxed twice too."

I opened my mouth to ask him what boxing was, decided not to halfway, and searched for something appropriate to say. Sunshine lay over my shoulders, a warm, forgiving touch. I settled on a cautious, "I don't hold grudges."

"Everyone says that." He rolled his eyes. "And nobody *means* it. I know Father's pissed off, but her family's got all it can handle, all right? Can you just...look, please, just don't hold it against her."

Wow. "You really like her." I could have clapped both hands over my mouth *and* smacked myself at the same time. It just fell out. "I mean, sorry. You're really nice, Ben."

He brushed aside my faint attempt at a compliment with the contempt it probably deserved. "Yeah, well, listen. You won't stay golden forever, you know? You might need someone to help you out one of these days. Right?"

Duh. Then again, I couldn't blame him for thinking I was stupid. Maybe I am, but most of the time I just don't say a goddamn thing and people think I haven't noticed.

I do, though. All the time. "What do you want me to do? She and Gabby were, like, my only friends. I don't care about the rest of it, I just wish..." I couldn't even say what I wished. I settled for the most banal thing possible. "I wish she'd relax, okay? We're fine."

He examined me intently. Thin threads of hazel in his irises glinted. "Okay," he said, finally. "I'll tell her."

"Look, if Ingrid needs anything, all she has to do is tell me." I *remember her knocking Sandy Gibson over, before she even knew me.* "I can't control what Owen does, okay? But I'm not some backstabbing bitch. She's got nothing to worry about from me."

"Good." He looked like he wanted to say more, but someone called his name and he whirled guiltily away, setting off at a fast walk.

I stood there, in the sunshine, cold all over.

54

YOU NEVER ADMIT

"Dad?" I pulled my knees up on the futon couch, careful to still keep my boots dangling off the edge. No reason to get gravel or mud where he slept.

"Hm?" A splashing—he was washing his hands, again. He did that a lot, maybe trying to get the engine grease all the way out instead of just mostly gone. "You should go get some sun, dumplin'."

Was he trying to say he wanted some time to himself? I'd lived in places this size with Mom before, but maybe he needed some space. Still, I forged ahead. "Can I ask you something?"

"Sure." His elbow moved—he dried his hands on the neatly mended blue towels. I wished I'd said a more cheerful color, like deep orange, or bright green, or something like sunflowers. Instead, I'd picked boring old blue. "What's on your mind?"

There was no other way to say it. "Are you happy here?"

His elbow paused. His shadow moved, a restless little twitch, as he hung the towel up carefully. "Oh, I'm comfortable anywhere."

It was the sort of thing Mom might have said, so I persisted like I would have with her. "But are you *happy*?"

He opened the door the rest of the way and regarded me with his bright, bright blue eyes. His hair had grown a little bit, and it looked nice. Less military, a little softer. You could see the teenage boy he must've been, though it was weird to think of either him *or* Mom as my age. I mean, Mom was easier, but Dad...he might as well always have been a grownup, right? He just *looked* like it. Always serious, and always careful.

After a few moments of considering, he leaned gingerly against the doorway's side. "Just what are you asking, Val?"

"I want to know if you like it here, if you're happy." That summed it up. Mom would have understood what I was asking, and I felt a sharp uneasy pinch behind my breastbone. "That's all."

"You think I'm not happy?"

Did he mean he wasn't, and was just too polite to say so? Maybe I should try to read his mind. It was bound to be better than Travis's. "I want to be *sure*, Dad. That's why I'm asking."

"Well, I figure this is good for you. Someone always here when you're home from school, neighbors to help out, you know. Your friends, too. I never hear you talk about your old friends."

That's because I didn't have any. Well, there had been Tamara, but that was more like we'd been tossed into the snakepit together and took turns fending vipers off with sticks. It wasn't like we were soulmates or anything. "It's fine here." And it was. I was learning how to use what Sarah had given me, I was maybe doing some good...but there was Ingrid, and Owen, and that whole mess.

And there was *boxed*. What the hell was that? It sounded nasty, and there was something nagging at the back of my mind. Sooner or later it would come back, probably in the middle of the night when I had nothing else to think about.

Mom called that the Memory Fairy. *She likes to sneak up when you're not looking.*

"Just fine?" Dad nodded, a few quick little jerks of his chin, making a decision—or getting ready to make one. "I can rent another place. Not back there, they were gonna clean out a unit but I'm not sure they still will. Be a couple weekends of haulin, but we can do that easy. Hooker'll help."

I knew Hooker thought he was crazy to live with a bunch of Christers out of town, as he put it. But Dad was thinking *farm*, and *wholesome*, and things like *role models* and *safety* and *community*.

Then there was Clover. Would she still be around if we moved? Probably not, no matter what she promised. She wasn't going to choose to go off with some guy she pretty much just started dating and his teenage kid, not when she had a whole life here with people that knew her. Who called her *Queen Clover* behind her back, sure, but who also made lunches with her, sang with her, did laundry with her.

A place to belong, the thing she wanted most in the world. Who would give that up for some guy and his weirdo teenage kid? "I like it here." *Mostly.* "I just...I mean, I got dropped on you and then all this. I want to make sure you're happy."

"You didn't get dropped on me. You're my *daughter*." He looked almost angry, a simmering in his forehead, a spark in his pale, pale eyes. "I'm beginning to think I shouldn't have left you with your mom."

My jaw threatened to drop. I sat straight up on the futon, dropping my boots to the floor. "What does *that* mean?"

"I mean I thought she was the best place for you, but I'm not so sure now. No friends, living in that busted-down condemned place, and you thinking you have to—"

"There was nothing wrong with the farmhouse!" I didn't realize I'd yelled it until I found myself on my feet, everything inside me on fire. "Mom was *fine*! It was all *fine*!"

"Uh-huh. That's why she cashed every check she said she lost, or *someone* did." Dad had gone pale. His five o'clock shadow hollowed his cheeks, turned his chin into a defiant bristle. "That's why you're worried you *cost* too much. Sure, it was all fine." A slow, ponderous shake of his head. "I kept my peace, thinking it was good for a girl to be with her mama, but now, dumplin', I'm thinking I was wrong."

I don't think either of us quite believed he'd said it. My heart chakra lit up, red and furious, and my hands curled into fists, short nails digging hard into my palms. I could almost *hear* my knuckles creaking. "Well, if you thought she was so bad, why didn't you ever visit?"

"Because she'd take you and disappear like she did the first time." Dad's own fists loosened, his fingers spreading helplessly. "I know women do that, dumplin'. I figured as long as I kept paying, well, she'd have to stick around. I thought...never mind what I thought." He rubbed at his face, palms scraping bristles. "I shouldn't tell you these things."

"Did she say that?" My heart chakra rotated, a pinwheel of painful flame inside my ribs. "*Did she?*"

"Hell, whenever I asked, you guys took off to some-damn-other-state or another. I didn't need a dictionary to figure that out." He dropped his hands. "Val, honey, your mom was...complex."

Didn't I know it. I remembered things, too. Waking up in the middle of the night. *We have to go. Now.* How she wouldn't talk to him on the phone unless she needed money. Counting change out for the electric bill, and her staring at me like I could either make the bill smaller or the pile of cash we had larger—or like she couldn't believe this was her life, trapped with a kid instead of being on the road, free and wild and magic and beautiful like she was meant to be.

Oh, God. The pain was coming. Not a pinch or a poke or a stab, but a big orange-red monster I'd been pushing away, avoiding, hiding from all this time. "If it wasn't for me, you guys wouldn't have split up." My cheeks were so hot I thought steam was going to come off them. "Right?"

"What? No, Val. It's not like that—"

But it was. And now I thought about all the times she told me I was her *practical* starchild, how she would snatch the tarot cards away and say *oh, honey, don't try too hard*, how she always bemoaned I got none of her talent, how she told Nadine it was a good thing I had some looks because she despaired of me ever having anything but a wooden, numbers-and-lists head...

If Mom was here after Sarah pushed the button inside me, she would have acted thrilled that I could finally do all the things she talked about. But I knew better, way down deep where the things you never admit about the people you love crouch.

"Val. *Valentine!*" Dad called my name. I heard him through the fog, but I was already out the door, clearing the steps with a jolting jump, and crunching on gravel as I plunged into the hot midafternoon sunshine, bolting for the dark line of woods in the distance.

55

BOXED

Thud-thud-thud of feet in steeltoe boots, my skirt catching on all sorts of underbrush, my hair tapped and poked and clutched by sapling branches. Splashing when the ground went downhill, tripping and using my hands to pull up on roots and branches where it rose, I skinned my palms and didn't goddamn care. I went down once or twice, barking my knee a good one on a rock, letting out a weird choked sound halfway between a laugh and a scream. Leaves whipped my face, and when I finally spilled out into a solid flood of sunshine and tripped for the last time, I went face-first into fragrant meadow grass. It was only slightly damp; the impact bounced all the sense out of me and made me realize that sound was my own voice, shouting language that would have, in Mom's phrase, made a trucker blush.

I curled onto my side, knees pulling up, tight as a snail inside its shell. How were they able to *breathe* like that? I didn't know, but I knew if I uncurled, I would start screaming again. There were no tears, just the anger, the drythroat scrape-rusty ranting over and over. "I *hate* you!" I yelled into the grass. "*I hate you I hate you Ihateyou IhateyouIhateyou!*"

I don't even know who I hated. Dad, or Mom, even though the Universe would surely strike me down if I dared to say that to either of them or even *think* it? Sandy Gibson or the Bathroom Bro? Teachers? The whole fucking world? Myself?

All of the above?

I yelled and rolled around in the grass like a toddler having a meltdown in the candy aisle. It was stupid, it was childish, it was completely uncool.

I didn't fucking care. I writhed. I kicked the ground, the juicy smell of crushed grass and mud rising around me in a simmering green stink. I flailed and curled up again, flailed and curled up. It only took a few repetitions before I was exhausted, so I lay in the damp and the heavy sunlight, shady fingers creeping across one edge of the meadow as the trees reached up and the sun retreated.

It was exhausting. How do really young kids keep it up? I sagged, limp and defeated, against dirt and grass. My hair was probably full of bugs. The green and white T-shirt, a little too small on me, was never going to be clean again. I lay on my side, resting my head on my arm, hip and shoulder pressing into last year's dead stalks, this year's growth waving softly as the evening breeze came up. It wasn't full summer's oven-draft, but it held a promise.

At least the weather doesn't lie. Not for long, and you can't hold it against the clouds. They're just doing what they were made for.

It was just plain awful to think people might be the same way.

The rage was gone, but only for the moment. I could sense it, lingering in the back of my brain, beating thinly behind my heart. I was worn out, the anger wasn't. When I had more energy I'd be angry again.

Furious.

Relax, starchild. Take a deep breath.

I even hated hearing her inside my head. Remembering her cheekbones and her patchouli, the skirts we shared, her necklace even now tangled around my throat and pressing against my collarbone. Remembering how she would sometimes sing about flying away. She loved songs about escaping, leaving everything behind. But now she was in a shitty little box in a shitty little hole, stuck fast forever. The pictures, the gruesome awful pictures, revolved inside my head, and my stomach revolved too, protesting everything I'd done to it, ever.

When I finally pushed myself up on my dirty hands, wincing as my body twinged in several places, the shimmer over me turned into a steady heat. I couldn't even fuck myself up the right way, it would all vanish in a matter of minutes.

That brought up the question of just how much damage—my own, or someone else's—I could heal, and what it would feel like. All Mom's books said that a lot of healers just took the sickness into their own bodies and defeated it somehow; shamans were real big on that. Was that what was happening? Or would I, all of a sudden, run out of the shimmer and all those hurts would come back, like in the book I read about scurvy and sea voyages?

I'd made a list of experiments, but that was before the fire. Maybe I should do another one.

You and your lists, Mom's voice whispered inside my head. I shook it away. Had she really threatened to take me away? Or kept coming back because at least Dad would pay her to keep me? Was that what he'd been doing, paying her to keep me out of *his* hair? Now she was...gone...and I couldn't ask her, could I?

"Not gone," I found myself saying, pulling my knees up. I hugged them, even though the ass of my skirt would be crunched deeper into the damp. Laundry was going to be hell this week. "Not *gone*. Say it. Out loud."

I didn't want to. Not again. Saying it was worse than thinking it, was worse than anything.

Well, you said it to Clover. Might as well say it to yourself, too. Name it. Names have power.

Was it all bullshit? If she could *really* read auras, really read the cards, why had she been so disappointed, over and over again? Why hadn't she known where to get enough money?

She kind of knew. From Dad.

So she took his money, cashed checks she said she'd lost...

She loved me. Mom loved me. Dad loves me.

But then, *why?* Why anything? Her tarot cards were gone, probably in her purse while she was driving. I could get another deck without much trouble. If I laid them out, what would I see?

Pretty pictures? Nothing at all?

I struggled to my feet, blinking. All my skin crawled. I probably looked like I'd been dragged behind a truck. *That* thought made me shudder. I set off, pulling my T-shirt down again and finding out it had torn across the back. At least my bra was in okay shape, though I had to pick leaves and grass out of it. Thank God there was nobody around to see me settling my tatas in the cups again.

Underwires are stupid uncomfortable to throw a tantrum in.

I didn't know where I was heading. Evening was already gathering under the trees, whispering to itself as I wandered aimlessly. There wasn't enough acreage to get lost in, right? Everything sloped up the ridge or down, sooner or later I'd find the fields, or the small creek threading downhill to join the one on the valley floor, or something.

Somehow, I'd gone on a tangent. I figured that out because I stumbled out into a hacked-clean clearing on the north side of the paddocks. I recognized it, and maybe something in me had been subconsciously prodding me in that direction even when I ran away from the mod.

This time, the clearing was getting dark, shadows pressing around its edges. In the middle, metal gleamed dully. Winter hadn't done the three original locker-things any harm, but they were no longer shiny. The three new ones, matching the three old ones, were all bright-penny, and while I stood there, my hand on a young tree bolting to get ahead of the trash-bushes on the fringes of the clearing, my jaw hanging loosely, I figured something out.

Wider than a locker, and taller than me. Big enough to fit a person, if they weren't Dad-sized. The person just couldn't turn around. The slats along the sides would let in enough air, maybe.

Boxed. The word sent a chill through me.

It was ridiculous, though, right? Nobody would lock someone else in one of those.

Why were there new ones? Were they used for smoking meat? They couldn't be, there was nowhere in them to start a fire. You wouldn't smoke stuff that way, you'd have a shed you could mostly seal up. There were falling-down smokesheds at the farmhouse, one still solid enough for me to have baby thoughts of turning it into a play-house or just a place to retreat.

Boxed.

I stood there staring for a little while before hauling my mouth closed with a snap. Then I turned, my head full of a strange buzzing, and headed downhill. I'd get some clean clothes, wash the gunk out of my hair, and talk to Dad.

At least, that was the plan.

56

BLUE DOOR

I MADE it into the laundry building's warm quiet, took a deep breath of the good smell of fabric softener and dryers working overtime, and hoped nobody was in there to see me. I wanted a couple towels and something to change into. That would mean I could go to the shower building, lock myself in one of the stalls, and hope the nighttime rush was over. The instant heaters on some of the more recent showers were pretty good, but they tended to fizzle out after about ten minutes hot or fifteen warm. Which is enough time, sure, but it's not exactly optimal for soaking away a tantrum.

"Val?"

God, she was the *last* person I wanted to see.

Ingrid dropped the plastic laundry basket; it hit the concrete with a cracking sound. "Holy crap, what happened to you?" Her dark curling hair pulled back in a ponytail instead of a braid; she looked a lot like her sister. Now I wondered if Astrid, with her black lipstick and her perpetual sighing and folding her arms, was signaling for help. And if Ingrid's dad would tell me about *boxing*.

What I was thinking was impossible. It was ridiculous. Father Jim wouldn't do that to anyone; Clover wouldn't let it happen.

Nobody would *let* something like that happen to somebody else, especially here at Harmony. Right?

I hesitated, caught between asking Ingrid flat-out and caution. How the fuck do you ask about something like that? Was I wrong?

Maybe if I had asked, a lot of what happened might not have. I don't know.

"Val?" She stepped away from the basket, moving slowly, her hands loose and spread by her sides. "Val, are you hurt? What *happened*?"

My mouth worked for a second. "Nothing." I decided clean clothes and a shower weren't worth the questions. Besides, there were other people to ask. "I...I fell."

Which was kind of the truth, and kind of not. But I turned around and marched out of the laundry building, my boots dropping bits of grass, gravel, and muck, and took off for the biggest question mark of them all.

The Big House.

THE FRONT DOOR was rarely used. Mostly to get into the Big House you went around the side and knocked on the smaller, blue-painted door closest to the vans. That's what I did that night, too, though I had to walk all the way around the front to get there. I probably wasn't thinking very clearly.

Yeah. *Probably.* More like *definitely.*

I found myself at the blue door, running my hands over my hair to pat it down or maybe get some of the guck and sticks and leaves out of it. The detritus jabbed my palms, and I tried to straighten my torn T-shirt, too before I knocked. Three fast little raps, a pause, then another two, and I was already losing my nerve as soon as I heard footsteps on the other side.

Sometimes I wonder what might have happened if Owen opened the door, or Mother Carole, or whoever was visiting that night.

Everyone dropped in the Big House at any hour, with any problem, Father Jim was really clear on that. *You've got a problem, you come to me, children.*

Instead, the door squeaked, and I found myself looking at Father Jim himself, his sunglasses gone, his dashiki pulled a little askew, and the ankh and cross necklaces dangling at his neck gleaming. He squinted a little, haloed in gold, and I realized it was well past dusk and on into night.

Dad was probably worried. I should have just gone back to the mod, but I stood there, paralyzed, and Father Jim pushed the screen door open. "Daughter Val." He didn't sound surprised. "Come in, come in." He offered his hand, too, and I grabbed at it like a lifeline.

It's okay, his dark eyes said. *Everything will be all right, child.* The warmth around him was *definitely* heatshimmer, but I didn't care. Everything sort of fell away when he focused on you. It was like you were the only person in the world, and he was really listening, really interested. I'd noticed that when he talked to other people, but when it's directed at you, it's kind of different.

"I fell," I said, stupidly. "I...I have questions. I have to know."

"Of course." Still unsurprised, he drew me into the house. The screen banged shut behind me, and when he closed the blue door it made a soft definite sound, like glass breaking under a heavy blanket. "We all do, daughter. Yes, we do."

It should have sounded ridiculous, but it didn't. It sounded like he absolutely goddamn believed me, and, what's more, had felt just what I was feeling, and knew what it was like.

"Val?" It was Sarah, standing in the doorway of what looked like a living room. I could see a sagging plaid couch behind her, and the edge of run-down brownish carpet. I kind of expected the inside of the Big House to be more, I don't know, luxurious? Instead, the walls were pretty bare, and all the furniture was secondhand at best. "Hey, Owen, it's Val, she's all beat up!"

"What?" Owen, breathless. A book hit the floor, and I heard

hurrying sounds, but it was Mother Carole who appeared next, her thin face lighting up a bit when she saw me.

"Val," she said, reminding herself. "Oh, my heavens. What happened, sweetheart? Sarah, go get a towel and some washcloths. Owen, Owen..." She half-turned. "Oh, dear. You're too big. She needs clean clothes."

"Val!" Owen pushed past his mom, but gently. "Holy sh—uh, I mean, what happened to you?"

"Now, now." Father Jim put his arm over my shoulders. I didn't even mind him touching me, I just stood there, my tongue stuck to the roof of my mouth, and it hit me just how goddamn *tired* I was. Every single question crowding my brain tripped over the logjam that was other people standing around, and fell flat on its question-face. "Sarah, get *two* towels, and washcloths, and put them in the upstairs bathroom. Mother, now, perhaps *you* can find her some clean clothes? We'll go in the kitchen and talk, I'll call when we're done and you can run a bath. Owen, son, go to the hall closet and the tool-box, and bring the hammer."

"Yessir," Owen and Sarah chorused, and that was that.

I was so underwater I didn't wonder at any of it. Even the fury had turned to cold ashes. I thought he meant the kitchen building, and wondered at it, but instead he guided me further down the hall-way, through a dining room turned into a sort of office or study with an ancient green-monitored computer on a chunky old wooden desk and stacks of paperwork and bills—I guess it wasn't easy keeping Harmony paid up—neatly arranged in wire baskets. There was a swinging door, and once through the past curled over and ate every-thing because the kitchen was laid out just like the one at the farmhouse.

That is, if you had the floor taken care of and the stove and plumbing updated, as well as a reliable fridge carted in and a good coat of paint over everything that needed it. The sink, the stove, the counters, the cabinets were all in the same place, and I let out a little sound before I could stop myself. It was just as I imagined the farmhouse kitchen might look if Mom ever won the lottery and got the place renovated, right down to the cool black and white linoleum squares.

Why hadn't she used any of the college money Dad talked about? Wouldn't that have helped?

Father Jim barely paused. "Are you hurt, daughter?"

Yes. No. Only on the inside. "No," I mumbled. Then, louder, "No. It's just...I've never been in here before."

"Not quite what you expected?" His arm was warm, and heavy. It didn't feel like Dad's, and I pulled away as soon as I could.

"I'm gonna get everything dirty." If I focused on that, I wouldn't have to think about the rest of it.

"Dirt is a consequence of living, Daughter Val." Father Jim nodded sagely, and didn't seem to mind that I'd pulled away. "I've thought that many a time."

It had a kind of ring to it, I guess. But it was also depressing as fuck, and not why I was here.

Why *was* I here? "I have to...I have to ask you something."

"In a moment. Here." He headed for the sink and I trailed in his wake, trying not to look at the smudges my wet boots left on the floor. Their cups were all mismatched, just like all the stuff in the kitchen building. It was kind of reassuring. At least he didn't have matching stuff in here and leftovers out *there*.

He filled a glass and handed it to me. "There you go. Take a deep breath, and a little water. We'll get it figured out."

Well, good. Because it was about time *someone* got *something* figured out. I grabbed what was left of my courage. "I have to know about the—"

"Here it is." Owen barged through the swinging door, a black plastic carrying-case in his hands. "Is she all right? Val, what *happened?*"

"Set it down there, son." Father Jim pointed. "I said the hammer, not the whole thing."

"Be prepared?" Owen said, and it struck me as funny. I choked on a laugh, sucked at the water, and found out I was thirsty as all get-out. "Val." He looked at me, and under his tan, he was pale. Or maybe his eyes were a little too wide. Was he really that worried about me? "Are you all right?"

"I fell," I offered again inadequately. "I just...I have questions."

"Certainly." Father Jim pointed. "Stand there, please."

I did. I took the water glass with me, tried another gulp. "I apologize for bursting in, but—"

Father Jim shook his head. "You knocked, you didn't burst in. Son, stand right there, please. Put your hand on the counter. Yes, like that." He flipped the latches on the black plastic case, but I wasn't watching because that put Owen right in front of me, and with him standing that close...well, I had to look up at *him*, every inch of dirt and crushed grass on me itching, and I was suddenly very aware of the rip in the back of my T-shirt and the way the thin damp cotton clung to my front.

It's all right, Owen's eyes said, and his mouth moved a little as if he wanted to say it out loud, too. *Everything is going to be okay.*

God, I hoped so, and for a second I almost believed it.

Then Father Jim brought the hammer from the toolbox down on Owen's right hand, lying flat on the counter just where his dad had told him to put it. It was a good hit, swung from the hip probably, and the hammer was broader than a claw one you use for getting pictures hung up and pulling nails out of the wall. It was more like a mallet.

Bone crunched. Owen's face crumpled.

The pain hit me too, a walloping red-black shock up my own arm. Somewhere far away, glass shattered because my arm spasmed and I threw the water glass. Everything went dark for a moment, and there was another crunch and another bolt of agony, because Father Jim did it *again*.

Owen sucked in a tiny breath, and I knew in a moment he was going to scream. I knew it because *I* was going to scream, and just because he blocked out other people's pain didn't mean I could block out *his*. Maybe Sarah yelled upstairs, I think maybe she did but I had no way of knowing because my ears were stuffed with a funny cottony thudding sound.

I could say it hurt, but there are no words. The first shock wasn't even the worst, because it was just that—shock. Then the real pain came, rolling up through my shoulder, nesting in my head like whatever had hatched from the egg in my heart chakra had come back to dig in its claws and roost, or just plain eat its way out. It was like Sheba the dog, only different because it was *Owen*, and I *knew* him, and the pain wouldn't *stop* it just kept going and going while the roaring was a freight train all through me. Like a few places Mom and I had lived, when the trains come in the middle of the night and after a while you stop hearing it, but your body knows and stiffens up every time one passes. You find yourself gritting your teeth and wondering why, then you actually *hear* the sound and...

Blackness feathered over my vision. A throbbing noise, then little crackles. My hands spasmed, locked around something that quivered a little, like a tiny robin's egg cradled in my palms.

It was the bones. Owen's bones. In his hand. Moving back into position, sealing themselves back together without even a mark to show the break. Torn tissue repairing itself, the swelling going down, and Owen's other hand clasped around both of mine, cold and sweating. He blinked, rapidly, and I could see again in shutterclicks because my whole body jittered and my eyelids couldn't control themselves.

"No," someone was whispering. "No nononono *Owen*..."

It was me.

Father Jim crouched carefully amid broken glass, staring at me. His forehead gleamed with a few dots of sweat. The pain gave one final crunching burst and receded, but I couldn't stop shaking. I jittered, my teeth chopping up my desperate whispered refusal over and over again, and Owen's cheeks were wet. He didn't look at me, just up over my head, his pupils swollen and his mouth a little open. It made him seem really young.

"Oh, my child," Father Jim said. "You have indeed been blessed."

57

PEPPERMINT, CHECKED OUT

MOTHER CAROLE WANTED to come into the bathroom with me, like I was five or something. Or maybe she thought I'd try to crawl out the window, even though I never would have fit through *that* hole unless I could chop off my chest and half my hips as well.

I didn't want to get in the antique clawfoot bathtub shimmering with hot water. It was clean and white except for the chips in its enamel, and I was filthy. I just stood there for a little bit, looking at the water rippling back and forth, fat drops gathering below the faucet, trembling like I was for long moments, then dropping to land with a *plink*, losing themselves in the sea. Just like Harmonies losing themselves, everything blurring while the music swept through them.

Voices downstairs. I'd almost forgotten what it was like to hear sounds in a *house*, rather than an apartment or the mod. Steam veiled the mirror, moisture collecting on a cold flat surface. My hands hurt, the right hot with muscles between its bones twitching in remembrance, the left just aching. My palms were bright red, traces of mud and grass clinging to my skin.

I could probably take off my shoes, slide sockfoot down the hall, try to get out through one of the bedrooms. But why?

Because he hit his own kid with a hammer, right in front of you. Did it make it better that he knew I'd fix it? Jesus.

He said things like *blessed* and *chosen*. He also said things like *you were meant to come here* and *you have a destiny.* He'd even handed the hammer to Owen and told him, *son, if you want to, go ahead and pay me back for that tenfold.*

Owen just shook his head. Over and over again, a tossing motion like there was something stuck in his brain he couldn't get out. I kept hearing the crunch, and seeing Owen's face go that weird color under its tan, that shocked second before the pain really started.

I realized I was picking leaves and bits of branches out of my hair, dropping them on the worn yellow bathmat. Everything in here glistened with cleanliness. I wondered if Mother Carole scrubbed her own toilet or if there was a work detail for it. The big chore board in the kitchens was full of names and scheduled turns. I hadn't paid too much attention, because Clover said I was just supposed to help out where I could, but now I wondered.

I wondered a *lot.*

I came back to myself with a shudder. My hair hung, heavy and lifeless, and somehow I'd stripped off my T-shirt, my dirty skirt, and my bra. I'd climbed into the bathtub, water slopping against the sides, my panties clinging uncomfortably, the leg-holes bunching. There was a pile of material on the toilet—clean clothes Mother Carole thought would fit me.

Peppermint Castile soap, in a familiar blue bottle. They bought the stuff in job lots, peppermint, rose, almond, lavender, unscented. It was good for everything and biodegradable. Mom loved the almond scented stuff. You could even wash dishes with it, but I always felt kind of weird about that. Soap was soap, shampoo was shampoo, the two could mix, sure. But *dishes* needed the strongest stuff, and if it was full of chemicals, well, that was okay, because I'd had enough damn food poisoning in my life and didn't need anything clinging to my plates, for God's sake.

I blanked out again. When I came back I was under the water, holding my breath. My nose stung as if I'd already inhaled some, and it was no longer hot. Instead, it was tepid, and when I surfaced, the peppermint smell was thick enough to choke. I'd used most of the bottle, and a thick layer of silt moved along the bottom of the tub. My fingers and toes were all raisin-wrinkled. All the crap I'd washed off was probably going to clog the drain, but I pulled the stopper anyway, dangling its chain while soap-slathered water gurgled down a metal throat.

"Val?" A tentative tap on the door. "Val, honey?"

It was Clover. I stood in the sloshing silt, my head cocked, and shimmied out of my wet panties. Thank goodness nobody shared *those*. It was an unspoken rule of laundry everywhere. "Fine," I croaked. My throat hurt a little, too. "I'm fine."

That made her pause a bit. I could almost see her leaning intently forward, listening on the other side of the door. How long had I been in here? At least I was clean, though the peppermint fog made me nauseous.

"You don't sound fine." Did she have her hand on the doorknob? "Can I come in?"

"I'm, uh, not dressed." *Go away. Leave me alone.*

Alone didn't happen at Harmony. At least she didn't jiggle the doorknob, though. "Can you at least tell me what happened? Did someone hurt you?"

I did it all myself. "I, uh, had a fight with my dad." I don't know why I said it. "I ran out of the mod, I went to the woods, I fell down. That's all." A stack of clean, fluffy yellow and white towels stood on the tiled counter, I wrapped my hair up and scrubbed at the rest of me hard enough to hurt. No bruises I could see, or feel. No cuts from thrashing around or smacking my way through the underbrush. "Hold on."

The clothes turned out to be an orange and black skirt and a boxy, very soft black sweater with a wide ballet neck. They smelled of the familiar Harmony fabric softener and a touch of patchouli, and the skirt was a little too big but that was okay. They were *clothes*, and

I balled up the towels around my dirty ones and braced myself. My hair was going to tangle something fierce, but I didn't care. It reeked of mint in here, and the steam had turned clammy.

When I opened the door, I found Clover there, her forehead wrinkled with worry and her arms crossed. She stepped forward, her hands dropping, and grabbed me by the shoulders. "Are you all right? Ingrid said you looked awful, Father Jim's worried, what's going on?"

Ingrid? Oh, yeah. "I'm sorry. I just...Dad and I, we..."

"Did he hurt you?" Her fingers bit into my upper arms. "Val, honey, *did he hurt you?*"

"Oh, God, no. He would *never*. Jeez." I shook her away, barking my elbow on the doorway for good measure. "Ow! No, come on, Clover, he wouldn't ever hit me or anything. I just yelled at him."

"Are you sure?" She didn't grab me again, but it sure looked like she wanted to. "Because I went to your place, and he's not there."

"He's not..." The world did a weird sideways slide underneath me, came back. Everything I thought about maybe asking her vanished. "Oh, crap. He's probably out in the woods looking for me. I have to—"

"Val." Her tone warned me. "His car's gone. And...forgive me, but I looked in his dresser."

That same funny lurching movement happened underneath me. "His...dresser?" My body knew before the rest of me. My fingers were cold, and still shrunken from soaking. They turned numb, and I dropped the sodden mess of cloth. "No."

"Maybe he just needed to think about things." She bit her lip. "Val..."

I shook my head. "No." I didn't know what I was refusing. Everything, probably. "He wouldn't. He wouldn't just go off."

Except...Jesus. What if I'd driven him to it?

Clover took my shoulders again, but gently. Heatshimmer crawled over her, wrapped around me. "Val." Her pupils swelled, and all of a sudden I couldn't look away from her eyes. They were big, and dark, and very important. "Listen to me, sweetheart. Let me help you."

The worst Sunday of my life so far ended with me falling into Clover's steady gaze, while she whispered things that were very important. I didn't care. Everything inside me had gone quiet, like an empty room.

I checked out.

58

THEN IT TWISTS

I BARELY REMEMBER the last week of school. It's in there, I suppose. I know I went, I sat with the Harmony kids on the bus, I know each day except the last there were little origami notes in my lunch from Clover, and each time I looked at the scraps of folded paper my head would fill with a weird sound. Not a roaring, just...an echo, like in a wide-open space. Like my skull was an empty room, nothing but walls and floor.

Like the mod. It had been cleaned out because I slept in the Big House now, in an upstairs bedroom with Clover. Her breathing in the middle of the night wasn't Dad's heavy almost-snore, and I don't think she knew I would lie there listening, tears trickling into the pillow and my hair, filling my nose. If she had, she probably would have sat on the bed and sang to me, and my head would fill with that space again.

Nothing really seemed to matter much. Even the cactuses on their wire rack, set right by the south bedroom window where they could bathe in sunshine all day, didn't make a damn bit of difference.

The only time it got a little better was sometimes on the bus ride home, when I sat near the window and stared while the Harmony kids sang. Sometimes I could watch the edge of the road, gravel ribboning by, and if I concentrated on the sound of tiny stones rubbing together I could think for a minute or two; I would realize that something was horribly wrong, and not just the obvious.

Clover would be waiting at the bus stop, and as soon as I saw her the empty would come back. I would just nod and do whatever she suggested. It wasn't like she was *controlling* me, really. It was more like...she was helping.

The yellow Charger was gone. Dad's clothes were gone. The only things he left were two pictures, one in a silver frame—the ones from his dresser. Mom smiling with the sun in her hair, and me in that red sweater.

I figured that was his final comment on the whole thing.

The last day of school was a blur of nobody really going to class, a lot of crowds in the hallways, and kids swapping yearbooks. I went from one usual room to another when the bell rang, mostly because there was nothing else to do. I didn't have a yearbook, nobody asked me to sign theirs. I was invisible among the sunshine-powered hijinks, which was pretty much the way I liked it. It was a half-day, which meant tiny classes and no lunch, and why did they even bother to have us come in at all? Probably because if they didn't, the day before it would become the "last day" and then the day before, and eventually it would crawl all the way into September and kids would slouch on streetcorners and smoke and disobey their elders, right?

All of which meant I was alone most of the day, a drifting particle. The Harmony kids had yearbooks, and I guess they were so busy getting them signed I was forgotten. Also, I'm pretty sure the fact that I wouldn't usually say a damn thing *or* sing with them helped.

It was good, being invisible. Even the teachers didn't say anything to me, except Ms Shieldman, who gave me a long look at the end of the period and told me to have a good summer. I kind of wanted to apologize for her having Travis in her class, but decided not to. It was enough that he wasn't there and had left me mostly the fuck alone since Owen started walking me around. Gibson wasn't in gym, of course, she was in the lunchroom, her cast propped on a chair and all her orbiting planets clustering her. She was finally queen of the heap, the broken ankle giving her some extra popularity.

All of which meant near the end of the day, there was no Ingrid or Gabby in Greeman's vicinity. I left the gym early and decided to walk the long way around to the buses. It took me through the portables near the track, squat white things with inconsistent heat in winter and nonexistent air-conditioning when spring turned warm. I heard summer school was held in them, as an additional punishment for kids who couldn't make it during the regular year.

I turned around the corner of the building and stopped, looking down the long side of the 300 building. In the distance, the yellow of the buses glared, pulled up in long rows. Kids milled around, excited chatter floating on a warm breeze that pulled my skirt against the back of my legs and floated loose, recalcitrant blue-black curls over my shoulders, into my face. This far away, even the tugging of aches, pains, summer colds, persistent coughs, or bad bruises turned into a background noise. My hand rested against bricks, hot from thick gold sunshine, my fingers flexing a little. My nails had grown out some more and they scratched on the rough surface, a sensation that made my teeth hurt.

My head filled up again. Which sounds weird, but it's the only way to describe it. Like a big glorp of what made me *me* slid back in from somewhere above where it had been hanging out, just observing my body stumbling through the days. How many? I tried to think. *Sunday, Monday...okay, right, it's Friday. The last Friday of school.*

That made it five days, if you counted both Sunday and today. So Dad hadn't just gone to the grocery store or something. It wasn't a drive to cool off, like Mom sometimes did.

That thought hurt. I felt it slide, a knife between my ribs, so sudden-sharp it's barely felt at first. Then it *twists*. Was he in a ditch somewhere? Or in a new apartment, getting his stuff out of storage, happy to finally be swimming without a millstone-kid clinging to his neck?

Cold and sweating at the same time, I dug my fingernails into the bricks. It was like waking up after you've been sick, like the winter I had that bad cough and finally Mom took me to the ER because I was wheezing and it turned out I needed antibiotics for pneumonia. Once they started to work I realized how weird I'd felt, how underwater.

Some of it was probably shock. How many people would totally calm after finding out they could heal people with their hands? Not a lot, but at least I'd been raised by someone who didn't faint at the notion, right? So there was that going for me. But...Mom.

The fire.

Harmony.

Now Dad.

It was a gigantic shit sandwich, really; I was only sixteen and expected to clean my plate.

Where else did I have to go, really? Bert and Coral weren't likely to be any help. Maybe Nadine? Would she believe me? Her wife was a lawyer. Had Coral told her about Mom by now? I had her number on the paper Coral gave me. Why hadn't I just laid down with some rose quartz and thought things over?

You know why.

Clover's voice, calm and sure. *Let me help you.*

But she cared, right? She cared about me.

You thought Dad cared too, Val. Think about this.

I didn't want to think about it.

Something touched my shoulder. I jerked, tearing my hand away from the bricks, and whirled.

Travis the Bathroom Bro, a nasty grin stretching his mouth and his cloud of body spray almost visible on the summery wind, grinned at me. "Hey, *Val.*"

Jesus, go away. I folded my arms, defensively. "What do *you* want?"

His smile faltered a little. If I hadn't been inside his head once, I would have thought he looked...I don't know. Maybe a little scared.

"Nothing. I just, uh...Hey." He held out his yearbook. "You wanna sign it?"

Cold Ridge High, it said on the front, in scrolling font. The year, in a big silver-foil circle on the top right. A drawing of the school that looked like a third-grader had traced it finished the whole cover off, and the idea that someone had paid money for it just about choked me. "Oh." I tried not to back into the wall, edging sideways in case he wanted to pin me or something. "Why?"

"I just..." His face fell by a few fractions. "Look, you know I didn't mean it, right? About you being a lesbian."

What if I was? It wasn't like it was an insult or anything. "Okay."

"You got a number or something?" He offered the yearbook again. "I mean, we could hang out, maybe. My dad's gonna get me a car." Anxious, like a kid saying *I've got a new puppy*.

All I wanted was to get rid of him. *How is this even happening to me?* "You don't even know me." Sweat gathered under my arms, at the small of my back, behind my knees.

"Well, yeah. But you're cute." Was that his imitation of a fetching smile? "And you know shit. Like, history. And stuff."

If he was wanting me to believe my brains were a selling point to a Bathroom Bro, he was *so* barking up the wrong tree. "Uh, thanks. I should go, I ride the bus." In other words, I wasn't interested.

"Look." His cheeks had stained themselves fierce red. "I didn't mean it, okay? Sandy said you were talking shit about me, that's all."

And he'd just believed her? Man, what was *with* straights? "I barely said two words to her, *ever*."

"Yeah, well." He kept holding the yearbook out, like a waiter with a plate. "Sorry."

"Thanks." I wished I had textbooks to carry or *something* to hold. I was mad, sure, but then there was the little matter of his desk collapsing on him, and his nose broken, too. It had to have been *me* doing it, but that wasn't *healing*, it was *causing harm*. Did it make me a bully, too? I didn't even know how I'd done it. "Sure, I'll sign it."

Someone yelled, towards the buses. My head snapped aside and I saw Owen, the rest of the Harmony kids trailing him. He was moving at a good clip, not quite running but close, his hair a wild halo with gold streaks beginning to show under the sunshine and his face dead white.

"Oh, *crap*," Travis said, and for a second I heartily agreed with him. I slid away, along the wall, and headed to meet Owen.

Who went right past me, his shoulder knocking mine painfully, and punched Travis the Bathroom Bro in the face.

PART IV
CRESCENDO

59

NOWHERE ELSE TO GO

"HE DIDN'T DO ANYTHING," I repeated, but nobody was listening. Ingrid, Ben, and Gabrielle were singing, a lilting *a capella* that drowned out the Top Forty instead of talk radio. This driver, a substitute, was a lean woman with a nose ring who ignored everything other than the road, and as a result, the entire bus rolled and rocked like a drunken sailing ship.

"Dude, calm *down*." Kellan's shirt, askew, showed a slice of his chest, already furring up. He'd pulled Owen off Travis and hustled him for the bus before a crowd could gather.

"Fucking *kill* him." Owen was repeating himself, too. "I told him to leave her alone!"

"I'm right here," I tried to say. Amy, leaning over the seat behind me, kept patting my shoulder. She hummed along with the trio, obviously trying to get Owen and Kellan to play along, but the preacher's son had other ideas. His anger was a deep redblack bruise and sitting right next to him made it worse, alternately chilling and scalding me. "Jesus Christ, calm *down*."

"I told him." Owen smacked his fist into his open hand, a hard, nasty sound.

He wasn't going to listen, so I shut off, staring at the side of the road and trying to fit everything inside my head. My face hurt, dimly, and my stomach, because Owen had kicked Travis while he was down, too. It was a good thing Kellan was strong even though he was a head shorter than Owen, because I'd been afraid for a few seconds that Preacher Boy wouldn't *stop*. The rage pouring off him flushed me again, but my teeth wanted to chatter.

Breathe. That was Nadine's advice all the time, not to mention Mom's. I did, filling my lungs, letting the air out. *Center yourself,* Mom would say. So I did, and everything outside my own skin faded away.

When the bus stopped, Clover would probably be there waiting. Was she going to empty out my head again? Did she really think she was helping?

Part of me was sure she did. The other part wasn't, and it was winning the battle in a big way. What was I thinking?

Was I even thinking?

"Val?" Owen's hand on mine. "Val, you all right?"

So now he was worried. Jesus. The song on the radio died and the Harmony trio held their last note, a beautiful sound. It faded under the chug of the engine, and static swallowed the radio for a second. A silence just for me, and I couldn't figure out what to say except the stupidest thing of all. "He wanted me to sign his yearbook." I kept staring out the window. "Funny, right?"

"His yearbook?" He sounded baffled. Kellan, across the aisle, peered at me past Owen's shoulders. Amy swallowed her humming and thumped back into her seat.

"Yeah." Gravel on the side of the road. If I could just hold onto that awful crunching noise, the white line ribboning by, I could figure something, anything, out. "He's the only kid who asked me."

Ingrid began to sing again, something I'd heard before about a river flowing. Gabby joined in, and Amy, behind me, sang along too. Kellan and Ben, their voices distinct but blending, hopped in as well. For once, though, Owen was as silent as me, and his hand jumped away from mine as if it burned him. He stayed stubbornly quiet the entire way, but I couldn't tell anything else because I was watching the white ribbon on the side of the road, trying to decide if I was just an ungrateful bitch naturally, or everything around me was wrong instead.

Either way, I was caught in it, and it wasn't going to stop. I could feel something gathering around the corner, a big staticky sense of a thunderstorm approaching, and hoped I was just, as Bert would have said, *stressed the fuck out.*

Clover wasn't waiting at the bus stop. For a hot second I thought about turning around, getting back on the bus, and telling the driver I needed to go somewhere, anywhere else. The door closed, the engine coughed, and at least this driver didn't peel out. I watched the back end of the bus vanish, my hands turning into fists, and trailed the rest of them as they headed for Harmony Home. They didn't cluster around me as usual.

Probably because they sensed, like I did, that I had nowhere else to go.

I DIDN'T HEAD for the Big House. I hung back while Owen went that direction with Kellan, Kell saying something in his ear and Ben on his other side, his head down and just a last long lingering look at Ingrid as she linked arms with Gabby and headed for the mods. Amy sped up and trotted for the barn with the goats. She liked anything on four legs. *Better than people*, she said once, and I kept checking her for that heatshimmer. She didn't have it, but I wondered if she had a button. A small oval one, buried somewhere deep inside her head.

Yeah, I felt like I'd woken up after a nap in the middle of a hot afternoon, when you sleep too long and get up thirsty with your head a little too big for your body. You know you're not going to be able to get any rest before two-three in the morning and that's if you're lucky and it cools off, so you put on whatever clothing you can find that won't drown you in sweat and go looking for shade, water, or air-conditioning. It's usually the first two, almost never the second. AC is for the straights. Sometimes I prowled the apple trees outside Mom's farmhouse on summer nights, pretending I was a real true witch like Maya always talked about, or the survivor of some big apocalypse. Nobody left in the hot darkness but me, and a whole world full of nothing dangerous except animals.

I skirted the paddocks and plunged into the welcome shade of the woods, dark negatives of leaves dancing, branches swaying. My entire skin felt tight and tingling, blood and nerves stealing back into a compressed leg. Some dim part of me was aware of a change in the air, Harmony's usual singing a little louder. A tiny nagging urgency prickled all down my back.

The clearing with the boxes looked just the same. They were all empty, as usual. I stood there for a few moments, staring at them, then turned toward the pond. I didn't want to put my hands on the sun-warmed metal and see if psychometry was a new, thrilling creature feature, so to speak.

I found the right path and worked down it. A lot drier than last time, but there were still pockets to catch an unwary foot and branches to grab a skirt. This one was Clover's so it was a little too long for me, and I didn't even remember putting it on this morning. Had she dressed me like a doll? A living, breathing doll that could bring a dog back and mend the bones in a shattered hand.

That flash of red, off to my left. I stopped, peering through the thickened branches. Yep, there it was.

I could flounder straight through the woods to get there, or I could look for a trail. I stood there, trying to decide, and that's when Sarah said, "What are you doing?"

You ever heard *I jumped out of my skin*? I'm here to tell you that is exactly, absolutely what it feels like. My heart almost shot out through my throat and I may have let out a strangled, half-hissed "*Shit!*"

"You said a swear." Wedged in the spreading branches of a

really old apple tree that had obviously only been pruned once in its life, Sarah grinned hugely. Her hair was full of leaves, like she'd stuck them in deliberately. A yellow T-shirt and jeans completed the picture of a kid determined to get a start on summer vacay ASAP.

"Well, you frightened the shit out of me, so of course." I pressed my hand against my chest, trying not to gasp. "Jeez, kid."

Her grin widened, if that was possible. "What are you doing?"

"I'm heading for that." There was no reason to lie.

"The Red House?" She studied me, her face furrowing and pinching in on itself. "Why?"

"Because." I didn't need a reason, for God's sake. I was sixteen, and if I wanted to go exploring, I would. Still, it sounded like something a grownup would say to a kid, especially a straight, and the thought pinched at me. "I need to."

She shimmied along the branch, which swayed alarmingly. "Why? I mean, you don't wanna go there. It's bad."

I wanted to ask her why it was bad, but there were other considerations. "You're gonna fall and hurt yourself."

"Am *not*." She dangled her red Connies, kicking in the moving shade, before dropping lightly. I guess when you're that small, you don't land as hard. "See?"

When was the last time I'd climbed a tree? I couldn't remember. "Well, good. I'm glad you didn't break a leg."

"You could fix it." In true kid fashion, it came right out of her mouth without stopping for a filter. She rubbed her hands on her T-shirt, adding streaks of green and brown. "Don't go to the Red House. I mean it. It'll make Father mad."

"I'm not sure I care." I folded my arms. "Sarah...does he make you fix things?" *Like a broken hand?*

"Sometimes. Small things. I can't do the big ones." She copied my pose, sticking out a hip slightly, tilting her head, folding her own thin arms. "You can."

"How do you know?"

"The button. It was bigger." A slow blink, two. "He made me bring back kittens, once."

"Bring back?" My stomach turned over. Everyone else would be at the kitchens to grab lunch before scattering to find somewhere to eat. The people on Rest Day would be taking lunch to everyone in the fields. "What do you mean, bring back?"

"You know." She crossed her eyes and stuck out her tongue, made a gargling noise. "Bring back dead things."

Oh, Jesus. "Kittens?" I asked, stupidly.

"If you get to them soon enough, probably. Remember the blue egg I showed you? It wasn't right inside. You fixed it, but it still didn't hatch. I had to break it open and check when the others did. It was fine, though."

Just when I thought I had a handle on this, something new popped up to hit me. "Why didn't you tell me?"

"You didn't *ask*." Her tone plainly said *obviously, getting older has made you stupid.* "Hey, can you lick your elbow?"

What did that have to do with anything? "The inside of it, I guess. Not the outside."

"Huh." Sarah shifted her weight a little. Shadow-leaves moved across her face, masking her expression for a moment. "If you really want to go to the Red House..."

I waited. Everything on me was cold, despite the warm breeze rustling the trees, a secretive mouthing.

"Don't do it," Sarah said, finally. "At least, not before everyone's at dinner. There's a path next to the pond. I can show you."

That was better than nothing. "Okay."

"But only if you promise not to go now."

Oh, for the love of... I crammed impatience back into its own little box inside my head. "Why?"

"Because." She forgot she was copying me and hopped on one foot, shaking her small hands out. The leaves in her hair bounced a little. She'd grown since I met her, getting a little more angular, deciding what she wanted to be. The process happens in increments, and if you live with someone all of a sudden you look up one day and *bam*, they've changed. "I'll show you a bird's nest. And snakes. There are snakes now, it's warm."

"Maybe not snakes." It's not that I didn't like them, they were earth energy and really powerful, right? It was just that they stayed where they wanted to, and I stayed somewhere else. "Can you fix people?"

"Nope, only animals. I like them better."

Didn't we all. "Me too."

"*You* can fix people. That's what Father wants."

"Oh." *You won't stay golden forever*, Ben had said. I decided it was probably better not to say what I was thinking about *that*. "I'm not too big on snakes. But I like birds."

"Okay." That grin came back, sunshine on her narrow, feral face, and it occurred to me that she was, after all, just a kid. I mean, I was too...but she was *really* a kid. How did she know she couldn't bring back bigger things?

How did she know she couldn't fix *people*?

60

DO ANYTHING RATHER THAN

WE WERE both dirty and hot by dinnertime. Coming out of the woods at the edge of the long line of mods, Sarah ran ahead. I'd managed to convince her to let me braid her hair, telling her two *little* ones wouldn't make her head feel funny. Really, I just wanted to sit her down and ask questions. Trying to worm complicated stuff out of an eight-year-old with a gnat's attention span is hard work.

All I got for my carefully phrased trouble was *They only box you if you're bad, then Father forgives you.* And, *Father had me try to bring back a goat. It was too big. Bet you could do it, though.*

It was a warm, breezy evening, but I shivered. I trudged past the mod where I'd lived with Dad. It was closed up now, all its furniture redistributed. All I had were some clothes that someone else could wear if they got to the laundry before I did and the two pictures, one in its heavy silver frame. Everything belonged to everyone at Harmony Home, so I couldn't really complain about the futon Dad had slept on or the dresser he'd put the pictures on or anything else, really, could I? Even that ugly lamp.

I *liked* that lamp.

At least I still had Mom's necklace. How long would it be before I lost that, too? I was losing everything, bit by bit. Things were peeling away, dropping into the dirt and the dark.

I stopped on the gravel walk right past the mod. Sarah, two braids bouncing behind her, vanished towards the pavilion. There was a special dinner planned for the end of school, she said. Maybe they'd be so busy they wouldn't notice I was gone. Hopefully, everyone would assume someone else had seen me.

I figured I had two choices. I could try to get out to the road and walk towards civilization, maybe break into the storage space with Mom's stuff, if Dad hadn't cleaned it out, and head for the farmhouse. It was still empty, and God alone knew if the lights were on, but at least there I could *think*. There was the well, and the apple trees, and I could bus into town and scavenge food from supermarket dumpsters. I had until winter to figure something, anything out.

Or I could turn around, go back into the woods, and use what daylight was left to find out what was really in the Red House. Because Sarah had said something else, too.

Boxing's better than the Red House. Which meant someone could be taken there, right? It wouldn't be that hard, especially if Clover was involved. She'd say she wanted to help you, and you'd be there before you realized it, and then...

It didn't take a genius to figure out I was ridiculously stupid even to think Dad might be there. But at the very least, I would *know*. If he was, it would mean he hadn't given up on me. If I found him, he'd know I hadn't given up on him either.

Still, I hesitated. People left you, it was what they *did*, especially if they'd never wanted you around in the first place. If I just would have made up my mind, or if it hadn't been summer and the days getting longer, maybe he wouldn't have seen me.

Footsteps on gravel, the little rocks crunching together like tiny broken bones. "*There* you are. I've been looking everywhere." Owen had changed his T-shirt. His knuckles were still swollen-scraped, and his hair was a mess. He loped easily towards me and skidded to a stop, out of breath. "Sarah said you were right behind her."

Goddammit. I nodded. Hopefully I could get away without saying anything.

Unfortunately, he had other ideas. He kept going, right over the border of my personal space, and threw his arms around me. "God. Listen, I have to talk to you. I'm sorry. I thought Miller was hassling you, and I just saw red, okay? I didn't mean to scare you."

He smelled like fresh air, fabric softener, worry, and *boy*. He was warm, and tall, and he blocked out the world around us.

I buried my face in his chest and hugged him. It was only partly because I needed a second to figure out how to get away.

"I'm sorry," he said into my hair. He didn't seem to care I was dirty. The heat-haze wrapped around me, relief that turned my knees into peanut butter instead of bone. "I thought you were coming home with me, then I looked around and you were gone. Don't do that, okay? I was worried."

It wasn't what he said, really. It was the *feeling* from him, wrapping around me. I knew what to call it because I'd felt it before. A tearing high in the chest, right under the stomach, a weird metal taste on the back of the tongue, a fierceness running along fingers and toes.

It was the exact same way I felt when I was worried about Mom. Or Dad.

All of a sudden everything seemed, well, manageable. Everything about boxing and the Red House was just a bad dream. I had to be misunderstanding something. I mean, Harmonies had all sorts of funny terms for things. Any group of people was going to have in-jokes and weird terms, right? Drum circle, pagan group, or even a gathering of straights, they all had their own vocab. Maybe boxing was more like a Meeting Circle or a public apology, an empty ritual.

Everyone wants to belong, and the instant you do, you'll do anything rather than give it up. I hadn't belonged in Mom's world, and I was pretty sure I didn't in Dad's. Was Harmony so bad, if I belonged there? Or if I just belonged with one person? Like, say, with Clover, or the guy with his arms around me, repeating he was sorry, he'd been worried, just God don't disappear on him like that?

I knew what it was like when someone disappeared on you. He hadn't given up on me, even when I'd been a bitch to him. "Owen." My breath made a hot circle against his T-shirt. "I didn't think you'd worry."

"Christ, of *course* I do!" He hugged me harder. "Your house burned down and your dad left, and your mom—I mean, Jesus, I can't even imagine. And you just button up and won't let anyone help you."

"Nobody wants to," I mumbled. Clover did, but was it help?

"*I* do." He actually sounded insulted. Muscle moved in his chest. He was warm and the evening was warm too, but I didn't mind the double sweat.

Not very much, anyway. "Why?" Fucking *hell*, that was always my question. But I needed to know.

"Gravity." His left hand moved up, cupped the back of my neck. "Okay? It's not gonna change, so stop asking."

I wanted to ask how he knew it wouldn't. It would be really handy to have that sort of information, but instead, I just shut my eyes and listened to the blessed quiet all around us. Nothing else trying to get in, nobody's pain tapping and teasing. Just him, and me.

Finally, I turned my head a little, resting my cheek against him. He didn't move. "Owen?"

He put his chin on my head, rubbing slightly. The entire world was a hush, for once. "You remember the first day you came here? Out in the woods?"

"Yeah." *Not like I could forget.*

"That was right after it happened, right?" Careful and soft, like he was afraid I'd pull away. "Your mom?"

"Yeah." Why the hell was he asking?

"I kept wondering why you were so goddamn sad." A deep breath, his ribs moving against me. "I couldn't get you out of my head, all right?"

Maybe it was because of Sarah. "Maybe Sarah—"

"No. Not Sarah, not anyone else, not even my goddamn father.

You. All right?" His shoulders hunched a little. He said *father* like it was a dirty word, and I suddenly knew, all the way deep down inside, that Dad would never have left me. Father Jim might leave his kid, or bash his own son's hand with a hammer, but my Dad—slow, stolid, too big for everything around him, full of engine grease and coffee and the smell of doughnuts—he wouldn't. Even if I was awful.

Sometimes you can only see something clearly when you're shown its exact opposite.

I hugged Owen. Tight. Tighter. If he knew where my dad was, he'd tell me, right? Was it possible he didn't? "All right."

Just for those few moments, in the lengthening dusk, we held each other. His heartbeat thudded all through me, the hazy shimmer cinching us together until I couldn't tell when he was breathing or I was, if it was really his heart or my own making that comforting thudding in my ears.

"There's a bonfire tonight," he said, finally. "You coming?"

Where else did I have to go? The Big House? "If you are."

"I have to. Plus, you know, fire. Fun."

"Yeah." I didn't tell him about dancing skyclad with Maya and the Wiccans under the full moon while flames leapt. Instead, I tensed, and he did too. "I need you do something."

"Anything." He even said it like he meant it.

"Stay with me." Could he manage that much? "Keep Clover from emptying my head out again."

"She can't do it if you're—"

Special. Talented. "Yeah, she can." *She has.* Maybe because I let her, but I didn't want it again. Now I was awake, I was thinking, and I was ready. "Promise me. Stay with me."

"Okay." No hesitation at all.

∼

I believed him, too.

61

WELCOMED

IT WASN'T LIKE the Wiccan bonfires. For one thing, the singing was constant, and for another, we kept our clothes on. But there was grape juice and cherry punch and iced tea and lemonade, and pieces of giant sheet cakes you could eat with your fingers—vanilla and white frosting, chocolate and chocolate, a vegan and carob chip cake, a yellow one with chocolate frosting. No barbecue, but plenty of hamburgers and hot dogs, the potato salad—Cass, Mother Carole's nurse friend, made it with smoked paprika—that had a special bite, all sorts of snacks and good things on the tables in the pavilion. It wasn't just one fire, either, there were three, in a field they were keeping fallow for the year.

Do you know what it's like to be welcomed? To have people say your name and smile, to have them genuinely care where you were and if you look all right? Cass, the streak of iron grey in her hair, kept telling the kids to eat because "dancing takes energy." Sister Agneta, Ingrid's mom, kept refilling pitchers of punch and ice water and fretting at everyone to stay hydrated. Scarred Big Tom, almost as tall as Dad but leaner, with an amused gleam in his dark gaze, built the fires and appointed a watcher for each one to make sure the really little kids didn't get too close. Robbie V—Brother Vee, to distinguish him from Brother Rob and Brother Roberto—had Sister Pam's little boy Tom on his shoulders, and Tom handed out sparklers bought in job lots with all the seriousness a five-year-old could muster.

After all, sparklers *are* serious business.

The Harmony teens danced with the smaller kids, laughter and shrieks rising with the music. Brother Kwanze had an acoustic guitar and Brother Roberto a couple drums that wouldn't have been out of place at an Enlightened Souls gathering. Sister Rebecca had a real violin, and when she wasn't singing, the bow flashed over the strings and it sounded like angels laughing. Sparks flew, riding the smoke from the three leaping piles of flame feasting on broken-up pallets, and bits of stumps and deadwood pulled out or gathered up.

Sarah shrieked with joy when she saw Owen again; he caught and twirled her in a circle while she laughed. Fireflies gleam-flickered through the trees, probably wondering which of their cousins had grown massive enough to produce lights the size of planets, to them. I once wanted to catch some fireflies in a jar, but Mom went pale at the thought and asked me to imagine being trapped in a jar, no air, nothing but glass walls. So I never did.

Neither did the Harmony people. Sarah coaxed the fireflies out of the dusk and dark. They swirled around her, glittering and winking, a cloud of stars. What little girl hasn't wanted to dance like a princess with firefly attendants? And the Harmonies didn't act like it was any big deal.

They handed out the soma, strangely heavy sugar cubes. Father Jim himself brought them over to the fire the teens had taken over. Owen tossed his far back, and I tried to shake my head and smile away the one Father Jim had for me. But Ingrid grinned and Ben had his arm over her shoulders and Amy said, *Val, you're one of us, we always take it at the end of school* and they were passing it out even to the little kids. Not the babies, but to Sarah and Tom and Pete and Pedro and the elementary-school kids.

It tasted bitter, even through the sugar, and that's when the night started to spin.

6 2

TO SEE YOUR DAD

EVERYTHING BLURRED, and was really warm. I rested my head on Owen's shoulder, watched the fire leaping, and after a while my throat felt funny. I touched my mom's necklace, a wooden bench lugged from the pavilion rocking a little under us, and found out I was singing. Not very loudly, but it didn't sound horrible. Or at least, it didn't sound horrible to me, and nobody around acted like it was, either. My voice merged into theirs, beautiful colors dancing from my ears to my brain.

No wonder they were happy. How can you *not* be when everything is deliciously soft and all the loneliness you've ever felt is washed away?

Some of them sang hymns. Brother Kwanze did a fair rendition of some Dylan and Hendrix—Mom would have approved. People took turns on the drums, and when they felt like dancing they just got up and moved. Ingrid's little sister wasn't wearing the black lipstick for once, and sat next to her classmate Georgia, both of them giggling in that way only middle-school girls can—closing out the rest of the world, painfully awkward and fiercely proud all at once.

Ingrid and Ben sat together. Maybe she figured it was better to have someone who wanted her, who knows? I do know Ben looked dopey-happy, and kept staring at her profile whenever she looked away. Gabby had her legs in Wolf's lap; Sierra and Annie were unashamedly making out between long drinks of ice tea sweet enough to rot your teeth straight out. I preferred the lemonade, a slight citric rasp and marvelous coolness in my throat.

I didn't see Clover for hours. Father Jim and Rebecca and Big Tom vanished intermittently too, but at the time I was too busy watching the flames turn weird colors to notice, columns of heat and light and smoke rising from their pyramid glow. Dusk turned into night, and the songs quickened. People began the second round of eating—fried chicken instead of barbecue, more hamburgers and hot dogs, home fries done in one of those big deep fryers you can fit a whole turkey in. Sister Amica did huge batches of frybread, blushing with pleasure at the oohs and aaahs that rose when she brought a fresh one out. So much food, and everyone laughing, passing it from hand to hand, singing when they weren't chewing. Owen stuck with me the whole time, and I began to feel silly and we ran out of lemonade so he went to get some more.

I *told* him to, even.

That was when Clover appeared. Big Tom was behind her; he'd turned the fire-watching over to Sister Grace early on. Rebecca and Nina had drifted near the teens, and Father Jim gazed steadily at me as he settled into his chair, carried out and placed in the middle of the wide triangle of bonfire. The wind veered a little; the fireflies had disappeared.

After a short while Father Jim set his guitar down. He'd just strummed, not really playing; his fingers pressed the strings too hard. Mother Carole had settled on a folded blanket near his feet, Sarah cuddled against her sleepy-eyed. They looked alike—same narrow nose, same small mouth. I wondered if Sarah would grow up looking as dazed as her mother all the time, then I remembered Mother Carole was only her foster mother.

Maybe she looked like Mother Carole because she wanted to.

"Val." Clover touched my shoulder, attempting to smile. A dreamy sense of alarm stole through the soma. "Feeling good?"

I don't want you here. "Fine, I guess." Husky and slow. I sounded drunk.

It was funny. The ones with the brightest shimmer were all drifting in my direction. Big Tom's was slow and thunderous, Rebecca's sharp-edged, Nina's much softer and weaker. There were other Harmonies with the shimmer, but these were the most intense ones, and it was kind of strange to see them all together. Harmonies just *looked* different, and maybe it was the shimmer leaching out of the ones who had it, making them seem more solid, more real. More *there.* Maybe it was just that they were happy, they flat-out *knew* they were doing good things. Singing with each other. Living for each other. Feeding people at the soup kitchen. Being kind.

Who wouldn't want that? Who wouldn't believe that was Heaven itself?

Father Jim rose, slowly. The warmth around him wavered a little, sucking in all the good feeling around the fires. He smiled like it was enjoyable, like he was having a good time too, but his gaze was fixed on me.

Ben nuzzled Ingrid's dark hair. She was watching me too, a faint smile on her pretty face. It wasn't a nice expression. It looked like she knew something bad was going to happen, and it amused her. Gabby, her eyes half-closed, stared into the fire. Amy and Kellan still sang, their eyes closed and their hands entwined. Sierra and Annie were lost in a world that involved only each other.

"Get away from her." Owen dropped the two glasses of lemonade. He pushed Big Tom aside, or tried to. Tom just put out an arm, and it was no use—he was a brick wall. "Val, look at me. *Val!*"

I couldn't help it. I stared instead at Father Jim, who must have teleported across acres of empty space between us and now crouched in front of me, easily, resting his elbows on his knees and putting his palms together.

"Daughter Val." He leaned in, looking up at me. "You've had a hard time lately. It hurts us to see it, it really does."

My mouth sealed up. A rushing noise filled my ears, but it couldn't drown him out. Clover's hand on my shoulder was gentle and forgiving, a warm touch I could have found refuge in if I hadn't suspected...

"You've been given a gift," Father said, softly, privately. Like we were the only two people on earth.

"It's okay," Big Tom was telling Owen. "It's all right."

"Val!" Owen sounded very far away.

Father Jim held my gaze, peering like he could see into my skull. "And I know it's been hard, very hard, for you, but we need your help."

Well, that wasn't what I was expecting. I blinked, tried to think. My mouth unstuck itself a little. "You do?"

He nodded, thoughtfully. "Have you ever wondered why you were sent here, daughter? It's for a reason. You have a marvelous gift, and we need you. Will you help us?"

Oh, God. "Are you gonna box me?" I whispered.

He looked puzzled. "What?"

"Put me in the metal boxes?"

Clover sucked in a breath.

"Child, *no.*" Horrified, Father's pupils swelled a little bit. "Heavens, who tells you these things?"

Now Ingrid was staring at the fire. I know because I looked right at her, I couldn't help myself. Father Jim glanced over his shoulder, and I caught a flicker of...something...in the warmth around him.

"No," I said, my lips numb. "Nobody."

"Well, that's as may be." He turned back to me and rose, slowly, then offered his hand. "Right now, tonight, we need you. I'm sorry to call you away from the celebration, but it can't be helped. Will you come with us?"

I tried to say no. "Where are we going?"

A bright, gentle smile widened on his suntanned face. "To see your father, Valentine. To see your dear old dad."

63

FATHER KNOWS BEST

"What happened? Where was he?" It was dark and I stumbled, relief making my knees shaky. "Is he okay?"

Clover, next to me, helped me over uneven ground. We didn't go by the pond. In fact, I didn't realize where they were taking me until the woods peeled themselves slightly away; I didn't recognize the structure because I'd only seen it from the side. The porch was old but still solid, and it was dark, but when Clover opened the front door I caught a glimpse of the exterior in a wash of uncertain, trembling golden light.

Red. Brick red. A squat, red-brick cube.

I thought whatever was in the sugar cubes was wearing off, but instead, the warm, disconnected feeling came back twice as strong. Underneath it, though, my hands were cold and my heart slowed down. I stopped just on the threshold, Clover crowding behind me. Her mouth was set, and she was ghostly pale.

"No." I grabbed the side of the door. "No, I don't want to. No."

"Don't want to see Brother Earl?" Father Jim stopped next to a small table in the hall. Doorways opened on either side, all dark and empty, but the one at the end was lit up, showing linoleum flooring and a white, white wall.

Oh, God. I pushed back, against Clover, but Big Tom was behind *her*, and I was forced through the door. Once inside, it was Big Tom who loomed behind me, his size not at all comforting like Dad's. Clover reached for my hand, but I jerked away from her.

"It's all right," she said. "Val—"

"Shut up." I reeled, trying to push myself backward, but Big Tom was a mountain. I had wild thoughts of sinking an elbow into his stomach, stamping on his foot, anything. I should have taken those self-defense classes Nadine's wife was always on about. "Stop it. *Stop.*"

"Owen?" Father Jim folded his hands, gazed steadily over my shoulder. "Son, can you help Daughter Val forward, please?"

"Father..." Clover subsided when he glanced at her. She was still paper-white, though, except for two spots of red high up on her cheeks. Her braids were a little askew, like she'd forgotten and tried to run her hands through her hair. Her lips trembled slightly.

"She needs to see to choose, Clover. Just like you did." Slow, hypnotizing, Father Jim swayed slightly. Was he on the soma too? "Valentine, come see your dad. He's just down this hall."

"Leave her alone." Owen squeezed past Big Tom. "*Father.* It was my fault, I swear. Please."

Father Jim beamed at him. "Now look at that. What do you think is going on, son? We're just bringing her to see her daddy."

Clover gripped Owen's arm. "Calm down."

"The *fuck* I'll calm down." He tried to shake her away, but she held on, grimly, slim fingers sinking in. "Get *off* me. You leave her *alone!*"

"Owen." I swayed, too. "Don't." I had a sick feeling, way down low, that if he kept this up he'd be hurt. "Please."

"Listen to her," Clover said, softly. "Come on, Owen. Father knows best."

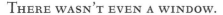

THERE WASN'T EVEN A WINDOW.

The room was white. Painted walls, a popcorn ceiling, creamy faded linoleum floor, old but clean. A metal gurney with a big white-shrouded shape on it sat in the middle. The *soma* burned in my blood, surging in tiny streams. I heard a dry, barking sob, and only after a few moments realized it was mine.

Dad lay on the gurney. His bare feet dangled off the end, but he looked...smaller, somehow. Hollowed out. He looked like he was sleeping, except he didn't snore through his half-open mouth and there was an IV pole next to the gurney, a sack full of some clear liquid hanging off it. There was tubing leading to his nose, too, and his cheeks were fuzzed with black beard-growth.

"What did you do to him?" I didn't recognize my own voice. I didn't sound like me. Or Mom. "What did you *do*?"

"He's sedated." Father Jim folded his arms, unfazed. His dashiki was spotless; you didn't see other people wearing those out of the laundry. "Do you remember the dog, daughter Val?"

"What?" I took two unsteady steps into the room. Clover's voice, low and urgent, talking to Owen. What was she telling him?

"The dog," Father Jim said, patiently. "It was dead, and you brought it back."

"I don't..." *Clover. She told him.* "It just...it was hit, by a car. A truck." No, it had been an Acura, I was the one who'd almost been hit by a truck. And the dog hadn't been dead, just dying. Maybe if I could just explain—

"You have made the blind see and the lame walk each Sunday," Father Jim continued, pitiless. "Oh, they attribute it to me, but God has not blessed me with that gift. God blessed *you*, and our little spark Sarah lit God's flame within you."

That was one way of putting it. But surely a little girl going around and pushing buttons wasn't a god-sized plan, was it? It seemed way more random. "I...I don't..."

"Do you remember the detective? The blind man was his brother, and quite wealthy. The good detective's been sniffing around us since we came here, suspecting venality." Father Jim shook his head. The light glowed in his surfer-kissed hair, and the warmth radiating from him was stolen heat, focused laser-sharp on me. "But really, daughter Val. Can you imagine what they would do to you, out there, if they knew what you could do?"

I didn't have to imagine, Mom told me about it all my life. *They still burn people like us,* she'd say, but really, it was just people like her. Special. Talented.

Gifted.

Father Jim headed for the long white-painted metal table behind Dad's gurney. "Sometimes," he said, "we don't know what we can do until we're forced to. Sarah, of course, is a little child, and she led us. But her gift isn't large enough for what must be done. She tells me yours is."

"Large enough?" The shaking was all through me, internal earthquakes sliding all my internal furniture around. The egg in my chest had hatched and it tore at my ribs form the inside, sharp stabbing pains. "For what?" It was a nightmare. I made my legs work, one at a time. If I could just get to the gurney, if I could just get to Dad...he just *lay* there. Sleeping. He had to be sleeping. Maybe they gave him soma and he was just really relaxed.

Except he wasn't snoring. When you're that big, you can't *help* but snore.

The table held all sorts of things. Surgical instruments—scalpels, forceps, other things, bright metal gleaming. There were also syringes. Real old heavy-duty ones, with glass barrels and big-ass needles. They lay in a neat row, uncapped, and he selected one that had been set a little aside. "Do you know when we're strongest, daughter?"

I couldn't keep up. I edged for Dad. I could wake him up, maybe. The heatshimmer blurred around me, a gathering like the unsteady air before a thunderstorm.

"We're strongest when we want to save someone we love." Father Jim smiled, tapping the glass cylinder. He turned, and pointed at the bag of liquid hanging from the pole. A tiny plastic thing below was already full of muddy black. It crept down more plastic tubing, heading for Dad's arm. The soma blurred everything, but I could *see* it, a river of black skulls pouring off a cliff, and Dad right underneath. "A little while ago, something was added to his sedative—a concoction of my own devising. Something to take away pain, something to seize the muscles, and something to stop the heart."

"No," I whispered. "*No.*"

"It's all right," Father Jim said, still smiling. "I have faith in you, Daughter Valentine."

6 4

CLOCKWORK

My head hurt.

Everything hurt.

Downstairs in the Red House, the rooms had concrete floors and walls, and the doors locked on the outside. There was a little circular drain in the middle. I lay against the wall, my cheeks on fire and my head pounding.

Bring him back, daughter.

My hands throbbed. They still felt Dad's arm underneath, my fingers sinking into his muscles. His arms were big and solid, from working on engines. When I was really little and he swung me around and around, it was like flying. And it was safe. Big hands cradling me, and he never let me fall.

A little scratching at the door, like a mouse. Sarah's voice, thin and quiet. *I told him. Unless there's a button, it won't work.*

Bring him back, Daughter. Bring your daddy back.

I tried. I pulled so hard everything inside me broke loose and floated. Someone was screaming, a harsh broken cawing sound.

Chemical suffocation. The body fights even when the person

inside it is gone. Iron bands around my paralyzed lungs. Black hole inside my skull.

His arms were so big. So was his chest, but he looked smaller, laying there. It worked, all right. Lungs and heart, blood and breath, bone and muscle. Like clockwork. Like an engine, coaxed back into service. Purring like a kitten, like a yellow Charger, signed over and sold to a lot on the other side of town.

I saw it, when everything inside me came loose. The shimmer moved from place to place, repairing, cleaning out arteries already narrowing from fried food, easing the strain on a heart tired from pumping through a body too big for this world, lungs scarred in places from where he used to smoke.

He gave it up when he started dating Mom. She didn't like the smell. Pot was fine, cancer sticks were not.

He lay there. Breathing just fine. Daddy.

Daddy.

Bring him back, Father Jim told me. I tried. I tried so hard.

Someone else screaming my name. Clover's face, deadly pale. Big Tom dragging me away. Father Jim shaking his head.

Bring him back.

God, I tried. Are you listening? God? Universe? Mommy? I *tried.* I tried so hard.

"SARAH," I whispered, through cracked lips. "The door's locked. Bring me the key." Her footsteps retreating, fast and quick and light, a little girl's high-pitched, terrified breathing. My own breath was the same. She vanished. *I told him. Unless there's a button, it won't work.*

Oh, I repaired the body just fine. I tasted the chemicals they'd pumped into him, they oozed out of his skin. His face firmed up, his heart stronger, his arteries clean as a whistle. Clean as the sink I scrubbed after doing dishes.

Valentine. Because you were our present.

The room next door was full of the smell of burning. I screamed until my voice broke, and he did too. I recognized his voice. He followed my yells pitch for pitch, break for break, singing with me. I screamed until my throat tore, I banged my head against the concrete wall and tasted blood. So did he. I knew who it was. It was Leaf.

Bring your daddy back.

His hands were so big. He never let go; I was safe. Until I wasn't.

THE BODY WAS JUST FINE. It breathed. It burned cellular sugar and took in oxygen and its blue eyes opened, staring at the ceiling, blinking in millimeters because that's an involuntary response. The body was beautiful, it was an engine, and it would last for years.

But Dad...my dad, my giant, beautiful daddy, was gone.

65

TWO THOUSAND YEARS AGO

I CAME BACK SLOWLY. I didn't want to. I wanted to fly out of myself up into the night sky, escape like Dad had. Maybe he'd even been in this room with the soft, weak, bare light bulb in the middle of the ceiling, the door with its slot on the bottom that a tray came through three times a day, the bed that was just a metal shelf with a thin foam pad, the tiny indifferent metal toilet that didn't really flush, just sort of trickled. The metal shelf was too solid to pull free, and even with the prickly wool blanket it was chilly.

Every time the slot on the bottom of the door slid sideways and the tray came through, it had a different little origami animal perched next to the sandwich, or with the carrot sticks, or next to the flimsy paper cup of juice, or nestled between plastic bottles filled with tapwater. Each time, too, there was the breathing on the other side. Soft, and quiet.

Baby Mine, she would sing. *Don't you cry.* Or *sleep, my baby, rest, my loved one.* Lovely lilting tunes, and at first I thought they were for me.

Sometimes, on the other side of the right-hand wall, Leaf would sing back in a cracked tenor. He knew all the words. When her voice trailed off, he would sometimes call to her.

"Clo. Clo, don't leave me here. Clover!"

He kept yelling long after her footsteps went slowly down the hall for the stairs.

I didn't open the notes. I tried not to eat. You can only be thirsty for so long, though. How long were they going to keep me in here? I had no idea. I hadn't done what Father Jim wanted. At least, not all the way. They'd kept Dad for over a week, and Leaf—how long was he in here?

They'd taken my boots, so I couldn't even kick. Sometimes I lay by the slit at the bottom of the door, trying to work it open, my fingers leaving little bloody prints on the metal. If I could talk to Leaf...but what would I say? Maybe we could get out of here somehow.

What would I do if I got out, though? Go to the cops? *Hi, I can heal people with my hands, and also make their desks collapse. My dad's a vegetable because of it. Help me.* Right. Sure.

Maybe I could try again to wake Dad up? Why hadn't it worked? *Unless there's a button...*

Either Sarah was right, or I just hadn't tried hard enough. I suspected it was the last one. Because I was always fucking failing.

The slit on the bottom of the door finally opened. I almost got the tray in the face, too. Maybe she didn't expect me to be there. "Clover." My voice was harsh, probably because I hadn't used it except to scream.

The tray paused. "Val? Thank heavens. I was afraid you were never going to talk."

Yeah? Whose fault would that be? "Let me out."

"Val..." A long pause. Cloth moving. She settled down to sit on the other side of the door, and her soft, pretty fingers ran along the side of the orange plastic tray. "Father wants to be sure you won't do anything to hurt yourself."

"Really." I could have kicked myself for sounding sarcastic. "How long are you going to keep me here?"

"Not long." She paused. "Well, Father is...there's things you don't understand, Val."

"Enlighten me." *It's not like I'm going anywhere.*

She shifted a little, folding her hands. Her skirt was blue, with a zigzag pattern. Her nails were bitten down all the way, too. "Father was in a car accident. It was very severe. He died in the ambulance, but was sent back. That changed things for him."

I moved impatiently. I knew that, I'd seen the news reports.

"He had a vision while he was gone," Clover continued softly, reciting like a good little girl. "A world without pain, without fear, without death. He saw that there are special people, with special gifts, and it was his job to find them. They could make the world better. He *saw* it, and when he came back, he knew what he had to do."

It was all right as a story in a newspaper. But here, inside this concrete cube, it was fucking terrifying. "What about Sarah?"

"Her mother was a drug addict. She was...well, it wasn't pretty, Val. But Father saved her, and we all worked to make her feel safe and welcome. Then we found out what she could do. She's our spark."

"Pushing buttons inside people." My mouth tasted bad, so the words were bitter.

"Yes. Well, we found out by accident." Clover sighed. "My brother was the first."

"Is that why he's next door?"

A long silence. Finally, Clover shifted a little, uneasily. "I always knew he was special. He didn't think so until Father showed him. His gift is...well, it's very strong, and sometimes it gets away from him."

Oh, I'll just bet. "Like when he burns down people's houses? Like that?"

She didn't even wince. "Father needed to bring you here so we could protect you."

Did she believe that? My hip hurt, pressed against the concrete floor. Were they going to bring me clean clothes? Maybe if I behaved.

That was how this worked, right—behave, and you get what you want. Don't behave, and you're locked in a cube.

Just like the straights. *Do what I want, and I won't hurt you.* Except that was a filthy lie. They hurt you no matter what. "Protect me from what?"

"There was someone else who healed the blind and the sick, Val. Two thousand years ago. You know what happened to *him*."

Oh, hell no. Mom would have demolished their stupid little argument posthaste, but I could only yell. "I was fine until you guys started fucking with me!"

"Were you?" She was *smiling*, I could tell by the sound. "Were you really?" She moved, pushing the tray forward, and I had to roll back.

I grabbed the tray-edge and yanked, then scrambled back to the slit and jammed my hand through. It was wide enough that the water bottles could come through laying on their sides, but I skinned my knuckles anyway. "Let me out, Clo. Come on. I can't stay in here. I'll try again with Dad, I'll do it right this time!"

Yeah, I actually said that. I'm a coward, okay? After a few days locked up with only the sound of your own screams to keep you company, you'd beg too, I bet.

"Oh, sweetheart. It wasn't your fault." She grabbed my hand, warm fingers, slender and strong. The heatshimmer washed through me. "Your dad didn't have a gift."

Yes he did. He was my father. He made everything safe and he was big and gentle and he could put together a desk without getting frustrated. That was, as far as I was concerned, a *bunch* of gifts. A cornucopia. A damn *embarrassment* of gifts. "Let me try. Please. Just let me try."

"We'll take care of him for the rest of his life, Val. Just like we'll take care of you." She patted my hand, then started sliding the slit on the bottom closed. "I have to go, sweetheart. I'll be back. It's almost Sunday."

I clung to her. "No. Don't leave me in here. Or just leave that open. Please. *Please, Clover, just leave it open!*"

She worked herself free, and I had to snatch my hand back so it wouldn't get closed in the metal. I dimly heard Leaf start to yell from next door.

I lay on the hard, dusty concrete floor. Finally, I made it halfway up and crawled to the shelf-bed. I took the wool blanket and pulled it over my head, and in the darkness, I went back to trying to figure out anything that would help me escape.

I failed at that, too.

66

ABSOLUTELY TRUTHFUL

IT WAS SCARRED, fever-eyed Big Tom and willowy, smiling Nina—
without her usual lacy shawl—who came with a tray of breakfast I
couldn't eat early that first Sunday. They took me out of the concrete
room and to the showers, one on either side, Nina's arm through mine
and Big Tom looming on the other side. Nina even went *into* the
shower with me, just gently shaking her head when I almost refused
to strip, her braid moving heavily against her back.

I couldn't have run away even if I wanted to. Where would I go?
Also, they had Dad.

It was Nina who had the sugar cube with its bitter cargo, and I
didn't want it but Big Tom stiffened a little and I had a vision of
him holding me down with his big, impersonal, callused hands
while Nina plugged my nose and forced the cube into my mouth,
so I gave up and let her put it on my tongue.. There was no chance
to spit it out, either, because they hustled me through predawn grey
to the Pavilion, where Mother Carole fluttered her hands and
blessed all three of us and said *we're not ready* in a monotone while
moving around in vague circles near the table, setting up the cubes
and the paper cups. The Harmonies filed in and began helping

with the other chairs and benches, but I was put up on the stage, Nina on my right and Big Tom overfilling a folding chair on the left.

I stared at foot-polished wooden planks, trying not to let my eyes focus. *Just get through this.* How soon would the soma start working? They would have to leave me alone sooner or later, maybe to go to the bathroom. Then I could...what?

"Val?" A tiny whisper. It was Sarah, big-eyed and pale, scrubbed and miserable-looking, not a trace of dirt on her shoes and her damp hair tightly braided.

I held out my arms and she clambered into my lap. The soma *had* started its work, filling me with disgusting relaxation. I tried to imagine my body rejecting it, my cells zapping a chemical invader, but the singing started and I couldn't focus.

I think they gave me a double dose that Sunday. Blobs of color filled the Pavilion. Sister Jacqueline was at the piano instead of Owen. Her playing wasn't as fluid, but nobody noticed. *I* barely even noticed, because the draining sensation when they let the outsiders in through the big double doors started almost immediately even with Sarah on my lap. She wriggled and fidgeted, twisting to look at my face, but I squeezed my eyes shut and listened to the singing.

Every time Father Jim started to speak, that rich resonant voice crawling between cracks, cajoling, enticing, I curled my left hand into a fist, forcing broken nails into my palm. The soma swallowed the hurt, but it still gave me something to think about, to focus on.

Their hurts filled me up, pulled out wave after wave of that horrible swirling, losing sensation through my middle. Father Jim made a gesture and Mother Carole began another hymn, her voice crystalline above a low grumbling chorus.

I raised my head.

Near the back, inside the double doors, was Owen. Clover stood beside him, her hand on his elbow, and I couldn't tell if the shimmer over her was forcing him to do what he didn't want to. He just stood there, staring at his father with hot coals for eyes, and I longed to tell him it wasn't his fault, that I'd sent him to go get lemonade, that he'd done everything he could.

Clover watched me, a faint line between her eyebrows and smudges under her pretty dark eyes. Was she having trouble sleeping?

I hoped, with sudden vengefulness in the middle of the fucking soma's deep warmth, that she was.

In the second row back, a familiar high-and-tight haircut bobbed. It was the detective, sitting next to a man with his chin but a kinder curve to his mouth—probably his brother, they even sat the same way —who craned his next and looked around the Pavilion as if he could see the light and color in the air. The second man had a faint disbelieving smile, and every once in a while he clasped his hands and said *praise be*, lips shaping words lost in the singing and in Father Jim's rich, resonant lies.

Even now I wonder how much Father Jim really believed. Sometimes I think he was always lying, and sometimes I think he was telling the truth but could only see a part of it, like the story Mom used to read me about blind men and an elephant.

What scares me the most, even after a long time, is the idea that he was absolutely truthful. That he believed in every single bit of it, right down to believing he was doing the best thing for everyone and God's work in the bargain.

It's easier when I think he was scamming everyone. It really is.

The soma swallowed me whole, and when the service was finished Clover and Owen vanished. When Sarah slithered off my lap Nina and Big Tom took me through a side door, Nina's arm through mine again and her back no longer aching, Big Tom's face oddly thoughtful since the twitching that happened under his scar— nerve damage—had quieted down.

The cop's brother had a small knot of people around him, and I heard a few words through the blurring and Nina's soft *don't, Sister Val, I'm asking you, please.*

"Amen," the cop's brother kept repeating. "I was sitting right in that spot when it happened. Like scales falling from my eyes, you know? This is my brother, he knows—the doctors couldn't do anything, the nerve was dead—"

It wasn't until we reached the woods that I realized they were going to put me back in the concrete cube, but when I tried to struggle in my slow sleepy soma-trance Nina tensed and Big Tom put his big paw around my other arm. Not hard enough to bruise, but I wasn't going anywhere.

Just for now, Nina cooed. *Just for now, Father's worried about you. It's for your own good, Sister Val. Please don't make a fuss.*

Maybe she believed what she was saying, too.

6 7

THE NEXT

THEY DID it the next Sunday, too. And the next.
I can't remember how many.

68

GRAVITY

"Val?" A hot, sliding whisper. At first I thought I was dreaming. But it came again, a soft scraping at the door, metal dragging on concrete, and the echoes form the hallway sneaking in through the opening slot on the bottom of the door. "Val? Wake up. It's me."

I pushed the blanket aside, took a stinging breath of chilly air. Last time I'd been awake I'd punched the wall; my scraped knuckles were already repaired. I'd watched the skin sealing itself up in the dimness under the blanket, slow and steady. My arms and legs felt clumsy, a little gooshy. Probably because I'd spent however-long laying on the bed, ignoring the trays Clover brought. How many? I couldn't remember.

I'd stopped eating after the last Sunday. I couldn't even tell what day it was. Maybe they wouldn't make me take the soma if I wasn't eating, or maybe they'd give me another high dose and I'd die from it because I had nothing else in my stomach.

When I thought about *that*, I felt only a weird, hazy, furtive relief, like when a bully begins picking on someone else.

The strip at the bottom of the door *was* open. I staggered across the floor, collapsed next to it, and shoved the flimsy red plastic tray away with a clatter. "Owen?" My voice cracked, I hadn't been using it except to scream every now and again. Listening to the sound bouncing off the concrete was almost like hearing someone else.

Not really.

"Hi." He stuck his hand through and I grabbed it, letting out a sob of relief. "God. Are you okay? I couldn't get out, they've been watching me. They've closed the gate, they're not letting anyone in this Sunday. And Clover..."

I don't care. I shook my head, as if he could see me. Held his hand in both of mine, pressed my cheek against his knuckles. I couldn't say a goddam word, I was too busy shaking, too busy with the relief that filled me up and choked me. My stomach growled, I ignored it. *I don't care. I just care that you're here.*

"Are you all right? Tell me." His fingers tightened.

I pressed them to my mouth again, finally found my voice. "I don't know." I gulped down another sob, I was probably getting snot and tears all over his hand. "My dad. Where's my dad?"

"In the Big House. He's...Val, what happened? No, never mind, you don't have to say anything. It's all fucked up. I brought you a sandwich."

I didn't want a fucking sandwich. I wanted my dad, I wanted to get out of here, and I wanted to punch something, anything.

"My dad." I took another shaky breath, pressed my lips to Owen's fingers again. "Is he okay? Is he—"

"He's, uh, a vegetable." Owen winced. The blessed, heavy warmth folded around us both. "Sorry."

"It's okay." Even though it wasn't, I knew what he meant. I squeezed my eyes shut so I wouldn't have to look at concrete, metal, and my own crusted fingerprints on the door. "Are *you* all right?" I had to think about the words before I said them, my word-finder was rusty.

He was quiet for a few seconds. His hand was warm, solid, *real.* The only real thing in the universe, right now. "You're asking me?"

"Uh, yeah." Funny, how someone else can make you real. Like

looking in a mirror until your own face seems like a stranger's, then blinking and thumping back into your body, a person again.

Owen moved again, his arm turning. He ended up stretched out on the floor, peering through the slot, and I don't think I've ever been so happy to see even a little slice of someone, *ever*. "Wow." It must have been uncomfortable, but he grinned with his cheek pressed against concrete. His cheeks were a little thinner, and rough with new stubble. "You're amazing."

"Huh?" *Don't leave.* My fingers ached, I was clutching so hard.

He'd have to rip his own arm off to get away. Someone here, talking to me, a relief from wondering and fretting and listening to the walls breathe. Except concrete didn't breathe. If it did, it would let me out of here when I begged, when I cried. It would feel sorry for me.

Did Clover? She never opened the door. And each time she took my untouched tray away she walked a little more slowly.

"You're asking if *I'm* okay. Sheesh." Owen squeezed back, hard, an almost-pain I welcomed. "What about you? Can I...I mean, do you need...what do you need?"

I was awake again, and frantic. *I need to get out of here.* "The door's locked." I figured that was the best place to start. "Where's the key?"

"Father keeps them. Clipped to his belt." He sucked in his cheeks. There weren't any hurts on him I could feel, but he was tense. "I brought you a sandwich. And some chocolate, we went into town."

Father keeps them. Plural. That meant there was more than one key, and he might have trouble finding the right one. Great. "How long are they going to keep me here?"

"I don't know."

"Did you know they had my dad here?" *Please tell me you didn't.*

"Jesus, of course not. I think it was Nina and Big Tom. Even Clover..." He closed his eyes and swallowed, hard. "Val..."

"You might not need a key." I pressed his knuckles against my cheek a little harder. "Maybe you can move the lock."

"And then what?"

It was a good question. "Then I get my dad, and—"

"What are you gonna do, steal a van and carry him to it?"

They were good questions, I decided. Still, they made everything inside me slip sideways again. This time there was no stopping, nothing to catch me before I spilled right over the edge. "I'm going to fix him."

Owen peered at me. "Can you?"

I wondered if I should lie. "I don't know."

"What if you can't?"

Another really good question. He was just full of them. My stomach growled again. "Then I get to the road and start walking."

"Jesus, Val." His hand tightened. Finger-bones creaked, but I didn't move. "You're serious."

Do I look like I'm fucking joking? "Owen. Help me. Please." Was he concrete, like the cell walls? Like Clover and Father Jim? Or was he something else?

If I was like Clover I could make him bring me the keys. How awful was it to even think like that, to wish you could force another person? To not care what happened to them as long as you got what you wanted?

"I gotta think." He finally opened his eyes again, and they were wide and troubled. He shifted a little more, settling himself; if he was uncomfortable on the bare floor he made no sign of it. "We'll need money."

Huh? "What?"

"Well, we gotta eat, right? I can pick up construction work, I guess. Or something."

My feverish cheek pressed against his knuckles again. I had to stop myself from kissing his knuckles again. "We?" *What the fuck?*

"If you're going, I am too." He stiffened, his head tilting back, and glanced up the hall. "Shit. I think someone's here." His hand yanked back, though I tried to keep it, and he shoved a paper bag through the slot. "Look, you gotta eat, I heard Clo telling Father you weren't. I'll come back when I can, okay?"

I stuck my fingers into the slot, hungry for just a few more seconds of his skin. "Promise?"

"I promise," he said, steadily, and then he was gone. I grabbed the bag and the slot closed. My hands tingled, and so did my cheek.

There was a sandwich. Lots of peanut butter, a layer of raspberry jam, homemade bread, all slightly squashed but still really good. A bar of Hershey's, full of wax and milk powder but still good too. And a square of paper, folded up. On it, in bold printing, was one word.

Gravity.

I folded it back up, pressed it to my cracked, chapped lips. Then I staggered to the shelf-bed, lay down, and slept, really slept, for the first time since they'd locked me up. Afternoon wore into evening, though I couldn't tell, locked inside where there was no such thing as day or night.

I should have known they wouldn't let a Sunday pass, though.

6 9

CHERRY PICK, CHASTISE

I WOKE up when the hinges creaked, the door opening with a groan like a horror movie. I thrashed out of the scratchy wool blanket, my heart blowing up like a balloon because I thought it was Owen, come back for me.

Then everything inside me collapsed. Because it *was* Owen, dead pale, his hair a wild mess and his eyes staring holes. Clover stood right next to him, her hand clamped on his elbow, and the heatshimmer over them both was sharp and unpleasant.

He was fighting her.

In front of them, calm and tall, Father Jim looked down at me. A draft of fresh air from the hallway flooded the room, and I found out how close and foul it was in here. I smelled bad with only one shower a week, the toilet smelled bad, the concrete was damp and rank. My scalp crawled, my skin did too. Father Jim just stood there and smiled gently for a few moments, and of all the times a straight's ever loomed over me, that one was the only time I really felt cold and small.

"Daughter, daughter," he finally said, that rich voice bouncing off the walls. "I'm so sad to see you like this."

It occurred to me that maybe he shouldn't have locked me up if he felt that way, but the thought vanished as soon as it appeared. I pushed the blanket down, swung my sock feet off the bed. My skirt was filthy with dust from the floor, and a rash was beginning on my thighs, under my arms.

Father Jim kept looking down at me. I gathered myself.

"Now, you might be angry," he said. "I can understand that. Clover tells me you're not quite clear on the gravity of the situa—"

I lunged off the bed, my arms windmilling and a rusty scream bouncing off the walls. My feet stung against the floor, I hit him hard and even managed to get my nails on his face, a long stripe of fire I felt on my own cheek. Owen made a small sound, and maybe I could have darted past Father Jim if he and Clover hadn't been filling up the doorway. As it was, Father Jim grabbed me, fingers biting like alligator jaws, and I gasped when he bent my arm a way it wasn't designed for.

"Now, now, child." He got an arm over my throat, too, and squeezed. Muscle swelled, and I choked. He lifted me off my feet, and I understood what every one of Mom's friends said about men in that single instant. Dangling there, kicking, my arm a bar of pain and black spots dancing in front of my eyes, I clawed at his forearm and got nowhere. "Shhh, hush. We're trying to *help* you."

"You. Killed." I choked again, kicked, and my lungs burned. "You *killed* my *dad!*"

"He's still breathing, daughter." Father Jim eased up a little, I swallowed a mineral taste and found out I could breathe again, just a little. "There's still hope. Now, will you listen to me?"

I struggled some more. It got me exactly nowhere.

"Listen," he said. "*Listen.* Tonight, I'm going to be in that same room, Daughter Val. I'm going to be injected with the same cocktail. I'm going to die."

I went limp.

Father Jim whispered into my wild, oily hair. "And you're going to bring me back, daughter. Or not, as you choose."

He dropped me. I hit the floor, my knees folded, and I spilled down into a puddle. Owen leaned forward, straining, but Clover had a good grip on him. His boots were muddy, grass clinging to them. Had they caught him sneaking around?

"I'm surprised." I wiped at my mouth with the back of one hand. My fingernails had little half-moons of dirt under them, like Dad's engine grease.

"Hm?" Father Jim's smile hadn't changed. Someone else might call it kind, but it was just the look of a straight who had you where he wanted you and wouldn't listen to any pleading, even if you were bleeding. The filthy satisfaction made me long to launch myself at him again.

"Surprised you're actually doing it yourself this time." Pushing myself up, straightening my dirty clothes, my T-shirt rasping with sweat under my arms. "Coward."

Clover actually gasped.

Father Jim's smile didn't waver, but something lit in his dark eyes. He took one step towards me. Two. His hand came up, and I braced myself.

The slap rocked my head back. Owen made a muffled sound, straining. His shimmer spread in concentric rings, the widest one almost, *almost* touching me. My cheek burned, swelling painfully. The pain faded, sinking away, and Father Jim watched hungrily as the reddened bulge shrank. A cut on the inside of my cheek bled a little, but as soon as my tongue found it, the edges fused together. Sealed up.

Even the rash wouldn't last.

"Behold," Father Jim said, softly. "I will chastise even my favorite children, as a father will his sons."

I cleared my throat. *What would Mom say?*

Like a gift, it came. She'd read the Bible and made me read it too, so I knew what the straights would cherry-pick to make whatever they wanted seem divinely commanded. *"Thou shalt not kill."*

That got a reaction. Dull red stained his face, rising from his throat. His hand twitched again, and I braced myself.

Clover cleared her throat, anxiously. "Father?" Pale and tentative. "Maybe I should take her to get cleaned up?"

"No," the god of Harmony said, finally. "No. We'll do this now."

NEGATION

It was the same room, sure, but the gurney had a nice comfy canvas-covered pad on it and candles had been brought in. Fresh flowers—irises, lilies, white roses. Big Tom loomed just inside the door, his scarred face impassive. Other Harmonies with the shimmer were in the hallway and the other rooms—I got a glimpse of bare white walls, floor pillows, more candles. Brother Sal and Sister Penny, who I didn't know because they didn't have kids, held my arms once Father Jim let go of me. The singing was hushed, and more of it came from outside. Was all of Harmony here? Did they know Leaf was locked up downstairs? How many of them had been boxed? Had any of them been locked up here, too?

How could you know something like that, and not *say* anything? Did they just not want to believe it was so bad? God knows I hadn't.

Sister Cass the nurse clucked her tongue at the sight of me, her hair pulled softly back and her lips glossy with beeswax-vanilla balm. "Father, she needs a shower and some clean clothes. Maybe we should—"

"The time is now, Sister." Father Jim settled himself on the gurney. Nina hummed in the corner, holding a tray of syringes, alcohol wipes, and other small things. Her pupils had swollen too, and the dragging warmth of soma filled the room. Cass wasn't on it, and neither was Clover, or Father Jim.

Or me. But now I wondered, if I'd eaten anything Clover brought, would I be? Or maybe Father Jim wanted me sober for this, who knew?

Cass subsided, and fussed at his arm. There was no IV pole, no bag of clear liquid. People shuffled, crowding at the door. Big Tom took Owen's other arm, and Clover watched me, a line between her eyebrows and her mouth pulled tight. There was a message in her dark eyes.

I didn't care.

Owen stared at me. He was still fighting, his shimmer sharp and spiking. Now I could see a bruise on his neck, and my arms hurt because his did. My back ached, but I couldn't tell if it was his pain or my own. We stared at each other, the rest of the world falling away, and I wished I could help him.

I wished I could help *anyone* right then. Including myself.

What if I managed *not* to bring him back? Clover knew I couldn't control it, though, I'd told her as much. Which meant Father Jim was probably counting on as much. What else had she told him about me and Dad? Stupid to trust her. Stupid to say *anything*. It was, really, all my fault.

Always. It always was.

Owen leaned forward, pulling against both Clover and Big Tom. "It's okay," I said, numbly. I didn't believe it, but what else do you say when you know nothing is ever going to be okay again? "Owen, it's okay."

Faces at the door. The shimmer tensed, expectantly, the whole house awash in it. Sarah had been pushing more buttons, I guess. Or maybe the glow could pass from one person to the next, like the flu.

"Father..." Brother Kwanze in the doorway, his entire face scrunched up. "Are you *sure*?" A murmur went down the hall behind him. Did any of them know what was downstairs? They had to, right?

What if they knew, and just didn't care? I shivered. My hands hung uselessly, and the print of Father Jim's strike on my cheek had gone away. I still felt it, though.

Not physically, but on the *inside*. Where did all the pain go? Was it just slopping around in there, and after a while I'd be full of it? What would happen then?

I didn't want to find out.

"I died once, Brother." Father Jim turned his head a little and smiled. "This time, I'll bring back the secret our little spark can't. Think of it—no more pain, no more death. All of humanity, bright and glorious as God intended."

My knees almost buckled. Was that what he was after? I mean, that's a great thing, it really is, but his methods were pure douchebag.

Cass folded up his sleeve, tenderly. Where was Mother Carole? Did she have any clue about any of this? Did Clover keep her in the dark, too? "This is wrong." My voice was a cricket's whisper. "This is *wrong*. You shouldn't be doing this."

Nobody paid much attention. Sister Nina just glanced at me worriedly, and Big Tom's mouth set itself even harder. A fine sheen of sweat stood out on Clover's pale forehead. Owen jerked, pitching sideways into Big Tom, but he couldn't shake free.

"This is wrong." I tried to think of what else to say. "You can't kill people. You just *can't*." I meant Dad.

Father Jim just fixed his gaze on Cass. "My blood is shed for one and for many. I am a willing sacrifice."

"My dad wasn't! Leaf wasn't either!" Another murmur greeted my words. "You can't do this! It's not right!" I just could not figure out what else to say. Couldn't they *see* it? Was I crazy? None of them looked like they had any second thoughts.

Except Owen.

"Do it, Sister." Father Jim's warmth was not a shimmer, but it still flexed and grew. "Set the timer, Sister Nina. Don't let Daughter Val bring me back until it's time."

There's a timer? I scraped up everything inside me and tried one last time. "Stop it! You can all stop this! You don't have to do it!" I lunged, but Sal and Penny had me, and they weren't letting go. *"You know this is wrong!"*

"Nina?" Sister Cass checked the old-fashioned syringe. It was full of thick, weird, magenta-tinted liquid. She tapped at the inside of Father Jim's elbow, professionally, and slid the needle home.

"Yes, Sister." Nina fiddled with something on the table—a rooster-shaped kitchen timer. She set it for six minutes, it began to tick, and the Harmonies began to sing louder.

And my hands, my stupid hands, began to hurt.

SIX MINUTES CAN BE A LIFETIME. Sal and Penny held me while I struggled, trying to get away, get out of the room before I felt it again, that awful *emptiness*, the cold that dragged Dad away from me.

When the timer rang and they let me go I couldn't help myself. My body didn't stop. It ran for the gurney and the thing it held. My hands hurt so bad, and they fused to the head of the thing on the table.

Thing. Not person.

Because what came back, while the Harmonies sang their beautiful doomed melodies, wasn't a *person*. Everything inside me turned black. Not even black, because black is a color. It was an *absence*. Nothingness.

No light. No color. No heat. No *anything*.

Except in the middle of it, something horrible suddenly *was*. My mother's necklace smacked hard against my breastbone, heating up like an electric element on a good stove.

Do you know what pure hatred looks like? Pure, unrepentant, gleeful, joyous *evil*? For an endless, hideous eternity I did, because I stared it in the face. It saw an opening, and mine were the hands holding the door open. I tried to slam the way shut, I did.

I didn't scream. I went stiff, my stupid hands clamped on either side of Father Jim's corpse-grinning head, and...

I really don't remember what happened after that, and even the thing I saw gets hazier when I try to think about it.

If I believed in God, or the universe, I would swear by both of them that I hope it stays that way.

STRONGER NOW

Nothing seemed very important. I sat on the shelf-bed in the concrete cube, my hands folded in my lap just as Nina had left me. My hair was damp. So were my cheeks, but with hot salt water. A clean sweater—white with green stripes—was too big for me, and tears dropped slowly onto its front. The skirt was one of Ingrid's favorites, also green and white, and the socks were a fresh pair. I had no idea how long I'd been there, no idea why I was crying. My hands hurt a little, a faraway soreness.

If I closed my eyes, I could look *inside* and see my heart, my lungs, my kidney, a long wormy thing that was my appendix and made faint nausea tinge everything rosy-yellow when I poked at it with invisible fingers. My chakras whirled, slow and clockwise, their colors not at all like how all the books said but I could see how they got there. I mean, how do you explain red to someone who's never seen colors at all? Or the difference between sky blue and periwinkle to someone who only gets black and white?

Mom's necklace was an arc of bright bold blue, reverberating with love and grief and a high thin note of stretch-strained metal and stone. Its edges dug into my chest, and I thought maybe, in some hazy way, it had saved me. My mouth hurt, because I'd bitten someone who tried to take the necklace away.

Everything belongs to everyone else, they said at Harmony. But not that. It belonged to *me*, and I wasn't giving it up.

Soft, stealthy sounds brushed all over me. I blinked. The bulb overhead dimmed when my eyelids fell, then brightened. I couldn't tell if it was because of blinking or something else. A metallic scraping, and a groan. My head turned, slowly, every crack and pore in the concrete wall across from me unreeling. If you looked close enough at anything, you can find the strangeness in it, and the beauty too. The opalescent feathering on a slug's back, the perfect edges of a footprint in dogshit, a map of burst red veinflowers on a drunk's mushroomed nose.

Everything could be beautiful. Except that *thing*, the thing that came back. Someone had screamed, and someone else had thrown up, and the thing's voice was Father Jim's but with a terrible power.

I am come to Bethlehem to be born, it said, and chuckled.

"Val?" A frantic whisper.

My head tilted some more. The bulb overhead dimmed further, and the boy took a sharp breath. There was more stubble on his cheeks; it looked like he'd aged, terribly and quickly—not a boy anymore, then. His chestnut hair was still the same, and his shoulders, but the cross on its too-short necklace was gone. There was only a thin red line where the leather had dug in. He set something down near the bed; backpack straps sat on his shoulders.

I tried to remember who he was. Something important stirred inside me, a tiny tapping, a bird-beak against the blank inside curve of a hard shell.

"Val." He was on his knees now, in front of me. My hands, holding each other so tightly the bones creaked and ached, warmed because he cupped them, gently. As if they were delicate. Breakable. "Talk to me. Say something."

How long had I been sitting here? My legs were stiff. My eyes, even though they were full of hot water, felt scratchy.

My mouth opened. A rustling sound came out. For one terrifying second I couldn't remember what words *were*.

Then they flooded back, and with them came my name. *Val. I'm Valentine Michaela Smith.* And his, too.

Owen. Owen Harrison.

I bent forward. My forehead hit his, not really hard but not gently either. He didn't move. My breath was sour, his was minty with toothpaste, and the two mixed while I rested my head against his and closed my eyes. I found the one word I wanted out of thousands. "Gravity," I whispered.

"Gravity," he whispered back. "Val…"

He was here. In front of me. When I could, I made my neck and my back work, and straightened.

The door was open. Not much, just a bit, a slice of light around its edges. I shuddered. *Close it. Close the door.*

How would I get out, if I did? At the moment, I wasn't sure I cared. "Something came back with him." I hoped he'd understand. The shimmer over him cloaked me, a warm blanket. "Something bad."

"I know." Owen's mouth turned hard. "I've got your boots, and your backpack. I stole all the money I could. We're getting out of here."

"What happened?" I didn't want to know, but I said it anyway, and hoped he wouldn't say.

"I can't…" He shuddered. "Don't ask, okay? Come on." He pushed himself upright, and since he held my hands, I had to go with him. My legs weren't all that steady, but he was. "I don't know where Clover is, or Big Tom. We've gotta *go*."

It was weird to have someone help me into my shoes. The last time anyone did was when I was, I don't know, four? Five? My fingers were swollen and clumsy, and I had trouble tying so Owen did it; he held my backpack too, so I could slip my arms through the straps. It was heavy, but not bad. No worse than textbooks.

I didn't ask what he'd packed; I didn't care.

He stepped out into the hall, hunching his shoulders and looking both ways. "Come on."

I stopped on the threshold. Closed my eyes, hopped over. Doors were going to give me trouble for a long time, I could just tell. "Wait."

"What?" He strained on his toes, leaning for the stairs at the end of the hall.

"Leaf." I pointed with one of my swollen, tender hands. "He's in there. Do you have the keys?"

"I don't need keys, it's stronger now. Val—"

Yes, it's much stronger now. "Please." I set my feet, stubbornly. "He's locked up, Owen. Come on."

"Fine." He tugged me along after him, stopped in front of Leaf's door. "Jeez."

The other doorways along the narrow central hallway—three on each side—were open. Maybe I should have been grateful there weren't *more* people down here. Right now, though, I was just trying not to puke while Owen held his hand near the handle-bar and the deadbolt keyhole, his shimmer intensifying. Maybe he'd been practicing. Was it like a muscle—the more he moved, the more he *could* move?

Or was it that Sarah just called it a button, and it was more like critical mass? Like cosmic debris gathering itself, glomming more and more and getting hotter and heavier until it began to burn and a star was born?

Snick. Owen shoved the handle down and pushed. Leaf's door swung in. I lost the battle with my stomach and retched, but it was just an empty, bile-laced, very painful burp.

The room was the same as my cell, only reversed so the plumbing in the wall could be shared. The bulb overhead fizzled and flickered, and Leaf, in his fringed jacket and well-worn jeans, crouched facing the far corner, rocking back and forth. He was way thinner than the last time I saw him, and his hair was long and feathery-lank. The room was full of a thick, smoky smell, body odor and lit matches. A pink plastic tray was set neatly to one side of the door, the plate on it gleaming clean, a crumpled smudge of folded, charred paper in the exact middle of the white moonface. The water bottle, twisted and half-melted, added a sharp plastic stink, and I wondered how the hell he breathed in here.

"Leaf?" My voice trembled. I hung back. Stepping into that room was just a little bit too far. I had enough trouble getting *out*, I wasn't going back *in*. Nuh-uh, no way, no day.

He kept rocking. Owen worked his hand free of mine; I didn't want to let go. I backed up, but there was an open door *behind* me, too. Not fun. Still, I hugged myself, the backpack straps cutting into my shoulders, and found out I was rocking, too. Of course Owen was going to help Leaf stand up, it was just who he was, and I would be an asshole if I tried to stop him.

It didn't mean I wasn't tempted. *Let's just get out of here,* I wanted to say. *Please.*

I didn't. I just concentrated on not retching again, and trying not to think of openings, of places where *things* could squeeze through. All sorts of black, grinning things, just waiting for a moment of pride and vanity to open a tiny crack.

"Leaf." Owen reached him, bending to touch his shoulder. "Hey. Brother. The door's open."

Leaf kept rocking. He hummed, a cracked melody I recognized. It had to be one of Clover's favorites. *Sleep, my baby, rest, my loved one.*

I heard something else, too—a soft footstep, a chiming of two thin bracelets. My head turned to the left, slowly, my neck creaky as an old piece of leather.

At the other end of the hall, brightly lit stairs rose one at a time. Standing in the rectangle of golden light was a slim, dark-haired shape. It blurred, and for a second I thought it was Mom, somehow showing up to rescue me. Everything was a huge, hideous mistake, and God or whatever had just figured it out and pressed a reset button. Relief warred with acid in my throat, and both died on a wave of terror.

It was Clover. She dropped the tray and began to run, straight down the hall.

Straight for me.

~

I BLURTED out a horrified warning and Leaf jerked upright, almost knocking Owen over. Clover's brother bolted for the open door and I stumbled back, saving myself from falling through the one opposite by clutching the side, ripping a couple of my nails down to the quick in a flash of red pain I barely felt. Leaf skidded out and almost toppled into me, the fringe on his jacket fluttering more than it should have. He was in the same T-shirt he'd been in *weeks* ago, before school ended, when I saw him at the apartment complex playground. His sock feet slapped the concrete hard enough to bruise, and a hot draft kissed my raw cheeks. Owen piled out right after him, almost falling over when he saw Clover at the end of the hall and Leaf barreling right for her.

Clover spread her arms, the shimmer over her intensifying and her mouth opening. Maybe she might have been able to stop her brother if Owen hadn't yelled and thrown both his arms out, a color-less ripple streaking down the hall, popping over Leaf as he tripped and went down to hands and knees, scrabbling. The ripple hit Clover right in the stomach, and she flew backwards onto the stairs with a heavy, sickening thud.

I felt it, of course. All the breath shocked out of me, sharp edges digging into shoulders, the middle of my back, right across my ass, the back of my head smacked hard. I might've passed out, knocked breathless, if Owen hadn't grabbed me, making the pain that wasn't my own vanish, his hand tight around my upper arm as he dragged me down the hall. "*Quick!*" he yelled. "*Before she can talk!*"

He didn't need to tell me twice—if we'd gotten stronger, she probably had too. We scrambled past, galloping up the stairs higgledy-piggledy hands and knees once when he tripped and took me with him. We made it to the top level, and I thought the smoke was just Leaf's funky smell before I realized the Red House was burning.

72

I'M HOME

We ran, hand in hand, slipping and stumbling, through a balmy, sweet late-summer night. We didn't have to worry much about figuring out where we were or what direction to go, because there was a trail lit up in garish, fiery stripes.

Where Leaf went, things *burned*.

You ever heard the phrase *like a hot knife through butter*? He cut a swath a good twenty feet wide, burned all the way down to bare dirt in the middle and crisped at the edges. Trees warped in the shimmering heat, leaves bursting into orange and gold as if autumn had come early. He knew where he was going—down the hill, veering only a little, staying away from the pond, and eventually, when the ground leveled a little bit, bursting out of the treeline.

Right through the mods.

Metal warped and buckled. Siding burst into flame. They didn't catch fire so much as *explode* when he veered drunkenly past, Owen and I scrambling after him but never quite catching up. It was pretty obvious where he was heading, and Owen's frantic certainty beat inside my head like my own pulse. I don't know if I knew what he was thinking, or only guessed.

Either way, we both knew. The Big House

And that was where Sarah was likely to be. Plus, even though Father Jim was horrible, he was Owen's dad, and oh God but the thought of a father filled me up with panic.

Coughing from the smoke, cinders crunching underfoot, we chased the bobbing, weaving, twisting ghost of Leaf's jacket through the mods to the edge of the small goat paddock. Fencing burst into crackling life, and that couldn't have been when the screaming first started, but that was when I heard it.

Leaf's head snapped aside. He looked at the Pavilion. The high peaked roof burst upward, shingles and splinters flying, and a gout of greasy orange flame belched through. Mod windows shattered, broken glass flying. The barns still stood, dark and silent, but animals inside figured out what was happening somehow and began to shriek. Or maybe it was people caught in the mods, or whoever was in the kitchen attached to the Big House when the walls caved in on three sides and flame gulped everything inside.

"*Sarah!*" Owen yelled, and my mouth moved with the word. We jolted across the gravel, small stones skipping up and falling back like popping popcorn, lurid dancing flamelight everywhere.

The Big House slumped, oddly untouched. Leaf staggered to a stop at the bottom of the porch stairs, his sides heaving and his cheeks bright red. I saw it, clear as day, because Owen aimed us for the side of the house and I glanced over as he yanked me around the corner, between the house and the carport.

Leaf began to yell, too. Or maybe he'd been yelling all this time and I only just heard him.

"*FATHER! FATHER COME DOWN! COME DOWN AND TALK TO ME!*"

"OhGod," someone sobbed, in a high breathy voice, and it was me. "OhGod ohGod no, no no no—"

Owen hit the blue door going full-speed, the shimmer flexing and spiking around him, and it exploded inward. "*Sarah!*" He dropped my hand and vanished into the rest of the house, leaving me in the utility room, my head suddenly full of high thin whining blasts of heat. Splinters pattered down—the swinging door had simply shattered as Owen barreled through it.

I staggered after Owen, another retch coming up when I realized I had to go through *yet another* doorway, and the memory of that horrible hateful thing in that infinite nothingness pitched me sideways. My shoulder hit the jamb, splinters scraping my sweater-sleeve, but I was already through, lurching down the hall. Everything was twisting, rippling, changing, and I stumbled to a halt when I saw Owen frozen in the hall to the living room. I peered over his shoulder and choked afresh.

Father Jim was on his knees in front of Sarah, whose dark eyes were huge and lusterless. "Do it!" he yelled, shaking her slightly. Her little head bobbled.

Mother Carole stood, stiff as a stick, next to the rosewood cabinet near the fireplace. Her narrow back was to the room, and she was looking for something in a drawer, with the dreamy movements of a sleepwalker. Leaf kept yelling for Father Jim to come down and talk, and things slowed down the way they do in nightmares.

"Do it!" Father Jim demanded, and Sarah's head bobbled again. Tears slicked her small cheeks, and the entire world went quiet. "*Do it, Sarah!*"

Sarah's gaze flicked over his shoulder and met mine. Understanding flashed between us. *He wants her to push the button further,* I realized. All the way, instead of only half.

I even *saw* it, a small round yellow nugget oozing pus, Sarah's thin child-fingers resisting as her internal hand was dragged clumsily closer to it.

The thing I'd seen was *inside* him somehow, now. Was it what he'd been looking for? I didn't know.

I *did* know that if Sarah managed to push that button all the way down, something very bad would happen. I lunged through the doorway, its terror suddenly paling beside an even deeper panic. Owen, right in front of me, went down in a heap, and I did too.

That's probably what saved us both when the front windows blew in.

My ears popped. That's what it felt like, a wall of pressure moving overhead and my body struggling to cope. Father Jim toppled sideways and Sarah's face was an openmouth howl of dismay, her eyes black wells and her tiny body shaking itself loose of Father's grasp. Mother Carole whirled, flinching, and the thing filling her hand was a dull metallic gleam.

Owen made it to hands and feet, jolting forward as Leaf's yelling got closer. He was on the porch now, and thick smoke drifted down the hall behind me. The front door shuddered as something huge and invisible hit it, the entire house rocking on its good stone foundation.

Mother Carole took one slow step. Another. Owen scuttled past his father and grabbed Sarah, shoving himself upright, his arms locked around her. He kept moving, and I realized he was heading for the big hole where the front window used to be. A cold breeze poured past—the fire, taking a deep breath.

"Jim," Mother Carole said, calmly. Her arm, stiff and straight, pointed the snub-nosed gun straight down. "Oh, Jim. Forgive me."

The front door exploded. I got to my feet in a scrabble, my hands both burning from grinding against broken glass, my skirt bunched around my knees before falling to tangle at my shins.

"CLOOOOOOOVER," Leaf cried in the front hall. "CLOOOOOOOVER, I'M HOOOOOOOOOME!" The fire took another deep breath, and he began to laugh.

Mother Carole squeezed the trigger.

Veins of flame gobbled the paint on the living-room walls. Burning bits fell from the ceiling; I crawled on carpet going sticky-soft from heat; I should have been trying to get to the window. My hands bled, the smoke choked me, my eyes blurred. How do you fall on your face while you're crawling? I don't know, but I did, and my cheek got a rash-burn from melting nylon. I rolled over, half on my back, coughing.

Leaf stood in the doorway, his arms spread. Flames lapped at his arms and legs, and he laughed while his skin blackened and melted. I *felt* it, the bubbling of blisters, and the smoke turned sickly-sweet.

"*Val!*" someone screamed outside, over the roaring of the fire.

Mother Carole on her knees, the gun tumbling from her nerveless hand. Her face contorted, a mask of agony. Father Jim's body twitched, one eye gone, the other rolling madly as the hateful thing inside him sucked at everything living it could reach, clawing with invisible, misshapen tendrils.

Father Jim's bloody, burning hands shot up. They closed around Mother Carole's throat, and *squeezed*. I gagged, my tongue suddenly too big for my mouth, caught between Leaf's burning body and Father Jim's, Mother Carole's suffocation fighting for me as well. A bone between three dogs, a rope yanked back and forth, and I just wanted it to be over.

Pow. Thunder. Was it raining? I couldn't tell. *Pow.* Another huge sound. *Pow*, another, and everything went black as I struggled to breathe, to do something, to move. Hands on me, I fought, feebly, but it wasn't Father Jim. The hateful thing trapped in his dying meat screamed, but it couldn't hold on.

"Hold on!" someone yelled. "*Hold on, Valentine!*" Hysterical strength pulled me upright, and of all the people I thought would run into a burning building for me, I never in a million years suspected...

PART V
CODA

73

CODA

"I HAD TO," Owen said, dully. Sarah sagged against him in the van's middle seat and I coughed again, a miserable racking sound. "You know that, right?"

"I do." My chest hurt, my lungs scoured. The smoke-smell wouldn't go away, even if my hands had healed under a mask of dried blood and my cheek was fine again. I held Sarah's leg, the clean heat of the shimmer pouring into her tiny body, and she sighed, her eyes half-closed.

"Bad," she whispered. "*Bad.*"

"Can you help her sleep?" Clover, in the driver's seat, wiped at her cheeks again. She held the van steady on the curve, and the windshield lit up with red, blue, yellow lights heading up the ridge. Someone had noticed Harmony Home was burning. There would be questions, investigations—had anyone survived? "It's the best thing for her now."

I hunched my shoulders, wedged uncomfortably behind the shotgun seat. I'd've thought Owen would have saved me.

But it hadn't been. He'd been too busy trying to bend the flames away from the window so *she* wouldn't get roasted. Clover hadn't even hesitated, he told me. Just gone right in, yelling my name. And it was Clover who had keys to one of the big white church vans, its back loaded with necessities.

"It's all okay." I tried to sound sure, holding Sarah's sleep-lidded gaze with my own as the van straightened out and Clover feathered the accelerator. More flashing lights, but we were almost home free. Once she could take the left turn onto Sluyker Road we could get to the highway. At least, I was pretty sure that's what Clover had in mind. "You can rest now, Sarah. It's all over."

"Bad," she whimpered again, and snuggled more firmly into Owen's side. I checked her body again, looking with that funny internal vision. Everything looked like it should, so I peeled my hands away and clasped Owen's knee. He made a funny half-coughing sound as the shimmer poured into him, hot and pure.

"Something was inside him." Owen shuddered. "He wasn't...he wasn't *him* anymore." It was strange to see a big husky guy look so scared.

"I know. I saw it." I focused; his lungs were full of smoke damage, but the shimmer ate all of that. My own chest eased when he could breathe deeply again. There was an icky wad of mucus in his throat, but I couldn't erase that. I suppose I was grateful he wasn't hawking a loogie onto the floor or anything.

"Everyone who didn't have..." Owen kept shaking; I felt it in my own arms and legs. "You know, anyone Sarah couldn't push her goddamn button in, he...he just..."

I didn't want to hear him say it again. I did, so he wouldn't have to. "He just sucked them dry. They just fell down." I could even see how he'd done it. The knowledge was just *there*, whole and terrible, memories not my own but bleeding into my aching, tender head.

Clover made a soft, strangled sound. Like a sob.

I had exactly zero sympathy. "I hate you," I said, conversationally, my chin on my shoulder so Owen wouldn't think it was him.

Clover made another soft sound, but when she spoke, the words were hard. "I'm so sorry, Val. I...I believed in him. In Harmony."

"I *hate* you." My fingers bit down on Owen's knee, and he leaned forward a little, touching the back of my hand.

"We have to stick together." His hair was a wild mess of soot and crap, and mine was no better. I hadn't questioned the wisdom of getting the fuck out of there, even with *her* driving. I was seriously reconsidering, at this point. I looked through Owen's body one last time, avoiding any of his, um, you know, his underbits, even though they were just masses of blood and tissue as far as the shimmer could tell. He finally relaxed, his head tipping back and his eyes half-lidding too, and by the time I slid my hands away, he was asleep as well.

I figured he'd need it.

I wormed my way up into the shotgun seat as the van coasted to a stop at the bottom of Cold Creek Ridge. There was the familiar stop sign, and the blue and white sign for Sluyker. "The highway's left," I said, tonelessly, buckling myself in.

"Yes." Her knuckles were white too, her hair a ragged mess and her cheekbones standing out sharply; Clover clutched the wheel like it was trying to escape. "Val—"

"Don't. Don't even try to talk to me." I leaned against the window, cool on my fevered forehead. "Wait, no. My dad."

"He was in the Big House." Clover exhaled, raggedly. Through her half-open window, a hot damp smell of cut grass came, and cricket-song, rising and falling in waves under the purr of the engine. "I'm sorry, Val. I really am. You may not believe me, but—"

"Fuck *off*." My hand leapt for the door-handle. I ran broken fingernails along the chrome bar. Pulling would unlock the door, I could hit the latch on my seatbelt and bail.

Except where in the whole, wide, goddamn world would I go? "Where are we going?"

"Anywhere. Away."

Well, I can't argue with that.

"I figure we'll drive until daylight, and find a motel. Clean up, and look over everything I managed to pack." Clover's hands didn't relax. This was a country road, and even with a fire up the ridge, you could wait for a long time before someone else came by. "Money won't be a hard problem to solve. The bigger thing is getting you and Owen through school, and Sarah too. We'll have to be careful, we can't let people know—"

"Jesus *Christ*." It exploded out of me, and the van rocked slightly. Sarah made a sleepy little moan, scared and trembling. I shut my eyes, but that was no good because I could see the *thing* when I did that. It would take a while for that to fade, I was betting. "You killed my dad, Clover."

"Val—"

"Why did you even bother saving me?" I didn't want to know but I couldn't help myself, either. The night breathed outside us, calm and warm and dark as if the world was normal, as if didn't mask deep, hungry insanity. "Why didn't you just let *me* burn too?"

She was silent for another long moment. Finally, her hands loosened on the wheel. "I promised I'd take care of you." A hitching, inward breath. Her profile was set, serene, bathed in the spectral dashboard light. "I promised my brother too. I couldn't save him." She settled further in the seat and flicked her left-hand blinker. "I know you hate me. You have the right."

I did, on both counts. She was goddamn right. She didn't take her foot off the brake, and I was so tired.

We have to stick together, Owen said.

"Please, Val." Her right hand floated, pale and still, in empty air. She reached across the big hump between driver and passenger seats, the plastic thing on top of it with cupholders and a map holder and the swirled grain of fake wood. "Please."

I folded my arms. I didn't reach for the door again, though. Maybe I was too tired, maybe I was weak. On the other hand, where on earth would I go? To Bert and Coral? To Nadine? There was nowhere—and no-one—else.

She sat there for a while. The engine rumble-purred. She finally put her hand back on the steering wheel, and a sharp, clear, precise pain went through me. I couldn't tell if it was mine, or hers.

She helped kill your dad, I thought, and the answer came back clear as day.

You gave up on him too, Val. You didn't look.

I guess we were both failures. Except I was a kid, and she was a grownup. What was the difference between the two fuckups, I wondered? She could just *force* me to stay, right?

But with the Big House burning down, she had to have the van keys beforehand, right? She'd snuck around packing it, that much was certain. She'd been coming back with a tray and another bunch of keys. Planning on at least taking Leaf out, right? Maybe me too, who could tell.

And she ran right into the burning house for me.

They were supposed to take care of us, she said. She was trying. Like Dad.

Oh but it hurt to think of him. It hurt to wonder if *he* would forgive *me*. Or if Sandy Gibson, or Travis, or anyone else would.

When Clover finally took her foot off the brake and turned left, I didn't move. The shimmer moved around me, tentatively reaching across empty space. Her hands and arms prickled with blisters, her throat was raw and full of a heaviness that had very little to do with the smoke. Her back ached, and her legs, and her eyes. She was so tired, but she just set her jaw and looked at the road. The shimmer worked on her, easing, repairing, soothing.

I FELL ASLEEP AROUND DAWN, but Clover kept driving. Right before I dropped off, she wiped at her eyes again.

Softly, gently, she began to sing.

FINIS

385

ABOUT THE AUTHOR

Lilith Saintcrow lives in Washington State with her children, two dogs, two cats, and a library for wayward texts.

ALSO BY LILITH SAINTCROW

Strange Angels

Tales of Beauty and Madness

Dante Valentine

Jill Kismet

Steelflower

...and many more

Lightning Source UK Ltd.
Milton Keynes UK
UKHW022044300619
345311UK00005B/19/P